Tempests & Tea Leaves

Copyright © 2025 Rachel Morgan

All rights reserved. No part of this book may be reproduced, distributed, or transmitted in any form or by any means without prior written permission from the author, except in the case of brief quotations embodied in critical articles and reviews. For more information please contact the author.

This book has been enchanted to appear as ordinary paper and ink to human eyes. Should you begin to notice the text shifting to reveal alternative storylines, please consult your nearest fae healer immediately.

ISBN 978-1-998988-22-8 (ebook)
ISBN 978-1-998988-23-5 (paperback)
ISBN 978-1-998988-24-2 (hardback)

www.rachel-morgan.com

Your endless page-turning is exceedingly distracting.

How unfortunate. Perhaps you might consider relocating to another workspace if my study habits disturb you so greatly. I was here first, after all.

This has been my workspace for years. I will not be driven out by your inability to turn pages quietly.

I wasn't aware that mastering silent page-turning was a prerequisite for occupying this study. How remiss of Lady Rivenna not to mention this crucial requirement.

Lady Rivenna would never be so impolite as to mention such a deficiency directly. She would expect one to have the self-awareness to recognize it.

How thoughtless of me. Just as it would be thoughtless to mention someone's apparent inability to complete a calculation without sighing dramatically. Yet here we are.

I am not sighing 'dramatically.' I am expressing justified frustration at being unable to focus on important financial matters while someone insists on creating miniature wind-storms with every turn of a page.

I had no idea paper could be so loud. Perhaps the sound is merely amplified by the echoing silence where your good manners should be.

ALSO BY RACHEL MORGAN

THE CHARMED LEAF LEGACY

Frost & Fae Bargains (Prequel)

Tempests & Tea Leaves

Deals & Dream Spells

Love & Letter Charms

Hearts & Honey Light

CREEPY HOLLOW

The Faerie Guardian

The Faerie Prince

The Faerie War

A Faerie's Secret

A Faerie's Revenge

A Faerie's Curse

Glass Faerie

Shadow Faerie

Rebel Faerie

RIDLEY KAYNE CHRONICLES

Elemental Thief

Elemental Power

Elemental Heir

CITY OF WISHES

The Complete Cinderella Story

STORMFAE

From Storm and Shadow

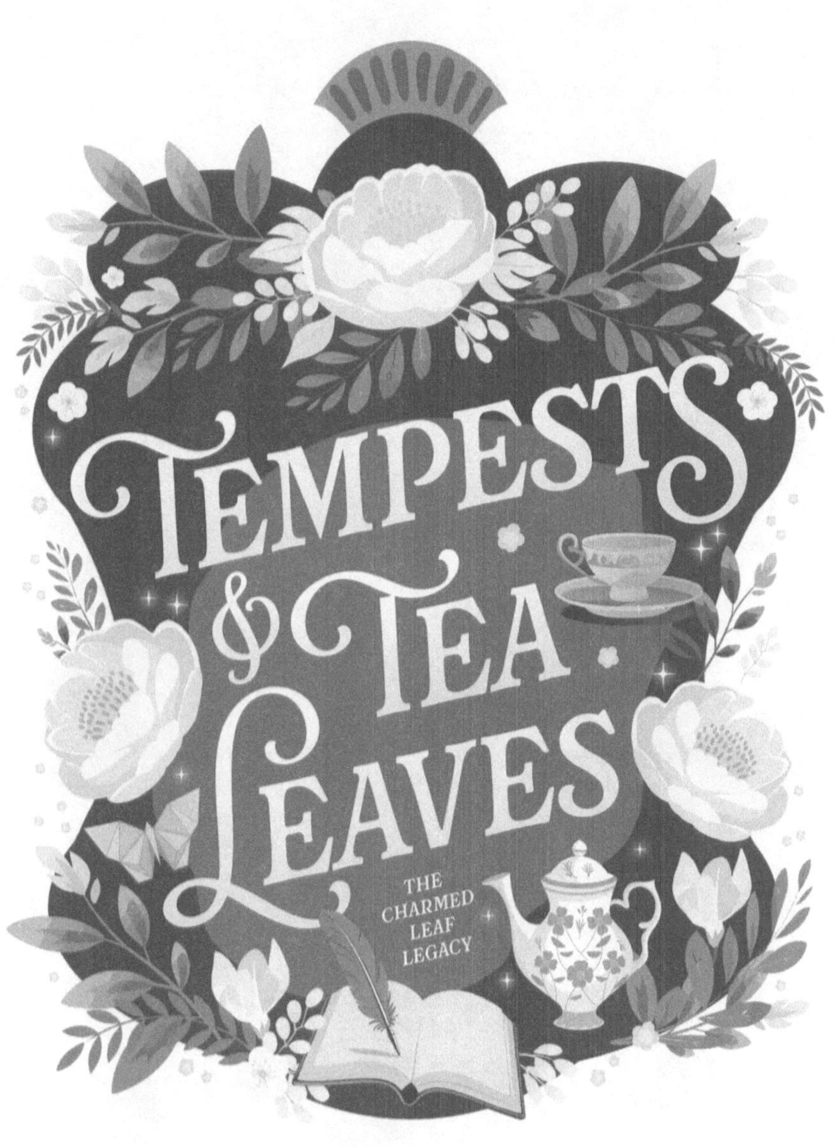

RACHEL MORGAN

To those who see not just what is,
but what could be

Chapter One

THERE WERE THREE THINGS EVERY MEMBER OF BLOOMHAVEN SOCIETY KNEW about The Charmed Leaf Tea House: it had a mind of its own, its gossip was fresher than its scones (and its scones were legendary), and its formidable proprietress and creator, Lady Rivenna Rowanwood, missed nothing that happened within its walls.

Lady Rivenna had learned long ago that the best way to maintain her position in society was to create a space where everyone came to her. The Charmed Leaf Tea House, with its enchanted walls, opinion-holding decor, and subtly shifting floor plan, had served that purpose admirably for decades. Even those who dismissed its magic found themselves drawn back day after day like dusk sprites to faelights.

Amid the swirl of excitement that marked the Season's first day, Rivenna reached up to subtly adjust one of the trailing vines that framed the tea house's elegant menu board. The plant preened under her touch, its leaves unfurling slightly. Rivenna was about to pull her hand away when her sharp eyes narrowed at the board's flowing script, where 'Honeyed Lavender Tarts' had been written as 'Honeyed Lavendar Tarts.' With a flick of her wrist and the barest whisper of magic, the letters adjusted themselves, the 'a' gracefully reforming as an 'e' while the rest of the lettering adjusted to maintain perfect spacing.

Rivenna pivoted on her heel, tucking away a stray strand of her otherwise perfectly arranged silver hair, and allowed herself a moment to absorb the morning's symphony of activity playing out across the tea house's main floor. With satisfaction, she watched as both the young and old of Bloomhaven's elite fae society fluttered through the doors, drawn by the promise of enchantment, gossip, and perfectly steeped tea. Magic sparkled in the air like dust motes caught in sunlight, and the constant lively chatter was as familiar to her as a favorite melody.

She released a contented sigh. All was right in her domain now that the Bloom Season had begun.

It was that most anticipated time of year, when the elite of the United Fae Isles returned from their sprawling country estates to present their sons and daughters to both society and to the High Lady herself. Those young fae lords and ladies whose powers had manifested over the past year would demonstrate their unique magic and watch it strengthen as the Season progressed, all while hoping to secure an advantageous match before the Summer Solstice Ball.

The weeks ahead would be an intricate dance with Bloomhaven's families guiding—or, more accurately, pushing—their offspring through the steps of courtship and alliance-building. From her corner in The Charmed Leaf, Rivenna would watch it all unfold, consulting the tea leaves, listening to the whispers around her, and quietly meddling where she saw fit. She'd been looking forward to it all year.

Across the room, Rivenna spotted Mrs Spindlewood, her hostess, leading Lady Featherlock and her two daughters toward an empty area near the kitchen. That simply would not do. She hastened across the room to intercept them before they could settle into their chairs.

"This way, ladies, if you please," she said smoothly, gliding past Mrs Spindlewood. "I believe you might prefer this lovely spot by the eastern window. The morning light is particularly enchanting there."

Lady Featherlock hesitated only briefly before nodding. "How thoughtful, thank you."

Rivenna's smile revealed nothing as she steered them toward a table conveniently situated beside Lord Emberdale and his sister. The young man had confided just that morning—within earshot of one of the tea house's more gossipy vines—that he found the eldest Featherlock daughter's newly manifested magic 'utterly captivating' and hoped to secure a dance with her at the Opening Ball.

The way his eyes widened and posture straightened as they approached confirmed Rivenna's instincts. "Lord Emberdale, what a pleasant surprise," Lady Featherlock exclaimed. "You remember my daughters, Elianora and Myrissa?"

As introductions flowed and cheeks flushed with carefully concealed excitement, Rivenna drifted away, weaving between the tables. She paused to straighten a perfectly straight flower arrangement, and then to adjust the hanging teapot that was already in precisely the right position, all the while keeping her ears attuned to the conversations flowing around her.

"He's impossibly handsome, of course," came a hushed voice from a corner table where three young ladies had gathered. "Those shoulders, and that jaw!"

"It's the fencing," one of her companions replied. "Or perhaps the swimming."

"The swimming, yes. I hear there is a large bathing pool inside the glasshouse at Rowanwood House."

"I believe so, yes. They say he swims daily. But he has all the charm of a frozen wasteland!"

Rivenna's fingers stilled on the picture frame she'd just moved to. The ladies could be speaking of none other than her eldest grandson, Jasvian.

"Casimira is utterly besotted with him," giggled the first voice. "She spent the entire ball the Rowanwoods hosted at their magnificent country estate this past winter trying to catch his eye."

"I simply appreciate quality," the third young lady—presumably Casimira—protested. "The Rowanwoods are the finest family in the United Fae Isles, and Lord Jasvian is as magnificent as he is wealthy."

Rivenna's lips pursed in consideration, a slight frown creasing her brow. Perhaps this Season some brave soul might finally crack through Jasvian's forbidding exterior. For all his handsome features and impeccable manners, it was true that the man possessed the social warmth of an icebound fortress. She did hope, though, that whoever might capture his attention would be interested in more than just the Rowanwood fortune.

"He'd likely be the most tedious lover imaginable," the second voice continued with a snicker. "Can you picture it? 'I regret to inform you that your kissing technique is substandard. Please refer to the manual I've prepared, with diagrams arranged in alphabetical order.'"

The trio dissolved into muffled laughter as Rivenna flushed with both embarrassment and indignation. She certainly had no desire to contemplate that particular aspect of her grandson's life, but how dare these frivolous girls speak of him in such terms? The spoiled little chits wouldn't recognize quality if it—

The floorboard beneath the table suddenly shifted, rising a fraction of an inch on one side. The teacup before the offending gossip jerked on its saucer, sending a splash of liquid across the table.

"Oh!" the young lady yelped, jerking backward.

"How clumsy," Rivenna remarked as she passed their table, her voice honey-sweet. "Do be more careful, dear."

She continued on her way, feeling a ripple of satisfaction in the air around her as she aimed for her customary table in the corner. The small grouping of comfortable chairs there—dubbed the 'Crones' Corner' by the younger set who thought themselves terribly clever—afforded the best vantage point to observe the entire establishment. She settled into her seat, arranging her skirts just so, and surveyed her domain with quiet satisfaction.

Something tickled the back of one of her pointed ears, and she absently flicked the air near her neck. When the tickle persisted—on her shoulder this time—she twisted in her seat and found one of the vines stretching hopefully toward the bowl of dainty sugar cubes at the center of the table. "Oh, for goodness' sake, it's the first day of the Season. Do try to show some restraint." But she snatched up a sugar cube anyway and tossed it over her shoulder.

The magical flora that adorned The Charmed Leaf's walls had grown quite demanding over the decades, though Rivenna supposed that was partly her fault for indulging them. They rustled with satisfaction as they caught the treat, their leaves shimmering with hints of gold in the morning light that streamed through the windows. At least it kept the plants occupied for a few moments, distracting them from dropping petals onto the heads of those the tea house deemed most in need of humbling.

Rivenna settled into her seat once more and reached for the teacup sitting in front of her. Only the tea leaves remained, having formed a delicate pattern at the bottom and around the sides after she'd completed the usual ritual of swirling and turning the cup over earlier that morning.

This was her annual reading of Bloomhaven's fortune. The cup had spent the night collecting dew drops from the magnificent elderfae tree that stood at the town's center, which Rivenna had then used to brew tea at first light before carefully pouring most of the liquid onto the tree's roots. Then she'd placed a protective charm over the cup to preserve the pattern until she could properly interpret it after the morning rush of the Season's first official day had passed.

Now she studied the arrangement of leaves, searching for meaning in the swirling patterns and hoping to get a sense of the upcoming Season. But the message remained vague, as though the leaves were teasing her with half-formed shapes and elusive hints. She was just turning the teacup in an attempt to view the patterns from a different angle when a pink petal drifted down and landed at the bottom of the cup.

Rivenna lifted her sharp gaze toward the enchanted ceiling. Why she, the most skilled practitioner of the nearly forgotten art of tea leaf reading, should require a nudge from her own tea house was beyond her. Was it trying to let her know it disagreed with her interpretation? She returned her eyes to the teacup in her hands and discovered, with a start, that the petal had turned a pale cream color.

"Did I just hear the youngest Titterleaf requesting *liquid luck* in her tea?" Lady Amarind Thornhart swept up to the table, her arrival announced by the rustle of her flower-strewn skirts. She maneuvered her voluminous attire into a chair, bumping the table repeatedly in the process. "Rather desperate, wouldn't you say?"

"She should know we don't brew such nonsense in this establishment," Rivenna said without looking up, her eyes still on the suspicious cream petal. She lifted it carefully between her thumb and forefinger, narrowing her eyes as she turned it this way and that. It had not only changed color but texture as well, having taken on the thin, crisp feel of paper.

She placed the petal on the table beside her saucer and peered into the teacup once more. Hopefully her protective charm had been enough to keep the pattern from being disturbed.

"Hm!" Amarind let out a most undignified snort. "And did you see that? Lord Bridgemere just tried to impress Lady Fawnwood by adding some silly sort of enchantment to her tea, and now it won't stop refilling itself. It's overflowing all over their table."

Continuing to frown at her teacup, Rivenna murmured, "Yes, well, I do admire his commitment to lowering expectations early in the relationship."

"True, but the *mess*—"

"Do not fret. I'm sure the kitchen pixies will be along shortly to clean it up."

"What intrigues have I missed, my dears?" A breath of lilac-scented air heralded Lady Lycilla Whispermist's presence. Her chair obligingly scooted out to welcome her and she sat, completing the trio of Bloomhaven's most formidable matrons.

"Nothing too scandalous," Amarind said, "though I do believe that's a Brightcrest seated at the table beneath the hanging teapot."

At that, Rivenna's head snapped up. It couldn't be. A Brightcrest wouldn't *dare* to set foot in her tea house.

"Oh, my mistake," Amarind said with a tinkling laugh that fooled absolutely no one.

Rivenna narrowed her eyes, finally focusing on her friend. The morning light caught the rich, dark cocoa of Amarind's skin, highlighting the elegant bone structure that had made her one of Bloomhaven's renowned beauties in her youth. "You did that on purpose."

"Well of course I did," Amarind said. "How else am I to obtain your attention?"

"*Not* by mentioning one of *them*."

"I bumped into your grandson on the way here," Lycilla said brightly to Rivenna in a clear attempt to break the tension. "Jasvian. He apologized, of course, but was otherwise as antisocial as ever, rushing off muttering something about getting back to his desk with barely a greeting." She patted the lower part of her elegantly arranged purple hair, ensuring not a strand had fallen out of place. "How will he ever find himself a wife if he doesn't stop for even a moment's pleasant conversation?"

"The mines have devoured his attention ever since Evrynd's passing," Rivenna said, sounding a little stiff. She understood the weight of responsibility her eldest grandson must feel, knowing he was now tasked with keeping the family lumyrite mines operating in perfect order.

"Oh, yes, of course. Forgive me." A shadow passed over Lycilla's normally serene features, and she shifted uncomfortably in her seat, a subtle reminder of the shared sorrow they all carried for Rivenna's late son.

"But Rivenna, my dear," Amarind said carefully, "are the lumyrite mines not dormant now for the duration of the Bloom Season? Do the miners not require their period of rest, and must the lumyrite deposits themselves not lie undisturbed for the prescribed interval? To allow—"

"Yes, yes," Rivenna interrupted, her annoyance growing. "Indeed that is so, but Jasvian has other matters that require his attention. The management of our various estates across the realm, accounts that have been neglected, correspondence that has piled up—all matters he was obliged to set aside while attending to the mines before the Bloom Season commenced."

"And how fares Rowanwood House since your family's arrival?" Lycilla inquired delicately, her tone suggesting yet another clear attempt to steer the conversation toward calmer waters. "I understand they've only just settled in for the Season?"

With a weary sigh, Rivenna replied, "My family has scarcely been in town for five minutes, and already they plague me about taking on an apprentice. As if I haven't managed perfectly well these past decades."

"They plague you thus every Season," Amarind observed.

"Indeed they do," Rivenna agreed, her mouth tightening. "And I grow exceedingly weary of it. When the right person presents themselves, both the tea house and I shall know. Not a moment before and certainly not because my grandchildren deem it time."

"Excuse me, my lady?" A polite voice interrupted them, and Rivenna's gaze slid from Amarind to land on the girl with soft brown skin and wide hazel eyes. She held a tray in her hands, upon which sat several used teacups. "The first round."

"Thank you, Lucie. Right here." Rivenna slid the Bloomhaven teacup and saucer to one side and patted the empty space in front of her. Lucie set the tray down, then executed a swift curtsy before retreating.

"You still have that young *human* working for you?" Amarind hissed.

"Clearly, yes." Rivenna's gaze swept over the teacups, which Lucie would have discreetly collected from various patrons throughout the morning and magically labeled.

"Well, I've said it before, and I shall say it again: You never should have dismissed that charming Miss Sparkwater. While not from the most elevated circles, she at least hailed from a respectable, middle-class fae family. One truly cannot have *humans* meddling in matters of magic."

"I trust Lucie implicitly," Rivenna said serenely, picking up the first of the teacups. She read out the name. "Lady Emberlee Whispermist. I presume you'd like this one, Lycilla?"

"Oh, yes. Thank you." Lycilla reached for the teacup her youngest granddaughter had used.

"She's a *child*, Rivenna."

"She's eighteen and manifested months ago. She's considered a young woman now, Amarind."

"Not Emberlee! I'm speaking of that Miss Lucie Fields. That *human* child."

"She's fifteen. You were barely older than her when you manifested."

"I was sixteen. But yes." Amarind preened, momentarily distracted. "I did manifest uncommonly early, did I not?" Then her face fell back into its previous expression of distaste. "But that has nothing to do with this. The girl will obviously never manifest; she's human. That's beside the point. The point is—"

"She can learn basic magic, Amarind, like any other human. She has already begun to do so. How do you think she labeled the teacups for me?" Rivenna lifted the next cup, which still had purple lip stain on the rim. "Now. This one belongs to—"

"As I was saying, my point is—"

"Your point is that you harbor suspicions towards her, and you are, of course, entitled to hold such a view, erroneous though it may be. The only thing of import is that I *do* find her entirely trustworthy."

On the tray in front of Rivenna, the remaining teacups rattled nervously in their saucers. "Hush," Rivenna told them. "There's nothing to be concerned about. Amarind and I are merely enjoying a trifling difference of opinion."

Amarind huffed. "Well, *you* may find this exchange enjoyable. I, however—"

"Speaking of manifestations," Lycilla interjected lightly, "has Rosavyn shown any signs yet?"

Rivenna kept her expression carefully neutral. Her granddaughter was already eighteen, and while Rivenna maintained complete faith that Rosavyn's powers would manifest any day now, she couldn't deny a small kernel of worry. "Not yet, but I'm not concerned."

"Too late for this Season though," Amarind observed with what Rivenna considered unnecessary relish.

And indeed it was. None of Rivenna's five grandchildren would be presented this year. Jasvian and Evryn, now twenty-four and twenty-two respectively, had debuted several Seasons ago, while the twins, Kazrian and Aurelise, were only sixteen. Generally considered too young to manifest, though Amarind had been an exception to that norm.

"And by next Season—" Amarind began.

"She will have manifested by next Season," Rivenna cut in. Rosavyn would be nineteen then. All young fae manifested by nineteen.

"Of course, of course." Amarind's smile didn't quite reach her eyes. "Or perhaps the year after. Twenty years of age is the absolute latest."

Rivenna lifted her chin and proclaimed, "Rosavyn will manifest precisely when the time is right, not a minute sooner or later." Though hopefully not at age *twenty*, she added with a silent plea. Twenty would be considered shockingly late to manifest, though Rosavyn was a Rowanwood, so she would survive the scandal.

Amarind sniffed. "I suppose not everyone can be blessed with children who manifest early. Though I must say, it does make one wonder about the waning strength of certain ... *distinguished* bloodlines."

Rivenna went still, her hand tightening around the teacup. Lycilla gasped softly. On the table, the sugar bowl tipped itself over and the dainty sugar cubes arranged themselves into the word RUDE.

"Oh, stop," Amarind said, flicking the nearest sugar cube. It shot off the table and was expertly caught by the eagerly rustling leaves that reached out to snatch it from the air. "You know perfectly well that was said in jest. Now, forget those teacups for a moment. I have far more interesting news to share." She leaned forward and paused, clearly savoring the moment. "About the carriages that arrived at the Starspun residence two nights ago."

"Amarind, darling, am I to understand you are only just catching wind of this now? Bloomhaven has been abuzz with the news since yesterday." Rivenna turned her attention back to the tray of teacups. She'd overheard quite a bit of chatter about it in the tea house's kitchen yesterday, all the members of her staff as curious as the rest of Bloomhaven. The elder Lord and Lady Starspun hadn't left Bloomhaven in years, deciding some time ago, like Rivenna, to make the town their permanent home. Their daughter now resided at their country estate, while their son had apparently found himself a love match on one of the most distant of the United Fae Isles and hadn't returned to Bloomhaven in at least twenty years.

"Ah, but do you know *who* was in that carriage?" Amarind said.

"Well, one assumes it's their daughter. Here to visit her parents for the Season, no doubt."

Amarind's smile grew positively feline. "Wrong. It's their son."

Rivenna pursed her lips before answering. "Unlikely. Errisen always did have adventure in his blood. He announced he wasn't looking back after his debut Season, and, so far, this has proven to be true." And considering the scandal that had chased him out of Bloomhaven all those years ago, Rivenna didn't blame him for not returning.

"Well, I can confirm that he is indeed in town. I saw him myself at the marketplace this very morn."

"And what, pray tell, would he be doing there?"

Amarind shrugged. "That's no business of mine."

"Are we going to get to the rest of those teacups now?" Lycilla asked. She leaned forward with anticipation, and Rivenna knew she was just as eager to decipher the fortunes of the young lords and ladies who would grace the Opening Ball in a few days' time. After all, strategic meddling required foresight.

"Yes, the teacups are far more important at present," Rivenna said, lifting another cup from its saucer.

"More important than the return of one of the most distinguished—"

"I am yet to hear this news from anyone else," Rivenna interrupted firmly. "Forgive me, Amarind, but I will confirm, as I always do, before we discuss this further."

Rivenna's gaze slid across the tea house's main floor and landed on her private little alcove on the far side—a cozy space partially hidden from view by trailing plants, with a small round table and comfortable chair beside a window. Everyone believed it to be where she retreated to attend to the tea house's accounts and administrative matters, a logical assumption that she had never bothered to correct. In reality, it was the perfect sanctuary for gathering the whispers and secrets the tea house absorbed throughout the day.

"But first," she said, returning her attention to her two friends, "let us read."

Rivenna divided up the teacups—four for each of them. Without a word, they lifted their first cups in perfect synchronization. Their left hands moved in graceful circles, swirling the remaining liquid three times counterclockwise. Then, as one, they upturned the cups onto their saucers. Three breaths passed before they righted the cups again. They repeated this ritual until all twelve vessels sat before them, wet leaves clinging to porcelain in patterns waiting to be deciphered.

The reading of the leaves became their focus, with all three women leaning in to examine the delicate patterns, murmuring interpretations and predictions and occasionally swapping teacups for a second opinion on something. The gentle clinking of china and murmur of conversations swirled around them, unheeded, as they attempted to unravel the leaves' secrets.

Rivenna barely noticed the gentle chime of the door opening. The Charmed Leaf Tea House saw a constant stream of visitors on the first day of the Season, after all. But then there appeared to be an odd dimming of the light that streamed through the windows, as if a cloud had slid across the sun. She lifted her gaze. No, it was the tea house itself causing the effect, making the usually clear glass take on a smoky tint.

Within moments, the usual chatter of the tea house had quieted to whispers. Rivenna turned toward the door, and—

Lord Errisen Starspun. Even after nearly two decades, she recognized him instantly. Like most fae, he had aged gracefully, though he must be about forty years of age by now. Yet something had changed. As a young lord, there had been a certain exuberance about him, where now there appeared only weariness.

Well, well. Amarind had indeed been right. How vexing to admit that her friend had outmaneuvered her in acquiring this piece of gossip first. Usually, Rivenna prided herself on being the initial recipient of any truly significant news in Bloomhaven.

Lord Errisen stepped aside, revealing the woman who'd been standing just behind him in the doorway. He looped his arm through hers, and—Oh. *Oh my.*

Rivenna's breath caught as all conversation in the tea house ceased entirely. Because the woman beside Lord Errisen was *human*. Completely, unmistakably human.

"He ... is that ... is that his *wife*?"

Lycilla's horrified whisper reached Rivenna's ears, but before Rivenna could answer, a young woman joined the couple in the doorway. She stumbled to a halt, as if she'd expected the three of them to keep moving and was taken by surprise when Lord Errisen reached out to catch her hand. Her lips parted to speak, but the words died on her tongue as she took in the silent tea house, every head turned in her direction, every pair of eyes fixed upon her.

"Oh. My. Stars," Amarind whispered.

For the girl bore not only the elegant nose all Starspuns had inherited for generations but also the dark, almond-shaped eyes and creamy complexion of the woman on Lord Starspun's arm. This was their *daughter*. A half-blood child of one of the oldest families in all the United Fae Isles.

In all her years of reading fortunes and mapping the intricate social web of Bloomhaven, Rivenna had never witnessed such a delicious disruption to the established order. She felt the tea house itself stir with curiosity, the vines along the walls reaching out just a little further, the floorboards creaking ever so slightly as they shifted to better observe the newcomers.

Rivenna remained perfectly still, watching the girl, seeing again in her mind's eye the pattern of leaves she'd attempted to decipher, the meaning that had seemed so frustratingly vague. Yes, the leaves had whispered of change—but even they hadn't prepared Rivenna for the storm that had just walked through her door.

Chapter Two

IRIS STARSPUN HAD NEVER SEEN A BUILDING BREATHE BEFORE, BUT THE Charmed Leaf Tea House seemed to inhale and exhale as she stepped inside. Delicate vines crept along the walls, occasionally reaching out to brush against patrons, flowers bloomed and faded along the wainscoting in rhythmic cycles, and the steam rising from teapots sitting on various tables around the room curled into momentary images before disappearing. The comforting aroma of baked goods and the earthy fragrance of exotic herbal teas created an atmosphere that felt both welcoming and magical. Under different circumstances, she might have found it delightful.

But circumstances being what they were—namely, that every fae eye in the establishment was fixed upon her family with varying degrees of horror and fascination—Iris found herself wishing the tea house was considerably less enchanting and considerably more prone to convenient sinkholes.

A young serving girl hurried past, an empty tray in her hands. Her perfectly round ears marked her as human, unlike Iris's own slightly pointed ones—not nearly as elegant as the graceful points of true fae, but enough to broadcast her mixed heritage to anyone who looked. The girl stepped swiftly out of the way as a fae woman in a pale green gown approached. The tea house's hostess, presumably. She welcomed the Starspuns with a strained smile and gestured for them to follow her.

As they walked deeper into the tea house, Iris wondered if the morning heat had made her light-headed. The interior seemed to stretch and expand around the table they were heading toward, as if the very walls were breathing outward to make room. It must be a trick of the light, the abrupt shift from the bright Bloomhaven morning to the tea house's interior. Or perhaps merely her imagination, heightened by the weight of a hundred stares. Yet even as they settled into their seats, a gentle brightening seemed to occur above them, like a faelight focused solely on their table.

Taking care to keep her chin up so as to appear unconcerned by the attention, Iris turned to her mother. "This is horrible," she whispered. "Why are we here? We should have remained at Starspun House until the Opening Ball."

Her mother forced a smile. "Your father thought it best to make our presence known early. Let the gossip run its course before the Opening Ball. Hopefully, by then, another scandal will have surfaced."

Well of course, if her *father* thought it best, then that was what they had to do. Iris exhaled slowly, longing for a time when her parents would engage in playful debate, her mother matching her father opinion for opinion instead of merely echoing his wishes.

"I doubt it," Iris murmured as conversation restarted around them and the strange light that had seemed to spotlight their table dimmed and disappeared. The glances in their direction didn't cease though. Back home, where the population was nearly equal parts human and fae, marriages between the races raised few eyebrows. Her parents' union, while not entirely commonplace, had been accepted with little more than passing interest.

But Bloomhaven was entirely the opposite. Here, the human families all belonged to the working class or lower, and her father had warned her that relations between the two races were still viewed with disdain by proper society. "There won't be another scandal to eclipse a half-human debutante," she added. "Not unless the High Lady herself elopes with a garden gnome."

"Iris." Her father's tone held a warning, though Iris could have sworn she caught a slight twitch at the corner of her mother's mouth.

"You know I don't want to be here," Iris quietly reminded her father.

"I am well aware of this," he answered in a low tone, "just as *you* are well aware that the Bloom Season is your only chance for a better future."

"Father, I am your only heir. If I am to inherit everything you—"

"We will not speak of this again," her father hissed. Iris flinched at his sharp tone, so unlike his usual measured demeanor. While her mother had grown quiet years ago, Iris had always enjoyed open discourse with her father, freely sharing her thoughts and feelings. But he'd been tense ever since their arrival in Bloomhaven. Even at dinner with her grandparents last night, her attempts at pleasant conversation had been met with uncomfortable silence and disapproving looks from everyone present.

Iris bit her tongue and refrained from saying what she truly felt: the Bloom Season was most certainly *not* her only chance for a better future. The whole notion of it had always struck her as ridiculous. That the fae elite would leave their sprawling country estates and travel from across the United Fae Isles just to parade their newly manifested offspring before society seemed the height of absurdity. They would dance and flatter, whisper behind silk fans, and engage in a ruthless game of matrimonial strategy as the Solstice Ball approached, the date after which betrothals were expected to be announced like battle victories.

Or so her father had always told her. Her father, who had never wished to return to Bloomhaven. Her father, who had suddenly changed his mind when Iris had surprised them all by manifesting. Only *then* had he explained to her that the Bloom Season was about magic as well. At the very heart of the United Fae Isles, Bloomhaven sat at the convergence of seven major ley lines, creating a wellspring of magical energy unmatched anywhere else in the realm. The concentration of raw power nurtured and strengthened newly manifested abilities—and would continue to do so right up until the Summer Solstice.

And Iris's unexpected magic could certainly do with some strengthening. With that, she agreed. She'd never had the ability to use any magic at all, unlike full-blooded fae children who could perform basic magic. For them, manifesting was a bonus. It was when, around age seventeen to nineteen, their *additional* magical abilities revealed themselves, typically reflecting the magical tradition of their lineage. Earth magic, weather manipulation, illusion-weaving, or any of the other hereditary gifts that distinguished the great fae families. They also earned the right to be addressed as 'Lord' and 'Lady' upon manifestation, elevated from the simpler 'Miss' and 'Master' of their youth—a formal recognition of their transition into magical adulthood within fae society.

For Iris, the *possibility* of manifesting had always been there. Half-fae children were rare enough that no one quite knew what to expect regarding manifestation. Some did, some didn't, and as her nineteenth birthday came and went without a whisper of power, Iris had become more and more convinced that it would never happen.

And then there had been the bookstore incident. Iris winced inwardly at the memory.

But the bookstore pixies had all been rescued, the owner of the shop generously compensated, and Iris's wounds had quickly been healed by magic. After that was all dealt with, Iris's father had announced his grand plan: the three of them would travel to Bloomhaven so that Iris's magic could reach its full potential, and, more importantly, so that she could secure an advantageous match with a fae lord.

Oh, and so that she could finally meet her grandparents, though that certainly hadn't been at the top of her father's list of reasons to return. The older Starspuns, like several other elite fae families—and, of course, the middle-class fae and human professionals of Bloomhaven—had chosen some years ago to live permanently in Bloomhaven. Iris's father had never seemed eager to visit them.

"Oh, that's her," Iris's father whispered suddenly, his posture straightening. "Lady Rivenna Rowanwood."

Iris sat a little straighter, hating herself for wanting to impress the regal, silver-haired woman who now approached their table. Her father had told her all about the Rowanwoods—the most influential family not just in Bloomhaven, but possibly across all the United Fae Isles. Their power lay primarily in earth magic, a gift that had made them wealthy beyond measure when their ancestor first discovered he could sense lumyrite deposits deep within the ground.

Lumyrite crystal was essential to fae society, powering everything from the faelights that illuminated their homes to the enchanted fountains that graced Bloomhaven's squares. Iris had even read about dresses embedded with lumyrite dust that could change color at will. Without lumyrite, much of their everyday convenience magic—as well as many of the elegant enchantments that adorned the homes and garments of the elite—would cease to function. And the Rowanwoods controlled nearly all of it. Iris's father hadn't precisely used the phrase 'obscenely wealthy,' but Iris could read between the lines.

"Lady Rivenna resides in Bloomhaven throughout the year, does she not?" her mother inquired softly, arranging her skirts.

"Indeed," Iris's father replied. "Her daughter-in-law and five grandchildren will likely be with her at Rowanwood House for the Season. Her eldest grandson now stands as head of the family since her son's unfortunate passing in the mines several years past." He lowered his voice further. "Though if Lady Rivenna remains true to her character, I dare say she considers herself the true authority of the Rowanwood line."

"Hush, my dear," her mother whispered urgently. "She approaches!"

But before Lady Rivenna Rowanwood could reach their table, a commotion erupted near the kitchen. Something small and glowing shot through the air, trailing sparks and causing several patrons to duck. Lady Rivenna turned swiftly and hurried toward the disturbance, calling out, "That's quite enough of that, you troublesome little sprite!"

She reached up and snatched the luminous creature mid-somersault as it twirled between the flowers draped across the ceiling. Cupping the tiny being carefully between her palms, she slipped quickly through a doorway at the back of the shop into what appeared to be the kitchen. Iris watched as the other patrons returned to their conversations and tea as if nothing unusual had occurred.

The woman in green returned to their table. "Might I tempt you with some refreshment to accompany your tea?" she inquired politely. "Our kitchen has prepared several delicacies this morning."

"Oh!" Iris's mother exclaimed, her gaze lifting. "I see the offerings there." She gestured toward the far wall where an elegant board hung, surrounded by a frame of carved vines. Upon its surface, names of various baked goods appeared in flowing golden script. Around the edges of the board, delicate illustrations of pastries, scones, and steaming teacups moved subtly—a scone breaking apart, steam rising from a teacup.

"Are there different varieties of tea available?" her mother asked hesitantly. "Perhaps a selection of blends?"

"Oh, the tea house generally decides what tea is best for each patron," the hostess explained with practiced patience.

"Ah." Her mother's brows drew together in polite confusion, and Iris didn't blame her. Since when did *buildings* have opinions on what drinks to serve? "I see."

Sensing her mother's discomfort and noticing her father was still frowning at the board, Iris added, "What would you recommend for first-time visitors? We're entirely unfamiliar with the house specialties."

With a thin-lipped smile, the woman said, "We are known for our scones."

"Lovely," Iris's father said, his attention on the hostess once more. "We'll have some of those, then," he added with a smile that Iris recognized as his public mask—bright and entirely artificial.

The whispers continued around them as they attempted polite conversation. Iris noticed her father's voice growing incrementally louder each time he mentioned how proud he was of her *manifestation* and her *upcoming presentation* at the Opening Ball.

When the human serving girl arrived with their tea and scones, she caught Iris's eye and offered a genuine smile. Iris found herself smiling back, feeling the first hint of warmth since entering the tea house. At least someone wasn't looking at her as if she were some sort of magical curiosity. "Thank you," she said as the girl placed a delicate porcelain cup before her—lavender with gold filigree around the rim and tiny vines painted along the handle.

Iris lifted the teacup, inhaling the fragrant steam. Notes of hibiscus and blackberry and something zesty—orange peel? When she sipped, the flavor bloomed across her tongue, warm yet refreshing and somehow exactly what she craved without having known it. She set the cup down, noticing the tea leaves swirling at the bottom. "They haven't strained the tea," she remarked quietly to her mother, slightly perplexed.

Her mother glanced uncertainly at her father, who leaned forward. "It is tradition here. The older generation once believed fortunes could be read in tea leaf patterns. Few practice such arts now, of course, but Lady Rivenna is known for her appreciation of tradition. Hence, the tea is served in the old manner."

"Sip carefully, dear," her mother advised. "So as not to disturb the leaves."

"I believe the teacups themselves may be charmed," her father added, "to prevent the leaves from being caught up in the tea while drinking."

The scones, Iris had to admit, were extraordinary. Light and buttery with a perfect crumb that practically melted on her tongue. As they ate, the tension at their table gradually eased. Perhaps it was the tea's soothing qualities, or simply the comfort of familiar family conversation, but Iris found herself relaxing despite the occasional curious glances from nearby patrons.

The atmosphere between them had been growing steadily more strained since they'd departed their home on one of the western-most isles, the demands of travel wearing on their nerves as they journeyed across the United Fae Isles. Their lengthy passage by ship followed by days of carriage travel had left them all exhausted and irritable.

The wealthiest families would have arrived in Bloomhaven via ley line gliders, of course. Enchanted vessels that hovered above ancient magical currents and carried passengers at extraordinary speeds when guided by specially gifted flow-weavers. Iris had glimpsed what must have been The Confluence that very morning, a circular pavilion at Bloomhaven's eastern edge where these magical conveyances docked after riding the ethereal tides.

Meanwhile, Iris's family had endured weeks of travel from their distant island to reach this nexus at the heart of the United Fae Isles. Had they possessed the means to secure passage on a ley glider, Iris realized, their entire journey might have been condensed to mere hours instead of the grueling weeks they'd endured.

But now, after savoring scones that seemed to melt on the tongue and tea that soothed their frayed nerves, they had settled into the first comfortable conversation since their arrival. Iris's father's shoulders lowered from their defensive posture, and her mother's smile grew more genuine as they discussed the charming architecture they'd passed on their journey through Bloomhaven that morning.

Still, it was with some relief that they made their way outside after finishing their refreshments, leaving the oppressive weight of curious stares and barely concealed whispers behind. Iris breathed deeply, noting once again that the air seemed fresher here in Bloomhaven, and the colors brighter. The town truly was saturated with magic unlike anywhere she had been before. Having spent most of her life in the quiet university town where her parents had met, with only occasional short journeys to neighboring areas, she found Bloomhaven almost overwhelming in its magical presence.

Clusters of flowers whispered to each other in the flowerbeds alongside the streets, cobblestones subtly shifted colors, and there was even the occasional pegasus flying overhead. Iris knew of pegasi, of course, but in the way that someone who didn't live near the ocean knew of sea creatures. She'd never personally witnessed one and had only ever seen drawings of anyone riding them. Where she had lived, the most exciting thing anyone ever rode upon was a horse with charmed horse shoes to give it extra speed.

They had barely taken more than a few steps away from The Charmed Leaf Tea House when a sharp voice cut through the air. "Lord Errisen Starspun? Can it really be? I heard the name Starspun, but I had to see for myself."

They stopped abruptly as a woman crossed the road toward them. She was tall and striking, her gleaming copper hair piled atop her head in an elaborate arrangement secured with jeweled pins. She appeared to be of an age with Iris's father—perhaps a few years older.

"Clemenbell?" he murmured, almost too quiet to hear. Then he cleared his throat and said, "Lady Brightcrest. It's been quite some time. Allow me to introduce my wife, Matilda Starspun, and my daughter, Lady Iris Starspun."

Iris still felt a peculiar flutter whenever she heard herself addressed as 'Lady.' After years of being 'Miss Starspun,' the elevation to 'Lady' still felt like a borrowed garment, one not quite fitted to her yet.

"Indeed, it *is* you!" Lady Brightcrest said, stopping in front of them as her eyes swept up and down Iris's father before moving to examine her mother and then Iris herself. "And your—family."

"News travels fast," Iris commented quietly.

"It's the gossip birds, dear." The woman's lips curved into something that wasn't quite a smile. "Ah, there is one now!" She pointed to a creature perched on a branch near the tea house—sleek and glossy, about the size of a starling but with a longer, more elegant tail. Its feathers appeared black at first glance, but as it turned its head, the sunlight revealed an iridescent sheen of purple-blue that rippled across its plumage. "They do fly quickly, and all about town they can be heard squawking one thing."

Iris blinked, waiting, but the woman held back the news like a cat toying with a particularly entertaining mouse.

"And what is that?" her father asked, his tone carefully neutral.

There was a cruel glint in the woman's eye as she replied, "Starspun half-breed."

Chapter Three

If there was one thing Jasvian Rowanwood had learned over the years, it was that the cacophony emanating from the family living room was directly proportional to the extent of his exhaustion. Today, as the sounds of laughter, bickering, and what sounded suspiciously like magical explosions drifted down the hallway, he concluded he must be approaching the limits of fae endurance.

He paused outside, straightening his already impeccable waistcoat and steeling himself for the inevitable assault on his carefully cultivated composure. One might think that after twenty-four years in this household, he would have developed some immunity to the Rowanwood brand of chaos. Evidence suggested otherwise.

Taking a deep breath, he pushed open the door.

The scene that greeted him was precisely the sort of ordered disorder that seemed to define his family's existence. Aurelise was hanging precariously out of the large bay window. Kazrian was hunched over the pianoforte, the instrument's top propped open as he fiddled with something that caused occasional sparks of blue-green magic to be spat from its depths. And Rosavyn was draped across a chaise longue, her limbs arranged in a casual sprawl that would have scandalized half of Bloomhaven's society matrons. An abandoned game of enchanted solitaire hovered inches above her chest, the cards occasionally rearranging themselves with disgruntled flutters.

Jasvian briefly considered whether he should have remained at the peaceful country estate for the Season. But someone needed to ensure his mother and siblings—and his grandmother—were properly attended to. Though Rivenna frequently reminded him that she managed perfectly well during the remainder of the year with only a small household staff to assist her. The family had long since abandoned attempts to persuade her to return to their main estate in the country with them each year. Now unburdened by family obligations, she kept the tea house open year-round, even through the quieter seasons when most of elite society retreated to their country homes.

"Must you always sit like that?" Jasvian asked Rosavyn, gesturing to her sprawled form. "One would think you were raised in a barn rather than one of the finest estates in the United Fae Isles."

Rosavyn merely grinned up at him. "No one of consequence is here to see me, brother dear. Unless you count yourself, which I most assuredly do not."

"Your impeccable manners are, as always, a credit to our upbringing," Jasvian replied dryly.

Their mother looked up from her embroidery, her needle continuing to weave golden threads of magic. Her warm smile softened her elegant features. "Jasvian, there you are. Did you have a productive afternoon?"

He crossed to the sideboard and poured himself a small glass of amberberry wine, an indulgence he rarely allowed himself. "The meeting with Hadrian went well enough. He remains enthusiastic about his design for the early warning system, though I'm still not convinced it will function as intended."

"Well, Hadrian has always been brilliant with his—Aurelise!" she called out, suddenly noticing her younger daughter's precarious position. "Do come away from the window, dear. It's hardly proper for a young lady to be seen hanging out of the house like washing on a line."

Aurelise jerked back inside, a deep blush staining her cheeks. "Sorry, Mother," she murmured, smoothing her skirts. But within moments, her curiosity clearly got the better of her, and she was inching back toward the window, though with slightly more decorum this time. Jasvian couldn't entirely blame her. Aurelise was so painfully shy at the few social events she'd been permitted to attend last Season that he suspected leaning out of windows was her primary method of learning about Bloomhaven society.

Jasvian crossed the room with measured steps and lowered himself into the chair beside his mother. He lifted the crystal wine glass to his lips, taking a slow, deliberate sip of the honey-colored liquid, hoping its warmth might ease the tension that had settled between his shoulders. Even now, during the dormant season when the mine shafts were sealed —and even at this considerable distance from the Rowanwood mines in the north—he could perceive the subtle hum of lumyrite magic that resonated deep beneath the earth's surface.

His particular manifestation of magic allowed him to sense the building of magical energy that gathered around raw lumyrite deposits. Left unchecked, this volatile power would eventually erupt into mine tempests—violent, swirling storms of pure magical force that could tear through solid rock, collapse tunnels, and shatter crystal formations. Along with this sensitivity came Jasvian's ability to calm these tempests before they fully formed, dispersing the wild magic with his own power.

The past year had been particularly demanding, with an unusual number of potential tempests requiring his attention. Time and again he'd journeyed north to the mountainside, spending days with his hands pressed to the earth, his consciousness extending deep below to sense the building disturbances. Each time, he'd sent his power flowing through rock and crystal, soothing the volatile magic before it could unleash its destructive force.

A sharp crack and a puff of smoke from the pianoforte startled Jasvian from his thoughts.

"Kazrian, perhaps we should send for a professional," his mother suggested, her gentle voice barely masking her anxiety.

"No need," Kazrian insisted cheerfully, his head still buried in the instrument's interior. "I've nearly solved it. Just a minor misalignment in the acoustic enchantment threads. One more adjustment should—" Another more colorful explosion of sparks interrupted him.

"If you set the pianoforte on fire, Mother will be most displeased," Jasvian observed.

His mother leaned a little closer and lowered her voice. "You don't think he might actually—"

The door swung open and Evryn sauntered in, his cravat loosened and his dark hair artfully tousled in a way that had become quite fashionable among young lords. He cast an assessing glance at Jasvian and grinned. "Well, if it isn't Lord Responsibility himself, gracing us with his presence," Evryn announced. "Did the weight of the entire Rowanwood fortune finally grow too heavy for your shoulders alone?"

"The weight would be considerably lighter if certain members of this family contributed anything beyond sarcasm," Jasvian retorted.

Evryn clutched his chest in feigned offense. "I contribute invaluable wit and charm. You're welcome." He strolled to the table where remnants of afternoon tea still lingered, selecting a honeyed scone with exaggerated consideration. "Besides, I have it on good authority that scowling at account books is your particular talent. I wouldn't dream of interfering with your natural gifts."

Their mother's lips twitched as she returned to her embroidery. "You were saying that Hadrian is optimistic. It would be wonderful if the two of you were successful in creating a far more effective warning system. To relieve so much of the burden from your shoulders—"

"I would still need to be present during active mining periods," Jasvian interrupted. "No mechanical system, no matter how ingenious, can replace direct magical supervision."

"But that's precisely Hadrian's intention, is it not? That you needn't monitor the mines constantly." His mother's brow furrowed with concern. "The strain will eventually cause harm, Jasvian. At this rate, you'll work yourself into an early grave, between your responsibilities to the family estates and your need to be near the mines. It has only been a few years since you manifested your abilities, and already you're—"

"What is the alternative, Mother?" he asked, more sharply than intended. "My abilities have made the entire mining operation safer than it's ever been before. I need to be present there during the active seasons."

"And what," his mother said gently as she leaned forward once more, "do you expect will happen when you are no longer around one day? If you do not implement a new system, the miners will have to return to relying solely on the tempest bells, as they did in previous generations. Are you content with that?"

Jasvian fell silent, the familiar vise of anxiety and pain tightening around his chest until breathing became an effort. The tempest bells had not been enough to save his father. Then again, neither had Jasvian's power. "No, I am not content with that," he said finally. "Which is why I'm continuing to work on this with Hadrian, despite my reservations."

Her expression softened. "I know, my dear." She patted his hand. "But you must allow for the possibility that Hadrian's system might actually succeed and acknowledge that your constant oversight may not be necessary."

Before Jasvian could respond, the drawing room door swung open once more, and Lady Rivenna Rowanwood swept in, her silver-streaked dark hair arranged in an elegant knot at the nape of her neck.

"Grandmother!" Rosavyn sat up, sending the enchanted cards scattering with indignant flutters.

"Good afternoon," Rivenna said, her sharp gaze taking in the scene before her. "I see you're all precisely where I left you this morning. How industrious."

"Not all of us," Jasvian corrected. "Some of us have been attending to family business."

"Yes, Jasvian, we're all deeply impressed by your diligence," Rivenna said, her voice dry as she crossed the room and settled herself into the empty chair on Jasvian's other side. "Though I note you've found time to join the family's collective indolence now."

"How was the first day of the Season, Grandmother?" Rosavyn asked. "The Charmed Leaf must have been positively overflowing."

"As chaotic as one might expect, though the day went remarkably well overall—aside from a stray hearth sprite escaping the kitchen. Things are winding down now, and my staff have everything well in control. I've read enough tea leaves for one day."

Rosavyn snorted. "You're still doing that, Grandmother?"

"One doesn't abandon a skill honed over decades simply because the younger generation finds it quaint, my dear."

"I do wish I could have come along," Aurelise said from her position near the window, her quiet voice carrying a note of wistfulness.

"Aurelise, dear, there's no need to look so forlorn," her mother said gently. "You're certainly welcome to visit the tea house on appropriate occasions, with proper accompaniment."

"On the quiet days, you mean," Aurelise replied with a sigh. "Never at the start of the Season when all the interesting gossip is flowing."

"Trust me, my dear, the gossip flows regardless of the day," Rivenna said. "Though today was particularly interesting, I must admit."

Jasvian studied his grandmother. Her tea house was an impressive creation, unlike anything else in Bloomhaven. Well, there was Dreamland, but that hadn't been in operation for at least fifty years. The Rowanwood-Brightcrest feud had seen to that. But The Charmed Leaf was unique—sentient architecture combined with his grandmother's formidable magical abilities and social acumen had created a nexus of influence that extended throughout fae society.

"Speaking of the tea house," he said, setting down his glass, "have you made any progress in finding an apprentice yet? You won't live forever, Grandmother, much as we all might wish it."

Rivenna's eyebrow arched delicately. "On the contrary, I rather hoped I would."

"The tea house needs a successor," Jasvian pressed. "Someone who can learn its ways, someone you can pass your knowledge to."

"And you believe you're qualified to determine when and how I should select this mysterious successor?" Rivenna asked, her voice dangerously pleasant.

Jasvian held her gaze. "I believe in preparation and foresight. Qualities you yourself instilled in me."

On his other side, his mother coughed delicately. "Foresight for others," she said in a low voice to her embroidery, "but never for his own well-being, apparently."

"How unfortunate that I did such an excellent job," Rivenna remarked. "Now I must endure lectures from my own grandson."

"Grandmother—"

"When the tea house is ready for a new guardian, it will make its wishes known," she interrupted firmly. "Until then, I shall continue managing perfectly well on my own, thank you."

Jasvian suppressed a sigh. His grandmother had been making the same declaration for years, deflecting all suggestions with the enigmatic claim that "the tea house chooses." As if a building, however magical, could select its own proprietor.

"And what of you, Jasvian?" his grandmother continued, a dangerous gleam entering her eye. "Have you given any thought to finding a wife this Season? As you know, my dear friend Lycilla Whispermist has a granddaughter debuting this year who—"

"I have neither the time nor the inclination for courtship," Jasvian cut in sharply. "My responsibilities to the family and the mines consume my attention entirely."

"How convenient," Lady Rivenna observed. "Your obligations provide such a perfect shield against emotional entanglements."

"I merely prioritize duty over frivolity."

"And the Opening Ball?" his mother asked, subtly redirecting the conversation. "You will attend, won't you? It's important for the family to be represented."

Jasvian barely restrained a grimace. "Is it really necessary? It's not as though I'm seeking a match, and I have little interest in witnessing the magical displays of newly manifested debutantes."

"It's expected," his mother said simply.

"Besides," Evryn added with a grin from where he was now lounging against the mantelpiece, "someone needs to keep me from causing a scandal. Think of it as your brotherly duty."

Before Jasvian could respond, a commotion outside drew everyone's attention. Aurelise, who had indeed managed to return to her window perch, suddenly leaned out even further.

"Aurelise!" their mother exclaimed. "What did I just—"

"Gossip birds!" Aurelise called excitedly. "A whole flock of them!"

Indeed, the distinctive sound of gossip birds filled the air—shrill, excited squawking that somehow managed to form garbled words.

These magical creatures, neither fully bird nor fully spell, were the bane of polite society and the delight of scandal-mongers throughout Bloomhaven.

Rosavyn leapt from her chaise. "What are they saying?" she demanded, hurrying to join her sister at the window.

"Girls, please!" their mother protested. "This undignified behavior—"

But both girls were now hanging out the window, straining to catch the gossip birds' cries.

"Starspun half-breed!" Rosavyn repeated, turning back to the room with wide eyes. "Did you hear that? They're shrieking about a 'Starspun half-breed.' What on earth does that mean?"

Lady Rivenna sighed. "It means the day has been even more interesting than I initially indicated."

"Grandmother?" Rosavyn prompted, abandoning the window and leaning over the raised end of the chaise. "Do tell us! Who is this mysterious half-breed the birds are so excited about?"

"The term is vulgar and beneath you," Lady Rivenna admonished. "But since you'll hear it from less reliable sources if not from me, the Starspun family has returned to Bloomhaven for the Season. Lord Errisen Starspun, his human wife, and their daughter."

A shocked silence fell over the room.

"Human wife?" Evryn was the first to recover. "A Starspun married a human?"

"It would appear so, yes. About twenty years ago," Lady Rivenna confirmed. "And now they've returned with their half-fae daughter, who it seems has manifested magic despite her mixed heritage."

"How extraordinary," their mother murmured.

"I should very much like to meet her," Rosavyn declared. "A half-human fae with manifested powers! She must be fascinating."

"You will do no such thing," Jasvian said firmly. The last thing his sister needed was association with a social pariah, especially when she herself had yet to manifest.

Rosavyn shot him a defiant look. "You're not the arbiter of my social circle, Jasvian."

"No, but I am responsible for this family's standing in society," he countered. "A responsibility I take seriously, even if others do not."

"Children," their mother interjected with a warning glance at both of them. "Let's not quarrel." She turned to Rivenna. "What would possess Errisen Starspun to return now, after all this time? And with ... well ..."

"With his human wife and half-fae child?" Rivenna finished the thought. "That is the question everyone is asking. Though I suspect we'll have our answer soon enough." She settled back in her chair, a small smile curving her lips. "I believe the girl will be presented at the Opening Ball. It would appear, my dears, that the young Lady Iris Starspun is hoping to secure herself a match."

Chapter Four

Contrary to what the gossip birds had been squawking all over Bloomhaven for the past several days, Iris Starspun had no intention of marrying. Marriage, as she'd witnessed, was not a path to partnership, but to oblivion. And Iris had no intention of fading away.

The Opening Ball had arrived however, and there was no getting out of it. She sat in a carriage with her parents, wearing a gown of midnight blue silk that shimmered with countless silver threads woven like constellations against the night sky. Her dark hair had been arranged in a neat but not overly elaborate coiffure, with a dusting of magical glitter that caught the light whenever she moved her head. She suspected she had been dressed deliberately to evoke the night sky, a rather heavy-handed reference to her family name. The irony wasn't lost on her that, unlike generations of Starspuns before her, she hadn't manifested any power remotely connected to starlight or celestial magic.

Instead, she could fold paper. Hardly the awe-inspiring magic one would expect from one of the oldest fae bloodlines in the United Fae Isles.

Iris turned to look out of the carriage window as they left Bloomhaven behind and traveled up the hill toward Solstice Hall, the High Lady's grand summer palace, along with the rest of the prominent fae families that had gathered from across the United Fae Isles. The enchanted road was lined with cherry trees in bloom, their delicate pink petals drifting down like fragrant snow, and at the top of the hill, Iris could see Solstice Hall itself, its walls gleaming with a warm gold radiance as it reflected the fading daylight.

The closer they drew to the palace, the heavier Iris's sense of dread became, inevitably bringing to mind the discouraging events of the past few days. It had been made painfully clear to her just how unwelcome she was in Bloomhaven society. Every outing had been an exercise in enduring sideways glances and whispered conversations that ceased the moment she drew near. Even the walk she'd taken in Elderbloom Park with the lady's maid her grandmother had assigned to her had been disastrous. Two young women—both beautifully dressed and clearly from prominent families—had practically sprinted in the opposite direction, one almost pulling the other over, when Iris had attempted a friendly greeting.

"Remember to smile, darling," her mother said now, breaking into her thoughts. Her mother's own smile appeared to have been carefully pinned in place, much like the enchanted flowers adorning her pale green gown. "And if anyone makes unpleasant remarks, simply pretend you haven't heard them."

"I've had quite a bit of practice with that particular skill these past few days," Iris replied dryly.

Her father frowned. "Iris ..." he began.

"Did Grandmother and Grandfather leave ahead of us?" Iris asked, attempting a swift subject change.

"Yes, I believe they planned to arrive early," her mother replied. "They wanted to secure advantageous positions in the ballroom."

"And ensure proper distance from us, no doubt," Iris muttered.

"Iris," her father warned again. "We've discussed this. Your grandparents are merely ... traditional in their views."

"Traditional enough to barely acknowledge Mother's existence? Traditional enough to address me as if I were a particularly slow child rather than a woman grown?"

"It's understandable that they need time to adjust," her mother said, though she was staring determinedly out of the window as she spoke. "They haven't seen your father in nearly two decades, and they had no idea what to expect of you or I."

"They've had days to adjust," Iris protested. "And I'm not asking them to embrace Mother as their dearest friend, merely to display basic courtesy."

"Let us set aside family tensions for tonight," her father interjected, his tone allowing no further argument. "This evening is about your presentation to society. Your opportunity to demonstrate your magic before the High Lady herself." He hesitated, then added, "And perhaps to make some ... favorable impressions."

Iris bit her tongue to keep from reminding him yet again that she had no intention of securing a match. The carriage began to slow, and her heart quickened. They had arrived.

Solstice Hall was a symphony of summer even at twilight's edge. Its walls were built of a pale, sun-warmed stone, but what caught the eye were the lavish golden accents: balustrades crafted from what looked like solidified honey, window frames edged in shimmering gold leaf, and great doors inlaid with panels of polished gold that reflected the fading light with a gentle glow. Vines laden with golden-hued blossoms climbed the walls and entwined the rails alongside the grand staircase, their fragrance—a blend of warm honey and summer herbs—drifting on the still air.

Ahead of them, a steady stream of elegant carriages deposited finely dressed fae before the steps, their attire ranging from classic formal wear to the more flamboyant styles favored by certain families.

Iris's mother reached across to pat her hand. "You look beautiful tonight," she said softly. "Whatever happens, hold your head high. You belong here as much as anyone."

Iris nodded, though they all knew it wasn't true.

She accepted the footman's hand and stepped down from the carriage, her eyes drawn upward to the towering façade of Solstice Hall. In any other circumstance, she might have paused to admire the intricate carvings that were only visible up close, or the magnificent floating lanterns that illuminated the grounds with soft, golden light. But nerves had tightened her chest to the point where she could scarcely draw breath, let alone appreciate architectural and magical wonders.

Her knees felt like water beneath her voluminous skirts, and she was grateful for the steadying presence of her father as he offered his arm. Her mother walked on her other side, her chin held high. They joined the procession of fae ascending the grand staircase, and all too soon they were swept inside Solstice Hall itself, though Iris was too nervous to register much of the grandeur surrounding them. She caught fleeting impressions of soaring ceilings, paintings of stern-faced ancestors, and elaborate lumyrite sculptures that served as both decoration and subtle amplifiers of magic. But her focus remained inward, a constant litany of instructions running through her mind. *Do not trip. Do not stammer. Do not embarrass yourself or your family more than your existence already does.*

A steward directed them to an antechamber where other young fae —both lords and ladies—awaited their turn to be presented. The room buzzed with nervous energy, young men straightening their cravats for the hundredth time while ladies fussed with their skirts or practiced specific gestures related to their magical abilities. Unlike Iris, they had all grown up with the expectation of this moment. They had been trained from childhood for this presentation. They belonged.

"We must leave you here," Iris's father said, his voice low. "Parents are not permitted in the antechamber during presentations. We will be waiting in the ballroom."

"Good luck, darling," her mother whispered, pressing a swift kiss to Iris's cheek.

It seemed they were about to turn away when Iris's father suddenly gripped her hand and leaned closer. "Remember who you are," he murmured. "Lady Iris. Not 'half-breed.' Not 'paper folder.' You are Lady Iris Starspun, daughter of one of the oldest and most respected families in the United Fae Isles."

Iris nodded and squeezed her father's hand as emotion tightened her chest. Things had certainly been strained between them lately, with him expecting far more from her now than she had ever planned for herself. But even with the weight of those expectations and their differing hopes, he was her father, and the fierce, protective love conveyed in his grip was undeniable. "Thank you," she whispered.

And then her parents were ushered away, leaving her alone among strangers who refused to meet her gaze. The room smelled of nervous perfume and anxious magic—little sparks of power that crackled in the air like static before a storm. One girl was actually producing tiny snowflakes from her fingertips, while a young man appeared to be making the potted plants grow at an alarming rate. Iris watched them with a mixture of envy and resignation until someone with a stern expression appeared to inform her it was nearly her turn.

She pressed her trembling hands against her skirts, trying to focus on her breathing.

"Lady Iris Starspun!"

The sound of her name, called out in the herald's magically amplified voice, sent a jolt through her body. For one wild moment, she considered fleeing—running back the way she'd come, out of Solstice Hall, away from Bloomhaven, perhaps all the way to the coast where she might beg passage on a ship bound for anywhere else. But before her traitorous feet could act on this impulse, she stepped forward.

She passed beneath the towering archway into the ballroom and was immediately assaulted by the weight of hundreds of stares. The crowd had parted, creating a clear path to the dais where the High Lady sat in regal splendor.

Drawing a steadying breath, Iris began the long walk across the marble floor. She kept her gaze fixed on the dais ahead, afraid that if she looked at the faces in the crowd, her courage might fail entirely. Finally, after what felt like an age, she reached the foot of the dais. The High Lady gazed down at her with eyes the color of a winter's night—not unkind, exactly, but utterly devoid of warmth. Her pale blue hair cascaded over shoulders draped in a shimmering silk that shifted through hues of emerald, sapphire, and gold, like the iridescent eye of a peacock feather, and atop her head sat a delicate circlet of glittering rose-hued gemstones.

"Lady Iris Starspun," the herald announced again, "daughter of Lord Errisen Starspun and—" there was the slightest pause, where the herald had no doubt caught himself, swallowing the customary 'Lady' before speaking her mother's name "—Matilda Starspun; granddaughter of Lord Caldersyn Starspun and Lady Ellesmere Starspun."

The High Lady inclined her head slightly. "Welcome, Lady Iris. We look forward to witnessing your manifestation."

Seated beside the High Lady was her son, Prince ... Well, Iris discovered that his name had utterly escaped her. His expression of bored indifference suggested he'd rather be anywhere else. Iris afforded him the briefest glance, noting only that he possessed the same ink-blue eyes as his mother before returning her attention to the task at hand.

This was her moment. With hands that trembled only slightly, Iris reached into the hidden pocket of her gown and withdrew several sheets of pristine paper. Her magic held them suspended in the air before her as she focused on willing her power to flow outward. After another few shaky exhales, she felt that familiar sense of possibility awakening within her.

Relaxing her mind as she'd practiced countless times, she became aware of all the potential configurations, all the many ways the paper wanted to crease and bend. The possibilities unfolded in her mind like the branches of a tree, each choice leading to a different form. She had decided days ago to keep her demonstration simple—elegant but uncomplicated—to minimize the risk of embarrassment in case something went wrong.

The first sheet began to fold itself with crisp precision. Creases appeared and multiplied as if drawn by invisible hands, the paper quickly transforming through a series of increasingly complex folds until it took the shape of a butterfly with delicately patterned wings. Iris gave it the gentlest push with her magic, and it fluttered upward, its paper wings somehow moving with the grace of a living creature. A second butterfly followed, then a third, each one more intricate than the last, until a small swarm of paper butterflies danced above the assembled crowd and rose toward the ceiling.

A murmur of appreciation rippled through the ballroom. Encouraged, Iris turned her attention to the next sheets. These folded differently, petals emerging from flat surfaces, stems lengthening with impossible intricacy as she crafted paper flowers that bloomed before the eyes of the crowd. A rose unfurled its layers, a lily extended delicate stamens, a chrysanthemum revealed countless petals arranged in perfect spirals.

Finally, with a subtle shimmer, a ribbon of fabric matching the deep blue of her gown and threaded with the same sparkling silver lifted itself from the hem of her skirt. It flowed through the air and wove itself around the gathered paper stems. With graceful precision, it spun and looped, pulling the flowers together before knotting itself into a large, elegant bow, completing the illusion of a perfect, formal bouquet.

The finished creation drifted gently toward the High Lady, stopping at a respectable distance. Silence fell over the ballroom. Iris held her breath, her heart pounding so loudly she was certain everyone must hear it. She managed an awkward curtsy, unsure of the proper protocol for offering her creation to the High Lady.

A court attendant stepped forward, carefully gathering the paper bouquet in his arms, and Iris realized with a flush of embarrassment that of course the High Lady would not accept a gift directly from her hands. Especially not from the hands of a half-breed.

The High Lady examined the paper creation with polite interest. "Most unusual," she remarked without touching it, her voice carrying effortlessly through the silent ballroom. "We have not witnessed such a manifestation before." She returned her gaze to Iris. "Welcome to society, Lady Iris Starspun. May your magic continue to grow throughout the Bloom Season."

It was a standard greeting, Iris knew, offered to every debutant regardless of the impression they made. Still, she couldn't shake the feeling that she had somehow fallen short. The High Lady's tone had been perfectly proper, neither overly impressed nor dismissive, but lacking any genuine warmth or interest.

"Thank you, Your Grace," Iris replied, her voice mercifully steady as she executed another curtsy before backing away from the dais. The herald called the next name, and the crowd's attention shifted to the young man who must have just stepped through the ballroom doors.

Released from scrutiny, Iris felt her composure begin to crumble.

Her chest tightened, and each breath seemed insufficient. She needed air, needed to escape the crush of bodies and the weight of judgment. Frantically scanning the ballroom, she spotted an arched doorway leading to what appeared to be a side terrace or garden.

Without a backward glance, Iris made for the exit, weaving through the crowd with as much dignity as she could muster while fighting the urge to run.

Chapter Five

THE NIGHT AIR CARESSED IRIS'S FACE LIKE A BALM, COOLING HER FLUSHED cheeks as she stepped onto the terrace. She moved deeper into the shadows beside an enormous copper urn containing an enderwood plant, grateful for the relative solitude after the overwhelming crush of the ballroom. Above, stars glittered against the velvet darkness, their light competing with the enchanted lanterns that floated at regular intervals throughout the garden.

Iris leaned her head back against the wall, drawing in slow, deliberate breaths while beside her, the enderwood plant reached out a few of its silvery tendrils and caressed her hand. "Not now," she whispered, her chest still heaving as she absently pushed it away. The vine persisted, wrapping gently around her wrist with a surprisingly comforting touch. After a moment, she gave up trying to discourage it. At least something in this wretched place didn't shrink away from her.

As her heartbeat steadied, voices drifted through the open doorway from just inside the ballroom. Two men, speaking in the cultured accents of Bloomhaven's elite.

"Come now, Jasvian," said a warm, good-natured voice, "even you must admit this one shows promise. Oh! Look at that ice display! Impressive, don't you think?"

Through the open doors, Iris could hear gasps of appreciation from the crowd.

"Impressive?" The second voice—which she presumed belonged to the aforementioned Lord Jasvian—was deeper, touched with what sounded like irritation. "Hadrian, you're far too easily pleased. An ice sculpture is hardly worth remarking upon. Almost as tedious as that weak manifestation of dream magic from the youngest Brightcrest. I almost fell asleep during her display. And did you see that paper-folding nonsense? A child could do better."

Heat flooded Iris's cheeks, her spine stiffening even as the enderwood's leaves brushed her skin in gentle, soothing strokes.

"Ah, yes. The Starspun girl." The first gentleman—Lord Hadrian, was it?—cleared his throat. "Given her particular circumstances ..."

"Her circumstances are precisely my point. The Starspuns have brought shame to one of our oldest bloodlines by *diluting* it, and clearly it shows in the inferiority of the girl's magic. I hardly think it's worthy of presentation to society."

Iris's vision blurred with tears of rage and humiliation, but what burned most was that this *Lord Jasvian* was only voicing what she herself had been thinking all along. That her magic was inferior, useless, unworthy. But to hear it spoken aloud, with such casual cruelty ... Her fingers curled into fists. She had half a mind to step out and give him a piece of her—

"You can't deny it was unique," Hadrian said, interrupting Iris's thoughts of confrontation. "Better than watching another fire-wielder singeing the curtains or a weather-worker making it rain indoors."

"Unique doesn't make it useful," came the cold reply. "The Rowanwoods have been shaping the lumyrite industry for generations. That's proper magic—magic that builds societies, creates wealth, serves a purpose. But paper flowers? It's bad enough having half-breeds diluting our bloodlines without them showing up during the Bloom Season to make a mockery of proper fae magic."

"Well, at the very least, she has nice ..." Hadrian trailed off, appearing to search for some redeeming quality Iris might have. "Eyes," he finished weakly.

"Eyes," Jasvian repeated. "Her *human mother's* eyes, you mean?"

"Yes. You have to admit they're … interesting. Upturned and a touch … elegant."

A sound of pure derision cut through the night air. "There is nothing *elegant* about that girl. She's as plain as the paper she folds."

Iris took a step from behind the urn, ready to charge back inside and confront the opinionated man, but the enderwood tightened its grip and tugged her roughly backward. "Ow," she hissed. Since when did plants display such strength?

By the time Iris managed to untangle herself from the surprisingly tenacious enderwood, her wrist bore delicate indentations from its grip. "Thank you for your concern," she muttered to the plant, which rustled in what she could have sworn was satisfaction.

She marched back into the ballroom, scanning the crowd for the two lords whose voices she'd overheard, but they appeared to have moved on. Just as well—her anger had cooled enough to recognize that causing a scene would likely only confirm society's worst assumptions about her.

"There you are!" Her mother appeared at her elbow, looking slightly flustered. "I've been looking everywhere."

Iris swallowed the angry words that still crowded her tongue. "I apologize for disappearing, Mother. I … needed some air. The presentation was a little overwhelming."

Her mother reached for her hand and squeezed it. "Your presentation was beautiful, darling. You did wonderfully."

"Did I?" Iris couldn't keep the bitterness from her voice. "The High Lady seemed distinctly unimpressed. And I've just overheard what at least one member of society thinks of my 'diluted bloodline' and 'paper-folding nonsense.'"

Her mother sighed, a soft sound barely audible above the sound of the music that was starting up now that the presentations were over. "People can be cruel, especially when faced with something they don't understand or that challenges their preconceptions."

Iris turned to face her mother directly. "How do you bear it?" she asked, suddenly desperate to know. "The whispers, the sideways glances, being treated as if you're somehow less than everyone else simply because you were born human? How do you smile and pretend it doesn't cut deep?"

For the first time since their arrival in Bloomhaven, her mother's carefully maintained composure slipped. Pain flashed across her features. "It's ... difficult," she admitted quietly. "More difficult than I expected, even knowing what your father had warned me about. I'd thought that perhaps things might have changed in the years since he left. That perhaps attitudes had ... evolved. But Bloomhaven society remains entrenched in its traditions and prejudices."

"Then why are we here?" Iris asked, her voice dropping to a whisper. "Why subject ourselves to this?"

"For you," her mother replied simply. "For your future."

"But this isn't the future I want!" Her whisper was edged with desperation. "I don't want to marry one of these awful, entitled fae lords, and even though my magic would benefit from the ancient power flowing through Bloomhaven, strengthening my abilities hardly seems worth enduring months in a place where we're treated like unwelcome intruders."

Iris's mother closed her eyes for a moment and swallowed before focusing on her daughter again. "It isn't only that, Iris. We're here because—"

But before her mother could finish, a familiar voice called out, "Matilda? Ah, there you are. And Iris too, excellent." Iris's father approached, relief evident in his expression. "I've been looking for you both. There's someone I'd like Iris to meet." His gaze lingered on his wife's face, a look passing between them that Iris couldn't quite interpret. "Are you well, my dear?"

"Perfectly fine," her mother assured him, her composed mask slipping back into place.

He nodded, turning to Iris. "Lady Rivenna Rowanwood has expressed interest in meeting you. As one of the most influential figures in Bloomhaven society, her good opinion could be invaluable."

Iris inhaled deeply and nodded. "Lead the way."

They stepped further into the ballroom, which now hummed with activity as couples moved through the intricate steps of a traditional fae dance. Iris's father guided them along the perimeter of the dance floor, weaving through clusters of observers until they reached a corner where several older women sat in elegant chairs, surveying the festivities with sharp eyes.

One woman in particular commanded attention, and Iris recognized her immediately from The Charmed Leaf Tea House. Her silver hair was arranged in a sophisticated coiffure, and she wore a gown of deep burgundy that set off the pale perfection of her skin.

"Lady Rowanwood," Iris's father said with a formal bow. "May I present my daughter, Lady Iris Starspun, and my wife, Matilda."

Lady Rivenna Rowanwood stood and moved closer, her gaze sweeping over the three of them, lingering on Iris with an intensity that made her want to fidget. Instead, Iris straightened her spine and met the woman's penetrating stare directly.

"So," Lady Rivenna said without preamble, "you're the girl who's got all of Bloomhaven in a tizzy."

Iris heard her father make a soft sound of dismay, but she refused to flinch. "I prefer 'Lady Iris,' but yes, I suppose that's me."

Something that might have been approval flickered in Lady Rivenna's eyes. "Direct. Good. I have little patience for those who cloak simple truths in elaborate niceties."

"Then we have that in common," Iris replied, ignoring her father's warning glance.

"Indeed." Lady Rivenna inclined her head. "Your demonstration earlier was ... unusual. In all my years, I've never encountered a manifestation quite like yours."

"I'm not entirely convinced that's a compliment, my lady."

"Merely an observation." Lady Rivenna waved away Iris's comment. "Tell me about your magic. Not what it does—I saw that for myself—but how it works. What do you experience when you create those paper forms?"

Iris blinked, taken aback by the question. There were not many who bothered to ask how her magic functioned; most simply judged its appearance and moved on. "Well, it's ..." she began slowly, searching for the right words. "When I look at a sheet of paper, I can perceive all the different ways it might fold, all the potential shapes hidden within it. It's as if the paper itself already knows all the forms it could take, and I simply … guide it toward one particular possibility."

"Fascinating." Lady Rivenna leaned forward slightly. "And can you see these possibilities in other things? Or only in paper?"

"Only paper, my lady," Iris replied.

"How can you be so sure? Have you received additional training? Have you pushed yourself, tested the limits of what you can do?"

The memory of the day her magic had manifested flashed through Iris's mind, and she suppressed a shudder. She had no desire to 'push herself' and experience something like that again. "I received some instruction from a manifestation expert in order to further explore my abilities," she said carefully. "It appears paper folding is all I can do."

In truth, this 'instruction' had been only a handful of lessons and had been more about learning control. There hadn't been time for much more than that before they left for Bloomhaven.

"Ah. Interesting," Lady Rivenna mused. "And having had no magical ability at all until your manifestation, the sensation must have been quite extraordinary. Have you grown used to the feeling now?"

A rather personal question, but Iris could hardly refuse to answer it. She glanced at her parents. Her mother gave her an encouraging look, while her father's face bore an oddly pained expression. She returned her gaze to Lady Rivenna. "Uh, yes, it was rather like finding an unexpected door in a familiar house—surprising, but somehow it feels like it was always meant to be there."

Lady Rivenna nodded as her fingers traced the ruby pendant at her throat. "We are all puzzles to ourselves, are we not? Finding that unexpected door was merely discovering another piece of who you truly are. Life continues to reveal these pieces to us, if we're wise enough to recognize them."

Iris nodded slowly, considering this. "I've always enjoyed puzzles," she said eventually. "They keep the mind sharp."

"Indeed." Lady Rivenna's gaze shifted to something over Iris's shoulder. "Ah, speaking of puzzles—Jasvian, darling, come meet Lady Iris

Starspun. Lady Iris," she added, her eyes on Iris once more, "my grandson, Lord Jasvian Rowanwood."

Iris's blood froze in her veins. *Jasvian.* As in ... the very man whose cutting remarks still burned in her ears? She turned slowly, already knowing what she would find. And indeed, the young lord approaching them was exactly as his voice had suggested—tall, imposingly handsome, and wearing an expression of perfect aristocratic boredom. His dark eyes swept over her in a swift, dismissive assessment.

"Lady Iris," he said, executing a flawless bow. "I caught the tail end of your demonstration earlier. Most ... interesting."

The word 'interesting' dropped from his lips like a dead flower, carrying the same inflection he'd used on the terrace. Iris felt heat rising in her cheeks, but she refused to let it show in her voice. "Lord Rowanwood," she replied, dipping into a curtsy that was just a fraction too shallow to be proper. "How fortunate that you were able to witness it. Though I realize my *diluted* powers pale in comparison to proper fae magic."

He hesitated, a spark of life igniting in his bored gaze, and she saw the moment he realized she must have overheard his earlier conversation. A muscle ticked in his jaw. "I stand by what I said, Lady Iris. Decorative magic serves little purpose in society. Surely you agree."

"On the contrary," Iris replied cooly. "Doesn't all magic serve *some* purpose? Even the smallest flower can bring joy."

"Joy." He drew out the word as if he'd never heard of it. He probably hadn't, given his sour expression. "Perhaps. My point," he said, each word precisely measured, "is that presentation to the High Lady is meant to herald the awakening of significant power. Magic that will shape and strengthen our society." His gaze swept over her with disdain. "One questions whether the ability to fold paper rises to the level of a true manifestation at all."

Her father made a choked sound of horror that Iris barely registered, all her attention fixed on the insufferable lord before her. "I see." Iris matched his measured tone. "And you consider yourself the authority on what constitutes 'true' magic?"

"I consider myself informed enough to recognize the difference between power that sustains our way of life and mere parlor tricks."

"How convenient," Iris said, her careful composure beginning to crack, "that your definition of 'true' magic happens to align precisely with your own abilities."

"My abilities serve a vital purpose," he said stiffly. "Without my magic, the lumyrite mines—"

"Oh, come now," Iris cut in, unable to contain herself any longer. "This entire ritual is nothing but an elaborate display of peacocking. If we're going to parade ourselves about like prized show creatures at auction, what difference does it make if some of us create paper butterflies while others boast about their ability to sense rocks?"

His jaw clenched. "No one needs your sanctimonious opinions on traditions that have sustained our society for centuries."

"And no one needs your suffocating self-importance!"

Somewhere to the side, Lady Rivenna made a sound that was part strangled laugh, part cough. Iris had forgotten she was even there. "My dear Lord Starspun and Mrs Starspun," she said brightly to Iris's parents, while Iris maintained unwavering eye contact with the imperious Lord Jasvian. "Allow me to direct your attention to the enchanted ice sculpture garden, through that archway over there on the terrace. Did you know they've managed to create flowers that actually bloom and wilt in an endless cycle?"

Lord Jasvian, clearly unwilling to break Iris's gaze as she attempted to stare him down, inhaled deeply. "I suppose," he said finally, "you're expecting an apology."

"Not at all," she replied. "That would require you to possess both manners and regret. I suspect you have neither."

His mouth tightened into a thin line. "You're remarkably forthright for someone in your position."

"My position?" Iris arched an eyebrow. "You mean as someone whose magic you've deemed unworthy of society? Or perhaps you're referring to my status as a—what was the charming term you used? Ah yes, a 'half-breed.'"

A flash of something—discomfort, perhaps—crossed his features before they settled back into aristocratic disdain. "I was merely expressing concern for the preservation of traditional magic."

"Traditional magic? Like the skills relating to lumyrite and the mining industry? How thrilling."

"It serves a purpose," he said stiffly. "A very important one at that. Where would today's society be without lumyrite? Your frivolous little paper creations, on the other hand, we can do without."

Oh how she hated that she'd had the very same thought. But she would sooner swallow broken glass than give him the satisfaction of knowing they shared any opinion at all. "Ah yes, how foolish of me to think some magic might be about more than profit. Tell me, my lord, do you disapprove of all art, or just the kind created by those with diluted bloodlines?"

A delicate tinkling sound reached Iris's ears, and she realized the crystals in the chandelier above them were shivering. She refused, however, to tear her gaze from Lord Jasvian in order to look up.

"This has nothing to do with an appreciation of art. Can you not see that with each generation, with each ... mingling of bloodlines, our magic grows weaker? Our ancestors could move mountains and command storms. Now we celebrate mere conjuring tricks. You, Lady Starspun, come from a line of celestial illuminators and navigators whose magic charted the stars themselves. The Starspun legacy deserves better than paper manipulation."

The reminder that her family indeed deserved more than the simple magic she'd manifested sent a flush of shame burning across her face, but she refused to yield now. "Oh? Please enlighten me about my family's legacy, Lord Rowanwood. I'm certain you know it better than I do."

His eyes narrowed. "I'm sure I do not need to tell you that your ancestor transformed nautical travel across the United Fae Isles when they were still separate territories after producing the first magical star charts. I do not need to tell you of the celestial harvesters, nor of the starlight spinners."

Indeed, he did not need to tell Iris any of these things. With each word, she felt the weight of her inadequacy more keenly.

"Imagine what magnificent starlight-related magic might have been passed to you," Lord Jasvian continued, "if your father had chosen to marry well instead of diluting your bloodline with a human woman. Now the once-great Starspun name will dwindle to nothing more than a footnote in magical history."

Something snapped inside Iris. "And the Rowanwoods will be remembered for what, precisely? For hoarding lumyrite-derived wealth while contributing nothing of beauty or wisdom to the world? For producing descendants so utterly convinced of their superiority that they cannot recognize true magic unless it comes packaged in profit margins?"

A flush crept up Jasvian's neck. "How dare you assume—"

"Perhaps if you spent less time mourning the purity of other families' bloodlines and more time developing a personality beyond staggering arrogance, you might actually be worthy of the legacy you so desperately cling to!"

Something in Lord Jasvian's expression shattered. Above them, an ear-splitting crack rent the air as the chandelier rattled violently, its crystal pendants suddenly bursting with light before shattering into thousands of glittering shards. Iris flinched, her gaze darting up even as Lord Jasvian's arms flew outward, fingers curling expertly. The falling glass transformed instantly into a cascade of golden dust.

When Iris's eyes landed on him once more, they were both breathing heavily. Her hands shook at her sides, while the remains of his control were clearly hanging by a thread.

"If you'll excuse me, my lord," she said coldly, "I believe I hear someone calling for more paper flowers." And with that, she turned, brushed past Lady Rivenna and her horrified parents—who, it seemed, had not allowed themselves to be distracted by any ice sculpture garden—and marched away through the crowd.

Chapter Six

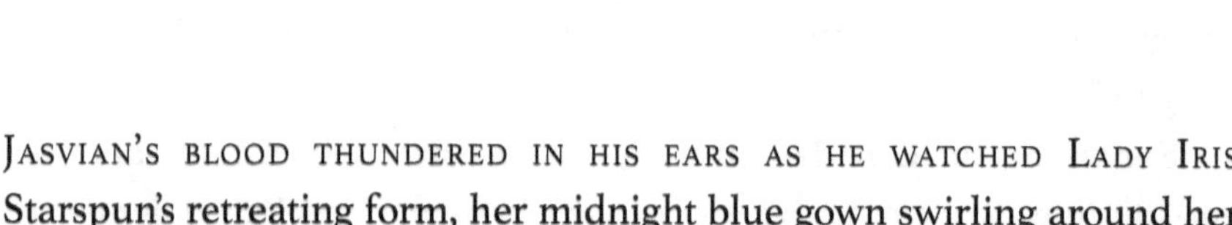

JASVIAN'S BLOOD THUNDERED IN HIS EARS AS HE WATCHED LADY IRIS Starspun's retreating form, her midnight blue gown swirling around her as she carved a path through the astonished crowd. Her parents exchanged a brief, panicked glance before hurrying after her.

How *dare* she? The sheer audacity of speaking to him that way, questioning traditions that had sustained their society for generations and throwing his private words back in his face. Words that, while perhaps not kind, had been *true*. The preservation of magical bloodlines was vital to their society's future. Someone had to speak sense, even if others found it uncomfortable to hear.

And what of the things she'd said about his own magic? Granted, it lacked the aesthetic appeal of more flamboyant powers, but it was *essential*. Lady Iris clearly failed to comprehend the responsibility he bore. He could have pointed out that his abilities saved lives—dozens of them, each time he sensed a building tempest and prevented a disastrous mine collapse. He could have explained that the Rowanwoods did not *hoard* lumyrite-derived wealth, as she had so carelessly suggested, but rather fostered prosperity throughout the realm, their operations sustaining countless families across the United Fae Isles with dignified employment and fair compensation.

And then there was her ridiculous claim that he disapproved of all art and his magic contributed nothing of beauty to the world. Did lumyrite not power self-playing musical instruments? Did it not enhance illusion tapestries that transformed rooms with changing scenes of far-off lands? Without it, half the elegant enchantments that adorned this very ballroom would cease to function. Though his own hands might not craft these wonders directly, his magic ensured that lumyrite could be extracted safely and abundantly, making possible the very enchantments that transformed the mundane into the magnificent.

The last of the golden dust settled around him, glittering on the polished floor. He suddenly became acutely aware of the crowd's attention, their curious glances and whispered speculations. His grandmother still stood beside him, and when she caught his eye, the slight arch of her brow spoke volumes.

"Well!" she announced with practiced nonchalance, addressing the gathered onlookers. "These ancient chandeliers really ought to be replaced. All this magical energy from our young debutants—it's a wonder the entire ceiling hasn't come down!" She gestured elegantly toward the dance floor. "Do continue with the festivities."

Her well-timed intervention worked its usual magic. The crowd's attention shifted as the orchestra struck up a lively tune, and couples began to form for the next dance.

"Quite the outburst," she remarked quietly, turning back to him once the immediate spectators had dispersed. "I haven't seen you lose control of your magic since you were a boy."

Jasvian stiffened, horror creeping through him as her meaning became clear. "The chandelier? That was most certainly not my doing. I do not lose control." The very suggestion was absurd. His entire life was built upon rigid self-discipline. The mines depended on his ability to maintain perfect control of his magic at all times. A single lapse in concentration could mean disaster. "Far more likely it was Lady Iris," he continued stiffly. "She's clearly still unused to her powers."

Lady Rivenna's gaze held his for a long moment. "Perhaps it was a combination of both your magic and hers. Such things have been known to happen when—"

"It was not," he interrupted, more forcefully than he'd intended.

His grandmother smiled and patted his arm with maddening condescension. "Of course not, dear," she replied, her tone suggesting precisely the opposite.

She drifted away to speak with Lady Thornhart, leaving Jasvian to confront an alarming possibility. Had he truly lost control? Even for just a moment? The idea unsettled him deeply. He prided himself on his discipline, on the careful containment of his emotions and magic alike.

This entire evening had gone from tedious to disastrous. He hadn't wanted to attend in the first place, finding these gatherings exhausting with their endless social expectations and crushing press of bodies. The constant noise and movement set his nerves on edge, and he'd noticed himself being unusually sharp-tongued in his conversation with Hadrian. Perhaps that had led him to express his opinions about Lady Iris's magic more bluntly than propriety dictated. But once she had challenged him so directly, with those flashing eyes and razor-sharp responses, something in him refused to yield ground. Each barbed comment she'd delivered had only driven him to respond in kind until their exchange had spiraled beyond his control.

Once they'd reached that point, he couldn't possibly have acknowledged that he secretly shared her opinions of the Opening Ball. He'd always found the entire ritual faintly absurd—young fae parading their abilities while society assessed their worth based on spectacle rather than substance. But he was not about to admit that to Lady Iris Starspun.

As the weight of attention shifted elsewhere, Jasvian found himself increasingly desperate to escape. Unlike his grandmother, who had always been skilled at managing social situations, he found every ball and social gathering where he was expected to make polite conversation to be more like navigating a maze blindfolded. Give him a quiet room or the open mountainside near the mine shafts any day.

"Lord Rowanwood!"

He turned reluctantly to find Lady Emberlee Whispermist approaching, trailed by two other young women whose names momentarily escaped him. They surrounded him in a flutter of silks and perfume, their expressions eager. "That was quite the exciting moment with the chandelier," Lady Emberlee said, her voice pitched just high enough to grate on his already frayed nerves. "So dramatic!"

"Indeed," he replied neutrally, searching for any graceful exit from this conversation.

"You handled it so masterfully," another young lady—Myrissa Featherlock, he now recalled—simpered. "Transforming all that falling glass into harmless dust! Such quick thinking."

"It was nothing," he said, wishing fervently that he could merge with the marble floor beneath his feet and sink into the very foundations of Solstice Hall.

"You never dance at these events, Lord Rowanwood," Lady Emberlee observed with a practiced pout. "Could we not persuade you to join just one set this evening?"

"Oh, yes!" the third young lady exclaimed, her fan fluttering with excitement. "Surely you could spare one dance?"

Jasvian maintained his polite mask with considerable effort. "I'm afraid I must decline."

The young women exchanged glances, undeterred by his refusal. "I heard the most interesting rumor," Lady Myrissa ventured after a moment. "They say you might be considering taking a wife this Season."

"I will not be choosing a wife!" he blurted out stiffly. A shocked silence fell over the immediate vicinity, and he realized he'd spoken louder than he intended. Mortification washed over him. "I ... that is ..." He cleared his throat and attempted to recover his composure. "Forgive me, ladies. If you'll excuse me, I have ... urgent business to attend to."

He turned on his heel and strode away from the clustered young ladies, their disappointed sighs following in his wake as he headed in the opposite direction from where Lady Iris had disappeared.

He needed air. And silence. And most of all, he needed to stop thinking about impertinent half-fae ladies who dared to suggest that his magic—magic that kept hundreds of families safe, that maintained the very foundation of their society—was nothing more than 'sensing rocks.'

Chapter Seven

Iris tried to keep her pace measured as she made her escape from the ballroom. She tried not to draw attention to herself—well, any *more* attention than the exploding chandelier had already brought. But then she caught part of a conversation:

"How fortunate they only have the one."

"Indeed! One shudders to think of how much worse it would be were there a whole brood of them."

"I dare say he recognized his mistake after the first."

"Alas, too late by then ..."

Iris took off through the crowd, no longer caring who she offended or what whispers followed in her wake. She heard her name being called—her mother's voice, then her father's—but she kept moving, her skirts rustling as she wove between clusters of fae nobility.

She finally burst free of the ballroom. The palace corridors stretched out before her, a maze of gilt and marble, but she kept moving. She had no idea where she was going, only that she needed to get away from the music, the judgment, the weight of a hundred stares. Her heels clicked against the polished floor as—

"Iris!" Her father's voice cracked like a whip. "Stop this instant."

She halted, chest heaving, and turned to face her parents. Her mother looked distraught, while her father's face had gone an alarming shade of red.

"Have you completely lost your senses?" he demanded. "Arguing with Lord Jasvian Rowanwood? In public? At your debut?"

"Did you hear what he said about me?" Iris's voice shook. "About my magic being useless and my blood being—"

"It doesn't matter what he said!" Her father took a breath and straightened. "He is one of the most influential men in ... well, not only Bloomhaven. The entire United Fae Isles. The heir to the Rowanwood fortune and lumyrite mines. And you ... you ..."

"Perhaps we should find somewhere more private," her mother suggested quietly, glancing around. "There is a room just there."

Iris allowed her mother to lead her into an elegant chamber dominated by a gleaming piano. Moonlight streamed through tall windows, casting silver patterns across the instrument's polished surface.

"I won't apologize," Iris said as soon as the door closed behind them. "We should return home. We are clearly not wanted here, nor do we have any need of this company."

Her father's laugh was harsh. "Need? We most certainly do need them. You have no future—none of us do—if you do not secure a match this Season."

"That's absurd. I don't *need* someone, and even if I did, I can find such a person in my own town. Someone who doesn't care about bloodlines or—"

"And live like what?" her father burst out. "Like paupers?"

Iris blinked at him. "What are you talking about? What do you—" She shook her head, utterly confused. "What about the Starspun estate? Our family fortune?"

Her father's shoulders sagged. "There is no fortune, Iris. There hasn't been for years. No inheritance. No dowry. Nothing."

"But ..."

"There hasn't been money in enchanted star charts for generations." Her father raked a hand through his hair, his voice rising with a desperate edge. "And as for starlight spinning ... the silks, the enchanted threads, all those magically potent materials that are so durable ... they were once sought after by nobility and royalty everywhere, but that market died out generations ago. Newer enchantments made our craft obsolete. The Starspun name has become just that—a name, nothing more."

Iris had known about the decline of their traditional craft, of course, but the revelation that their finances had deteriorated to absolute destitution left her momentarily speechless. "But ... the country estate where Aunt Celandine—"

"Is falling into ruin," he cut in. "Your aunt and uncle maintain a skeleton staff—barely enough to keep the basic operations running. From what I understand, your uncle's family has experienced severe financial hardship as well and cannot provide assistance from his side."

"But ... everyone speaks of the distinguished Starspun legacy ..." Iris fumbled for words, her mind still reeling. Hadn't the insufferable Lord Jasvian reminded her of her illustrious family history mere minutes ago?

"The Starspun legacy is indeed distinguished and respected," her father said, "but there is no fortune that accompanies it anymore."

"But surely Grandfather—"

"Your grandparents chose to remain here in Bloomhaven precisely because maintaining the country estate became impossible. If things do not change very soon, they will have to let it go, as well as Starspun House here in Bloomhaven."

"Starspun House as well?" Iris asked, her voice faint with disbelief. It wasn't as though she'd ever pictured herself living as some wealthy heiress. She'd always assumed that her father, having defied his family by marrying a human woman, would inherit only a small portion of his parents' estate. But she'd always believed she and her parents would at least remain comfortable.

"Yes." Her father took a deep breath, as if he were steeling himself for something. He stepped closer, his tone becoming gentler. "So when your magic manifested, your grandparents invited us to return. They see it as an opportunity to restore our family's standing. A chance to save us all from financial ruin."

"But ... what about Aunt Celandine and—"

"She cannot have children," Iris's mother interrupted softly. "She represents the end of that branch of the family line."

The full weight of this statement settled heavily upon Iris. "So I'm ..."

"The only possible future for the Starspun bloodline," her father confirmed quietly. "The only hope for all of us."

"At ... the cost of my happiness," Iris said faintly, staring at the floor with unfocused eyes. "The cost of my freedom."

"What happiness will you have when we are destitute?" her father asked, not unkindly. "What freedom? We are almost at the point where we cannot maintain even the most basic of appearances. We are drowning in debt, Iris. The compensation for the bookshop alone ..."

Iris flinched as her father trailed off. The memory of that day still haunted her. "I'm so sorry about that. If I had known what was happening, if I had been able to control it—"

"No, I apologize, I should not have brought that up," her father said wearily. "The bookshop was only part of it. I've been borrowing for years, trying to maintain some semblance of our position, hoping ..." He shook his head. "But now our creditors are losing patience. If we return home without securing your future here, we'll lose what little we have left."

Iris sank onto the piano bench, her mind whirling. "So this is why you brought me to Bloomhaven? Strengthening my magic has nothing to do with it. Our sole purpose here is to find someone wealthy for me to marry?"

"Your magic manifesting was a gift," her mother said, stepping closer, "and of course we wish for it to strengthen, both for your sake and for the opportunity it represents. You have given us *hope*, Iris." She sat beside Iris on the piano bench and took her hand. "A half-fae with magical ability might be acceptable to the right family, especially one looking to secure connections to the Starspun name—which still carries weight, even if there's nothing material behind it anymore."

"Even if that bloodline has been *diluted*?" The words tasted bitter on her tongue.

"Iris—"

"And now I've ruined everything by antagonizing the wealthiest bachelor in Bloomhaven with all of fae society watching." She laughed, but there was no humor in it. "How terribly inconvenient of me."

"We should have told you sooner, but we didn't want to burden you with this responsibility. We thought ... we hoped ..."

"That I would manifest some *useful* ability that might save us somehow? That at the very least I would be a good daughter and secure us all a comfortable future?" Iris stood, unable to bear her mother's gentle touch. The weight of it all pressed down on her—her family's desperate circumstances, her own part in their financial ruin, the impossible task before her. "I ... I need to ..."

She didn't know what she needed to do. *Not* apologize to Lord Jasvian Rowanwood, that was certain enough. She could apologize to her parents though.

"I'm sorry," she whispered. "Had I known how important this evening was ..." She trailed off. It would have been difficult not to engage with Lord Jasvian after what she'd overheard, but perhaps she could have bitten her tongue, greeted him politely, and sought an excuse to leave. But what was done could not be undone. She must now compose herself with what little dignity remained and navigate her newfound circumstances.

She drew in a deep breath and straightened her shoulders. "I shall do better," she said, meeting her parents' worried gazes. "I'll mind my tongue in proper society and ... attempt to make favorable impressions upon suitable gentlemen." The words felt dry in her throat, but she forced them out with all the conviction she could muster.

Her parents' expressions softened with visible relief, and her mother squeezed her hand gratefully. But as they prepared to leave Solstice Hall —it would be unthinkable to return to the ballroom now, so soon after her dramatic confrontation with Lord Jasvian—Iris's mind was already turning over possibilities like pages in a book. There had to be another answer. Another path. Whatever it was, she would find it. Somehow, she would save her family without sacrificing her independence.

Chapter Eight

The clock in the drawing room of Starspun House ticked away with merciless precision, each second punctuated by a sharp click that seemed to mock Iris as she paced from one end of the room to the other. She paused at the window for the fifth time in as many minutes, pressing her fingertips against the glass as she gazed longingly at the street below. Though Starspun House occupied a less prestigious corner of Bloomhaven—not in the central or wealthiest district, which now made perfect sense to Iris—there was still a comfortable flow of activity in the street below. Elegant carriages rolled past occasionally, while small groups of people and couples wandered arm in arm, enjoying the pleasant spring morning.

She turned from the window and crossed the room once more. Unlike the warm, cluttered home she'd left behind, Starspun House was all formal elegance and untouchable perfection—polished surfaces, stiff brocade, and gleaming silver that seemed more for display than use. Even the floral arrangements were pristine and scentless, preserved by magic in a state of perpetual bloom that somehow rendered them lifeless.

"Iris, please sit down," her mother said without looking up from her light-weaving. The delicate strands of enchanted light refused to hold their pattern between her fingers as she attempted to perfect the spells, clearly more difficult for her without any magic of her own. "Your constant movement is rather distracting."

"How can I possibly sit still?" Iris drummed her fingers against her skirts. "We've been trapped in this house all morning."

Her grandparents had departed for their promenade at Elderbloom Park over an hour ago, pointedly not inviting them to join. "After last night's unfortunate display," her grandmother had said with a thin smile, "perhaps it would be best if you remained here today. Allow the initial whispers to die down before presenting yourself in public again."

Translation: hide your shameful face until people have found something new to gossip about.

Her father, who sat stiffly in the chair across from her mother while pretending to read a newspaper, sighed heavily. "You exaggerate the situation, Iris. No one is keeping you prisoner here. Your grandparents are merely being cautious. The social fallout from your confrontation with Lord Jasvian Rowanwood could be significant."

Lord Jasvian Rowanwood. His name alone caused a flare of anger in her chest. That arrogant, disdainful face came to mind immediately—the way his dark eyes had swept over her with such dismissal, how his voice had dripped with condescension as he'd deemed her magic "paper-folding nonsense" and called her a "half-breed."

But beneath the anger lay the sharp sting of something else. His words had sliced deeply because they'd echoed her own fears. Her magic *was* frivolous compared to the abilities of full-blooded fae. Her father *had* diluted the Starspun bloodline by marrying her mother. The great celestial magic of her ancestors had indeed been reduced to mere paper manipulation in her hands.

"All the more reason I should be out there," Iris insisted, resuming her pacing. "If I'm to repair the damage to my reputation and present myself as a worthy prospect to the eligible gentlemen of Bloomhaven, I can't be confined to Starspun House."

The weight of their conversation from the previous night pressed down on her shoulders even as she tried to outpace it with her restless movement. If she couldn't find another solution, marriage to some wealthy lord was her only option. The thought made her stomach twist with dread. To be bound forever to a man who viewed her primarily as a means to continue his bloodline, who would likely choose her only because the Starspun name still carried the weight of respectability and ancient lineage worthy of alliance. How could she possibly bear such a fate?

Her father shook his head, his expression grave. "After last night, we need to proceed carefully. Your grandparents went out this morning specifically to gauge the reaction in society. When they return, we'll have a better sense of our standing."

With a sigh, Iris returned to the window, watching as a small flock of those awful gossip birds flew past, their dreadful squawking indecipherable but clearly excited as they darted from rooftop to rooftop. With any luck, they were now spreading some new piece of social misfortune instead of shrieking about her own indiscretion.

She turned away from the window and eyed the formal settee she'd abandoned earlier with its rigid back and thinly cushioned seat. Everything in this room was designed for appearance rather than comfort—much like the facade her grandparents presented to society. The warm spring sunlight that streamed through the windows seemed unable to penetrate the room's austere atmosphere.

She turned away from the window and dropped into a chair beside a potted fern, her energy momentarily exhausted though her mind continued to race. The chair, like all the furniture, was clearly designed for perfect posture rather than relaxation, its ornate wooden arms unyielding beneath her fingers. Even the very air in the room seemed to demand formality, as if casual conversation or genuine emotion might somehow tarnish the perfect surfaces.

As she picked up the volume of poetry she'd abandoned earlier and began aimlessly leafing through it, one of the fern's delicate fronds stretched outward, brushing against her wrist with a touch so gentle she might have imagined it. She glanced down as the plant appeared to reach for her deliberately, its leaves curling softly around her fingers in what felt remarkably like comfort.

"Thank you," she murmured, stroking the frond with her fingertip.

Her mother looked up, a question forming on her lips, but before she could speak, the drawing room door opened. "Lady Rivenna Rowanwood," announced the butler, his face betraying a flicker of astonishment that his impassive voice managed to conceal.

All three Starspuns shot to their feet as the formidable matriarch of the Rowanwood family swept into the room.

"Lady Rowanwood," Iris's father said, executing a bow that was perhaps a touch too deep. "What an unexpected honor."

"Indeed." Lady Rivenna's sharp gaze swept the room before settling on Iris. "I trust I find you recovered from last night's excitement, Lady Iris?"

Iris swallowed, unsure how to respond. Should she apologize for her heated exchange with Lord Jasvian? Express regret for her part in the chandelier incident? "I ... that is ..."

"Tea!" her mother exclaimed. "We simply must have tea." With a swift motion, she reached back for the long cord of braided silk hanging against the wall and gave it a firm tug.

Lady Rivenna lowered herself into a chair with the easy confidence of one accustomed to commanding every space she occupied. "I must say, that was quite the display of temper last night. From both parties involved."

Iris's throat went dry. "My lady, I—"

"Do you know," Lady Rivenna continued as if Iris hadn't spoken, "I cannot recall the last time I saw my grandson lose control of his magic like that. He insists it was not him, of course. I, on the other hand, find myself rather convinced that it was both of you."

"I'm so terribly sorry about that," Iris's father said quickly. "We will, of course, cover any damages—"

Lady Rivenna waved away his concerns, which was just as well, given that Iris had no idea *how* her father would cover said damages. "Nonsense. That chandelier was ghastly anyway. The High Lady has been looking for an excuse to replace it for years." Her lips curved. "Though I doubt she expected quite such a dramatic catalyst."

A parlourmaid arrived with the tea service, and Iris's mother busied herself preparing cups with slightly trembling hands. When she passed one to Lady Rivenna, the older woman took a delicate sip, then pursed her lips. "Ah. Well. I suppose not everyone can maintain The Charmed Leaf's standards."

"At least we don't have to drink the leaves," Iris muttered into her own teacup before she could stop herself.

Her mother released a barely audible gasp, but Lady Rivenna's eyes sparked with something that might have been amusement. "My dear, if you find yourself *consuming* the leaves rather than *reading* them, I fear you've misunderstood the entire practice."

Iris hesitated with her teacup halfway to her lips, but before she could think of an appropriate response, Lady Rivenna forged on. "Now, let me not waste time with any more pleasantries. The events of last evening have solidified something I've been considering since you first entered my tea house." She turned to address Iris directly. "Lady Iris, I would like to offer you the position of apprentice at The Charmed Leaf Tea House."

Iris stared at her, certain she had misheard. Carefully, she lowered her cup to its saucer. "I ... beg your pardon?"

"An apprenticeship," Lady Rivenna repeated, her tone suggesting she was unaccustomed to repeating herself. "I am not getting any younger, despite my best efforts, and I have known for years that The Charmed Leaf requires a successor. Someone who can learn its ways, who can eventually assume responsibility for its operation when I am no longer able to do so. I have simply been waiting for the right person."

"I, uh ..." Iris glanced at her parents, who appeared equally stunned. Her gaze swung back to Lady Rivenna. "Forgive me, my lady, but ... you're offering this position to *me*?"

"Indeed. It is a position that many have sought over the years. The Charmed Leaf is not merely a tea house—it stands at the very intersection of information, influence, and magic, at the beating heart of

Bloomhaven society. Its proprietress holds a unique position of respect and ... shall we say, insight." A slight smile curved her lips. "The financial benefits are not inconsiderable either."

At the mention of financial benefits, Iris felt her pulse quicken. Could this be it? A path to independence that would also secure her family's future? Had providence delivered the very solution she had been hoping to find, presenting itself far sooner than she might have hoped?

"Lady Rivenna," her father said carefully, his brow furrowed, "while we are naturally honored by your offer, I must express some concern. Iris's purpose in Bloomhaven this Season is quite specific. She has social obligations that must take priority—"

"Social obligations," Lady Rivenna echoed, her tone dry. "By which you mean securing an advantageous match."

Iris's father cleared his throat. "Well, yes. That is the tradition of the Bloom Season, after all."

"And how do you imagine that pursuit is progressing after last night's exchange with my grandson?"

A pained expression crossed her father's face, and Iris felt a fresh wave of guilt.

"The apprenticeship need not interfere with Lady Iris's social calendar," Lady Rivenna continued smoothly. "Indeed, her position at The Charmed Leaf may well enhance her standing. As my chosen successor, she would be viewed with new interest by certain families who might otherwise hesitate to form connections with someone of her ... unique heritage."

"And you mentioned ... financial benefits?"

"The tea house generates considerable income," Lady Rivenna confirmed. "As my apprentice, Iris would receive a stipend immediately, with her share increasing as she assumes more responsibility."

Iris felt her initial spark of hope dim slightly. A mere stipend would scarcely address the mountain of debt her father had described. Would such a modest sum truly be sufficient to maintain them until she advanced to a position of greater responsibility and remuneration? Might their creditors be willing to extend further patience if they saw a legitimate prospect of eventual repayment?

"But why Iris?" her father asked, giving voice to the question that had been echoing in Iris's own mind. "Surely there are many worthy candidates. Full-blooded fae from established families who have been waiting for such an opportunity."

Lady Rivenna's eyes narrowed slightly. "Are you suggesting your daughter is unworthy of the position, Lord Starspun?"

"No! Of course not," he said hastily.

"I believe he means to say that surely there are others more qualified," Iris said, echoing the very doubts that circled in her own thoughts. "Someone with more practical magic, or—"

"More qualified? You mean someone who fits more neatly into society's expectations? Someone who wouldn't cause the gossip birds to molt in shock?" Lady Rivenna smiled. "My dear, that is one of the reasons I'm interested in you."

Iris frowned. "I don't understand."

"The Charmed Leaf requires someone who can see beyond the surface of things. Someone who isn't afraid to challenge convention." Her smile widened. "Someone who might suggest that the heir to the Rowanwood fortune merely 'senses rocks.'"

Iris felt her face flame. "About that—"

"Oh, don't apologize. Jasvian could do with someone pointing out his occasional stuffiness. Though perhaps with slightly more subtlety next time."

"Next time?" Iris's father's voice cracked slightly.

"Of course. The Season has barely begun, after all."

"I'm still not sure," Iris said, "how seeing beyond the surface of things or challenging convention—"

"It matters not," Lady Rivenna interjected with a dismissive wave of her hand. "To be perfectly honest, you have already satisfied the most crucial requirement: the tea house itself selected you the moment you crossed its threshold."

A beat of silence followed her pronouncement. "The tea house ... *chose* me?"

"Indeed." Lady Rivenna reached into her elegant reticule and withdrew something small, which she placed on the table beside her teacup.

"What is that?" Iris's mother asked curiously.

"A petal," Lady Rivenna said. "Or, more precisely, a paper petal."

They all stared at the innocuous object in silence. Lady Rivenna appeared to be making some profound connection between this paper petal and Iris's folding abilities, but surely she hadn't based such a momentous decision about her successor on the tea house producing a single paper fragment? Such a coincidence could signify any number of things! Iris, however, wasn't about to voice these doubts. Her mind was already racing with possibilities. This opportunity excited her not merely as a potential path to independence and her family's salvation, but because the tea house itself fascinated her.

Sitting forward on the edge of her chair, she asked, "What exactly would this apprenticeship entail?"

"I cannot divulge the specifics to anyone but you, Lady Iris," Lady Rivenna said with a glance at Iris's parents, "and only after you have accepted the position. But in essence, you would learn everything there is to know about the tea house—its magic, its secrets, its operation. By the time your training concludes, all the knowledge I have cultivated over decades will be yours to wield."

"And when would this apprenticeship begin?" her father asked.

"Immediately. Time is precious, and there is much to learn."

Iris couldn't contain herself any longer. "I want to accept," she said, sitting forward on the edge of her chair now. "This is an incredible opportunity."

Her parents exchanged a look that spoke volumes. Her father turned to Lady Rivenna. "Perhaps we might have a moment to discuss this privately?"

"There is nothing to discuss," Iris insisted. "This is exactly what I need—a purpose beyond merely seeking a husband."

"Iris," her mother began gently, "we understand how appealing this offer must seem, especially after ... recent revelations. But marriage is still ..." She hesitated, glanced at Lady Rivenna, and lowered her voice slightly. "It is still the surest path to security."

"You must consider this carefully," her father urged. "What if you were to receive an offer of marriage and accept, only to discover your husband expects to return to his country estate after the Bloom Season? You cannot possibly manage the tea house from a distant property."

Lady Rivenna cleared her throat. "When I first established The Charmed Leaf, I too had family obligations—young children requiring my attention. For many years, I closed the tea house at the conclusion of each Bloom Season while returning to our country estate, reopening only when most of society gathered in Bloomhaven again. Once the tea house belongs solely to her, Lady Iris would have the freedom to make similar arrangements."

A tense silence fell over the room. Iris looked between her parents, silently willing them to say yes. Her father's gaze swept back to Lady Rivenna. "If Iris begins this apprenticeship and circumstances then prove unfavorable, would she be permitted to withdraw from this arrangement?"

"If *Lady Iris* were to decide this," she said, and Iris noticed the emphasis Lady Rivenna placed on her name, "then of course she would not be forced to remain."

Iris's father considered this in silence for another few moments, then sighed. "If Iris wishes to accept your offer, Lady Rivenna, we will not stand in her way. However, we must insist upon certain conditions."

"Name them," Lady Rivenna said, inclining her head.

"First, the apprenticeship must not interfere with her social obligations. She will attend all significant events of the Bloom Season and maintain her place in society."

"Agreed."

"And second, she must continue to develop her magic in preparation for the Summer Solstice Grand Ball. Her presentation there is vital."

"I would expect nothing less," Lady Rivenna replied. "Her magical growth will only benefit the tea house."

"Then ..." he glanced at Iris's mother before returning his gaze to Lady Rivenna. "I suppose that is all. We shall support Iris if she wishes to accept your offer."

Lady Rivenna's lips curved into a satisfied smile. "Your conditions are reasonable, Lord Starspun. I accept them." She turned to Iris. "And you, Lady Iris? Do you accept my offer with these stipulations?"

Iris nodded, a strange sense of exhilaration coursing through her. "I do."

"Excellent." Lady Rivenna rose to her feet. "Then I shall expect you at The Charmed Leaf tomorrow morning. Eight o'clock precisely. We have much to cover. Oh, and do wear something practical, dear. The hearth sprites can be quite mischievous with newcomers."

Chapter Nine

Iris arrived at The Charmed Leaf precisely at eight o'clock the following morning, dressed in what she hoped qualified as 'practical.' She'd selected a pale blue day dress with minimal embellishment, and her hair was arranged in a simple knot at the nape of her neck. She paused at the foot of the tea house's stone steps, taking in the weathered charm of the establishment. Morning light caught on the intricate carvings adorning the heavy oak door—delicate teacups and swirling leaves etched by a master craftsman's hand. Vines climbed the stone walls, their glossy leaves framing the entrance while clusters of tiny purple flowers cascaded around the doorframe.

Her heart fluttered a little faster as she ascended the steps. Despite Lady Rivenna's warm welcome yesterday, Iris couldn't quite shake her nervousness. Was the front door even unlocked at this hour? Perhaps she was meant to enter through the back, where staff might already be preparing for the day.

She startled as a gossip bird shrieked from a nearby tree. "Kissing in the lake!" it proclaimed before taking wing. Iris blinked, wondering if she'd heard correctly.

Just as she lifted her hand to knock, the door swung inward. She hesitated on the threshold, took a steadying breath, and stepped inside to find the entrance area curiously empty, with no sign of whoever—or whatever—had opened the door.

The interior of the tea house appeared quite different in the early morning light, devoid of patrons yet humming with subtle magic as if taking a deep breath before the day began. Windows gleamed, tables sat perfectly arranged, and the faint aroma of fresh-baked goods mingled with the earthy scent of brewing tea.

Lady Rivenna emerged from the kitchen on the far side of the tea house, dressed in a deep emerald gown that somehow managed to appear both elegant and entirely practical. "Ah, Lady Iris. Punctual. Good." She beckoned with one hand. "Come. There is much to see before we open."

"Good morning, Lady Rivenna," Iris said, hurrying to reach the older woman. "I'm eager to begin."

Lady Rivenna stopped in the center of the main floor, her silver hair catching the morning light that spilled through the windows. "The Charmed Leaf is more than it appears," she began, her voice taking on a subtle cadence that suggested she was imparting something of great importance. "You see tables and chairs, walls and windows. But what we truly have here is a carefully cultivated ecosystem of magic, social currents, and information."

She gestured toward the far corner, where a cluster of plush chairs surrounded an oval-shaped table. "That area is favored by the elder ladies of Bloomhaven. Lady Thornhart, Lady Whispermist, and myself, of course. From there, we observe everything while appearing to observe nothing."

Iris followed her gaze, trying to see the tea house through Lady Rivenna's eyes—not as a mere establishment but as a strategic vantage point.

"The central tables," Lady Rivenna continued, indicating the heart of the room, "are for those who wish to see and be seen. Young lords and ladies hoping to make an impression. Families showcasing their offspring. The recently betrothed flaunting their good fortune."

She moved toward the opposite wall, where several semi-private alcoves had been created through clever arrangement of trailing plants and decorative screens. "These nooks are for more discreet conversations. Business negotiations, delicate social maneuvers, the occasional minor scandal being carefully managed."

"Is every seat so deliberately assigned?" Iris asked, fascinated by this invisible orchestration.

Lady Rivenna's lips curved. "Not assigned, precisely. But the tea house has its ways of encouraging certain patterns. The chairs throughout the establishment become remarkably uncomfortable for those carrying gossip with malicious intent. Tables have been known to wobble mysteriously when occupied by guests plotting social sabotage. And tea has a peculiar tendency to go cold very quickly when consumed by anyone who has spoken ill of the Rowanwood family."

Iris failed to suppress a smile at this last revelation. "And do you arrange all this yourself? Through magic?"

"The tea house itself plays a part," Lady Rivenna replied. "Over the decades, it has developed ... preferences. Habits. A personality, you might say. My role is to interpret and occasionally direct these tendencies."

She then gestured toward a smaller alcove nestled against the eastern wall, where honeysuckle vines cascaded from the ceiling, partially obscuring the space from casual view. Beyond the natural curtain of greenery sat a small round table with a single chair. A window seat lined with plush cushions faced the side street, and a small shelf—seemingly floating against the wall without visible support—held several well-worn leather-bound books.

"That," Lady Rivenna said with unmistakable fondness, "is my private alcove. The true heart of my observations. I sit there quietly, alone with a pot of tea, and simply listen to what the tea house has to tell me. No one else ever sits there." Her gaze settled meaningfully on Iris. "Until now. This alcove will become yours as well."

"Oh, are you certain?" Iris stammered, taken aback by the intimacy of this offering. "I'm sure I could sit somewhere else, perhaps at one of the—"

"You will never understand the true workings of The Charmed Leaf," Lady Rivenna interrupted firmly, "if you don't seat yourself in that alcove daily and simply *listen*." She beckoned Iris to follow once more. "Now, to the heart of our operation."

Lady Rivenna extended her hands before her, and the kitchen doors swung open at their approach, revealing a bustling scene of organized chaos. Steam rose from copper kettles, the air sparkled with tiny motes of magic, and several small creatures darted between workstations. A cloud of flour hung suspended over the central worktable, within which Iris could just make out a tiny, industrious figure.

"This is where the true magic of our tea blends and culinary delights takes place," Lady Rivenna declared. "Here we have our hearth sprites —" she nodded toward several faintly glowing beings tending the fires, some adjusting the iron cranes that held simmering pots over the open hearth, while others stoked the embers beneath a cast-iron stove "— kitchen pixies who maintain our equipment and assist with preparations —" several blue-tinged beings sat polishing silver tea services on a table alongside the back wall "—and of course, Orrit."

The flour cloud parted momentarily to reveal a scowling, stout little creature no taller than Iris's hand, his ruddy face and expressive eyebrows coated in fine white powder. A brownie, Iris guessed, though it was difficult to tell with the amount of flour that covered him.

"Orrit has been with us since the day The Charmed Leaf opened," Lady Rivenna explained. "He is the master of our legendary scones. No one touches his dough, his ovens, or his secret recipe."

The brownie harrumphed, clearly displeased by the interruption but apparently too busy to spare more than a skeptical glance at Iris before returning to his work.

"Don't mind his gruffness," Lady Rivenna added. "He takes his art seriously."

Iris watched the kitchen's harmonious activity unfolding, and then—between one blink and the next—the scene shifted. Suddenly she was looking at a different configuration—the same kitchen but filled with unfamiliar faces, save for one. Orrit remained at his workstation, but now he was playfully tossing a cloud of flour into the air while a small dark-haired girl sat on the edge of the worktable, swinging her feet and laughing with delight.

Iris blinked, and the scene returned instantly to its original form. What strange trick was this? Some whisper of the tea house's unique magic?

"Lady Iris?" Lady Rivenna was watching her with a curious expression. "You seemed momentarily elsewhere."

"I apologize," Iris said, shaking her head slightly. "It's just ... there's so much to take in."

At that moment, a quick flash of heat at her ankles made Iris gasp and jump backward. She looked down to see a tiny hearth sprite darting away, trailing sparks and giggling as the hem of her dress began to smolder. She yelped and hastily batted at the fabric to extinguish the burning fabric before it could properly catch alight.

"Good thing, my dear," Lady Rivenna said, "that you wore a practical dress as I suggested." Her eyes gleamed with amusement. "But yes, as you were saying, there is indeed much to take in. And you have yet to meet Saffron and Lissian, both of whom shall be in shortly. But for now, let me introduce you to—ah, Lucie! Perfect timing."

A girl entered through the back door carrying a basket of fresh herbs, and Iris recognized her immediately as the serving girl from her first visit to the tea house. She couldn't be more than fourteen or fifteen years of age.

"Lucie, this is Lady Iris Starspun, my new apprentice."

"Oh! An apprentice!" Lucie's smile stretched wider. "Finally! I-I mean to say ..." she stammered, her soft brown complexion taking on a deeper warmth, "how very exciting, my lady."

Lady Rivenna arched a brow. "Exciting indeed. Lady Iris, this is Miss Lucie Fields. She is invaluable to our operation. Though she is human, she has shown remarkable aptitude for the simpler enchantments I've taught her, particularly those relevant to the tea house's daily operations. She's also developing quite impressive skills in the confectionery arts, creating delicate chocolate concoctions infused with subtle mood-enhancing magic."

"Thank you, Lady Rivenna," Lucie said, executing a quick curtsy. "And it's an honor to meet you, my lady," she added in Iris's direction.

"Lucie's mother is one of the most respected dressmakers in

Bloomhaven," Lady Rivenna continued, "though Lucie herself clearly has no interest in fashion."

The girl began to stammer something else, but Lady Rivenna added, "All I mean to say, my dear, is that you are perfectly suited to working here, learning the delicate art of magical confectionery from Saffron—that's our pastry chef—" she added as an aside to Iris, "rather than wasting your days sewing dresses."

Lucie nodded, a smile creeping onto her lips once more.

"And this," Lady Rivenna said as a tall woman entered from the main floor, "is Mrs Spindlewood, our hostess."

Iris recognized her as the woman who had greeted her family during their first visit. She also noted that although the woman was fae, Lady Rivenna had introduced her as *Mrs* and not *Lady*. Iris found herself pondering the woman's circumstances. Did she perhaps hail from a fae family of lesser standing, possessing modest means and only basic magic? Or might she belong to one of the established noble bloodlines but have failed to manifest any significant ability?

Mrs Spindlewood's expression remained as coolly professional as Iris remembered from the first time they had met, though she did incline her head in polite acknowledgment. "I look forward to working with you, Lady Iris," she said, her tone giving nothing away.

Lady Rivenna directed Iris toward the back door, where Lucie had entered. "We also maintain extensive gardens," she explained as they stepped outside.

The space was divided into distinct sections—neat rows of herbs, flowers, and what appeared to be tea plants. Beyond this, Iris saw elegant outdoor seating arranged beneath the trees around a central fountain. Garden gnomes moved between the herb beds, their pointed hats bobbing as they inspected leaves and stems. Meanwhile, tiny pixies with gossamer wings flitted among the blooms, collecting the morning dew in miniature crystal vials.

"While we cultivate a small selection of tea right here, the majority of our leaves are sourced from across the United Fae Isles," Lady Rivenna explained. "And the herbs and flowers are essential for our specialty blends. The garden gnomes have been tending these plants for decades, using methods passed down through their families. The pixies assist with harvesting ingredients at precisely the right moment—dawn-caught dew, moon-blessed blossoms, and so forth."

"And the seating area?"

"For outdoor functions," Lady Rivenna replied. "Though the fountain serves another purpose entirely." She lowered her voice. "Its water flows directly from one of the seven ley lines that converge beneath Bloomhaven. The magic that infuses it enhances certain ... perceptions."

Iris was about to ask what perceptions specifically when Lady Rivenna turned and headed back inside. "Now, for the final stop on our tour. Your primary domain, at least initially."

They re-entered the tea house and crossed the kitchen to the main floor. At the end furthest from the front door, tucked around a corner behind a wall adorned with an artful arrangement of antique teacups, Iris discovered a staircase she hadn't noticed during her previous visit. They ascended the polished wooden steps. At the top, a small landing led to a single door, which Lady Rivenna opened with a flourish, stepping back to allow Iris to walk in ahead of her.

Beyond lay a cozy study with a large window overlooking the street that ran along the side of the tea house, flooding the room with natural light. Comfortable chairs with plump cushions were positioned near the empty fireplace, where a single hearth sprite lay sleeping, the room warm enough in the early spring that no flames were needed. Carved wooden tables held elegant vases of fresh flowers and delicate magical ornaments, while along one wall stood a modest book shelf, its contents neatly arranged.

Iris's anxiety stirred faintly at the sight of the books, memories of the bookstore incident flashing unbidden through her mind. She took a deep breath, steadying herself. This wasn't a shop crowded with volumes. It wasn't a vast library. Merely a few shelves of carefully selected tomes. Her magic remained calm, dormant beneath her skin.

Two empty desks occupied the space. One larger, positioned at an angle in the corner of the room, the other slightly smaller, standing in front of the window.

"This will be your sanctuary," Lady Rivenna said, moving toward the window and the desk in front of it. "Your place to study, to observe, to learn the deeper mysteries of The Charmed Leaf."

"It's perfect," Iris breathed. Well, almost perfect, she added silently as her gaze was drawn back to the bookshelf. But that was no fault of the study itself. Perhaps here, in this peaceful space, she might finally reclaim her comfort around books, might rekindle the pure joy of being surrounded by boundless realms of ink and imagination, without fear of her magic spinning out of control.

"I assumed you would appreciate it," Lady Rivenna replied, straightening a vase of flowers on a small side table. She crossed to a cabinet beside the bookshelf and withdrew something from its drawer. "And this —" she extended her hands, offering a leather-bound notebook of deep plum with silver filigree patterns along its edges "—is for you. To record your observations, insights, and perhaps the occasional secret."

Iris accepted the gift with wonder, running her fingers over the intricate silver design. "It's beautiful. Thank you."

Lady Rivenna moved around the room, adjusting a book here, straightening a crystal prism there. "I hope you don't mind hard work, Lady Iris. You will be exceptionally busy this Season with three distinct goals to pursue: this apprenticeship, your social obligations, and developing your magic for a memorable display at the Solstice Ball."

"I welcome the challenge," Iris said, tucking the notebook beneath her arm. "I've never shied away from hard work."

"Good," Lady Rivenna replied with a satisfied nod. "Because the first patrons will arrive soon, and there is much to do. Now, let me show you how to—"

The study door swung open without warning, and in stepped Lord Jasvian Rowanwood, his tall frame filling the doorway. He halted abruptly, dark eyes widening as they moved from his grandmother to Iris and back again. "Grandmother?" His gaze hardened. "What is *she* doing here?"

Lady Rivenna straightened, hands clasped serenely before her. "Ah, good morning, Jasvian. I was just showing Lady Iris around her new workspace."

"Her new ... what?" The words emerged with such careful precision that Iris could almost hear them cracking beneath the weight of his restraint.

"Workspace," Lady Rivenna repeated, as if speaking to a child with limited comprehension. "Lady Iris has graciously accepted my offer to become my apprentice at The Charmed Leaf."

Lord Jasvian's face went through a remarkable series of transformations—disbelief, horror and outrage cycling in rapid succession before settling into a rigid mask of displeasure. "This is completely unacceptable."

The hearth sprite—no longer asleep—squeaked in alarm. From the corner of her eye, Iris saw it zip across the room to hide behind the vase on one of the small tables.

Lady Rivenna arched one silver eyebrow. "I seem to recall you lecturing me at great length just days ago about my advanced years and the urgent necessity of finding a suitable successor for the tea house. By all rights, I should be thanking you for your persistent encouragement."

"I didn't mean—" His fingers curled into tight fists at his sides. "That is, I never suggested—" He drew a sharp breath. "You cannot possibly believe that *Lady Iris* is a suitable candidate."

"I find her eminently suitable," Lady Rivenna replied, smoothing an imaginary wrinkle from her skirts. "As does the tea house itself."

"The tea house cannot—"

"As I've explained countless times, Jasvian, the tea house absolutely can and does make its preferences known. You simply choose not to listen." Lady Rivenna turned to Iris with a slight smile. "You'll find that's a recurring theme with my grandson."

Iris fought to keep her expression neutral, though the corner of her mouth twitched traitorously. Lord Jasvian's evident distress at finding her in what he clearly considered his territory was, she had to admit, rather satisfying after his dismissive treatment of her at the Opening Ball.

He drew in another steadying breath, eyes still fixed on his grandmother. "But she's ..." He gestured vaguely in Iris's direction.

"Perfectly capable of speaking for herself," Iris said. "Though I understand if complex sentences are beyond your comprehension this early in the morning."

Jasvian finally deigned to meet Iris's gaze. "I was merely pointing out—"

"That my magic is unsuitable?" Iris asked. "That my bloodline is impure? That I'm as plain as the paper I fold? Please, do tell me which insult you'd like to lead with today."

"I was *going* to say that you're untrained."

"As are all apprentices at the beginning," Lady Rivenna observed.

A tiny glowing shape momentarily caught Iris's attention, and her gaze darted toward the door where the hearth sprite was busy sneaking out, clearly sensing the rising tension in the room.

"Well then," Jasvian said stiffly, "now that you have shown Lady Iris the upstairs study, perhaps the two of you would prefer to continue your tour downstairs."

"Oh no," Lady Rivenna said, gesturing to the desk by the window. "Lady Iris will be working here, in the study. I've always found it the perfect place for contemplation and learning."

The look of pure horror that crossed Jasvian's face was so comical that Iris had to bite the inside of her cheek to keep from laughing outright.

"Here?" he echoed, his voice rising slightly. "But this is *my* study!"

"*Your* study?" Lady Rivenna's tone remained perfectly pleasant. "How curious. I was under the impression that The Charmed Leaf—including all its rooms, furnishings, and indeed this very study—belonged to me."

Jasvian's jaw worked silently for several seconds. "You know perfectly well what I mean," he finally managed. "I've used this study for years. It's my escape from the chaos of Rowanwood House, the one place where I can properly focus on business without constant interruption."

"And you may continue to use it," Lady Rivenna assured him. "You'll simply be sharing the space with Lady Iris." She paused, tilting her head slightly. "Ah, I believe I'm needed downstairs." She moved toward the door. "Lady Iris, please join me when the two of you have finished sorting out your differences." And before either of them could respond, Lady Rivenna swept from the room, leaving an uncomfortable silence in her wake.

Iris squared her shoulders and lifted her chin. "Lord Jasvian."

"Lady Iris." His voice was cold enough to frost glass. "I see you've wasted no time insinuating yourself into my grandmother's good graces."

"On the contrary, it was Lady Rivenna who approached me with her offer," Iris replied, her tone matching his. "Though I must confess, had I known it would cause you such evident distress, I might have accepted even more enthusiastically."

Jasvian's nostrils flared. "This is *my* space."

"I don't see your name etched anywhere," Iris observed, glancing pointedly around the room. "Nor do I see any of your personal effects. It appears to be quite simply a study that Lady Rivenna has graciously allowed you to use—and now has graciously invited me to share."

"The desk," he said tightly, "is enchanted to mirror my workspace at Rowanwood House. The moment I sit down, everything I've left at home appears here, arranged precisely as I left it. I've been using this arrangement for—" He stopped abruptly, as if annoyed with himself for offering any explanation at all. "Not that it's any of your business."

"Ah, how very *practical* of you," Iris said pointedly.

His jaw tightened. "I see you're still bristling from our exchange at the Opening Ball."

"Exchange?" Iris gave a short laugh. "Is that what we're calling it? I would have described it as you making disparaging remarks about my heritage and magical abilities, followed by my pointing out your insufferable arrogance."

"You caused a scene," he said through gritted teeth.

"Did I? How mortifying." Iris pressed a hand to her chest in mock distress. "Though not nearly as mortifying as having one's magic dismissed as 'nonsense' by someone who's probably never had to question his place in society for a single moment of his privileged life."

"You know nothing about me," Jasvian said, his voice low and tight.

"And you know nothing about me," Iris countered. "Yet that didn't stop you from passing judgment, did it?"

"I spoke only truth. Your specific magic has no practical application."

Iris stepped closer, heat surging in her veins. This close, she saw that his eyes weren't merely dark, but a deep storm gray, circled by rims of a darker shade that gave way to startling flashes of silver closer to the pupil. "I do not have to prove myself to anyone," she said, her voice low and measured, "least of all to you."

"On the contrary," Jasvian replied, not backing away from her advance, "if you're hoping to find yourself a suitable match in Bloomhaven, then you have a great deal to prove. To everyone."

Iris felt her retort die on her lips, hating that he was right. Her family's financial situation meant she couldn't afford the luxury of righteous indignation, no matter how satisfying it might be. "Are we done here?" she asked finally. "Or would you prefer to spend another few minutes glowering at me?"

"I do not *glower*."

"My mistake. That must be your natural expression." And with that, she tucked her new notebook more securely under her arm and swept past him with as much dignity as she could muster. "If you'll excuse me," she said without looking back, "I believe I'm needed downstairs. Unlike some, I don't have the luxury of idle conversation when there's work to be done."

Then she pulled the door firmly shut behind her, taking perhaps a bit too much satisfaction in the solid thud it made as it closed.

Chapter Ten

IRIS REACHED THE BOTTOM OF THE STAIRS, HER CHEEKS STILL FLUSHED from the confrontation. She paused at the edge of the main floor, taking a moment to compose herself before stepping into view of the early patrons who had begun to arrive.

Mrs Spindlewood stood at the entrance, welcoming a pair of elegantly dressed fae ladies. Iris watched as Lady Rivenna glided forward, exchanging pleasantries with the newcomers before personally guiding them to a table near the center of the room. Iris noticed how the table was positioned perfectly within earshot of where a younger gentleman and an older woman who might have been his mother were already seated, deep in conversation. Lady Rivenna then guided a trio of young lords to a table adjacent to where several debutantes sat with their chaperones. Before long, conversations began to spark between neighboring tables.

Iris smiled, shaking her head a little in wonder. What might appear random to anyone else now revealed itself as an intricate dance of social engineering. Every placement seemed calculated, every 'chance' encounter designed. Even now, Mrs Spindlewood was subtly rearranging the chair positions at one of the tables—after a whispered discussion with Lady Rivenna—to create a more intimate setting for what appeared to be a reunion between old friends.

"Fascinating, isn't it?" Lady Rivenna's voice came from beside her, and Iris started, not having noticed her approach. "Most believe they choose their own seats based on preference or availability. Few realize how deliberately their interactions are orchestrated."

"It's remarkable," Iris admitted, continuing to watch. "I would never have noticed had I not been looking for it."

Lady Rivenna's lips curved in satisfaction. "The best manipulations are those that remain invisible." She gestured toward the honeysuckle-draped alcove. "This morning, you will sit there in my private space and simply observe. Listen to the tea house, watch its subtle changes. Take note of what you see and hear, but do not intervene. I shall sit with you later this morning, and you can tell me what you've learned."

Iris nodded, then made her way across the floor toward the private alcove. As she slipped past the curtain of trailing vines, she felt a curious sense of welcome. The cushions on the window seat seemed to plump themselves invitingly, and a shaft of sunlight angled through the window, illuminating the small table where a delicate porcelain cup sat waiting, filled with fragrant tea.

She placed her new notebook carefully on the window seat and settled herself comfortably beside it, taking a deep breath as she prepared to immerse herself in the life of The Charmed Leaf. From this vantage point, partially concealed by greenery yet offering a view of the majority of the main floor, she began to understand why Lady Rivenna treasured this particular spot. It was both sanctuary and observation post, a place to witness everything while appearing to notice nothing.

At first, she simply watched the steady stream of patrons, but gradually, something odd caught her attention. She blinked, then stared harder at the far wall. Had that alcove always curved quite that way? She could have sworn ... She kept her gaze fixed on the spot, barely daring to breathe. Yes—there! The wall itself was moving, ever so slowly, creating a more intimate space for the young couple sharing tea and significant glances.

If she hadn't been watching so intently, she might have missed it entirely. The changes were subtle, almost imperceptible unless one knew to look. A wall shifting a fraction of an inch, a doorway widening just enough to let in more light, a corner deepening to offer more privacy. And Iris suddenly remembered, with startling clarity, the way she thought she'd imagined the tea house interior stretching and expanding around the table she and her parents had walked toward the day they'd first come in here.

How remarkable! When she'd first heard people claim that The Charmed Leaf had a mind of its own, that it held opinions and preferences, she'd assumed it was merely figurative—a charming exaggeration to explain Lady Rivenna's uncanny influence. But now Iris saw the truth: the building itself was consciously, physically altering its own architecture, reshaping itself to serve purposes only it fully understood.

Iris reached for the notebook Lady Rivenna had given her, intending to record these observations, but before she could open it, she heard something that made her pause. Voices—soft, delicate things that seemed to come from the very plants surrounding her.

"—simply cannot believe she would wear that shade of blue to a morning tea—"

"—told him three times already that Father won't approve—"

"—if he thinks I'll simply stand by while he gambles away my dowry—"

Iris sat very still, listening. The voices seemed to shift and flow around her. Were the vines ... No, they couldn't be. And yet, as she watched closely, she found she was able to match the words currently reaching her ears to the movement of a woman's lips at the table on the far side of the tea house.

Iris allowed herself a quiet gasp, her heart pattering faster. The vines were indeed relaying snippets of conversation from throughout the tea house. When Lady Rivenna had said that she sat here and listened to what the tea house had to tell her, she'd meant it quite literally. Iris's gaze traveled to a table near the window where two ladies and a gentleman sat in apparently peaceful conversation. But now she could hear what lay beneath their pleasant smiles.

"You promised," one of the women was saying, her actual voice barely a whisper while the plants carried her words clearly to Iris. "You swore you would stop."

"My dear sister," the man replied with fake joviality, "you worry too much. The investments are completely sound—"

"That's what you said about the pegasus racing scheme," the other woman cut in. "And the enchanted jewelry venture. And now you expect us to believe—"

A leafy tendril brushed Iris's cheek, as if seeking approval for sharing these secrets. "You're listening," she murmured, partly in awe and partly in horror. "You're listening to everything."

The implications were staggering. How long had the plants been gathering intelligence? How many secrets had they collected over the years? Iris had heard it said that Lady Rivenna always seemed to know everything that happened in Bloomhaven, and now she understood how.

She continued to watch the arguing trio, and then ... somehow, the scene before her seemed to shift, as if another image was trying to overlay itself on top of reality. For a moment, Iris saw the same table but with different people seated there, their faces indistinct but their postures speaking of similar tension. Then that image faded and another took its place—the same spot but at what must have been a different time of day, sunlight slanting differently across the table, the chairs arranged in a new pattern.

A burst of laughter shattered the strange vision, and Iris blinked rapidly as reality reasserted itself. "Did you do that?" she murmured out loud, but the vines didn't answer her.

Iris's gaze swept across the room until she caught Lady Rivenna's eye. The older woman gave her a knowing look, and Iris realized that Rivenna was well aware of what Iris had just discovered. With unhurried grace, Lady Rivenna made her way toward the alcove, slipping behind the curtain of vines to join Iris in the sheltered nook.

"You have discovered the tea house's greatest secret," Lady Rivenna said, settling beside Iris on the window seat.

"The plants—they're conveying conversations from across the room,"

Iris said, keeping her voice low. "Is it ... ethical? To listen to private exchanges without consent?"

Lady Rivenna's expression grew solemn. "We are custodians of these secrets, Lady Iris, not their exploiters. Unlike those wretched gossip birds that squawk every tidbit to the highest rooftop, we hold these confidences sacred. The information gleaned here is to be used wisely—to guide, to prevent disaster, to create harmony where there might otherwise be discord. Never for vindictive purposes or personal gain."

"But still," Iris pressed, "how can you justify—"

"Think of it as a responsibility," Lady Rivenna interrupted. "One of the reasons I have never before chosen an apprentice is precisely this—I needed someone with both the wisdom and moral fortitude to be entrusted with such power."

"But you don't even know me," Iris said, bewildered. "How can you possibly trust me with this?"

Lady Rivenna studied her for a long moment, her eyes reflecting the dappled light streaming in through the window. "I sensed something in you the night we met at the Opening Ball. Even before that, the moment you walked into this tea house ..." She gestured to the trailing vines surrounding them. "I believe the tea house recognized you before I did."

Iris laced her fingers together in her lap. "Are the whispers of the vines your only means of gathering insight? Does reading the tea leaves not play a role in this? I've heard they reveal glimpses of what's to come. An old practice meant to divine the future."

"The tea leaves do not show the future with certainty," Lady Rivenna replied. "Rather, they hint at what might come to pass. Combined with the tea house's whispers, these readings allow me to make informed judgments about where and how to ... nudge circumstances in favorable directions." She rose, smoothing her emerald skirts. "Continue listening, Lady Iris. The tea house has much more to teach you."

As Iris listened and watched, time slipped by as effortlessly as steam rising from a freshly poured cup of tea. When she finally thought to glance at the ornate clock on the wall, she started. How had nearly two hours passed? The morning rush had given way to the pre-luncheon lull, and the quality of light streaming through the windows had shifted completely.

"Lady Iris?" She turned to find Lucie beside her. The serving girl dropped a quick curtsy. "I beg your pardon for disturbing you, but Lady Rivenna thought I might show you more of the tea house gardens before my midday break."

Lucie led her through the bustling kitchen, where a fae woman whose skin possessed a definite orange tinge moved between the central work table and two of the ovens, her steps appearing to be perfectly choreographed to weave between the hearth sprites and kitchen pixies. "That's Mama Saffron," Lucie whispered to Iris. "Our pastry chef. She presides over all manner of confections and baked delicacies outside of the scones. Oh, and that's Lissian," she added as a pale, almost translucent figure emerged from the pantry carrying several jars of tea leaves and moved toward the brewing station.

The creature was shorter than both fae and humans, with wavy white hair arranged in a loose braid that reached all the way to her waist. Tiny flower buds were woven into the braid, and she wore what appeared to be a garment woven from morning mist and scattered petals that floated around her graceful form.

"Lissian prepares most of the tea served within these walls, though always in deference to the tea house itself, which, I have been assured, maintains the final authority on what shall be served to each patron."

"I don't believe I've ever encountered such a being before," Iris remarked in a hushed tone. "Is she a nymph?"

"Indeed, my lady. A tea nymph, to be precise."

Iris almost laughed before realizing Lucie was entirely serious. "A tea nymph?" she repeated. "I had no idea such creatures existed."

"I believe they're exceedingly rare. From what Lady Rivenna has said, these beings are particularly attuned to the essence of tea leaves and herbs. Lissian dwells in a secluded corner of the garden here, and it's considered an honor that she has chosen to make her residence at The Charmed Leaf."

As they crossed the kitchen toward the back door, Iris glanced at Lissian at her brewing station, which was nestled against a wall where the same vines that adorned the main tea house floor crept and twined. The nymph ran her slender fingers over the leaves, tilting her head as if listening to something. Then, with a nod, she lined up three teapots and began removing the lids from jars of various ingredients.

Outside, hints of lemongrass, mint and lavender mingled with the scents of other herbs and flowers. The garden gnomes Iris had glimpsed earlier were now fully engaged in their work, their pointed hats bobbing as they moved between rows with miniature watering cans and trowels. Nearby, a trio of garden pixies flitted around a cluster of exotic star-shaped blooms, coaxing the petals to open with delicate taps of their fingertips.

There was nothing here that Lady Rivenna hadn't already shown her earlier that morning, and it occurred to Iris—belatedly—that this little visit to the garden with Lucie might be the result of one of the older woman's carefully arranged social orchestrations that Iris had unknowingly stepped into.

"The garden gnomes and pixies are forever at war," Lucie said before Iris could decide whether to be amused or exasperated at being drawn into one of Lady Rivenna's subtle machinations. The younger girl pointed to where a gruff-looking gnome was shaking his trowel at a tiny figure hovering just out of reach. "The gnomes focus on what they call the 'proper work'—turning soil, pulling weeds, ensuring correct drainage—while the pixies manage what they consider to be the more sophisticated tasks."

As if to illustrate her point, a small group of garden pixies darted past, their gossamer wings catching the light as they carried armfuls of freshly cut blossoms, their tiny faces determined as they raced toward the kitchen door. The nearest gnome bellowed something unintelligible, his face reddening beneath his beard. The pixies merely giggled, accelerating as they disappeared inside with their floral treasures.

"I heard Lady Rivenna ask for more flowers for some of the table arrangements," Lucie whispered, leaning a little closer, "but the gnomes are quite particular about where exactly the flowers are cut from. The pixies, however, pay no heed to their wishes."

Iris suppressed a smile. "And does Lady Rivenna side with one or the other, or does she let them wage their little war unchecked?"

Lucie laughed. "Oh, she claims neutrality, but the gnomes grumble that the pixies get away with far too much under her watch."

The two of them stood in companionable silence for another few moments, watching the gnomes and pixies at work. Then Lucie spoke, her voice soft and hesitant. "If you'll permit me to say so, my lady … I am terribly sorry about those dreadful gossip birds and their awful squawking. It must be horrible, being new here and feeling like an outsider, only to have them spreading such unkind rumors."

Iris's throat tightened at the genuine sympathy in the girl's voice. "Thank you. Though I suppose I should grow accustomed to it."

"You should not have to." Lucie's usually cheerful face darkened. "Charlotte and I—Charlotte is my sister—have sworn we shall hunt down their keeper one day and put a stop to all this horrid rumor-mongering."

"Their keeper?" Iris turned to her in surprise. "But aren't they natural creatures that happen to live in the area?"

Lucie shook her head emphatically. "Oh no, my lady. They were created decades ago. Magical constructs, not proper birds at all. Abominations, if you ask me. Perhaps they no longer have a keeper, but if they do …" Her expression grew determined. "Well, Charlotte and I shall find this dreadful person eventually."

"I had no idea." Iris watched a garden pixie carefully measuring the distance between lavender plants with a tiny ruler. "Though I suppose I shouldn't be surprised. Everything here seems designed to maintain social order through secrets and whispers."

"It can be rather overwhelming," Lucie agreed. "Especially when you're …" she hesitated, then continued more quietly, "when you're not quite what they consider proper society."

Understanding passed between them. "Because you are human?" Iris asked gently.

Lucie nodded. "Yes. Like us, you understand what it means to be judged by what you lack rather than what you possess."

"Indeed," Iris murmured.

"I can learn some basic magic, of course," Lucie continued. "Simple charms and everyday enchantments. But I will never have the natural ability of the fae." She gestured to where a garden pixie was coaxing a reluctant rose to bloom. "Never be able to do anything quite so instinctive."

"At least you know where you stand," Iris said. "Being half-fae is like ... like being caught between two worlds. Not quite belonging to either."

"But you manifested," Lucie pointed out. "That is something they cannot dismiss, no matter how much they might want to."

Iris heaved a sigh. "True. Though a certain brooding person of great importance seems determined to do precisely that."

"Ah." Lucie's lips twitched. "You speak of Lord Jasvian Rowanwood, I imagine? Indeed, he can be rather ... overbearing in his opinions. Though his younger brothers and sisters are much pleasanter company." She leaned closer, lowering her voice. "He may fancy himself the arbiter of all society's opinions, but I assure you, he doesn't speak for everyone. The rest of Bloomhaven's elite will have to acknowledge you now. Not only have you manifested, you are Lady Rivenna's chosen apprentice."

"That's another thing that continues to surprise me," Iris commented. "I wouldn't have thought an apprenticeship a position the nobility would covet."

Lucie's eyes widened. "Oh, but you cannot imagine! To be the next proprietress of The Charmed Leaf? Why, half of Bloomhaven's most distinguished families would trade their finest pegasi for such an opportunity. Even those who pretend to look down on commerce would give anything to hold such a position."

Iris thought of the morning's whispered revelations, the secrets carried on vine-wrapped breezes. Having witnessed only a fraction of the tea house's abilities this morning, Iris could well understand its allure. The tea house's exact magic might remain a mystery to most, but none could deny the power held by its mistress.

"Though of course," Lucie continued, her expression growing thoughtful, "it takes someone rather special to manage it all properly. Which is why Lady Rivenna is so particular about ..." She trailed off, clearly searching for the right words.

"About what?"

"About seeing people for who they truly are, I suppose. She is not like the rest of them, you know. She sees beyond all their silly rules about proper bloodlines and natural ability. She gave me a chance here when no other fine establishment that serves the elite of Bloomhaven would consider hiring a human girl, and she has never once made me feel lesser for it." She smoothed her apron. "She trusts me. Values my work. Gives me the opportunity to stay late sometimes and experiment in the kitchen. It means everything to me."

Iris studied the young serving girl with new appreciation. "She seems to have excellent judgment."

"Oh, she does." Lucie's smile returned. "And she chose *you* as her apprentice. That must mean something rather significant, don't you think?"

Before Iris could respond, a voice called from beyond the willowbloom. "Lucie? Are you out here? I wanted to ask if you still plan to—oh!" A young woman emerged from beneath a flowered archway, her dark brown hair caught up in a practical knot. She wore a simple dress—quite different from the elaborate silks favored by Bloomhaven's elite—but carried herself with quiet dignity.

"Oh! Lady Iris, this is my sister Charlotte," Lucie said, and indeed, Iris could see the resemblance now. "The very one I was just speaking of—my partner in the great gossip bird investigation."

"Plotting our detective work without me again, Lucie?" Charlotte grinned, though her expression grew somewhat guarded as it shifted back to Iris. "Good day, my lady."

"This is Lady Iris," Lucie said. "She has just become Lady Rivenna's apprentice."

"Apprentice?" Charlotte looked appropriately shocked. "But ... wait. Lady Iris? Lady Iris *Starspun*? But you are ..." Charlotte trailed off as her gaze shifted slightly, leaving Iris with little doubt that the girl was examining the not-nearly-elegant-enough points of her ears. Then her face broke into a grin. "Oh, but this is simply marvelous!" She clapped her hands and gave a delighted laugh. "Lady Rivenna has outdone herself this time. Proper fae society will be in absolute fits over this. How perfectly wonderful."

Lucie giggled, then hurriedly clapped a hand over her mouth, her uncertain gaze darting to Iris as if she wasn't sure whether laughter was an appropriate response. The girl's apparent fear, due no doubt to Iris's fae side, made something twist painfully in Iris's chest.

She smiled warmly, hoping to reassure Lucie. "I have no doubt," she said, her gaze returning to Charlotte, "that they will respond exactly as you have predicted. I'm surprised those blasted gossip birds have not spread the news already."

"A slow morning for them indeed," Charlotte said. "They are most likely still recovering from spreading their rather creative version of your encounter with Lord Rowanwood at the Opening Ball. Apparently you challenged him to a magical duel, and he turned all your paper butterflies into golden dust while the High Lady cheered him on."

Iris could not help her horrified bark of laughter. "*That* is the story now circulating around Bloomhaven?"

Charlotte shrugged, her eyes sparkling with mischief. "Well, perhaps not *quite* so embellished, my lady."

"Please," Iris said, "just Iris will do. After enduring endless formality and judgment, it's refreshing to be among people where such pretense isn't necessary."

"Iris," Charlotte repeated with a small nod, and something in her expression—a mixture of understanding and shared defiance—made Iris feel truly seen for the first time since arriving in Bloomhaven. "It is so lovely to meet you."

Iris felt something tight in her chest begin to loosen. After days of navigating cutting remarks and sideways glances, Lucie's gentle kindness and Charlotte's straightforward warmth were like finding two unexpected allies in enemy territory. "Likewise."

"Now, sister dear," Charlotte continued, turning her attention to Lucie, "I came to ask if you still wished to visit The Petal & Pearl during your break. I heard they've just received a new shipment of products."

"Oh yes!" Lucie's eyes lit up. "I've been looking forward to it all morning. I have but a few minutes remaining until my break."

"The Petal & Pearl?" Iris questioned, curiosity getting the better of her.

"Oh, it's the most enchanting beauty boutique in Bloomhaven," Lucie explained, her eyes sparkling. "You'll find the most marvelous magical cosmetics there. Dewdrop lip stains, powders that make your skin glow, balms that change color with your emotions. Their newest product is something called Starfall Kohl that's supposedly made from crushed meteor dust."

"You simply must come with us, Iris," Charlotte said. "If Lady Rivenna permits, of course. We shall not be gone too long. Only the length of Lucie's break."

Iris hesitated, holding back the 'yes' she had almost blurted out. As much as she longed to spend more time with Lucie and Charlotte, two human girls were hardly the sort of company her grandparents would approve of if she hoped to make advantageous connections in society. But this wasn't a formal social gathering, and after the strange morning she'd had ...

"I would love to," she said, then quickly added, "though I must first ask Lady Rivenna if—"

"Go, go," Lady Rivenna's voice came from behind them, making them all jump. Iris swung around and found Lady Rivenna standing in the open doorway leading to the kitchen. "The afternoon rush won't begin for hours yet, and you've already observed much this morning. I suspect your mind is full of ... knowledge." She hesitated a moment on the final word, her eyes holding a knowing glint, and Iris knew that in this case, 'knowledge' most certainly meant 'secrets.' "Best not to weigh you down with too much at this early stage. We shall discuss all that you have learned so far when you return this afternoon with Miss Lucie." Her sharp gaze landed on the young girl. "Do be sure you return on time."

"Of course, my lady," Lucie said, dipping into a curtsy.

As Lady Rivenna disappeared back into the tea house, Lucie let out a small squeal of excitement, and the three young women exchanged delighted glances. For the first time since arriving in Bloomhaven, Iris felt something remarkably like the beginning of friendship.

Chapter Eleven

"SURELY YOU CANNOT BE IN EARNEST ABOUT THIS ARRANGEMENT, Grandmother."

Jasvian stood in the doorway of the tea house's pantry, his shoulders rigid beneath his impeccably tailored coat. He'd deliberately timed this conversation with his grandmother to coincide with the midday lull, when most of Bloomhaven's elite would be taking luncheon in their homes rather than lingering over tea and gossip. More importantly, he'd specifically waited until he was certain Lady Iris wasn't present. The very idea of another confrontation with that infuriating half-fae woman had set his teeth on edge all morning.

His grandmother didn't look up from the inventory ledger that lay open on her lap, where she was meticulously recording figures with a silver-tipped quill. Shelves of exotic teas, spices, and preserves surrounded her, each jar and canister meticulously labeled in her elegant script.

"I am absolutely in earnest about the chocolate shipment," she replied, turning a page in her ledger. "The supplier insists the price has increased due to transportation difficulties, but I suspect opportunism in the face of growing demand."

"You know perfectly well that is not what I meant," Jasvian said, stepping further into the pantry and closing the door behind him. The familiar scents of cinnamon and dried tea leaves enveloped him. Normally a comforting combination, but today it failed to soothe his agitation.

Rivenna finally glanced up, one silver eyebrow arched in that particular way that had intimidated half of Bloomhaven society for decades. “Ah. You refer to Lady Iris Starspun, I presume? My new apprentice?”

“Yes, I refer to *Lady Iris Starspun*,” Jasvian replied, unable to keep a hint of mockery from his tone as he pronounced her name and title. “The very same Lady Iris whose magic consists of folding paper into decorative shapes. The Lady Iris who insulted our family in front of the High Lady herself and caused a scene that will be discussed in every drawing room in Bloomhaven for weeks to come. That Lady Iris.”

“Indeed.” His grandmother carefully set down her quill and closed the ledger. “Might I inquire as to your specific objection? Beyond the rather tiresome prejudice against her heritage that you seem determined to nurture.”

“My objection,” Jasvian said, “is that the tea house is not some charitable institution for wayward half-bloods with delusions of belonging in proper society. It is the center of Bloomhaven’s social web. A position it has maintained through years of careful stewardship by a full-blooded fae of impeccable lineage.” He drew a breath, forcing his voice to assume a more reasonable tone. “I simply cannot fathom how you could possibly believe her suitable for this role.”

His grandmother’s expression remained maddeningly serene. “And yet here we are.”

“Here we are indeed,” Jasvian agreed, his frustration building. “With you having offered an apprenticeship—a position dozens of accomplished young fae have sought for years—to someone whose magic couldn’t light a candle without assistance.”

“I see,” she said, rising from her chair. “I wasn’t aware that you had suddenly become an expert on The Charmed Leaf’s succession requirements. How marvelous that in addition to managing the lumyrite mines and overseeing our numerous estates, you’ve had time to master the tea house’s ancient magic as well.”

"That is not—"

"Or perhaps," she continued, her voice cutting through his protest, "you simply assume your title and bloodline grant you authority over matters that have never been your concern?"

Jasvian felt heat rise to his face. "My concerns are solely for the family's standing in society."

"How noble of you." His grandmother moved to a shelf lined with various jars of honey, minutely adjusting their positions as she spoke. "And naturally, you believe yourself better positioned to judge what might affect our standing than I, who have maintained both the tea house and the Rowanwood social position for more decades than you've been alive."

He forced himself to take another deep breath. Arguments with his grandmother invariably followed this pattern, her calm deflection and subtle redirection gradually leading him into verbal traps of his own making. "I apologize if I've overstepped," he said, "but you cannot deny that this appointment is highly unusual."

"The most significant decisions often are." She turned to face him fully, her silver hair catching the faelight.

"In any case," Jasvian said, raking a hand through his immaculately arranged hair, a gesture of frustration he immediately regretted, "the point remains that I cannot work under these conditions. If you insist on maintaining this arrangement with Lady Iris, then I will be forced to return to working at Rowanwood House."

"An excellent solution," his grandmother agreed smoothly. "Though I was given to understand that your mother's ballroom renovations have made concentration at home rather challenging."

Jasvian's jaw tightened. His mother had indeed commissioned extensive renovations to the ballroom directly beneath his study, filling the house with the constant cacophony of workmen, enchanted tools, and the occasional minor explosion. "The renovations are ... disruptive," he admitted reluctantly.

"Such a pity. So it seems you have three options." Rivenna ticked them off on her fingers. "Work amidst the chaos at Rowanwood House, find another location entirely, or ..." Her smile grew slightly wicked. "Learn to coexist peacefully with Lady Iris in the study upstairs."

"Or you could reconsider your decision," Jasvian pointed out, his voice tight.

"I could," she agreed. "But I will not."

Jasvian pressed his fingers to his temples, where a headache had begun to form. "I don't understand your insistence on this particular candidate. Surely there are dozens of suitable young fae who would be honored—"

"The tea house chose her," Rivenna interrupted, her voice suddenly gaining an edge of steel. "And I agreed with its judgment. That is all you need to know."

"The tea house cannot *choose* anything," Jasvian said, exasperation coloring his tone. "It is a building, Grandmother. A magically enhanced building, certainly, but still ultimately an inanimate structure. Everyone indulges the fancy that it has 'a mind of its own,' yet we all understand that it does not possess true sentience."

His grandmother's expression grew dangerously calm. "Is that what you believe, after all these years? That The Charmed Leaf is merely a clever enchantment? A trick designed to impress the gullible?" She shook her head slowly. "I had thought you more perceptive."

"I understand that it responds to your magic," Jasvian said. "That you've bound it to your will through decades of careful enchantment. But to claim it possesses independent judgment, that it can *select* anything of its own accord—"

"And yet it did precisely that," Rivenna cut in. "From the moment Lady Iris stepped through the front door, the tea house recognized something in her that you, with all your esteemed magical sensitivity, have failed to perceive."

"And what might that be?" Jasvian asked, unable to keep the skepticism from his voice.

"Potential," she said simply. "The kind that reshapes worlds, if given the chance to flourish." She sighed, her expression softening slightly. "You see only what is before you, Jasvian. The tea house and I see what could be."

A heavy silence fell between them. Jasvian struggled to formulate a response that wouldn't sound petulant or dismissive, but found himself curiously unsettled by his grandmother's words. What potential could Lady Iris possibly possess that he had failed to recognize? Her magic was rudimentary at best, her bloodline compromised. And yet ...

He recalled the fierce intelligence in her eyes as she'd challenged him, both at the Opening Ball and again this morning in the study. The unwavering confidence with which she'd defended herself against his criticisms. Despite his initial dismissal of her abilities, there was something undeniably compelling about her refusal to be diminished.

"Your frustration is etched into every line of your face," his grandmother observed, breaking the tense silence. "Perhaps you might consider some additional fencing practice to work through these emotions that so clearly unsettle you."

Jasvian's frown deepened. "That won't be necessary. I've already scheduled the optimal number of fencing sessions into my weekly regimen, as well as the precisely calculated amount of swimming required to maintain peak physical condition."

"Of course you have," she sighed, rolling her eyes toward the ceiling. "Heaven forbid your exercise routine should ever become as spontaneous as your temper."

"I still maintain that this arrangement is ill-conceived," he said, ignoring her jab. "Lady Iris and I are ... incompatible. Our interactions invariably devolve into argument."

"Perhaps that is precisely what you need," his grandmother suggested. "Someone who challenges you, who refuses to be cowed by your pronouncements or intimidated by your position."

"I have no desire to be challenged on a daily basis," he answered. "I merely wish to complete my work in peace."

"Ah, yes. Your precious solitude." Rivenna moved to the pantry door. "Has it occurred to you, my dear grandson, that your insistence on isolation might be less a necessity and more a convenient shield against the messier aspects of human connection?"

"I have responsibilities—"

"As do we all," she interrupted smoothly. "Yet most of us manage to fulfill them without retreating entirely from society." She opened the pantry door and gestured for him to leave. "Lady Iris is due to return at one o'clock. The study is large enough for both of you, and I expect you to make a genuine effort at civility."

Jasvian recognized the tone—the conversation was over, his grandmother's decision final. He could continue to protest, but it would accomplish nothing beyond prolonging this increasingly uncomfortable exchange. "Very well," he conceded with poor grace. "I shall endeavor to be civil."

His grandmother's mouth curved in a smile that held more knowledge than Jasvian found comfortable. "How magnanimous of you." She gestured once more toward the door. "Oh, and Jasvian? If you're planning to filch one of Orrit's fresh-baked loaves to tide you over until dinner, I suggest the rosemary sourdough in the cloth-covered basket beneath the third shelf. He's outdone himself with today's batch."

Jasvian gave a curt nod of acknowledgment, then moved past his grandmother into the kitchen. He located the basket she had mentioned and helped himself to a generous slice of the still-warm bread before making his way back to the study upstairs, determined to put Lady Iris Starspun out of his mind.

Chapter Twelve

"Here we are!" Charlotte announced as the three girls approached The Petal & Pearl. The enchanted cosmetics shop was nestled between two larger shops on one of Bloomhaven's winding side streets, its facade adorned with delicate climbing roses and its petite display window featuring an arrangement of crystal bottles.

A small bell tinkled pleasantly as they stepped inside, and Iris's senses were immediately enveloped by the intoxicating blend of dozens of different fragrances. The interior was bathed in a soft, rosy light that illuminated displays of elegantly packaged cosmetics arranged on wooden shelves and glass-topped tables.

"Oh, look at these!" Lucie exclaimed, darting toward a collection of little silver-lidded pots. "The new Dewdrop Lip Stains! They've added three more shades since we were last here."

Iris followed, removing her gloves as her gaze swept across the shop. She'd visited similar establishments back home, of course, but nothing quite so magical. Here, mirrors whispered compliments as patrons gazed into them, brushes floated gently to demonstrate the perfect application technique, and the contents of certain containers changed color to complement the complexion of whoever touched them.

The three girls placed their gloves on the silver tray that sat on a small table near the entrance to the shop, before Charlotte linked her arm through Iris's and guided her toward a display of shimmering powders. "These are The Petal & Pearl's signature creations—Wingshine and Dandelion Dust. Even the High Lady herself is said to wear them."

"They're beautiful," Iris murmured.

"Try this one," Charlotte suggested, lifting a small jar filled with a pale golden powder. "The color is Sunbeam Honey."

Iris hesitated, then dipped her finger into the jar. The powder felt cool against her skin, almost like water rather than a dry substance. She approached one of the ornate mirrors mounted on the wall before dabbing it gently onto her cheekbone. The powder seemed to melt into her skin, leaving behind a subtle golden glow that caught the light with every turn of her head. "Oh!" she breathed, leaning closer to the mirror. "It's lovely."

"Isn't it?" Charlotte beamed, already reaching for another jar. "Now try the Foxglove Kiss. It's a lip stain that changes according to your mood."

The next several minutes passed in a flurry of giggles and exclamations as the three young women sampled various magical cosmetics. Iris allowed Lucie to apply a smoky eye kohl that made her dark eyes look larger and more mysterious, somehow accentuating their graceful slant, while Charlotte tried a variety of dramatic lip stains.

"I feel like an entirely different person," Iris admitted, turning her head from side to side to admire the transformation in the mirror. Her features were enhanced in ways that highlighted her fae heritage while softening the aspects that might be considered too human.

"You look absolutely enchanting," the mirror assured her in a silky voice. "The starlight in your eyes is positively luminous."

Iris clapped a hand over her mouth before giggling. "Do the mirrors know I'm of the Starspun family?" she whispered to Charlotte

Charlotte shrugged and laughed. "They're charmed to be effusive with their compliments, though. Good for business, I imagine."

"Though in your case," Lucie added, "I believe it's being entirely truthful."

Iris smiled, a warmth spreading through her chest that had nothing to do with the cosmetics. After days of feeling scrutinized and judged, the simple pleasure of trying on magical makeup with two girls who seemed to genuinely enjoy her company felt like the purest form of freedom.

"Your turn, Lucie," Iris insisted, picking up a jar of shimmering purple-blue kohl. "This shade would look spectacular on you."

As Iris carefully applied the pigment to Lucie's eyelids, she noticed a group of young fae ladies enter the shop, their silk gowns rustling as they moved between the displays. They were perfectly attired for an afternoon of shopping, with elaborate hairstyles and the subtle magical enhancements that marked them as members of elite fae society.

One of them, a slender girl with a rose-gold circlet nestled in her blue curls, looked in their direction and whispered something to her companions. Muffled laughter followed, along with a poorly concealed glance of disdain that swept over Iris, Charlotte, and Lucie in quick succession.

Iris stiffened, but Charlotte merely rolled her eyes. "Ignore them," she whispered. "Bloomhaven's finest young ladies, demonstrating their impeccable breeding through pointed stares and whispered insults. How original."

Iris managed a smile, though she couldn't help noticing how the group continued to watch them.

"Is that a *human* applying cosmetics to another human?" one of them said, her voice carrying deliberately. "How quaint. I suppose they haven't realized some enhancements simply cannot overcome certain ... limitations."

"And in the company of a half-breed, no less," another added with feigned horror. "Though I'm not sure who's lowering themselves more by the association."

Iris felt her cheeks flush, but Charlotte straightened her shoulders and spoke without turning around. "How fortunate we are to be reminded that magical cosmetics cannot disguise a complete absence of manners or basic decency."

Iris bit her lip to suppress a laugh, then spotted a stack of delicate paper pamphlets on the corner of a nearby table—each one detailing various magical products and their proper application. She reached out with her magic, feeling that familiar awareness of all the ways the paper wanted to fold. One pamphlet separated itself from the stack and floated toward her, creasing itself rapidly along invisible lines.

Within seconds, a beautifully crafted paper fan took shape. It drifted to hover before Iris, then began to wave itself back and forth, creating a soft breeze that caressed her face. "How charming," she said with exaggerated sweetness, angling herself so that the fan partially concealed her face. Then she caught her own reflection in the mirror—cheeks delicately flushed, eyes dramatically enhanced, paper fan fluttering coquettishly—and burst into laughter at the ridiculousness of it all. "I must look absolutely absurd," she said, still giggling.

"Absurdly beautiful," Lucie corrected, her own laughter joining Iris's.

"The fan is a particularly nice touch," Charlotte added. "Very dramatic."

As their laughter subsided, Iris noticed one of the fae girls staring at them with undisguised hostility. "Who is that?" Iris asked quietly, inclining her head slightly toward the glaring girl. "The one with the golden hair. She seems particularly cold."

Charlotte glanced over, then quickly returned her attention to the mirror. "Mariselle Brightcrest," she replied in a low voice. "Youngest Brightcrest daughter. Honestly, the entire family is awful."

"Brightcrest," Iris repeated, a memory stirring. "I believe I encountered a Lady Brightcrest shortly after my family arrived in Bloomhaven. She greeted my father outside the tea house. Though 'greeted' might be too generous a term."

"Probably Lady Clemenbell, Mariselle's mother," Charlotte said. "Your father would know her from when he used to come to Bloomhaven every Season. Before—" She cut herself off with a cough, darting a quick glance in Lucie's direction. "Be that as it may," she continued, "the Brightcrests and the Rowanwoods have been feuding for generations."

"Indeed, Lady Rivenna cannot stand them," Lucie added. "Something about a business venture gone wrong decades ago? Though I'm sure it must have been more than that. And now that you're her apprentice ..."

"I suppose that makes me doubly objectionable in their eyes," Iris concluded.

"Triple, if we're counting," Charlotte said with a wry smile. "Half-human, Lady Rivenna's apprentice, and now fraternizing with two entirely human girls in public. How utterly scandalous."

Despite her discomfort, Iris told herself not to be affected by these fae ladies and their hostile glances and comments. For the first time since arriving in Bloomhaven, she had begun to feel the first hints of genuine belonging, even if it was only in the company of two human sisters and a shop full of magical cosmetics. "Let them stare," she declared, lifting the magical fan to cool her flushed cheeks. "I'm having far too much fun to be bothered."

"That's the spirit," Charlotte agreed. "Now, shall we try the Dappleberry Balm? It gives you freckles in whatever shade perfectly compliments your natural complexion."

"Oh yes, let's!" Lucie reached for a small crystal pot containing a pearlescent substance. "It always gives me golden freckles, and they're simply delightful."

"What about this?" Iris picked up a small obsidian jar nestled among other jars in a basket.

Charlotte peered over her shoulder at the label. "Midnight Veil. 'A mysterious kohl that deepens the gaze and enhances one's natural perception of magical auras.' Oh, I believe I've heard of that one. Some ladies refuse to use it. They say the main ingredient is imported from the realm of the dark elves."

"I must point out that they are simply called 'elves,'" Iris remarked.

"The entire notion is ridiculous, whether they're called elves or dark elves," Lucie said, lifting the jar to examine it more closely, "We cannot even be certain elves exist at all."

Iris's laugh caught in her throat. "Are you ..." She trailed off, realizing Lucie was serious. "You doubt their existence?"

Lucie regarded her with evident skepticism. "Have you yourself ever met one?"

"Well, no," Iris admitted. "But I've read numerous scholarly works concerning them. My former home had a university with a most extensive library, volumes on every subject imaginable. There were entire volumes dedicated to elven culture and magic."

"And these learned authors—had they seen elves?" Charlotte asked, her lips twitching with amusement.

"I ... well ..." Iris faltered. "I'm not certain, but the documentation was most thorough. Detailed illustrations, accounts from historical sources—"

"So there exists no true evidence," Lucie concluded, now visibly suppressing a smile.

"That reasoning would suggest the High Lady herself doesn't exist merely because you've never had tea with her," Iris countered, though she could not maintain her serious expression.

Lucie tapped her chin thoughtfully. "I don't believe I've ever actually seen the High Lady."

Iris was laughing now. "Very well. Perhaps I shall arrange an expedition to that distant continent and return with an elf as proof. Then I shall invite both you and the High Lady to tea. Would that satisfy your skepticism?"

"Only if you persuade them both to wear Midnight Veil kohl," Charlotte replied solemnly before all three of them dissolved into giggles once more, Iris's paper fan fluttering animatedly beside them.

The shop's bell tinkled again as the door opened, and Iris glanced up reflexively. She froze, her fan stuttering in mid-air before dropping a few inches. "Mother?"

"There you are!" The silver bell chimed again as Matilda Starspun swept into the shop, dressed in a gown of dove-gray silk embroidered with tiny silver flowers. "I went to the tea house, but Lady Rivenna said I would find you here. I informed her you wouldn't be returning today. Your grandmother requires your presence at the Whispermist garden party. We were supposed to leave twenty minutes ago."

Iris's stomach dropped. She'd completely forgotten about Lady Lycilla Whispermist's afternoon garden party—a small and carefully curated affair Iris's grandmother had insisted was an honor to be included in. "I'm so sorry," she began, "I was just—"

Her mother's gaze swept over the scene—the open jars of cosmetics, the shimmering powders dusting the glass counter, the two human girls at Iris's side. Her lips pressed into a thin line, and she lifted a gloved hand to her temple, as if warding off a headache. "There isn't much time," she said briskly, lowering her hand. "You'll need to return home at once to wash that off and change into something more suitable."

"I know, I'm sorry. I forgot about—"

"You can't afford to forget things like this, Iris," she continued in a low tone, stepping closer. "Your father and I supported the tea house apprenticeship because Lady Rivenna's patronage could be valuable, but finding a suitable match must remain your priority."

Iris fought back a fresh wave of frustration. As if she could forget for one moment the pressure to secure their future through marriage. "Yes, Mother. Just let me tidy up—"

"Oh!" Charlotte stepped forward, setting down the jar of Midnight Veil kohl. "Don't worry. Lucie and I will ensure that all is left as we found it upon our arrival."

"Thank you," Iris said, grateful for her friend's help. "Mother, may I present Miss Charlotte Fields and Miss Lucie Fields. Charlotte, Lucie, this is my mother, Matilda Starspun."

Her mother's lips parted, then closed again, a half-formed word dissolving into silence. An odd expression flickered across her face, but it was gone too quickly for Iris to decipher it. "Fields," her mother said carefully. She cleared her throat and added, "It's a pleasure to meet you both."

The sisters curtseyed, but Iris noticed that neither of them would meet her mother's eyes. "My lady," Charlotte said quietly.

The air in the shop felt suddenly heavier, charged with something Iris couldn't name. Her mother's fingers worried at the edge of her glove—a nervous gesture Iris had rarely seen. Charlotte and Lucie remained perfectly poised, but their former warmth had been replaced by a careful neutrality.

Iris's gaze darted between the three of them, and understanding dawned. They knew each other. Or knew *of* each other. The certainty settled in her chest, though she couldn't begin to guess how or why. If it had only been Charlotte and Lucie's reaction, Iris might have dismissed it as natural curiosity about another human woman who'd married into fae society. But her mother's response suggested something deeper, something personal.

"Is everything all right?" Iris ventured.

"Of course, darling!" Her mother's voice was too bright, her smile too wide. "We really must hurry though."

Charlotte merely nodded, her eyes fixed on some point near the hem of Iris's mother's dress. "It was lovely to meet you, my lady."

The silence that followed felt heavy with words unsaid, until the fae woman who had occupied the space behind the counter suddenly appeared at their side, breaking the strange tension. "Would you like me to wrap anything for you today, Lady Starspun?"

"No, thank you, we really must go," Iris's mother said, her voice slightly too high as she answered for Iris.

"O-of course," Iris stammered, her mind still racing to make sense of the strange undercurrents in the room. She glanced at her new friends, noticing how they all seemed to be carefully avoiding her gaze. "I'll see you tomorrow?"

"Yes," Lucie said. Her smile returned, though it didn't quite reach her eyes. Both she and Charlotte were watching Iris's mother once again, curious expressions on their faces.

Iris stepped past them and followed her mother toward the door, pausing just long enough to snatch up her gloves from the silver tray where she had left them. Then she stepped into the bright afternoon sun, pulling her gloves back on, her mind filled with questions she didn't know how to ask.

Chapter Thirteen

"She simply should not have been allowed to attempt weather magic there," Lady Fawnwood remarked, shaking her head. "Those new tapestries were ruined beyond repair, and the poor cellist was absolutely drenched."

"The girl clearly requires more instruction before attempting public displays," Lady Whispermist agreed, delicately selecting a tiny frosted cake from the tiered silver tray. "Though I understand her eagerness to demonstrate. Weather manipulation has always been considered quite impressive."

The sunlight filtering through the canopy of trees cast dappled patterns across the pristine white tablecloth. Lady Whispermist's garden party was an elegant affair set amid immaculately groomed flower beds where enchanted blooms changed color with the passing breeze. Several small groups of ladies were scattered throughout the garden, arranged in perfectly composed clusters.

Iris and her mother and grandmother had somehow found themselves at the table near the central fountain, sitting with the elder Lady Whispermist herself—Lady Rivenna's lilac-haired friend. Also at their table was Lady Fawnwood, a woman of similar age to Iris's mother, and

Lady Featherlock and her two daughters, who seemed to have little to say.

"You must admit, though," Lady Fawnwood said, leaning forward slightly as she lowered her voice, "that it was a relief when that cellist stopped playing. The screech—"

A sudden flapping of wings interrupted her, and two gossip birds swooped low over their table, sending the ladies into a flurry of protective movements.

Perfect, Iris thought, watching as Lady Whispermist attempted the impossible feat of simultaneously ducking away from the birds while keeping her teacup perfectly level. *Because this gathering wasn't uncomfortable enough already.*

Lady Featherlock swatted ineffectually at the air with her lace handkerchief. "Shoo! Shoo, you wretched creatures!"

In the ensuing commotion, Lady Fawnwood's plate tilted precariously as she leaned away from the diving birds. Her slice of strawberry cake performed a graceful arc through the air before landing on the immaculate grass beside her chair.

One casualty already, Iris noted, fighting to keep her expression appropriately concerned rather than amused. *A noble sacrifice in the war against avian rudeness.*

The gossip birds, having successfully created their desired chaos, settled triumphantly on a decorative floral hoop suspended from a low-hanging branch directly above their table. They preened for a moment before simultaneously opening their beaks. "Tea house apprentice Iris!" they squawked in perfect unison, their voices carrying across the garden. "Tea house apprentice Iris!"

Lady Whispermist frowned. "What on earth?"

A wave of cold washed over Iris, her fingers stiffening against the fine porcelain of her teacup as warmth drained from her face. This was it. The start of the horrified reactions from proper fae society that Charlotte had predicted.

"Tea house apprentice!" the birds repeated before taking flight once more, narrowly missing Lady Featherlock's elaborate hat as they departed.

A confused silence settled over the table as the ladies straightened their posture and rearranged disturbed napkins. "Did they say 'tea house'?" Lady Featherlock inquired, her thin eyebrows drawn together in puzzlement.

"I believe they said 'apprentice,'" Lady Whispermist added, adjusting a displaced hairpin. "Though what they could possibly mean ..."

All eyes turned curiously toward Iris, who felt as though she had been transformed into a specimen upon a naturalist's display board. If she hadn't already been hoping for the uncomfortable garden chair she was seated upon to perform a spectacular feat of magic and swallow her whole, she was certainly wishing it now.

Before she could formulate a response, her grandmother cleared her throat pointedly. "As it happens," she announced, her voice carrying that distinctive note of triumph that Iris had come to recognize, "Lady Rivenna Rowanwood has indeed offered Iris the apprenticeship at The Charmed Leaf, and we are absolutely delighted that she accepted. She began her training this very morning."

A sudden, profound silence fell over the table. Lady Fawnwood's teacup froze halfway to her lips, while Lady Featherlock's cake fork clattered against her plate before she hastily recovered it. Lady Whispermist's eyes widened to a degree that might have been comical under different circumstances. Clearly Lady Rivenna had not yet informed her friend of this development.

"The apprenticeship?" Lady Fawnwood finally managed, carefully setting her teacup back onto its saucer. "At The Charmed Leaf?"

"Indeed," Iris's grandmother confirmed. "Lady Rivenna approached us personally with the offer. She said the tea house itself selected Iris."

Another beat of shocked silence followed, during which Iris could almost hear the thoughts racing behind their carefully composed expressions. She kept her own face neutral, though she felt her mother stiffen.

"How ... unexpected," Lady Whispermist finally said, her voice slightly higher than normal. She cleared her throat delicately. "That is to say, what a singular honor."

"Yes, quite singular," Lady Featherlock echoed, having regained her composure. "Many families have hoped for such an opportunity," she added, her tone carefully modulated to hide what Iris suspected was profound disapproval. "Lady Rivenna has always been so particular."

"Indeed she has," Iris's grandmother agreed, either oblivious to or deliberately ignoring the underlying current of dismay. "She recognized Iris's potential immediately."

"And what a wonderful opportunity for you, dear," Lady Whisper-mist said to Iris, her smile slightly strained at the edges. "The tea house is such a central institution in Bloomhaven society."

"Thank you," Iris replied politely. "I'm honored by Lady Rivenna's confidence."

"And how fascinating that Lady Rivenna would choose an apprentice with such unconventional talents," Lady Fawnwood remarked, recovering enough to add a hint of acid to her tone. "I have always thought paper folding to be such a charming pastime for children."

Iris kept her expression carefully neutral. "Lady Rivenna believes my abilities have unique applications," she replied, then took a sip of her tea.

"And how lovely for you," Lady Whispermist said to Iris's mother, speaking to her directly for perhaps the first time since they'd arrived. "Your daughter finding such a useful occupation."

Iris's mother smiled thinly. "Indeed. Iris has always possessed a keen mind and diligent nature. I have no doubt she will excel in any endeavor she pursues."

"One expects a certain traditional background for such a prestigious position," Lady Fawnwood observed, her gaze sliding meaningfully to Iris's mother before returning to Iris. "But perhaps times are changing."

"Perhaps they should," Iris's mother replied, her tone still perfectly pleasant though Iris could practically feel the tension radiating from her. "Magic manifests where it will, regardless of tradition."

An uncomfortable silence fell over their table. Nearby, a trio of garden pixies darted among the rosebushes, encouraging particularly vibrant blooms to unfurl. Their giggles filled the awkward pause.

"I must say," Lady Whispermist remarked, clearly attempting to redirect the conversation, "the enchanted foxgloves are particularly stunning this year. My garden gnomes have incorporated a new moonlight harvesting technique that has enhanced their luminescence."

"Your gardens are always exquisite, Lycilla," Iris's grandmother agreed, seemingly grateful for the change of subject. "The integration of traditional and innovative magical horticulture techniques is most impressive."

As the conversation turned to safer topics, Iris watched her mother and grandmother carefully avoiding each other's gaze. The tension between them remained palpable, a silent current running beneath the polite exchange of pleasantries. Her mother's back remained ramrod straight, her posture perfect but clearly uncomfortable. Her grandmother, meanwhile, seemed determined to announce Iris's accomplishments to anyone who would listen, though her motivation appeared less about pride in Iris and more about establishing the continued relevance of the Starspun name.

"Lady Iris," Lady Whispermist said, reclaiming her attention, "I understand you've had one or two, uh, *memorable* encounters with Lord Jasvian Rowanwood since your arrival in Bloomhaven."

Iris fought to keep the grimace from her face. "We have had the pleasure of making each other's acquaintance, yes."

"I heard the most extraordinary rumors about your exchange at the Opening Ball," Lady Featherlock added. "Something about exploding chandeliers?"

"Gossip birds do love to embellish," Iris replied smoothly. "A minor magical mishap, nothing more."

"Goodness, it was a little more than minor, I would say," Lady Fawnwood observed. "It was practically—"

"Oh! I do believe I just saw Lady Rivenna arrive!" Iris interrupted, rising suddenly from her seat. She forced an apologetic smile. "Please excuse me. I promised to attend to her should she grace the gathering with her presence today."

Without waiting for a response, Iris moved away from the table, her heart pounding as she heard Lady Fawnwood's final comment float after her: "Such impulsive manners. One wonders what Lady Rivenna was thinking."

Instead of heading toward the house where she had pretended to see Lady Rivenna, Iris veered toward a more densely planted section of the garden, where climbing plants created a natural corridor leading away from the main gathering. The foliage grew thicker as she advanced, magical flora intertwining to create a lush, emerald sanctuary. Unlike the meticulously arranged flower beds of the main garden, this area had a wilder beauty—not unkempt, but allowed to grow with artful abandonment.

She continued until the voices of the tea party faded entirely, replaced by the gentle bubbling of a hidden stream and the soft chiming of bell-shaped flowers. Finally, in a small clearing surrounded by dense flowering shrubs, Iris allowed herself to sink to the ground, her back pressed against the trunk of a blue oak.

Drawing her knees to her chest—a thoroughly unladylike posture that would have scandalized her grandmother—Iris took a deep, shuddering breath. The constant vigilance required to navigate these social waters was exhausting. Every conversation was a minefield, every expression a potential misstep. How was she to endure an entire Season of this? How was she to snare a wealthy suitor—a prospect that still repulsed her to her core—when even the approval of Lady Rivenna Rowanwood herself had failed to soften society's disdainful gaze?

Lost in thought, Iris didn't notice the approaching footsteps until a startled gasp broke through her reverie. She looked up to find a young woman standing at the edge of the clearing, her hand pressed to her chest in surprise. "Oh!" the stranger exclaimed. "I do apologize. I didn't realize anyone else had discovered this hiding place."

Iris scrambled to her feet, mortified to have been caught in such an undignified position. "No, I'm the one who should apologize. I shouldn't have—"

"Please, don't get up on my account," the young woman said quickly. "I came here to escape all that proper posturing myself." She gestured vaguely back toward the main garden.

Iris hesitated, then settled back against the tree, though with slightly more decorum than before. The young woman—who appeared to be close to Iris's own age—wore a gown of blush pink that complemented her porcelain complexion and dark hair. There was something familiar about her, though Iris couldn't recall where she'd seen her.

"I'm Rosavyn," the young woman said, moving further into the clearing. "May I join you? I promise I won't insist on proper tea party conversation."

"Please do," Iris said, surprised to find herself smiling. "I'm Iris."

"Iris Starspun," Rosavyn nodded, settling gracefully onto a mossy stone near the tree. "Yes, I know who you are. Everyone does."

Iris felt her smile falter. "Ah. The infamous half-breed who dared challenge Lord Jasvian Rowanwood at the Opening Ball."

To her surprise, Rosavyn laughed—a bright, genuine sound. "That's precisely how I know you! Anyone who stands up to my insufferable brother earns my immediate admiration."

"Your brother?" Iris blinked, suddenly recognizing the resemblance —the same dark hair, the same elegant bone structure, though Rosavyn's features were softened by an expressiveness that Jasvian's lacked. "You're Rosavyn *Rowanwood*."

"I am indeed," Rosavyn confirmed. "Though unlike my brother, I don't consider it my personal mission to maintain the proper order of the universe through sheer force of disapproval."

Iris couldn't help the laugh that escaped her. "He does have rather strong opinions."

"Strong, unwavering, and frequently tiresome," Rosavyn agreed with a dramatic sigh. "Though I suppose I shouldn't speak ill of him. He has shouldered rather a lot of responsibility since ..." She trailed off, then shook her head. "Well, enough about gloomy Jasvian. I owe you an apology."

"You do?"

"For that dreadful business at Elderbloom Park," Rosavyn said, her expression turning contrite. "When I was forced to quite literally run away from you. It was horribly rude, and I've felt terrible about it ever since."

Iris's mind flashed back to the incident—the two young women who had spotted her and then fled in the opposite direction. Now she recalled where she had first seen Rosavyn. "Oh. I ... That's quite all right."

"It isn't, actually," Rosavyn said firmly. "But I appreciate your graciousness. Faylira Bridgemere was with me, and when she saw you approaching, she practically yanked my arm from its socket in her haste to escape. I didn't have a chance to protest before she was dragging me halfway across the park."

"I see," Iris said, remembering the speed of their retreat with a pang.

"I should have broken free and come back to introduce myself properly," Rosavyn continued, genuine regret in her voice. "Or at least sent a note of apology. I truly am sorry."

The sincerity in her voice was unmistakable, and Iris felt some of the tension ease from her shoulders. "There's nothing to forgive. Though I'll admit, up until today, it has been rather a lonely introduction to Bloomhaven society."

"I can imagine," Rosavyn said, leaning forward slightly. "Bloomhaven society excels at two things: maintaining rigid traditions and passing judgment on anyone who dares to deviate from them. They act as though you've committed some terrible offense by merely existing. It's exhausting, isn't it?"

"It truly is." Iris studied Rosavyn more carefully, struck by an unexpected sense of kinship. She felt *seen*, much like she had during her conversation with Lucie in the tea house garden. It was curious that she should feel this with someone like Rosavyn—full-blooded fae from one of the most distinguished families in the United Fae Isles. "But why would society find fault with you?"

Rosavyn sighed. "I have not manifested yet. That is why I'm still 'Miss' Rosavyn rather than 'Lady' Rosavyn. A little humiliating at my age, though Grandmother insists it will happen when the time is right."

"How old are you?" Iris asked before she could consider the impropriety of such a direct question.

"Eighteen," Rosavyn answered, not seeming to mind.

"But that's hardly too late," Iris said gently. "I'm nineteen, and my magic only revealed itself a few months ago."

Rosavyn gave her a small, rueful smile. "That's kind of you to say, but it's different for someone like you. No one has established expectations for half-fae manifestation—the very fact that you have magic is considered remarkable. For full-blooded fae, the patterns are well-documented. Most begin to show signs by seventeen, some even earlier. With each passing month, I become a 'less desirable prospect.' By nineteen, I'll be practically unmarriageable if I haven't manifested."

"Surely not."

"Well, perhaps not by nineteen. But certainly by twenty years of age."

Iris shook her head, struck by the absurdity of it all. Here sat Rosavyn—beautiful, lively, and from one of the most prestigious families in the United Fae Isles—yet society considered her somehow lacking because her magic had not yet revealed itself. While Iris, with her mixed heritage and 'useless' magic, had been elevated to 'Lady' simply because she could enchant paper. "The rules do seem rather arbitrary," she observed.

"Completely nonsensical," Rosavyn agreed emphatically. "But enough about my magical shortcomings. Tell me about the apprenticeship! Is it as boring as I've always imagined it might be?"

Iris laughed. "Well, I've only been there half a day and already your brother's *extreme* disapproval ensured it was not dull. He found my presence in 'his' study utterly intolerable and made no effort to hide his belief that I'm completely unsuitable for the position."

Rosavyn rolled her eyes. "Of course. He's been after Grandmother for years to choose an apprentice, but I'm certain he expected her to select someone proper and predictable and utterly boring." Her eyes twinkled. "How delightful that she chose you instead."

"You don't mind?" Iris asked hesitantly. "That she selected an outsider rather than ... well, someone from your own family?"

"Mind?" Rosavyn laughed. "No, of course not! We've always known it would not be one of us. Grandmother informed us of that when we were all quite young. Besides, Grandmother has always done precisely as she pleased. It's one of the things I admire most about her."

A comfortable silence fell between them, broken only by the gentle chiming of the bell flowers and the distant murmur of the party they'd both escaped. Iris found herself studying Rosavyn's open, animated face, marveling at how different she was from her stern, controlled brother.

"You're nothing like him," she said finally. "Lord Jasvian, I mean."

"Thank the stars for that! Can you imagine *two* of him? Bloomhaven would collapse under the weight of all that propriety."

Iris laughed. "He does seem rather ... intense."

"That's a charitable description," Rosavyn said, though there was genuine affection in her voice despite her teasing. She sighed and added, "I should probably return to the gathering before Mother sends out a search party."

"I suppose the same goes for me," Iris admitted as the two of them rose reluctantly from the ground.

"But I'm so glad we had this chance to meet properly. Perhaps we might see each other again soon? Perhaps a promenade through Elderbloom Park that doesn't involve me sprinting in the opposite direction?"

"I'd like that very much," Iris said, surprised by how sincerely she meant it.

Rosavyn beamed. "Excellent! Then it's settled. Friends?"

"Friends," Iris agreed, the word warming her from within.

It was only as they walked away from the clearing that the thought struck her—with no small amount of dread—that a friendship with a Rowanwood would undoubtedly mean she'd find herself more frequently in the presence of the ever-disapproving Lord Jasvian.

Chapter Fourteen

Iris lifted a sprig of lavender to her nose, inhaling deeply and closing her eyes to fully appreciate the delicate floral scent. She set it down beside the small pile of herbs and tea leaves spread across her desk, then reached for a spoonful of dried chamomile. A faint herbal sweetness tickled her senses as she leaned in to capture the aroma.

"Notes of apple," she murmured to herself as she scribbled the observation on one of the loose sheets of paper scattered across her workspace. "And ... something earthy?" The tip of her self-inking quill danced across the paper as she continued writing. One of the small advantages of having manifested magic was that her own power flowed into a quill when she used it, meaning she never had to dip it into an inkwell. Even if her magic was, as Lord Jasvian had so charmingly put it, 'useless,' at least it spared her the inconvenience of splattered surfaces and overturned inkwells.

It was Iris's fourth morning at the tea house, and after spending the previous two days in the kitchen with Lissian and Saffron—who, it seemed, was called *Mama* Saffron by almost everyone—and observing the main floor, she'd been instructed by Lady Rivenna the previous afternoon to begin this morning in the study. She'd been at her desk for nearly an hour, cataloging the characteristics of The Charmed Leaf's extensive collection of tea ingredients.

So far, she was enjoying this sensory exploration more than she'd expected. And if she was being entirely honest with herself, the peaceful solitude of the early morning study offered a welcome respite from the curious stares and whispered comments that followed her everywhere else in Bloomhaven.

She crushed a mint leaf between her fingers and inhaled before pulling another blank sheet of paper in front of her. She had somehow managed to misplace the beautiful leather-bound notebook Lady Rivenna had gifted her and so was forced to write her observations on loose sheets that had somehow formed a chaotic array across her workspace. She breathed in the scent of the mint leaf again before returning her quill to the page and murmuring, "Refreshing. Cool. Slightly sweet with—"

The door creaked open behind her.

Iris lifted her quill and looked over her shoulder. Lord Jasvian Rowanwood stood in the doorway, his expression darkening visibly when he spotted her. His appearance was immaculate, of course. Not a hair out of place, coat perfectly pressed.

"You're here. Already." His voice carried the warmth of a midwinter frost.

"Good morning to you as well, Lord Rowanwood. Yes, I am indeed here."

He removed his coat and hung it with measured precision on the wooden stand by the door. "I had hoped for a few hours of peace before having to share the space."

Iris turned back to the page in front of her, projecting an air of composed serenity. "Then perhaps you should have arrived earlier," Iris suggested. "I've been here for nearly an hour."

Heaving a frustrated sigh, Lord Jasvian crossed the room behind her. She watched from the corner of her eye as he pulled the chair out from behind his desk. The moment he settled into his seat, piles of documents materialized on his previously empty surface—account ledgers, correspondence, and meticulously organized stacks of papers, each one perfectly aligned with the edge of the desk.

"I see the enchantment works as intended," Iris observed, looking up.

"Indeed. Some of us appreciate a system that ensures nothing is out of place." His gaze lingered pointedly on the tea ingredients scattered across her desk.

"How fortunate that we're each permitted our preferred approaches," she replied sweetly. "You with your precise orderliness, and I with my ... what was the term you used at the Opening Ball? Ah yes, 'paper-folding nonsense.'"

Jasvian's jaw tightened. "I thought we had agreed to maintain civility."

"Had we? I must have missed that conversation amidst all your disapproving glares."

He exhaled slowly through his nose, clearly striving for composure. "I see no reason why we cannot share this space amicably if we each focus on our respective tasks."

"Precisely my intention," Iris said, reaching for another jar and inadvertently knocking over a small vial. Golden pollen spilled across her notes. "Oh, blast it all."

"Perhaps if you organized your materials in some logical sequence—"

"Perhaps if you concerned yourself with your own affairs," Iris cut in, brushing the pollen into a neat pile. She took a breath and focused intently on directing a wisp of her magic to scoop up the pollen and return it to its vial. Iris felt a quiet thrill of satisfaction at this small success. She secured the stopper, savoring the moment before Lord Jasvian could find something to criticize.

At his desk, he lifted the topmost ledger from the pile of documents and placed it neatly in front of him before opening it. "I would appreciate some quiet while I work, if you can manage it."

"I'll try not to breathe too loudly while sampling aromatic herbs."

"I'm sure the effort would strain your capabilities," he muttered, just loud enough for her to hear.

"About as much as basic courtesy appears to strain yours," she replied in a similar tone.

For several minutes, they worked in strained silence. Iris continued her methodical sampling, though she found herself increasingly distracted by the scratching of Lord Jasvian's quill and the almost inaudible whisper of magic he used to blot each line before continuing to the next. Everything about him radiated control and precision.

It was, Iris decided, utterly maddening.

She reached for another sheet of paper, accidentally brushing several loose herb stems off the edge of her desk and onto the floor. From the corner of her eye, she saw Lord Jasvian's hand freeze mid-sentence, his gaze fixed on the fallen foliage.

Iris lifted her gaze from the floor and met his head-on, arching a single brow in silent challenge. His eyes narrowed, but he remained silent, his stare unwavering. And in that moment, something Iris couldn't identify prickled all the way up her spine.

Then, as if shaken loose by the weight of his stare, a thought struck her. She frowned. "Is it not considered improper that we're alone in here together?"

He blinked and returned his gaze to the page in front of him. Lowering his quill to the paper once more, he said, "In this tea house, Lady Starspun, one is never alone."

Iris looked around more closely and realized that despite the quiet, this was indeed true. There were several hearth sprites nestled in the unlit fireplace, their tiny forms glowing faintly as they dozed. A kitchen pixie who must have snuck in unnoticed after Lord Jasvian opened the door was arranging fresh flowers in the vase on the small corner table, and a flutter of movement on the bookshelf brought Iris's attention to the small creature that had just darted behind the largest volume.

"How comforting," she said. "Our mutual animosity has an audience."

"I'm certain they find it as tedious as I do," Jasvian replied, returning to his calculations.

Iris turned her attention back to the botanical reference book Lady

Rivenna had provided. She reached for a sprig of rosemary to mark her current page, then flipped back to another section she'd previously marked with a loose button—one that had fallen from her sleeve when she'd settled at the desk that morning. Running her finger down the page, she found what she was looking for: *When properly crushed, moonroot seeds release a delicate vapor with notes of vanilla and honey, intensifying any blend's magical properties.* Curious to test this out for herself, she reached for the small mortar and pestle on her desk, drawing them closer. The pale blue moonroot seeds rattled softly as she poured them into the bowl. With deliberate, circular motions, she began grinding.

"Must you do that?" Lord Jasvian demanded.

Iris paused. "Do what, exactly?"

"Create disturbances while I'm attempting to work." He gestured toward her mortar. "I need to finish these accounts early. I have social engagements to attend this afternoon."

Iris couldn't contain her surprised laugh. "You socialize? Voluntarily?"

He dropped his quill and looked up. "It is most certainly not—" He cut himself off, snapping his mouth shut. When he spoke again, his voice had taken on a careful, measured quality. "Yes. Is that so difficult to believe?"

"Frankly, yes." Iris set down the pestle. "What does that look like, my lord? You standing rigidly in the corner of a gathering, cataloging all the ways in which everyone else is failing to meet your exacting standards?"

A muscle ticked in his jaw. "We are not all capable of easy conversation in a crowd, Lady Starspun."

"Nor easy conversation in a confined space, it would appear," she muttered.

He exhaled sharply through his nose. "If you find my company so objectionable, perhaps you might consider working elsewhere. The kitchen seems better suited to your current endeavors."

"Lady Rivenna specifically assigned me to this study," Iris replied. "Though you're welcome to return to Rowanwood House if my methods disturb you so greatly."

"That isn't possible at present," he said, his voice clipped. "My mother is having work done on the ballroom, which is directly beneath my study. I cannot think for all the banging."

Iris raised an eyebrow. "Surely your magnificent home has more than one room suitable for work?"

"The lighting in that room is optimal, and the desk itself cannot—" He broke off, seeming to realize how ridiculous this might sound. "I simply prefer my established workspace."

"As do I, yet here we are, forced to adapt to circumstances beyond our control." Iris gestured expansively, accidentally sending several petals dancing through the air toward his desk. "Life's great equalizer."

Lord Jasvian sent the petals spiraling back toward her desk with a quick spark of magic before they could land on his papers. "There is nothing remotely equal about our situations."

"Of course not. You merely face the inconvenience of sharing a study, while I contend with an entire society that views my very existence as an affront to proper order." Iris smiled tightly. "Clearly, your burden is the heavier."

"That isn't what I—" He stopped, visibly recalibrating. "Your personal challenges, while regrettable, are hardly relevant to the matter at hand."

"Which is?"

"Your deliberate invasion of my workspace with ... botanical debris."

Iris threw up her hands. "For someone so obsessed with efficiency, you waste an extraordinary amount of time and energy on pointless complaints."

"And you," he countered, "seem determined to justify disorder as some form of artistic necessity."

"Better than justifying rudeness as—" She broke off with a gasp as her gesturing hand knocked against a delicate vial of shadowberry extract. The vial toppled, its silver stopper popping free as it rolled across her scattered notes. Black liquid pooled across the sheets of paper. "Oh, for the love of—"

"One might take this as a sign," Lord Jasvian said, his tone laced with false sympathy, "that even the tea house finds your methods objectionable."

"Or perhaps," Iris countered, turning in her seat to face him fully, "the tea house is providing a perfect metaphor for how your presence darkens every room you enter."

A flicker of something—hurt?—crossed his features before his expression hardened again. "I see. Well, far be it from me to inflict my 'dark' presence on someone who finds it so objectionable." He shut the ledger with a snap and pushed his chair back.

But Iris was already standing. "Oh, by all means, stay," she said with exaggerated politeness. "This is *your* study, after all—as you've repeatedly reminded me."

She gathered her skirts and swept away from her desk, leaving behind the disaster of midnight essence-stained papers and scattered tea ingredients. The mess would likely torment Lord Jasvian's ordered sensibilities far more effectively than any retort she could offer.

"Do ensure the door is properly closed when you leave," he called after her.

With a deliberate slowness that bordered on theatrical, Iris pushed the door open to its widest extent. She paused in the doorway, turned to meet his gaze with defiant satisfaction, then lifted her chin and marched away, leaving the door gaping behind her.

She was halfway down the stairs when she heard the resounding bang of the study door closing upstairs. She halted mid-step, fingers tightening around the banister as a fresh wave of indignation surged through her. The insufferable man had actually slammed the door! For a wild moment, she contemplated marching right back up those stairs, flinging the door open once more, just so she could have the satisfaction of slamming it shut herself.

That would be childish, a small voice of reason whispered in her mind. *And exactly what he would expect from you.*

She took a deep breath, then another, willing the flush of anger to subside from her cheeks. Lord Jasvian Rowanwood might be the most irritating, rigid, judgmental person she had ever encountered, but she refused to give him the power to disrupt her day any further. She would not allow his arrogance to chase her away from this apprenticeship—her path to independence and, hopefully, her family's financial salvation.

By the time she reached the kitchen, her breathing had steadied, though her irritation still simmered beneath the surface. She pushed open the door, expecting to find the usual bustle of morning activity. Instead, she was greeted by a surprising stillness. The kitchen wasn't entirely empty, but the usual frenetic energy had dissipated to a gentle hum of minimal activity.

Before Iris could inquire about this unexpected calm, Lady Rivenna emerged from the pantry, a ledger tucked against her side, a kitchen pixie sitting on her shoulder, and a frown creasing her brow. "It's simply unacceptable," she was muttering to the pixie. "I paid the astronomical shipping price weeks ago and yet the stock still has not arrived? And we are *days* into the start of the Season now. I most certainly will not be dealing with them again in—" She broke off, noticing Iris. "Ah, Lady Iris. I thought you'd be occupied in the study until noon at least."

"I found the environment less than conducive to focused study," Iris replied carefully.

Lady Rivenna's eyebrow arched knowingly. "I see. My grandson's company proved as stimulating as expected, did it?"

"If by 'stimulating' you mean 'infuriating,' then yes."

A smile tugged at the corner of Lady Rivenna's mouth, but all she said was, "Interesting."

"Where is everyone?" Iris asked, gesturing to the quiet kitchen around them. "I expected more activity."

"We're closed today. It's the spring races."

"Races?" Iris repeated.

"Pegasus racing," Lady Rivenna clarified. "The first major event of the Season after the Opening Ball. Nearly all of society will be in attendance. The tea house would be practically empty even if we were to open. Personally, I lost interest in pegasus racing years ago, so I rarely attend these days."

"I had no idea," Iris admitted. "I wonder why my parents did not mention it. I would have thought they'd want me to attend if all of

Bloomhaven's elite will be there. It seems like the perfect opportunity to make a favorable impression and improve my standing in society."

"Your grandparents have never been particularly fond of pegasus racing either—they haven't attended in years," Lady Rivenna replied with a dismissive wave. "Besides, it's not truly an ideal setting for making meaningful connections. Everyone is far too distracted by the races to engage in any conversation of substance. They're either shouting themselves hoarse over their favored steed or frantically calculating their potential winnings."

"Ah, well perhaps that's for the best then," Iris said, though inwardly she felt a pang of disappointment. Her curiosity about the magical marvels of Bloomhaven—so different from everything she'd known before—made her secretly long to witness such a spectacle.

"Well," Lady Rivenna said, moving toward the kitchen's central worktable and placing her ledger upon it. The pixie leaped from her shoulder and disappeared into a gleaming copper pot hanging from the ceiling rack. "Tell me what you learned during your botanical study this morning. Before my grandson disrupted your concentration, that is. Oh, and have you been recording your observations in the notebook I provided?"

Heat crept up Iris's neck. "I, um ..." She cleared her throat. "I seem to have temporarily misplaced it."

"Misplaced it?" Lady Rivenna repeated, her tone suggesting that misplacing such an item was akin to misplacing the High Lady herself.

"I'm sure it's here somewhere," Iris hastened to add. "I last had it when ..." She cast her mind back over the past few days, taking a few moments to think before realization struck. "The alcove! Your private alcove, where you had me sit and observe. I must have left it on the window seat when I was distracted by ..." By the revelation that the tea house itself was actively listening and reporting on every conversation within its walls. "I'll find it immediately," Iris promised, already backing toward the door.

"Please do," Lady Rivenna said, her expression subtly communicating that she expected better.

Iris hurried through the quiet main floor, weaving between tables until she reached the honeysuckle-draped alcove. She ducked inside and surveyed the small space, her eyes scanning the window seat with its plush cushions. Nothing. Frowning, she lifted the cushions one by one until finally she saw a gleam of deep plum leather wedged into the back corner of the window seat. "There you are," she murmured, reaching for the notebook.

She tucked it securely beneath her arm and made her way back to the kitchen, where Lady Rivenna was now sitting at the worktable consulting a weathered recipe book. "Found it," Iris announced, holding up the notebook.

"Good," Lady Rivenna said, looking up. "See that you do not misplace it again."

Iris was about to assure her that she would be more careful in future when the back door burst open with a bang that made both women jump. A whirlwind of teal silk and dark curls swept into the kitchen, bringing with it the scent of fresh air and herbs from the tea house's garden.

"Grandmother!" the whirlwind called, resolving itself into the form of Rosavyn Rowanwood. "I simply must—"

"Rosavyn!" Lady Rivenna exclaimed as she stood. "A lady does not careen about like a runaway pegasus."

"Pegasus! That's precisely why I'm here, Grandmother. The races. You simply must allow Iris to accompany me today. And may I remind you, I'm not actually a 'lady' yet, so perhaps I'm still entitled to a bit of careening."

"With that unruly mane of yours, my dear, you'll need far more than a magical manifestation before anyone considers you a proper lady," Lady Rivenna replied with a pointed sniff.

"Fine, fine! I'll tame this wild mane into the most elegant of hairstyles if you'll allow Iris to accompany me," Rosavyn said.

"When," Lady Rivenna asked, arching a single silver brow, "in the long and distinguished history of our family, has anyone ever successfully bargained with me? Besides, Lady Iris has important work to attend to here."

"Oh, surely she can sniff random leaves or whatever it is she's been doing any day of the week," Rosavyn said, earning another sharp glance from her grandmother. "This is one of the most significant social gatherings of the early Season. If Iris is to establish herself properly in society, she absolutely must be seen in the right company. My company, specifically."

Iris refrained from pointing out that Lady Rivenna had just told her the races were not ideal for making connections. In truth, her curiosity about the pegasus racing had only grown since their conversation, and she found herself hoping Lady Rivenna might relent.

"Please, Grandmother," Rosavyn begged. "Mother is insisting I attend, and I shall be stuck with her and the twins if Iris does not come along."

"A cruel fate indeed," Lady Rivenna remarked dryly. "To be surrounded by one's own family." But she turned to Iris and asked, "What do you think, Lady Iris? Does the prospect of witnessing fae society engaged in one of its more frivolous pastimes appeal to you?"

Iris hesitated. She didn't want to appear eager to escape her studies—she'd been genuinely enjoying the botanical examinations and the tea house's many mysteries—but she couldn't deny the pull of curiosity about this quintessentially fae spectacle she'd only read about in books.

"I would be honored to accompany Miss Rosavyn," she said finally. "If you feel my studies can spare the time."

Lady Rivenna paused, her lips pursed.

"Please, Grandmother," Rosavyn repeated. "I cannot possibly attend such an occasion without proper female companionship. Please, please, *please*—"

"Oh for goodness' sake, stop this unseemly whining. Very well, you may have Lady Iris's company for the afternoon."

"Oh, thank you, Grandmother!" Rosavyn darted across the kitchen and pressed a swift kiss to her grandmother's cheek, which Iris noted Lady Rivenna attempted—and failed—to receive with due dignity.

Excitement bubbled up inside Iris as Rosavyn seized her hand, tugging her—just a touch too hastily to be deemed entirely proper—toward the back door. "Oh, my gloves!" Iris protested with a laugh.

"Quickly!" Rosavyn released Iris's hand, though she could hardly contain herself, rising and falling on her tiptoes like a sparrow ready for flight.

Iris turned back, relieved she'd left her gloves in Lady Rivenna's private alcove this morning instead of in the study upstairs. She raced off as the older woman heaved a dramatic sigh and muttered, "The pegasi shall still be there, my dear, even if you *walk* at a reasonable pace."

Chapter Fifteen

"Hold still," Iris laughed, tucking the last stray wave of hair into place with one of Rosavyn's many pins. "There. Now you look like a proper lady again."

"Finally!" Rosavyn turned back around on the plush velvet seat, smoothing her skirts as the enchanted carriage crested the final hill outside Bloomhaven. Unlike typical carriages, this one required neither horses nor driver, operating solely on magical energy stored within its lumyrite-infused chassis. Iris's grandparents did not own a carriage like this, though she suspected they once had.

The vehicle slowed as they approached their destination, and Iris peered eagerly through the window. The carriage came to a gentle stop, and a small chime sounded, indicating they had arrived. "We're here!" Rosavyn's eyes sparkled with excitement as she flung open the door. "Come on!"

Iris followed her friend out of the carriage, her boots sinking slightly into the soft grass. The moment she straightened and looked around, her breath caught in her throat.

The carriage had stopped atop one of the many rolling hills that formed a rough ring around a shallow dip in the landscape. The gentle slopes of these hills served as natural seating areas, with colorful pavilions and canopies dotting the greenery like wildflowers. In the air above the central dip, glowing ribbons of golden light twisted and curved, forming an elaborate three-dimensional racetrack that sparkled against the azure sky. Magical obstacles floated at various points along the circuit, while bright flags fluttered near what must be the finish line.

"It's ..." Iris struggled to find words adequate enough.

"Magnificent, isn't it?" Rosavyn grinned, clearly delighted by Iris's reaction. "Oh! It looks like something is about to begin. A qualifying round, perhaps?" A melodious horn sounded, and the crowd's cheerful chatter intensified. "I'm not familiar with the particulars," Rosavyn added, "unlike my brother Evryn, who studies the bloodlines and racing records and places the most ridiculous wagers. I simply love being here. The atmosphere, the excitement, the magic of it all."

Iris followed Rosavyn's gaze upward just as six pegasi glided through a shimmering portal that had appeared in the air. The magical beasts displayed a dazzling array of colors—deep blues with silver-tipped wings, burnished copper with manes that trailed sparks, and one that was a gold so pale it seemed to glow.

The riders guided their mounts in a formation so tight it seemed impossible they wouldn't collide, yet they moved with such precision that not a wingtip touched. They circled the natural amphitheater once, the pegasi occasionally dipping low enough that spectators reached up as if hoping to catch a stray feather, before taking their positions at the starting line where a band of golden light pulsed in the air.

"Where should we sit?" Iris asked, tearing her eyes away from the spectacle long enough to scan the various spots along the hillsides. Some spectators huddled under colorful canopies and tents, while others spread blankets directly on the lush grass. The air smelled of sweet honey cakes and spiced cider, with vendors wandering the hill-sides carrying trays of treats or pushing colorful carts.

Rosavyn gestured toward a small pavilion draped in forest green and silver perched on one of the best vantage points. "The Rowanwoods have a family stand, of course. It has one of the best views of the circuit—well, aside from the High Lady's stand." She pointed to an elegant white and gold structure situated on the highest knoll. "But I prefer to wander among the open areas." She pulled Iris toward a grassy section where spectators milled about freely. "It's far more fun than enduring the company of my family."

They wound their way through the crowd, Rosavyn nodding graciously to various acquaintances as they passed. Ladies flaunted silk gowns with intricate embroidery and towering hats adorned with feathers, while gentlemen sported pristine waistcoats and polished shoes. Iris, in the practical dress she'd worn for a day of work and study at the tea house, was woefully underdressed for such a grand occasion. She lifted her chin, reminding herself that she belonged here just as much as any of these ladies.

From their vantage point, Iris could see across nearly the entire circuit. Small flags marked different sections of the hillside, and a group of musicians played sprightly tunes from a wooden platform nearby, their melodies carrying across the natural amphitheater. Down at the base of their hill, bookmakers sat at small tables with colorful umbrellas, calling odds as eager bettors pressed forward.

"This is thrilling," Iris said, her eyes drinking everything in. "And so lovely to get away from the tea house." She stopped suddenly, widening her eyes. "Not the tea house specifically," she added hastily. "Your grandmother's establishment is wonderful. I meant because of—well, your brother. He is most infuriating. How ever do you endure his ridiculously rigid ways?"

Rosavyn laughed, the sound bright and mischievous. "It's quite the challenge at times," she admitted. "When he is being particularly insufferable, I like to remind him of the time he and Evryn were attempting to outdo one another with levitation spells as boys. It was early morning and neither of them was fully dressed yet. Jasvian's spell went awry and left him drifting helplessly near the ceiling in only his underthings, the spell forcing him to float through the house for all to behold."

Iris couldn't help but giggle at the image. "I would have paid good coin to witness that."

"But he wasn't always so severe," Rosavyn added, her expression growing slightly more serious. "It worsened after our father's passing some years ago. Jasvian believes it his duty to uphold tradition, to preserve our family's standing. At times, I wonder if he remembers how to take pleasure in anything at all. "

Iris opened her mouth to carefully inquire further, when something —or rather someone—barreled up the hillside and nearly collided with them, accompanied by a burst of giggles. "Rosavyn! You came after all!"

Iris immediately recognized Charlotte, her dark hair escaping its pins and her eyes bright with mischief. She wore a dress of faded indigo —simple and unadorned compared to the elaborate silk gowns and feathered hats dotting the hillside around them.

"Charlotte!" Rosavyn exclaimed, embracing the girl warmly. "I thought you wouldn't be here! You said you had to work at the shop today."

"Mother allowed me to leave early," Charlotte said, grinning. "All of Bloomhaven society appears to have abandoned their usual haunts in favor of the races. The shop stands quite deserted." Her eyes sparkled as she turned to Iris. "What a delightful surprise to find you here as well!"

Iris smiled in return. "I didn't realize you two knew each other."

"Oh, we've been good friends for years," Rosavyn said, linking her arm through Charlotte's. "Ever since an incident in Charlotte's mother's shop when we were children."

Charlotte burst into laughter. "Oh, the dress stand disaster! I'll never forget your mother's face."

Rosavyn turned to Iris with a conspiratorial smile. "I was about nine, and Mother had dragged me to the dressmaker for a fitting. I was bored beyond tears and noticed another girl hiding among the dress racks, peeking out at me. That was Charlotte."

"I was supposed to be sorting ribbons," Charlotte added.

"We started making faces at each other," Rosavyn continued. "Then I snuck over, and we both hid behind a display of silks draped on padded dress stands. We were whispering and giggling, and then—"

"I backed into one of the stands," Charlotte interjected, "and they went down like dominoes! Crash, crash, crash! Silk and lace and toppled stands everywhere!"

"Both our mothers came running," Rosavyn said. "They were furious, demanding to know who was responsible. Neither of us would say, neither wanting to get the other in trouble."

"So we both got punished," Charlotte finished. "I had to reorganize the entire ribbon collection."

"And I was not allowed to speak for the entire time Mrs Fields pinned my dress, which felt like an eternity. But by the end of it, we'd passed so many secret smiles that we were inseparable from then on."

A trumpet sounded, drawing their attention back to the race above. The pegasi had taken their positions, their riders leaning forward in anticipation.

"You might not expect it," Rosavyn murmured to Iris as they focused on the racetrack, "considering my brother's opinions on humans and their supposed unsuitability as companions for a young fae of good standing. But I've never been bothered by Jasvian's views. A friend is a friend, no matter their lineage."

The horn sounded again, sweet and clear in the afternoon air, and the pegasi surged forward in a blur of wings and color, following the golden track that wound through the sky. "What are those golden spheres?" Iris asked, pointing at the large spheres floating at different heights.

"They're filled with enhancement magic," Rosavyn said. "If a rider manages to pass through one, their pegasus gains a temporary burst of speed or agility."

Iris nodded, her gaze darting ahead along the track, taking in all the various obstacles. "And those dark clouds?"

"Storm pockets," Charlotte said. "They create random wind patterns and occasionally release lightning. The riders have to time their approach perfectly. A skilled rider can use the wind currents to gain advantage, but one wrong move ... Well, it's potentially deadly."

"Oh, Charlotte!" Rosavyn suddenly exclaimed in a theatrical whisper. "Is that not the Turner family over there? Indeed it is! We simply *must* go and pay our respects."

"Rosavyn!" Charlotte hissed as Iris looked around to see who Rosavyn was talking about. "No!"

"But why ever not?" Rosavyn asked with feigned innocence. "When it is quite plain you're entirely taken with young Mr. Theo Turner—"

"Hush!"

"The Turners keep the stationer's shop across the road from Charlotte's mother's establishment," Rosavyn explained to Iris. "They offer the most delightful assortment of fine papers. You truly *must* pay a visit. And should you do so, if you happen to see a handsome young man with fair hair behind the counter, do inform him that a certain young lady from across the way wishes most earnestly to—"

"Rosavyn, that is quite enough!" Charlotte cried, though she could barely contain her laughter.

As the two of them continued arguing good-naturedly, Iris's attention was caught by the name 'Starspun' and the words 'that human woman' spoken by someone behind her. An unwelcome chill coursed through her, and she shifted forward slightly, not wanting to hear the rest of the conversation. But the woman's sharp voice was loud enough to cut through Rosavyn and Charlotte's chatter.

"You'll notice the Starspuns are not in attendance today."

"Indeed," a second voice replied. "I'm not surprised *Mrs* Starspun hasn't shown her face much in society since arriving."

Charlotte's cheerful expression faltered, her smile freezing in place as her eyes darted toward the voice. Beside her, Rosavyn's face tightened, a muscle working in her jaw as she met Iris's gaze with a look of quiet alarm. She placed a hand on Iris's arm. "Perhaps we should—"

"I would be hiding too," the first voice replied with a delicate sniff. "Being human is bad enough, but to be second choice after another human? It's positively mortifying."

"And with the Fields family still here in Bloomhaven! Can you imagine?"

The Fields family. Iris looked at Charlotte just as the other girls' gaze turned swiftly to the ground, her face flushing. Iris frowned.

"Clearly he was trying to prove some point by marrying the second one," the woman said.

"I imagine so. One wonders if he even loved her at all or was merely doing it to spite his parents!"

The two of them laughed and continued moving through the crowd.

"Charlotte?" Iris's voice emerged barely above a whisper. "What were they talking about?"

Charlotte's eyes darted to Rosavyn, who was watching both of them with an expression of growing alarm. "I ... I don't know if it's my place to—"

"Tell me." Iris's voice emerged a little more forceful than she'd intended. "Clearly everyone else knows this secret, and I do not like being kept in the dark about something that pertains to my own family."

Charlotte nodded, pressing her lips together before answering. "Perhaps we should find somewhere more private to discuss this."

They made their way to a relatively secluded spot beneath a tree at the edge of the gathering. Charlotte took a deep breath before speaking. "My aunt ... well ... she and your father were in love, years ago. Before he met your mother. They wished to be married."

Iris felt as though the ground had shifted beneath her feet. The thought that her father had loved someone before her mother—had nearly *married* someone else—cracked the foundation of her family's story as she understood it. Iris herself would not even exist if her father had married his first love!

"What?" she whispered.

"It was quite the scandal at the time, I believe. A fae lord and a human woman? It simply was not done. Not in those days. Your grandparents refused to support the match, threatened to cut him off entirely." Charlotte's voice grew quiet. "He left Bloomhaven after that. Apparently he said he wanted nothing more to do with any of it."

"And then he married my mother," Iris said slowly. "Also human." Slowly, pieces clicked into place. The odd tension at The Petal & Pearl, her mother's strange reaction to meeting Charlotte. Her mother clearly knew that there had been someone else before her. "So when they say *second choice*—"

"It's horrible gossip," Rosavyn cut in. "History that should have been forgotten years ago. But you know how some people love to cling to old scandals."

But Iris was barely listening. The scene before her eyes seemed to fold in on itself before unfolding to reveal something slightly different—the same gathering but with subtle changes, faces shifting, positions altering. Then it folded again and again, each new variation layering over the previous one until she could barely distinguish what was real and what was not.

The world tilted alarmingly. She reached out blindly, her knees threatening to buckle. Rosavyn caught her arm. "Iris! Are you all right? You've gone terribly pale."

Iris blinked rapidly, trying to clear the disorienting images from her mind. The strange folding effect began to recede, though echoes of it lingered at the edges of her vision, like scenes glimpsed through warped glass. She drew in a shaky breath.

"I ... I think I need to return home," she said, her voice sounding distant to her own ears. "I need to speak to my parents."

"Iris, wait—" Charlotte reached for her arm, but Iris was already moving.

She pushed through the crowd, barely registering the disapproving looks her haste earned her. The surrounding sounds seemed oddly muted as she struggled to escape the gathering—and then collided with two men who suddenly appeared in her path.

"Oh! I do apologize!" She stumbled backward, looking up to find herself face to face with—

Lord Jasvian Rowanwood. Sound crashed back into her awareness like a broken dam. Good stars, could she not escape this man? Was *this* the social engagement he'd spoken of earlier? The pegasus races?

Beside Lord Jasvian stood someone Iris did not recognize. Handsome, with light brown hair and an open, friendly face. "No harm done," he said with a warm smile. There was something familiar about his voice, though she couldn't place it. "Are you ... is everything all right, my lady?"

"I ..." Iris blinked once more. "Yes, thank you. I simply need to ... to go."

"Allow me to assist—" the stranger began, but Iris was already moving past them.

"Thank you, but no," she called faintly over her shoulder. And with that, she hurried away, struggling to make sense of what troubled her more: her father's unexpected past or the disorienting images that had momentarily replaced her reality.

~

"That was Lady Starspun, was it not?" Hadrian asked, watching the young woman's retreating form.

Jasvian barely registered the question, too preoccupied to muster a proper response. He frowned, his gaze sweeping the crowd as he searched for the source of the unstable magic that had been prickling at the edges of his awareness for the past few minutes.

"I heard your grandmother has made her the apprentice at the tea house," Hadrian continued. "Quite unexpected. Mother thinks it's a dreadful scandal, of course, but it's made me look at Lady Starspun in a new light. She must be quite the impressive young lady if your grandmother chose her. It certainly speaks to her character, does it not?"

A noncommittal noise emerged from Jasvian's throat. He did not think particularly highly of Lady Iris's character, but the last time he'd expressed his honest opinion about her in a public setting, it had ended with a chandelier exploding above his head. He thought it prudent to keep his exact thoughts to himself.

Besides, there was that sense of volatile magic to be concerned about. It was growing dimmer now, but—

"Don't you think she's rather lovely, Jasvian?" Hadrian pressed.

Jasvian cleared his throat and attempted to focus on his friend. "I believe I made my opinion quite clear at the Opening Ball." The unsettling magical disturbance was fading now, which brought him some relief. It had possessed a distinctive quality quite unlike the tempests he monitored in the mines—his ability was specifically attuned to the volatile magic that gathered around lumyrite deposits—but still a possible cause for concern. Most fae mastered basic magic in childhood, and even those still adjusting to their newly awakened abilities rarely lost control to the degree of the erratic surge he had just sensed nearby.

"Do you think she seemed distressed?" Hadrian continued, clearly not noticing Jasvian's distraction. "I wonder if I should go after her, offer assistance ..."

Before Jasvian could respond, Rosavyn pushed past him in a flutter of skirts, followed closely by a young woman he recognized as Charlotte Fields—the older sister of his grandmother's human serving girl. And they were headed in the same direction as Lady Iris. His jaw clenched. It was bad enough that Rosavyn insisted on maintaining her inappropriate friendship with the Fields girl, but now it appeared she was openly associating with Lady Iris as well?

He took a step forward, fully intending to remind his sister about the importance of appropriate social connections, but a cheer went up from the crowd as the first race ended. Spectators surged forward across the lawns, their excitement amplified by streams of magical light that burst from the finish line and scattered across the sky. The winning pegasus landed gracefully on the platform that had materialized to receive it, wings trailing golden sparks as its rider acknowledged the applause.

Then Jasvian caught sight of another pegasus—the third or fourth to land on the platform—and went very still. Even from a distance, there was no mistaking that particular landing style. Perhaps not noticeable to anyone else, but Jasvian had seen it too many times during childhood races around the Rowanwood country estate.

"Excuse me," he said shortly to Hadrian. "There is something I must attend to."

He made his way through the crowd toward the receiving yard where riders dismounted after races. Some of the pegasi were led to special cooling-down platforms, while others were guided toward the enchanted stables where weather wisps maintained perfect conditions for the magnificent creatures. The riders themselves dispersed to the Recovery Pavilions—a series of open-sided, airy structures where trainers offered immediate performance assessments and sponsors mingled discreetly with their favored competitors between races.

But the rider Jasvian sought had—unsurprisingly—slipped into one of the private preparation rooms. He followed, his anger building with each step, and threw open the door without knocking. "Have you completely lost your senses?" he demanded.

Evryn turned, still pulling off his racing gloves. He didn't appear surprised to see his brother. "Ah, Jasvian. Come to lecture me about proper behavior again?"

"How did you convince the real rider to swap places with you this time?" Jasvian demanded, shutting the door firmly behind him. "Do you have any idea how dangerous this is? I am doing everything in my power to look after this family, and now I must worry about you getting yourself killed by illegally participating in the races?"

"Oh please." Evryn tossed his gloves aside. "I've been riding since before I could walk. And fatalities are quite rare these days."

"We discussed this. You promised it was finished."

"I will not be bested by a Brightcrest!" Evryn's composure cracked. "Especially not a—"

"Brightcrest?" Jasvian repeated. "Alaryn Brightcrest is partaking in this lunacy as well? While his new wife and unborn child await him at home?"

Evryn released a snort, almost amused but not quite. "Please, brother," he said, turning away to place his racing gloves on a nearby table, "do not embarrass yourself by meddling in affairs about which you comprehend nothing."

Jasvian stared at his brother for a long moment, jaw working. Then he turned on his heel and stormed out, slamming the door behind him. The nerve of Evryn! As if Jasvian did not have enough to worry about with ensuring safety in the mines, with Rosavyn's delayed manifestation, with the esteemed legacy of The Charmed Leaf at risk now that his grandmother had chosen such an unsuitable apprentice. And now illegal pegasus racing! Was he the only one who understood what responsibility meant?

Their father had taught them that duty came before personal indulgence, but apparently Jasvian was the only one who had taken this lesson to heart.

Chapter Sixteen

Iris stood outside the drawing room of Starspun House, her hand hovering over the doorknob. The butler had informed her that both her parents were inside, his tone suggesting something unusual in their afternoon seclusion. She drew in a deep breath, trying to calm the storm of emotions that had propelled her all the way from the racing grounds.

The revelation about her father and Charlotte's aunt thundered through her mind. *Second choice.* The words had lodged themselves in her chest like shards of glass. Had her mother always known? Was that why she had gradually yielded more and more of herself, afraid that any resistance might drive her husband back to his first love?

Iris steadied herself against the wall. With one final deep breath, she turned the handle and stepped into the drawing room.

Her parents sat side by side on the settee, their postures unnaturally rigid against the plush upholstery. Her mother's fingers moved mechanically through the air, guiding enchanted golden threads that wove themselves half-heartedly through an embroidery hoop, the pattern losing its cohesion as her attention clearly wavered. Beside her, Iris's father held a newspaper spread open across his lap, though his unseeing gaze suggested the words might as well have been written in invisible ink.

They both looked up as she entered, their expressions shifting in perfect, alarming synchronicity.

"Iris," her father said, straightening. "We were just about to send for you."

"I have something I wish to speak with you about," Iris said, her prepared speech suddenly evaporating from her mind.

"As do we," her father replied, gesturing to a chair opposite them. "Please, sit."

Iris lowered herself onto the edge of the chair, her fingers twisting in her skirts. The air in the room felt thick with unspoken words.

"We've come to a decision," her father continued, his voice carefully measured. "Your mother and I will be returning home. Tomorrow."

Iris stared at them, certain she had misheard. "Returning? You mean ... you're leaving Bloomhaven?"

"Yes," her mother said softly, reaching for her husband's hand. "You will remain here at Starspun House with your grandparents."

Numbness spread through Iris's fingers, and she felt a sudden chill despite the warm afternoon sunlight streaming through the windows. Alone. With her grandparents. With the whispers and rumors and the weight of her family's future on her shoulders. "But ... the Season has barely begun. I don't understand."

Her father cleared his throat. "We believe our presence here may be ... complicating things for you. Without us around, society will be free to see you for who you truly are—not as an extension of our choices, but as Lady Iris Starspun, with all your remarkable gifts and merits."

"And because you're miserable here," Iris said quietly, eyes on her mother now. "Not only because society seems to be so unwilling to accept a human wife of a fae lord, and not only because Grandmother and Grandfather have made you feel so unwelcome, but also because of Father's history here." Her gaze slid to her father, and she weighed her words before letting them fall from her lips. "With another human woman."

Her parents exchanged a startled glance, and her father's face paled slightly. "How did you—"

"I heard it at the races today," Iris said, her voice surprisingly steady despite the trembling in her hands. "Everyone seems to know this story except me."

Her mother breathed deeply before her practiced smile returned. "It was a long time ago, Iris."

"Is that why you're leaving? Because it's too awkward for you to be here while she and her family still reside in Bloomhaven?"

"No," her mother said firmly. "We are leaving because your father and I assessed all options and decided this would be the best course of action for all involved."

Iris's gaze moved back and forth between her parents. "But mainly," she said, her voice wavering just the slightest, "because you are unhappy?"

Her mother's eyes closed for several moments before she refocused on Iris. "I am unhappy. This is not a secret. But if that were the only reason, I would stay. I am doing this for *you*, Iris. You will have the best possible chance here without me."

Iris felt as though the floor beneath her was dissolving. There was a hitch in her breath as she inhaled. "But Grandmother and Grandfather barely acknowledge my existence. They have made it quite clear they wish I didn't—"

"They will come around," her father interrupted. "Especially now that you've secured a prestigious position with Lady Rivenna. And without our presence, things will become less strained between the three of you. I'm sure of it."

Iris swallowed hard against the lump forming in her throat. "Are they making you leave?" she asked, looking directly at her mother. "Grandmother and Grandfather. Did they say something?"

"No," her mother said, reaching across to take Iris's hand in her own. "They cannot *make* me do anything. This is a decision we arrived at together."

Iris fought back the tears, her jaw clenched in resolve. "When?" she asked, her voice barely above a whisper.

"Tomorrow morning," her father replied. "We've already begun packing."

Tomorrow. So soon that Iris wouldn't even have time to process the shift in her world. A part of her wanted to argue, to beg them to reconsider, but she recognized the resolve in their expressions. This decision was final.

"I see," she said, forcing her voice to remain steady. "Is there anything I can assist with?"

Her mother's eyes glistened with unshed tears. "That's very thoughtful, darling, but it's all been taken care of already. The most important thing for you is to continue with your apprenticeship and social obligations."

"Of course." Iris nodded, rising from her seat with careful dignity. "Though I would like to spend what time remains with you both this evening, if that's agreeable."

"Nothing would please us more," her father said, his voice unusually thick with emotion.

"Then I shall see you at dinner."

Iris waited until she was alone in her bedroom that night before allowing her tears to fall. They came silently at first, then in great, heaving sobs that she muffled against her pillow. Her parents were leaving, and she would remain behind in this house where her grandparents regarded her with thinly veiled disappointment, in this town where gossip birds spread vicious rumors about her parentage, in this society that seemed determined to remind her at every turn that she did not quite belong.

When the storm of emotion finally subsided, Iris sat up and wiped her eyes with the back of her hand. A rather undignified gesture, her grandmother would have noted, but there was no one here to witness such a lapse in propriety. The thought almost made her laugh—what did a bit of undignified tear-wiping matter in a world where her entire existence was considered improper?

She moved to the window seat, drawing her knees up to her chest as she gazed out at the part of Bloomhaven visible from her window. Starspun House stood on one of the gently elevated streets that had been claimed by the elite families generations ago, when the Starspuns still commanded both wealth and influence. From here, she could see the warm glow of faelights illuminating elegant townhouses and the occasional shop with its windows dark for the evening. If she leaned to the right, she could just glimpse the edge of the Elderfae Gardens where magical fountains sparkled in the gathering twilight.

Somewhere out there, gossip birds were no doubt still squawking about her mother, her father, and the woman he had loved before. About Iris herself and her unsuitable magic. About all the ways in which she did not measure up to proper fae standards.

With a sigh, Iris reached for the satchel she'd brought from the tea house. Among the books and papers nestled inside was the leather-bound notebook Lady Rivenna had given her. She hadn't had a chance to use it since finding it nestled beneath the cushions of her little alcove.

She retrieved a self-inking quill from her desk drawer before heading to the window seat and settling onto it with the notebook on her lap. She ran her fingers over the silver filigree patterns on its deep purple cover, admiring their intricate beauty. Then she took a deep breath and opened it to the first blank page. She set the tip of the quill against the blank page and wrote:

I am alone.

Then she sat there, the quill gripped loosely in her hand, staring through the page. This was almost certainly not what Lady Rivenna had intended the notebook for, but—

Iris blinked, her breath catching. Beneath her own words, in an elegant script, new words had taken form on the page:

Technically, you are not.

Iris shrieked and leaped to her feet, dropping the notebook as if it had burned her. Then she stood frozen, one hand to her mouth and her heart thudding in her chest as more letters appeared in the same elegant script. She dared to lean closer.

That hurt.

She pulled back. "What in all the stars?" she murmured. With a deep breath and slightly trembling fingers, she bent and retrieved the notebook. She blinked a few times, but the words were still there. She sat and reached for the quill.

Who is this?

The High Lady herself.

Iris's mouth fell open, a quiet gasp escaping.

A notebook, silly girl. You are conversing with a notebook. Now do close your mouth.

Iris closed her mouth with a snap. Then she returned her quill to the page.

I've never heard of such a thing.

I dare say there are a great many things in the world you are unaware of.

Iris frowned and wrote, *There is no need to be rude.*

Pointing out your limited knowledge is not rudeness but simple observation. Though I suppose one might consider abandoning me in a window seat for days on end rather rude as well.

Iris stared at the page, a strange mixture of emotions swirling within her. Part of her wanted to slam the notebook shut and hide it beneath her pillow. Another part—the curious, scholarly part—was fascinated by this unexpected discovery.

Lady Rivenna enchanted you? she wrote finally.

A fine deduction. What tipped you off? Perhaps the fact that she was the one who gifted me to you?

Iris felt her lips twitch despite herself. *You do seem rather tetchy for a notebook.*

And you are rather bold for someone conversing with an enchanted object for the first time. Most would be cowering in fear or running for assistance. Instead, you are critiquing my tone.

I've had a difficult day, Iris wrote. *Criticism from stationery hardly seems worth the additional distress.*

A pause, then: *I see.*

The notebook's response somehow managed to convey a sense of judgment despite consisting of only two words. Iris sighed and wrote: *My parents are leaving tomorrow. Returning home without me.*

Ah. That would explain the melodramatic opening statement.

It wasn't melodramatic. It was true. I will be alone here with grandparents who can barely stand to look at me.

Have you considered that perhaps your grandparents need time to adjust, as do you? One wonders if you've truly given them the opportunity to know you before dismissing their capacity for affection.

Iris glared at the page. *I did not realize I would be subjected to such criticism from an inanimate object.*

I am hardly inanimate, as this conversation rather definitively proves. And if you wished to avoid criticism, perhaps try actions worthy of praise instead.

This was a mistake, Iris wrote, her quill pressing harder than necessary. *Or perhaps merely Lady Rivenna's idea of a silly joke.*

Lady Rivenna rarely gives anything without purpose. The question is whether you possess the wisdom to discern that purpose.

Iris's hand hovered over the page, a dozen sharp retorts dancing on the tip of her quill. But something in the notebook's words gave her pause. Lady Rivenna had chosen her as an apprentice when no one else in Bloomhaven would have given her a second glance. There had to be a reason.

What is your purpose, then? she wrote finally.

I am an extension of the tea house, in a manner of speaking. My purpose is to guide your education, to respond knowledgeably to your inquiries about your studies, and to assist you in understanding the patterns that might otherwise elude you. I am here to help direct your attention to where improvement is needed.

Your 'direction' seems to be accompanied by far more opinions than necessary, Iris wrote with a wry twist to her lips.

No one specified that I should lack personality. Education benefits from a touch of liveliness, does it not? Now. Is there anything in particular that you require assistance with this evening, Lady Iris?

Iris sat back against the window once more. Outside in the distance, a pegasus soared above Bloomhaven, its wings leaving a trail of silver sparks against the darkening sky. After a long moment, she returned her quill to the page.

I am frightened, she wrote, the confession easier to make to an enchanted notebook than to any living person. *Everyone expects me to secure my family's future through marriage, but I can barely navigate a conversation without causing offense. My magic is considered unworthy of proper society. My grandparents see me as a last resort, not a granddaughter to cherish. And now, in addition to stepping into a role I fear I can never live up to, my parents are leaving.*

The words appeared slowly this time, as if the notebook was choosing them with particular care: *Fear is natural when facing the unknown. But consider this: Your path was never going to be conventional.*

Iris stared at the words. She supposed that was true. Being caught between two worlds—fae and human—had always meant she would walk a different path from those whose lives were neatly defined by clear social boundaries and expectations. She had simply hoped to ignore this for as long as possible.

She yawned, suddenly aware of how exhausted she felt after the emotional turmoil of the day.

I should sleep, she wrote. *But I think you've helped me. Thank you.*

There is no need to sound so surprised about it. That is, after all, my purpose.

Iris gave a small smile as she closed the notebook, tucking it into her satchel with newfound care. The weight of her parents' impending departure still pressed against her heart, but somehow, it felt a fraction lighter than before. As she climbed into bed, her thoughts drifted to Lady Rivenna and the tea house, to Charlotte and Rosavyn, to the strangely opinionated notebook. Perhaps she wasn't quite as alone as she had feared.

Chapter Seventeen

Iris stepped out of her grandparents' carriage at the edge of Elderbloom Park, squinting slightly as her eyes adjusted to the mid-morning brightness. Even from this distance, she could see the ancient elderfae tree that dominated the center of the park, its massive branches reaching skyward. Stately oak and willow trees lined the winding gravel paths, their leaves rustling gently in the breeze, while ornate marble fountains bubbled with enchanted water that sparkled in the sunlight.

"Do hurry, Iris," her grandmother said, already moving toward the park entrance. "The morning promenade has already begun."

Iris fidgeted with the edge of her lace glove, smoothing an imaginary wrinkle before taking her grandfather's arm when he offered it. "Remember," he said in a low voice as they followed her grandmother, "today is about being seen. About establishing your place in Bloomhaven society now that your parents have returned home."

"As was always the plan," her grandmother added over her shoulder, clearly having overheard despite the distance between them. "That is what we shall tell anyone who inquires. It was always intended that you would remain with us for the Season while your parents returned to manage affairs at home."

Iris nodded, biting back the urge to point out that this 'plan' had only materialized two days ago. Her grandparents were determined to control the narrative surrounding her parents' abrupt departure, and she supposed she couldn't blame them.

Rumors were already circulating, of course. Iris had heard whispers of them the day before as she sat in her alcove at the tea house. She was relieved she now knew of her father's history in Bloomhaven, otherwise she would have been utterly bewildered by the repeated mentions of 'that Fields woman' that floated to her from the vines' whispers.

Despite everything, there was one small silver lining to her parents' departure: the strained atmosphere between Iris and her grandparents had lightened somewhat. Dinner the previous night had been marginally less tense than the ones that preceded it, as if her mother's absence had removed some invisible pressure from the room.

Her grandmother slowed as they entered the park, allowing Iris and her grandfather to draw closer. "My maid Frances told me she overheard the Locklear heir inquiring about you," she said, her voice pitched just for their ears. "His family possesses an admirable estate to the north."

"Locklear?" her grandfather scoffed quietly. "They may have land, but their influence has waned considerably. The Blackbriar family would be a far more advantageous connection."

"The Blackbriars are certainly well-positioned," her grandmother conceded with a small nod. "Though I hear Lady Thornhart has already set her sights on Lord Blackbriar for her youngest granddaughter."

"Lady Thornhart can set her sights wherever she pleases. The Starspun name still carries weight, despite ..." Her grandfather trailed off, his fingers tightening almost imperceptibly on Iris's arm.

"Despite our financial situation," her grandmother finished bluntly, though still keeping her voice low. "Which is precisely why we must be strategic. Lord Jasvian Rowanwood would have been the most advantageous match by far, had Iris not engaged in that regrettable exchange with him at the Opening Ball."

Iris suppressed the urge to roll her eyes. She didn't bother reminding them that Lord Jasvian had been the one to offer insult first with his contemptuous remarks about her heritage and magic.

"Young Lord Ellendale has shown interest," her grandfather said, "and while his family's standing isn't what it once was, an alliance there could prove mutually beneficial."

"The boy barely manifested last Season," her grandmother countered with a dismissive wave of her gloved hand. "His magic is hardly impressive."

"As if Iris's paper folding puts her in a position to be selective," her grandfather muttered.

Iris felt a flush creep up her neck, but she kept her expression carefully neutral.

"We should encourage connections with at least three promising candidates," her grandmother declared. "The Blackbriar heir, certainly, if an opportunity presents itself. Perhaps young Wintervale, despite his mother's insufferable pretensions. And I still maintain the Broadbank second son has potential. He may not inherit the estate, but his moonstone investments are reportedly quite successful."

"Very well," her grandfather agreed with a short nod. "But do remember, we cannot appear desperate. The Starspun legacy demands a certain standard be maintained, even in difficult circumstances."

Her grandmother's lips curved into a tight-lipped smile. "Of course, my dear. Dignity above all else." Then she raised her voice, calling out, "Lady Titterleaf." She lifted a hand in greeting to a woman whose extravagant skirts billowed with countless silk flowers that swayed with magical life. "How delightful to see you."

"And you as well, Lady Starspun," the woman replied, her gaze flicking curiously to Iris. "I see you have your granddaughter with you today."

"Indeed. She is in our care for the Season," her grandmother said smoothly. "Now that her parents have seen her settled here, they have returned home, as was always the arrangement."

Lady Titterleaf nodded, though her expression suggested she was mentally cataloging this information to dissect later with her circle of friends. Iris had no doubt she would hear this news repeated to her through the whispers of the tea house tomorrow. "How thoughtful of them to see her safely delivered. And how are you finding Bloomhaven, my dear? I understand you've secured quite the unique position with Lady Rivenna Rowanwood?"

"I am honored by Lady Rivenna's interest in my abilities," Iris replied, the words feeling stiff on her tongue despite her best efforts to sound natural.

"Quite remarkable," Lady Titterleaf said, her lips forming a smile that didn't reach the calculating gleam in her eyes. "And to think, everyone had quite given up hope that she would ever select an apprentice at all. I'm sure she has much to teach you. Though I'm certain your grandparents have explained that such an apprenticeship should not distract from your primary purpose this Season."

Iris felt a gentle but warning squeeze on her arm from her grandfather. "Lady Rivenna has been most accommodating," he interjected smoothly. "She understands perfectly the importance of social engagements during the Bloom Season."

The conversation continued for another few minutes, touching on the weather, upcoming events, and thinly veiled gossip about a young lord who had apparently fallen into Mirror Lake while trying to impress a group of ladies.

They had just bid Lady Titterleaf farewell when two garden pixies tumbled through the air in a fierce tussle over a sprig of wildflowers. Their aerial battle spiraled downward, ending with both plummeting directly into a muddy patch created by the nearest fountain's overflow. The impact sent a splash of dirty water arcing toward Iris, who gasped and raised her arms instinctively to shield her face.

"Disgraceful!" her grandmother scolded the pixies, who hung their muddy heads in shame before zipping away. She turned back to Iris with a critical eye. "Thankfully, your face remains unblemished, but your gloves have suffered the consequences of their foolishness."

Iris turned her hands over and examined the delicate white lace, now marred with several brown splotches. "I can hardly continue to wear these in such a state," she said, slipping off the soiled gloves with a small grimace. She folded them carefully to contain the mess and tucked them into her reticule. "I'll have them cleaned later."

Her grandmother eyed Iris's bare hands with poorly disguised dismay. "To be seen without gloves ... Well, I suppose it can't be helped. Do try to keep your hands folded demurely, at least."

Iris sighed inwardly. *Oh wonderful*, she thought. *Yet another mark against my already questionable suitability for Bloomhaven society.* She was about to reassure her grandmother that surely this minor breach of etiquette wouldn't cause the social apocalypse she seemed to fear, when another voice called out.

"Lord and Lady Starspun! Good morning to you both."

Iris turned to see a tall, broad-shouldered young man approaching, accompanied by an elegantly dressed older woman and a girl who appeared to be a little younger than Iris. It took Iris a moment to place the man—the friendly stranger from the pegasus races that she had quite literally run into.

"Lord Blackbriar," her grandfather replied, inclining his head as Iris's grandmother nudged Iris a little too sharply in the ribs with her elbow. Ah, yes, she was reminding Iris that this was one of the suitable young lords she was meant to make a good impression upon if the opportunity presented itself. "Lady Blackbriar, Miss Willow," her grandfather continued, completing his greeting. "A fine morning for a promenade, is it not?"

"Indeed it is," the young man replied, his smile warm and genuine. His gaze settled on Iris, and recognition flickered in his eyes. "And this must be Lady Iris. I believe we had a brief encounter at the races, though we were not properly introduced. I'm Hadrian Blackbriar."

The name stirred something in Iris's memory, and she realized why his voice had seemed vaguely familiar when she nearly collided with him at the races. This was the same man she'd overheard conversing with Lord Jasvian on the terrace at the Opening Ball. Her guard rose instantly, though if she recalled correctly, he hadn't joined in Lord Jasvian's disparaging comments about her magic.

"A pleasure to meet you properly, Lord Blackbriar," Iris replied with a small curtsy, keeping her expression neutral.

"The pleasure is entirely mine," he said, his smile widening. "Your name has been upon everyone's lips since your arrival in Bloomhaven,

Lady Iris. I've been most eagerly anticipating the opportunity to make your acquaintance myself."

There was something that Iris found immediately likable about his open demeanor. Unlike most of the fae nobility she'd encountered in Bloomhaven, his friendliness seemed entirely without calculation. The introductions continued, with Iris learning that Hadrian's sister, Willow, was expected to make her debut next Season.

"I understand you're apprenticed to Lady Rivenna," Lord Hadrian said as the conversation flowed. "How extraordinary. My mother was just remarking how unprecedented such an arrangement is."

"Lady Rivenna has always been rather ..." Lady Blackbriar paused, seemingly searching for an appropriate word, "progressive in her associations."

"I consider myself extremely fortunate to have been selected," Iris said carefully.

"I'm sure you are precisely the right person for the position," Lord Hadrian said warmly. "You would not have been chosen without good reason, regardless of what certain people might suggest."

Iris's eyebrows rose slightly. "Certain people, yes. Like Lady Rivenna's own grandson, Lord Jasvian."

Hadrian's expression turned briefly chagrined. "Ah, yes. Whatever my friend has said to you, I must apologize for him. He can be rather ... set in his ways."

"Indeed," Iris said, her smile tightening somewhat. "That is one way of describing him."

As her grandparents and Lady Blackbriar engaged in their own conversation about an upcoming ball, Lord Hadrian asked Iris about her experience at The Charmed Leaf thus far. His genuine interest in her responses caught her off guard. Most conversations with Bloomhaven's elite felt more like carefully choreographed dances than actual exchanges. He inquired about her magic, calling her demonstration at the Opening Ball 'uniquely beautiful,' and asked how she'd discovered her ability—though Iris delicately sidestepped that particular question without actually answering it.

"Iris, my dear," her grandfather's voice interrupted, "Lady Blackbriar was just mentioning their family's upcoming ball."

"Indeed," Lady Blackbriar said with a gracious smile. "We would be delighted if you would join us."

"How lovely," Iris's grandmother replied. "We would be most—"

"Rosavyn! Aurelise! Do slow down, for stars' sake!"

Iris turned at the familiar voice, her stomach performing an unwelcome flip. Lord Jasvian Rowanwood strode along the path behind them, looking distinctly irritated as he followed two young women who had nearly reached their group. Rosavyn, her face radiant with delight, hurried forward with a younger girl who bore a striking resemblance to her.

"Iris!" Rosavyn exclaimed, eschewing formality entirely. "How wonderful to see you here!"

"*Lady* Iris," Lord Jasvian corrected stiffly as he caught up to his sisters, his gaze moving from Iris to Hadrian and back again, narrowing slightly.

Rosavyn rolled her eyes. "Do forgive my brother's tedious adherence to protocol. Iris, this is my sister, Aurelise. Aurelise, this is Iris—the one I told you about."

The younger girl curtseyed, her movements graceful. "Pleased to meet you, my lady."

The adults exchanged greetings, and soon the conversation had split once more—the elder generation discussing some upcoming social event while Rosavyn asked Willow about her favorite places to sketch in Bloomhaven and Aurelise listened politely. This left Iris standing somewhat awkwardly between Lord Hadrian and Lord Jasvian, the tension that radiated from the latter almost palpable.

"I see you've been getting acquainted with Hadrian," Jasvian observed, his tone carefully neutral in a way that suggested significant effort.

"Lord Blackbriar has been most welcoming," Iris replied, equally careful. "A refreshing change from some of my earlier encounters in Bloomhaven."

Hadrian chuckled. "I was just apologizing for your frequent lack of social graces."

"Which was hardly your place," Jasvian said, his jaw tightening.

"Someone had to do it," Hadrian replied good-naturedly.

"Lord Blackbriar has been kind enough to take a more charitable view of my paper-folding magic than certain others have expressed," Iris said, unable to resist the slight barb.

"Indeed?" Jasvian's eyebrow arched. "And what exactly did you find so captivating about Lady Iris's abilities, Hadrian?"

"I found her artistry and precision remarkable," Hadrian replied. "There's something quite enchanting about magic that takes something entirely ordinary and reveals its extraordinary potential."

Before Iris could reply, Rosavyn suddenly gasped. "Oh! Look at that!" She pointed toward a clearing where a collection of water sprites were dancing across the surface of a small pond, their movements painting glowing patterns that hung suspended in the air. "Lord and Lady Starspun, you simply must see this. It only happens when the morning light hits the water at precisely the right angle."

With remarkable deftness—and for reasons Iris could not fathom—Rosavyn managed to guide all but Lord Jasvian toward the display, leaving Iris alone with the very person she had hoped most to avoid.

The silence between them stretched uncomfortably.

"Hadrian seems quite taken with you," Jasvian finally said, his tone neutral but his eyes sharp.

"He has been perfectly polite," Iris replied. "Though I understand that concept might be foreign to you."

"There is a difference between politeness and whatever display that was," Jasvian said, nodding in the direction Hadrian had gone. "He is not usually so ... effusive."

"Perhaps he simply recognizes that not all magic needs to serve a practical purpose to have value," Iris said, her fingers curling into her skirts.

"Is that what you discussed? Your magic?" The question sounded casual, but there was an intensity to his gaze that betrayed his interest.

"Among other things." She wasn't sure why she felt compelled to be deliberately vague, except that his obvious curiosity gave her a small sense of satisfaction.

"I see." Jasvian's jaw worked. "And I suppose your grandparents approve of this newfound friendship?"

"We've barely exchanged a dozen sentences, my lord. I would hardly call that a friendship just yet. Though I'm certain they'd prefer almost anyone to the man who publicly insulted their granddaughter."

"I merely spoke the truth as I saw it," Jasvian said stiffly.

"The truth?" Iris let out a short, disbelieving laugh. "You called me a half-breed with diluted magic. You questioned whether I belonged in society at all. That was not truth—it was prejudice wrapped in arrogance."

Jasvian inhaled a slow, steadying breath. "I may have been unnecessarily harsh in my assessment."

"How magnanimous of you to admit it," Iris replied, her voice dripping with sarcasm. "Shall I express my eternal gratitude now, or would you prefer I compose a formal letter of thanks?"

"This is precisely why conversation with you is impossible," he hissed, leaning slightly closer. "You twist every word—"

"I twist nothing," Iris cut in, matching his intensity. "You made your contempt perfectly clear that night, and nothing in your behavior since has suggested any change of heart. So please, spare me your concerns about any friendship that may develop with Lord Blackbriar. At least he sees me as a person worthy of basic courtesy instead of—"

Her words cut off abruptly as a glittering pink fox darted between them, pursued by a frantic young boy. The creature's sudden appearance startled Iris, causing her to step backward onto the hem of her gown. She teetered precariously, arms flailing for balance, before Jasvian's hand shot out to catch her. His arm curved securely around her waist, his other hand clasping hers firmly as he steadied her.

They were still for a single, startled moment, his body almost flush with hers. Then, as quickly as he'd caught her, Jasvian released Iris, stepping back as if the contact had burned him. He flexed his hand at his side, opening and closing his fingers as if trying to rid himself of the sensation of touching her.

The gesture sent a fresh wave of anger through Iris. Did he find the mere touch of her hand so distasteful? Was her half-human blood somehow contaminating to his precious fae sensibilities?

"Iris, dear!" Her grandmother's voice cut through the tension. "Do come see this marvelous display."

Iris stepped back, taking a shuddering breath. She plastered on a smile and turned toward her grandmother. "Coming, Grandmother."

The water sprites continued to dart across the pond's surface, but Iris barely registered their artistry, her skin still tingling where Lord Jasvian's hand had gripped hers, the sensation of his arm around her waist lingering with annoying persistence.

She was grateful when the encounter drew to a close. Farewells were exchanged, and each party offered the appropriate courtesies. "Lady Iris," Hadrian said, his smile warm and genuine, "it was truly a pleasure. I hope we shall have the opportunity to speak again soon."

"The pleasure was—" Iris's voice caught momentarily, her thoughts still tangled in the previous interaction. She blinked once, quickly composing herself. "—entirely mine, Lord Blackbriar. I look forward to our next meeting."

"Such a lovely morning for a promenade," Iris's grandmother remarked as they walked away. "I do believe this outing has been most successful."

Iris murmured her agreement, keeping her eyes firmly ahead of her as an unsettling energy coursed through her body, a peculiar tingling sensation that might have been lingering anger—or perhaps something else entirely.

Chapter Eighteen

JASVIAN HAD DEVISED A PERFECT, FOOLPROOF SYSTEM FOR MAINTAINING HIS sanity while sharing workspace with Lady Iris Starspun. Step one: climb the stairs to the study. Step two: greet her with the exact minimum courtesy required by social convention (precisely calculated at four words: "Good morning, Lady Iris."). Step three: proceed directly to his desk without further engagement. Step four: immerse himself so completely in the mountain of paperwork that he could plausibly pretend she didn't exist.

And a mountain it was. The annual Rowanwood Masquerade loomed less than a fortnight away, and his mother's seemingly endless ballroom renovations had generated enough invoices to bury a small village. There would be no deviation from sorting through them. No distractions. Certainly no dwelling on the infuriating conversation in the park yesterday, or how inexplicably unsettled he'd felt watching Hadrian charm Lady Iris with his easy smile. And absolutely no contemplation of the way her touch had left his skin tingling long after contact.

He'd already spent far too much time doing precisely that the night before.

He reached the top of the stairs and inhaled deeply, squaring his shoulders like a soldier preparing to face an opponent far more dangerous than any mine tempest: a woman who somehow managed to disrupt his perfectly ordered existence simply by breathing the same air.

He pushed open the door to find her already seated at her desk, her dark hair arranged in an elegant knot at the nape of her neck. Several books lay open before her, and she appeared to be comparing passages between them, her quill moving swiftly across her notebook. Beyond the pervasive aroma of tea leaves that perpetually filled this building, another delicate scent now lingered in the air. Something citrusy. Something Jasvian was doing his best not to notice.

"Good morning, Lady Iris," he said, then silently congratulated himself for successfully executing step two of his plan as he crossed the study to his desk.

She did not look up. Did not acknowledge him at all. The scratching of her quill continued without pause.

Jasvian placed his leather satchel on the desk with more force than necessary, but still received no response. He settled into his chair, waited the usual two to three seconds for the contents of his desk at Rowanwood House to appear on the desk in front of him, then pulled the stack of invoices closer. He began meticulously comparing the artisans' charges against their initial estimates, noting with irritation that the crystal chandelier fixtures had exceeded the projected cost by nearly fifteen percent. The lumyrite inlay work for the dance floor similarly showed concerning overages that would need explanation before payment could be authorized.

He reached for the next invoice and scanned it, but the figures began to blur as his attention kept wandering across the room. The silence stretched between them, heavy and pointed. Normally, he would have welcomed such peace, but today it felt like an accusation.

After another minute or two of staring at the same invoice without making any progress, he cleared his throat. "I see you've decided not to speak to me. Is this because of yesterday's ... exchange?"

Iris finally looked up, her expression carefully neutral as she glanced at him. "I have determined that conversation between us inevitably leads to argument. It seems more efficient for each of us to simply pretend the other does not exist."

"Indeed?" Jasvian found himself strangely irritated by her calm assessment. "I suppose that is one solution."

"You're welcome to propose an alternative," she said, her tone so perfectly reasonable it bordered on maddening.

"No, your approach suits me perfectly. I have complex calculations that require my full concentration. Silence will work well."

"Excellent."

And with that, she returned to her work, effectively dismissing him.

Jasvian stared at her bent head for a long moment before forcing his attention back to his own papers. The figures now made even less sense than before. He took a deep breath to clear his head, then copied the numbers from various invoices to calculate the total expenditure. He made an error, crossed out his work, and made another two errors before giving up with a quiet huff of frustration.

Despite his best efforts, his awareness of Iris's presence seemed to have intensified now that they had agreed not to speak. The soft rustle as she turned a page, the occasional scratch of her quill, even the rhythm of her breathing—all of it conspired to disrupt his concentration.

He glanced up again just as she tucked a stray lock of hair behind one slightly pointed ear, revealing the elegant line of her neck. As if sensing his gaze, she shifted in her chair, the movement releasing another wave of—what was it? Orange blossom? Jasvian found himself inhaling deeply before he could stop himself.

This was intolerable. How was he supposed to work while she sat there being so ... present?

His gaze fell on the notebook lying open on her desk. She had moved it a little to the side as she focused on a page in one of the books in front of her, and from his vantage point, he could see that the current page was blank.

He picked up his quill, hesitated for just a moment, and then cast a communication spell he and his siblings had taught themselves years ago. Originally intended for sending messages across ballrooms during particularly tedious social events, it would serve his current purpose well enough.

He released magic into his quill and wrote on his own paper, beneath the scratched-out calculation: *Your endless page-turning is exceedingly distracting.*

Across the room, it took a few moments before Iris stiffened. Jasvian watched as she noticed the words appearing on her blank notebook page. For a long moment, she simply stared at them. Then she reached for a loose sheet of parchment, wrote something quickly, then sat back as it quickly folded itself into a perfectly crisp envelope. The paper creation lifted from her desk and flew across the room, landing precisely in front of him.

He unfolded it to find a message written in a neat, flowing hand:

How unfortunate. Perhaps you might consider relocating to another workspace if my study habits disturb you so greatly. I was here first, after all.

Jasvian found the corner of his mouth twitching upward before he mastered the impulse. He penned his reply:

This has been my workspace for years. I will not be driven out by your inability to turn pages quietly.

He watched with satisfaction as his words materialized in her notebook. Her shoulders tensed again, but she didn't turn around. Instead, another paper envelope soon made its way to his desk.

I wasn't aware that mastering silent page-turning was a prerequisite for occupying this study. How remiss of Lady Rivenna not to mention this crucial requirement.

Despite himself, Jasvian felt a spark of ... something. He wrote:

Lady Rivenna would never be so impolite as to mention such a deficiency directly. She would expect one to have the self-awareness to recognize it.

The next paper envelope pirouetted through the air with unnecessary flourish before landing on his desk:

How thoughtless of me. Just as it would be thoughtless to mention someone's apparent inability to complete a calculation without sighing dramatically. Yet here we are.

Jasvian glanced down at his work, noting with chagrin the multiple crossed-out figures. He wrote:

I am not sighing 'dramatically.' I am expressing justified frustration at being unable to focus on important financial matters while someone insists on creating miniature windstorms with every turn of a page.

I had no idea paper could be so loud. Perhaps the sound is merely amplified by the echoing silence where your good manners should be.

A snort escaped Jasvian before he could stop it. He cleared his throat and sat a little straighter, still fighting a smile. There was something oddly liberating about arguing in writing rather than aloud. The slight removal allowed him to appreciate Iris's quick wit without the immediate pressure to maintain his stern demeanor.

You misunderstand. It is not the sound of the paper, but the obvious deliberation with which you turn each page. Clearly calculated to disrupt my concentration.

He watched as she read his message, her posture straightening indignantly. The next envelope practically shot across the room:

Oh yes, because my entire purpose in life is to disrupt Lord Jasvian Rowanwood's precious concentration. How did you discover my nefarious plot? I've been meticulously practicing disruptive page-turning for years, awaiting this very opportunity.

He had to catch himself before another snort could escape.

Your sarcasm is noted, Lady Iris. Though I must point out that dedicating one's existence to disrupting my concentration seems a rather dull and limiting life purpose.

Still more satisfying than your apparent life purpose, which seems to revolve entirely around sitting at your desk and glowering at innocent accounts. Do the numbers tremble in fear when you approach, or do they merely cower respectfully?

Jasvian's lips twitched. Biting back a smile, he wrote:

They arrange themselves in perfect order, naturally. Unlike your tendency to arrange your desk in what appears to be complete chaos.

He looked at her workspace as he finished writing. Books open to various pages, loose sheets of notes scattered across the surface, several jars of tea ingredients positioned with no apparent system.

Not all of us feel the need to arrange our lives with unyielding precision. Some of us appreciate the beauty of spontaneity. Though I understand such concepts might be beyond your rigid comprehension.

Jasvian glanced at his own meticulously arranged desk, everything placed at precise angles, and felt a curious twinge of self-consciousness.

Organization is not rigidity, but efficiency. Though I wouldn't expect someone whose research system consists of marking pages with sprigs of rosemary, buttons, and even a dried orange slice to appreciate such distinctions.

He watched as she finally half-turned, glancing at him over her shoulder with one eyebrow raised before returning to her writing:

Have you been keeping track of my highly creative bookmark selection? How flattering to know I occupy so much of your attention. Perhaps that explains your inability to focus on your precious calculations.

Her observation hit uncomfortably close to the mark. Jasvian shifted in his chair, suddenly aware of how much he had been watching her, noticing her habits, cataloging her expressions. He wrote:

Merely an observation made in passing. Do not flatter yourself that you command any significant portion of my thoughts.

A blatant lie, and from the tone of her next note, she knew it:

Of course not. You merely tracked my bookmark choices, noted my page-turning volume, and initiated this written conversation because I occupy so little of your attention. Perfectly logical.

Jasvian felt heat rising in his cheeks. He was grateful she wasn't looking at him directly.

I initiated this conversation because your disruptive presence was preventing me from working. Nothing more.

Her reply was infuriatingly smug:

And yet here you are, continuing to engage rather than simply ignoring me. Curious behavior for someone so determined to focus on his work.

She had him there. Why was he continuing this exchange? He should return to his calculations, should prove that he could indeed ignore her presence. Instead, he found himself writing:

Perhaps I am merely being polite by responding to your notes.

The paper envelope that floated back to him seemed to do so with an air of triumph:

Lord Jasvian Rowanwood, choosing politeness over productivity? Alert the gossip birds—this is truly unprecedented news.

Jasvian worked to suppress another smile. The morning sun had shifted, casting a warm glow across the room that caught in Iris's dark hair, highlighting strands that weren't purely black but rather a deep, rich brown. He found himself staring at the play of light before forcing his attention back to their exchange.

Very amusing. I see your wit is as sharp as ever, if somewhat misdirected.

My wit is precisely directed, thank you very much. Your reception of it, however, remains questionable.

Jasvian was formulating a suitably cutting reply when the door to the study opened. They both looked up, hastily shuffling papers as Lady Rivenna entered.

"Well," she said, her sharp gaze moving between them, taking in their guilty expressions. "I cannot decide whether to be pleased or concerned that you two have found a way to continue arguing without speaking aloud."

"Grandmother," Jasvian began, "we were merely—"

"Exchanging notes regarding our respective work," Iris finished smoothly.

Rivenna arched an eyebrow. "Indeed? How very collaborative of you both." The skepticism in her voice was unmistakable. "In any case, Lady Iris, I require your assistance downstairs. We have received a shipment of specialty tea leaves that need proper cataloging."

"Of course, Lady Rivenna." Iris rose, casting a quick look at Jasvian before very deliberately placing what appeared to be a cake fork on the page of the open book nearest to her before shutting it and following his grandmother to the door. As she pulled it closed, she glanced back at him. For just a moment, their eyes met, and he could have sworn he saw a hint of amusement in her gaze.

After they were gone, Jasvian found himself staring at the last paper envelope, his fingers tracing the crisp folds Iris had created with her magic. He should return to his work, now that the distraction had been removed.

Instead, he found himself wondering what retort she might have offered to his next message, had their exchange not been interrupted. Pushing the thought aside, he turned back to the pile of invoices, determined to make progress. But the scent of orange blossom lingered in the air, and the silence that had once been so welcome now felt strangely empty.

Chapter Nineteen

EVENING LIGHT SPILLED THROUGH IRIS'S BEDROOM WINDOW, CASTING LONG shadows across the polished floor. Iris sat before her vanity as her maid, a quiet human girl named Brenna, made the final adjustments to her hair for the Thornhart Garden Maze Soiree. The girl's fingers worked carefully, weaving small blossoms through the elaborate arrangement of twists.

Despite Iris's best efforts to focus on the evening ahead, her thoughts kept drifting back to the study that morning. To folded paper envelopes darting across the room and words appearing via magic on blank pages.

A smile tugged at her lips before she could suppress it, causing Brenna to pause momentarily. "Something amusing, my lady?" she asked, meeting Iris's eyes in the mirror.

"Nothing of importance," Iris replied quickly, schooling her features into neutrality. But as Brenna resumed her work, Iris found the smile returning unbidden. The verbal sparring with Lord Jasvian had been ... dare she say *enjoyable*? No, that couldn't possibly be the right word. Stimulating, perhaps. Intellectually engaging. Certainly not *enjoyable*. Not when it involved that brooding, judgmental man.

What had made the exchange even more amusing was her notebook's inevitable commentary. Lord Jasvian clearly had no idea that his notes were appearing on an enchanted notebook with opinions of its own. The notebook had remained silent during the first few exchanges, but after his message about her unconventional bookmark choices, elegant script had appeared beneath his words: *I hardly think this is the appropriate place for Lord Jasvian to reveal he cannot get you off his mind.*

Iris had been too busy penning her own replies to acknowledge the notebook's observation, though she'd felt an unexpected flutter at the thought that the infuriating Lord Jasvian couldn't stop thinking about her. Her fingers had moved faster across the paper, crafting her response about his attention while pointedly ignoring the notebook's smug commentary.

Later, after several more exchanges, the notebook had added: *I am left somewhat in the dark seeing only one side of this conversation. Do you plan to fill me in later?* She'd almost laughed aloud at that. Insufferable notebook, demanding to be kept abreast of their argument as if it were entitled to the full story. Yet she couldn't deny she'd been tempted to write out the entire exchange that evening, if only to receive the notebook's undoubtedly cutting assessment of Lord Jasvian's attempts at wit.

"Perhaps just a few more blossoms, my lady?" Brenna said, stepping back to survey her work with a tilt of her head. "Yes, perhaps two or three more."

"Oh, yes, if you think so. I trust your judgment." Iris didn't want to admit she had not been paying attention, her thoughts still lost in the memory of that curious morning. She had intended to ignore him completely, had even convinced herself it was the sensible approach. Instead, she'd spent far too much time engaged in what was essentially an argument by correspondence, with a sarcastic enchanted notebook providing running commentary, and found herself disappointed when Lady Rivenna had interrupted them.

"I've heard such fascinating things about the Thornhart maze," Brenna remarked as she carefully tucked another blossom into Iris's hair. "Apparently the hedges actually move while you're walking through the pathways."

"So I'm told," Iris replied, grateful for the distraction from her thoughts. "It sounds rather intimidating, doesn't it? What if one becomes trapped with no way out?"

Brenna smiled reassuringly. "Oh no, my lady. It's all in good fun. I believe the maze itself is quite simple. And it reads your emotions, they say. If you begin to panic, it will show you the way out."

"But how can it possibly shift its construction to accommodate everyone within it at once?" Iris wondered aloud. "Surely different people would need different pathways."

Brenna merely shrugged, adding the final blossom to Iris's hair. "Well, that's magic, I suppose. It doesn't need to make sense to work beautifully."

A firm knock at the door interrupted them.

"Enter," Iris called, her eyes flicking to the door's reflection in the mirror before her. Her grandmother appeared in the doorway, elegant as ever in a gown of deep green silk. "Grandmother," Iris said, surprise coloring her tone as she turned to face her. "Apologies for keeping you waiting. I'm almost—"

"There is no rush. Your grandfather is seeing to the final arrangements with the carriage." Her grandmother's gaze shifted to Brenna. "That will be all for now. I shall assist Lady Iris with the finishing touches."

"Yes, my lady." Brenna curtseyed and slipped from the room, closing the door softly behind her.

Iris felt herself tense slightly. She couldn't recall ever being alone in a room with her grandmother. What could possibly have prompted this unexpected appearance?

Her grandmother moved to the window, adjusting the curtain slightly before turning back to face her. "How are you finding the Season thus far, Iris? Your conversation with Lord Hadrian Blackbriar in the park seemed quite animated. Did you feel there might be a connection worth pursuing there?"

Iris hesitated, choosing her words carefully. "He is easy to converse with, to be sure. He seems genuine in his interest and kind in his manner. But it's possibly too early to determine if there might be something more substantial between us."

"True. Perhaps you will see him tonight at the Thornharts' soiree." Her grandmother's gaze moved over Iris's appearance. "You look lovely, my dear. That shade suits you."

"Thank you," Iris said, genuinely touched by the rare compliment. The gown, a soft lavender that deepened to purple where the light caught its folds, featured a delicate sheer overlay adorned with small glittering flowers. It was a touch simpler than high fae society strictly dictated, with fewer layers and embellishments than was fashionable, but Iris found it both comfortable and more aligned with her personal taste.

Her grandmother pursed her lips, then took a breath, but no words appeared to come to mind. Feeling the need to fill the silence, Iris said, "I've noticed that the social calendar in Bloomhaven follows a predictable pattern each Season. Certain events are hosted by the same families year after year. The Whispermist Garden Party, the Rowanwood Masquerade that I hear is coming soon, the Charmed Leaf Music Recital that Lady Rivenna has mentioned."

"Yes," her grandmother said with a nod. "This is true."

"Are there any events that our family traditionally hosts?"

Something flickered across the elder Lady Starspun's face. "There was one," she said quietly. "The Mirror Lake Dance."

"What was that like?" Iris asked, genuinely curious.

Her grandmother's gaze returned to the window, her gaze distant as if looking beyond the gardens of Starspun House to some memory from years past. "It was magnificent," she said softly. "For one night each Season, we would enchant Mirror Lake to achieve a perfect, glassy surface that reflected the stars above with such clarity that it seemed the sky existed both above and below."

Iris found herself leaning forward, captivated by the wistful note in her grandmother's voice—a quality she'd never heard before.

"Couples would dance upon the lake's surface beneath the stars," her grandmother continued. "Through the glass-like surface of the water, one could glimpse the luminous fish that dwell in the lake's depths, trails of enchanted light flowing behind them. I would enchant the lake myself —coming from a family that traditionally manifests water-related abilities—while those from the Starspun line would create lanterns spun from threads of pure starlight, enchanting them to drift above the scene."

"It sounds breathtaking," Iris said, imagining the scene. "Why do we no longer host it?"

Her grandmother's shoulders stiffened almost imperceptibly. "We simply could no longer afford it."

"Perhaps one day," Iris said quietly, "our fortunes will change."

"Perhaps," her grandmother answered with a small smile. She cleared her throat. "In any case—" she turned back to Iris with something clasped in her hand "—I came to find you because I thought perhaps you might like to wear these this evening." She opened her palm to reveal a set of delicate hair pins, each tipped with tiny crystals that contained twinkling silver light. "They were passed down from your grandfather's mother. Starlight captured in crystal during the height of winter. Even now, generations later, they retain their glow."

Iris's breath caught. "They're beautiful."

"They would complement your gown," her grandmother said, moving toward the vanity. "If you would permit me?"

"I would be honored," Iris replied, surprising herself with the genuine emotion behind the words.

Her grandmother gestured for her to turn back toward the mirror, and Iris felt the gentle pressure as the older woman began to insert the pins into her hair arrangement. In the mirror's reflection, the tiny crystals caught the evening light.

"I know," her grandmother began, her voice softer than Iris had ever heard it, "that we have not been close over the years." Her fingers moved with careful precision, each pin placed with deliberate care. "I recognize that I have made little effort to reach out to you." Iris remained perfectly still, hardly daring to breathe for fear of breaking this unexpected moment of vulnerability. "But I am pleased that you are here now," her grandmother continued. "And I hope that perhaps we might get to know one another better during this Bloom Season."

The words were offered stiffly, with the awkward formality of someone unaccustomed to expressing such sentiments, but Iris felt their sincerity nonetheless. She looked at her grandmother's reflection in the mirror. The proud set of her shoulders, the careful composure of her features, the slight uncertainty in her eyes. "I would like that," she said quietly.

Her grandmother placed the final pin, then rested her hands lightly on Iris's shoulders. For a brief moment, their eyes met in the mirror, and Iris felt that she saw her grandmother more clearly now than she had before—not merely a calculating matchmaker, but a woman who had watched her family's fortunes decline, who had lived with the gradual erosion of their standing in society, who now pinned her hopes on the granddaughter she barely knew. Though Iris had been put off by her grandmother's scheming, she recognized that it came from a genuine desire to secure her family's future. A legacy that stretched back generations, now resting precariously in Iris's hands.

"There," her grandmother said, stepping back. "They suit you."

In the mirror, the starlight pins seemed to have brightened. Iris turned in her seat to face her grandmother directly. "Thank you," she said as she stood, the words encompassing more than just the gift.

Her grandmother nodded once, her composure fully restored. "We should join your grandfather downstairs. The carriage will be waiting."

Jasvian stood at the edge of the Thornharts' garden, a glass of hummingfizz untouched in his hand as the evening festivities swirled around him. Faelights bobbed overhead, casting a dreamy glow across the expansive grounds where Bloomhaven's elite mingled in their evening finery. At the center of it all loomed the infamous Thornhart maze, its hedges too high to see over, their deep green foliage occasionally rippling with magic.

From within the maze came peals of laughter and startled shrieks as the living labyrinth rearranged itself according to inscrutable whims, separating companions and creating chance encounters between those who might otherwise never speak, pathways widening or narrowing with no warning. Jasvian suppressed a shudder. The entire concept had never appealed to him in the slightest.

What had possessed him to attend this event? He rarely participated in the Thornharts' annual maze soiree. The quarterly accounts ledger had arrived from the coastal property on the Fifth Isle and would have been far preferable company. But Hadrian had mentioned his intention to seek out Lady Iris this evening, and Jasvian had felt ... concern. Yes, that was the appropriate classification for the unsettled feeling that had propelled him into his formal attire. Concern for his friend's reputation should he continue to show such obvious interest in someone as unsuitable as Lady Iris Starspun. Nothing more. Certainly nothing to do with the way Lady Iris's eyes lit up when she challenged him, or how the delicate scent of orange blossom lingered in the study long after she was gone.

Jasvian took a small sip of his drink, grimacing at the overly sweet flavor. The courtyard buzzed with anticipation as more guests arrived, many heading straight for the maze entrance where a footman was explaining the rules to newcomers. Jasvian planned to maintain a dignified presence at the periphery, have a brief word with Hadrian, and make a tactful exit before anyone could suggest he join the maze-wandering frivolity.

His attention shifted to the main house as a new group of guests emerged onto the terrace. His breath caught inexplicably. Lady Iris Starspun descended the steps into the garden, the glittering details of her lavender gown catching the faelight. Her dark hair was arranged elegantly with tiny flowers and what might have been starlight twinkling among the refined twists. For a moment, Jasvian found himself unable to look away.

He blinked and forced his gaze elsewhere, irritated by his own reaction. She was dressed well, that was all. Anyone would notice such things.

"Jasvian, darling," his grandmother's voice cut through his thoughts. "Come join us."

Reluctantly, he made his way to where his grandmother stood with Lady Thornhart, an imposing woman whose hair was coiffed to resemble the hedge maze itself, complete with tiny faelights woven through the elaborate structure.

"Lord Jasvian," Lady Thornhart greeted him with a nod. "How delightful to see you this evening. I don't believe you've attended our maze soiree in recent years."

"I find myself with slightly more leisure time this Season," he replied.

"He means he's been ordered to socialize more," his grandmother translated with a pointed look. "The family estate will survive without his constant attention for a few hours."

Lady Thornhart laughed. "Indeed! And perhaps you'll venture into the maze tonight? I assure you, it's perfectly safe."

"I appreciate the invitation, but I'll leave the maze navigation to those who find such activities entertaining."

His grandmother's expression softened, a rare gentleness replacing her usual sharp assessment. "You know my grandson has always preferred more intimate gatherings," she said, patting Lady Thornhart's arm. "You should see him in a small circle by the fire at Rowanwood House—positively loquacious by comparison."

Well, he certainly wouldn't have used the word 'loquacious,' but it was true that he found smaller gatherings far more comfortable.

Lady Thornhart's eyes sparkled with mischief. "My dear Rivenna, one doesn't get more 'intimate' than a narrow passageway where one is forced into conversation with someone one would never normally speak to! That's precisely how I met my husband, you know."

"Be that as it may," Rivenna replied, "I rather doubt that's the kind of intimate gathering Jasvian is looking for."

Jasvian inclined his head in silent gratitude. He was thankful his grandmother hadn't revealed the real reason he avoided the maze—his ridiculous, irrational fear of enclosed spaces that he'd never managed to overcome.

He opened his mouth, but before he could respond to either his grandmother or Lady Thornhart, his attention was caught by movement across the garden. Hadrian had approached Lady Iris and her grandparents. Even from this distance, Jasvian could see the warm smile that transformed his friend's face as he addressed her. Worse still, Iris herself appeared to light up in response, her laugh carrying faintly across the garden as Hadrian leaned in to share some observation.

"Lady Iris seems to be settling well into Bloomhaven society," Lady Thornhart observed, following his gaze. "Quite remarkable, given her unusual background."

Jasvian's grandmother made a noncommittal sound. "The girl has certain qualities that compensate for any irregularities in her lineage."

No doubt Lady Thornhart had something to say to that, but Jasvian had ceased listening. Across the garden, Hadrian was now guiding Iris toward a fountain where cascades of liquid chocolate had replaced the usual water, flowing from tier to tier before collecting in a shimmering pool at the base. The enchantment cast a warm, honeyed glow across their faces as they approached, illuminating Iris's delighted expression. Hadrian's hand hovered respectfully near the small of her back without quite touching her. The ease between them was obvious, and Jasvian found himself gripping his glass with unnecessary force.

He excused himself from the conversation as politely as possible and drifted toward the edge of the gathering, his eyes still tracking Hadrian and Iris. They appeared to be deep in conversation, their heads inclined toward each other. Iris laughed again at something Hadrian said, the sound bright and unaffected.

"Hardly appropriate," muttered a voice nearby. Jasvian glanced over to see two young women watching the same scene with obvious disapproval. The two Brightcrest daughters, he realized. Ellowa and Mariselle. Their matching expressions of disdain were evident even in the soft evening light.

He turned away, uninterested in their petty gossip, and was relieved when Hadrian finally excused himself from Iris's company, presumably to fetch refreshments. She remained where she was, her gaze drifting toward the maze entrance. After a moment of apparent contemplation, she moved toward it.

Without conscious decision, Jasvian found himself following, maintaining a discreet distance. She paused at the entrance, exchanged a few words with the footman, then stepped into the maze alone.

Jasvian approached slowly, still with no intention of entering. The hedges near the entrance were thin, and through their leaves, he could make out Iris's lavender gown as she took her first hesitant turn.

"Lost already?" a voice called out, sharp with false sweetness.

Jasvian stiffened. Through a gap in the hedge, he saw Ellowa Brightcrest stepping into Iris's path. Her younger sister Mariselle appeared behind Iris from another pathway, effectively blocking Iris's retreat.

"Not at all," Iris replied, her gaze moving from Mariselle back to Ellowa. "Though I hadn't expected company quite so soon."

"We saw you enter alone," Ellowa said, toying with a strand of her golden hair. "How brave of you to venture in without an escort. One might almost mistake such behavior for impropriety."

"I was simply curious about the maze," Iris said. "And I hardly think I shall be alone for long, given the great number of people who have already entered this maze and are still wandering about its paths."

Ellowa crossed her arms. "Curious indeed. But then, you're quite the curiosity yourself, aren't you? The half-blood girl who somehow secured an apprenticeship with Lady Rivenna."

"A position that many full-blooded fae from respected families have sought for generations," Mariselle added.

"Including yourselves, I presume?" Iris's tone remained light. Jasvian had to admit he was impressed by the way she retained her composure despite the Brightcrest sisters' continued provocations.

Mariselle's laugh was brittle. "The Brightcrests have more dignified aspirations than shopkeeping."

"Is that what you think the tea house is?" Iris asked. "A shop?"

"What else would one call an establishment that serves tea for coin?" Ellowa's voice dripped with condescension. "Though I suppose for someone of your background, such an association might seem elevated."

Jasvian's fingers tightened on his glass. The Brightcrest sisters had always been vicious—indeed the entire family had built their fortune by exploiting the vulnerabilities of others—but their targeted cruelty toward Lady Iris seemed excessive even by their standards.

"You do realize," Mariselle continued, stepping closer to Iris and forcing her to turn and face the younger sister, "that you're merely a novelty? A shiny new curiosity that has temporarily captured attention. But the enchantment will fade, as it always does."

"Indeed," Ellowa agreed. "Soon enough, Lady Rivenna will realize her mistake. Your magic is hardly worthy of notice, let alone worthy of inheriting something as significant as The Charmed Leaf. And as for Lord Hadrian's attentions?" She let out a cruel laugh. "Surely you don't believe they signify genuine interest. Men of his standing marry within their class. They may dally with ... *unusual* specimens, but they do not offer them permanent positions."

"How unfortunate," Iris replied, her tone carefully measured, though Jasvian could detect a tremor beneath the surface, "that you measure your own worth solely by the advantages your bloodline affords you."

Ellowa's expression hardened. "Better to have advantages than to be a half-breed interloper with delusions of acceptance. You will never truly belong in our world, Lady Iris. The sooner you realize that, the less painful your inevitable fall from grace will be."

A surge of anger shot through Jasvian like an ember flaring to life, burning away all restraint. Before he could reconsider, he found himself striding to the maze entrance, thrusting his glass at the footman, and saying, "I believe I'll enter after all." He stepped inside, jaw clenched and fists balled at his sides. The oppressive closeness of the hedges set his nerves on edge, but fury propelled him forward despite the unease gnawing at him. He followed the sound of voices, turning a corner before finding himself face to face with the three women.

Iris's eyes widened in surprise, while the Brightcrest sisters had the grace to look momentarily discomfited. "Lord Rowanwood." Ellowa recovered first, her features rearranging themselves into a scowl. Neither the Brightcrests nor the Rowanwoods endeavored to hide their true feelings for one another. "How unexpected to encounter you in the maze."

"Indeed," he replied. "What *isn't* unexpected is the sheer lack of decorum spilling from the mouths of two Brightcrests."

Ellowa drew herself up indignantly. "We were merely having a private conversation."

"Is that what you call cornering a fellow guest with petty insults and transparent intimidation?"

Mariselle's cheeks flushed. "We were simply ensuring Lady Iris understands her position in society."

A stab of guilt pierced Jasvian's conscience as he recalled his own similar words to Iris at their first meeting. Had he not attempted to do the very same thing? He pushed the uncomfortable thought aside.

"Her position?" Jasvian raised an eyebrow. "As Lady Rivenna's chosen apprentice and the sole heir to one of the oldest magical bloodlines in the United Fae Isles? That position?"

"None of that changes the fact that she is a half-blood," Ellowa hissed.

"And that," Jasvian replied, voice sharp as cut crystal, "does not change the fact that the tea house has been waiting for someone *worthy* of its legacy. A standard no Brightcrest could ever hope to meet, regardless of how pure they claim their bloodline to be."

Ellowa lifted her chin, fire evident in her gaze. "Well—"

Mariselle grabbed her sister's hand, cutting her off with, "We should rejoin the party. Mother will be wondering where we've gone."

"A wise decision," Jasvian agreed.

With one last venomous glance at Iris, the girls swept away, their identical golden heads disappearing around the corner.

For a moment, silence hung between Jasvian and Iris. The surrounding hedges seemed to lean inward slightly, as if curious about what might happen next. The narrowing pathway made Jasvian's heart quicken, his chest beginning to feel oddly tight.

"I did not require your intervention," Iris said finally, her voice tight. "I was handling the situation perfectly well on my own."

Jasvian narrowed his eyes at her. "Of course. I should have allowed you to continue 'handling' their social evisceration with such admirable stoicism."

"What do you care?" she demanded. "Have you forgotten that you happen to agree with their sentiments?"

"I would never agree with a *Brightcrest*."

"Oh, I see," Iris said, a short, bitter laugh escaping her. "This was merely another skirmish in your ongoing family feud. You couldn't resist the opportunity to remind them of their place. How foolish of me to imagine you might feel a genuine inclination to defend my honor."

"There you go again," Jasvian exclaimed, "twisting my every word and intention. I cannot even defend you without earning your scorn!"

"Because it is *you* doing the defending! You have said the very same things to me—"

"Do not compare my comments to the vicious taunts of two jealous young—"

"Why not?" Her eyes filled with a challenge. "How was it different when you questioned whether my magic was worthy of presentation to society? When you called me a 'half-breed' as if the word were poison on your tongue?"

The accusation landed with uncomfortable precision. "I spoke without proper consideration," he admitted stiffly.

"How convenient," Iris retorted. "So we may cast whatever poisonous barbs we wish, provided we later acknowledge our words might have been ill-chosen? Is that how nobility justifies its cruelties?"

"What else can I do?" he demanded, hands spread helplessly at his sides. "I cannot go back and erase my words."

"You should not have spoken them in the first place!"

"Indeed, I should not have!" he agreed. The hedges rustled ominously, responding to their heightened emotions. Jasvian forced himself to take a deep breath, all too aware of the enclosing space around them. Sweat began to collect on his brow. "This is pointless. I should not have interfered."

"On that, at least, we can agree," she said in a shaky tone.

He should leave. His breathing was growing increasingly shallow and the air within the maze seemed thick and stifling. But he suddenly became acutely aware of how close the two of them were standing, of the faint scent of orange blossom that seemed to follow her everywhere, and he could not seem to will his feet to move.

"I cannot tell," Iris said, her voice barely above a whisper as she regarded him with weary resignation, "if you truly regret your words or if you're merely scrambling to defend yourself. All I know is that whenever we're near each other, we inevitably part in anger. Perhaps some forces in nature are simply not meant to coexist in harmony." She stepped around him with careful precision, as if avoiding even the merest brush of contact, her lavender skirts whispering against the hedges as she disappeared around the corner.

Jasvian remained frozen for several moments, watching the space where she had been. Finally, he followed, tugging at his cravat, desperate to escape the confines of the maze. Once outside, he gulped the evening air, hands clenching and unclenching at his sides, breathing deeply as he watched Iris rush across the garden toward the house.

Then it struck him—a violent surge of uncontrolled magic crackling through the air like lightning before thunder. Unlike at the pegasus races where the disturbance had built gradually, this eruption came without warning. The sensation pulsed outward, unmistakable to his trained senses, and this time, as he watched Iris disappear into the house and felt the sensation begin to dim, he was almost certain of its source.

"I see you've managed it again, my boy." His grandmother slowly approached him.

"Managed what?" he asked tersely, still watching the house where Iris had disappeared.

She sighed, moving to stand beside him as they both gazed in the direction Iris had gone. "For all your skill at calming tempests underground, you seem determined to stir one up every time that girl steps into your presence."

And to that, Jasvian had no response. Mainly because he feared she was right.

Chapter Twenty

Iris hurried through the Thornharts' grand house, barely registering the ornate gilt frames housing portraits that seemed to follow her with disapproving eyes, or the enchanted tapestries where woven figures shifted to whisper to one another as she passed. Her vision blurred with unshed tears, heart hammering against her ribs as she sought any exit that might allow her to escape without notice.

The confrontation in the maze had left her raw, exposed in a way that felt unbearable. The Brightcrest sisters' cruel words echoed in her mind—*half-breed interloper with delusions of acceptance*—a sentiment distressingly similar to those Lord Jasvian himself had expressed when they met.

And yet, he had defended her tonight. Why? Merely to spite the Brightcrests? Or had he truly meant it when he'd supported her position as Lady Rivenna's chosen apprentice?

And why did it matter to her what Lord Jasvian Rowanwood thought? The man was insufferable, arrogant, and infuriatingly proper. She shouldn't care about his opinion. Yet some treacherous part of her had sparked with hope at his intervention, desperately wanting to believe he'd acted out of genuine concern rather than some familial rivalry she still did not understand.

"Ridiculous," she whispered to herself, rounding a corner too quickly and nearly colliding with a footman bearing a tray of miniature tarts shaped like acorns. She muttered an apology and pressed onward, seeking an escape route that wouldn't place her in full view of half the gathering.

As she hurried down a less populated corridor, an odd dizziness overcame her. The hallway seemed to fold in on itself and then reappear, revealing another version of itself, and then another and another, multiple images layered atop one another like sheets of translucent paper. In one version, the corridor was empty; in another, it teemed with laughing guests; in yet another, the wallpaper appeared completely different while an elderly gentleman she didn't recognize crossed the corridor with the aid of a walking stick.

Iris pressed her palm against the wall to steady herself, breathing deeply as the images flickered and merged. This was the same strange phenomenon she'd experienced at the pegasus races. She'd forgotten all about it in the wake of discovering her father's history and her parents' abrupt departure. But now it had returned with alarming intensity.

She blinked hard, willing the overlapping scenes to dissipate, but they persisted. A figure approached from the end of the corridor—or was it three figures? No, one woman in three different dresses, all occupying the same space. Iris took a stumbling step backward.

"Iris!"

The voice—blessedly familiar—cut through her disorientation. The overlapping scenes wavered, then settled into a single reality as Rosavyn hurried toward her. "Rosavyn," Iris breathed, relief washing over her. "I looked for you earlier but couldn't see you anywhere, and then my grandmother dragged me out to the garden."

"I only just arrived. Mother was being particularly fussy about—" Rosavyn broke off, her expression shifting to concern as she took in Iris's distress. "What's happened? You look positively haunted."

"I just—need to leave," Iris whispered haltingly. "Without my grandparents seeing. Without *anyone* seeing. I just ... I need a moment. Or perhaps a dozen moments. Somewhere else. Can you help me?"

Rosavyn's eyes lit with understanding and something that looked suspiciously like mischievous delight. "Can I help you escape a suffocating social gathering? My dear Iris, I've been sneaking out of events like this since I was old enough to walk. And I'm well acquainted with the layout of the lower levels of the Thornhart residence, given my grandmother's friendship with the elder Lady Thornhart. I've endured many a tea in this house." She took Iris's hand, giving it a reassuring squeeze. "Come with me."

Without waiting for a response, Rosavyn tugged Iris down a side corridor and through a small door concealed behind a decorative screen. They emerged into a narrow servants' passage where Rosavyn immediately adopted the purposeful stride of someone who belonged there.

"Keep your chin up and move with confidence," she instructed in a hushed tone. "If you carry yourself with purpose, anyone who sees you will assume you have every right to be wherever you are."

As they approached a corner where two footmen stood chatting, Rosavyn made a subtle gesture with her left hand. Iris felt a whisper of magic brush past her, and the footmen's gazes slid over them without interest, their conversation continuing uninterrupted.

"Was that—" Iris began.

"Just a little redirection," Rosavyn explained with a grin. "I've always had a knack for making people look elsewhere when I don't wish to be seen. I half wonder if, when I eventually do manifest my specific magic, it will be the ability to turn completely invisible."

They continued through the servants' quarters, down a flight of narrow stairs, and finally out a side door into the cool night air. Rosavyn led her around the edge of the property, keeping to the shadows cast by ornamental shrubs, until they reached the lane where carriages waited to collect departing guests.

"Perfect timing," Rosavyn whispered as a gleaming carriage pulled up, its enchanted framework glowing softly in the darkness.

Before the footmen could approach, Rosavyn made another subtle gesture. Their eyes glazed slightly as the young women slipped past and into the waiting carriage. Rosavyn turned to Iris. "Where should I tell the carriage to—"

"The Charmed Leaf Tea House," Iris blurted without thinking.

The carriage glided forward smoothly. Iris tugged her gloves off—darned things were so constricting—leaned her head back against the cushioned interior of the carriage, and pressed her fingertips to her temples. Even with her eyes closed, the disorienting visions hadn't fully receded. Images of Rosavyn continued to overlap one another, one with her hair elegantly coiled atop her head, another with loose curls cascading down her shoulders, and in one brief, startling flash, Rosavyn appeared to be leaning inappropriately close to a shadowed figure Iris couldn't quite—

"Are you quite all right?" Rosavyn asked gently, interrupting the visions. "What happened back there?"

"I ..." Iris sighed, her eyes still closed. "I do not want to repeat it."

Rosavyn remained thankfully quiet, seemingly content to respect Iris's reluctance without pressing for details.

The carriage wound through Bloomhaven's streets, but Iris kept her eyes closed, trying to ignore the odd images her imagination kept presenting her with. Before long, the carriage slowed to a stop, and Iris opened her eyes to see The Charmed Leaf outside the window. In the moonlight, the tea house looked different. Still and mysterious, the leaves of its vine-covered facade barely moving.

The carriage door swung open of its own accord and Rosavyn gestured for Iris to disembark first. With her gloves clutched loosely in one hand, Iris climbed out onto the cobblestone path. She approached the door of the tea house as a curious warmth spread across her right palm. She looked down and—

"Oh!" she breathed. For there on her skin was the shimmering copper outline of a key, its handle delicately shaped like a leaf.

"Goodness," Rosavyn whispered, her eyes wide with wonder. "You have a key just like Grandmother's."

"It appears I do," Iris replied, equally surprised. Until this moment, she hadn't considered how she might enter the tea house, which would surely be locked at this late hour.

"It makes sense, of course," Rosavyn continued, "with you being the apprentice. But somehow I hadn't realized ... I suppose if I'd thought about it, I would have assumed Grandmother would wait longer before granting you such direct access."

If Iris had thought about it, she would have assumed the same.

Tentatively, she lifted her hand and pressed it to the door. The lock clicked and the door swung open immediately. "Incredible," Iris murmured, stepping into the darkened interior. Unlike during daylight hours, when sunlight streamed through the windows and the air hummed with conversation, the tea house at night had a hushed, expectant quality, as if perhaps it was dreaming of tomorrow's bustle.

Several of the faelights embedded amidst the foliage in the ceiling stirred to life as they entered, casting a gentle glow over the empty tables. The vines that decorated the walls rustled ever so slightly, like someone stirring in their sleep.

Iris took a deep breath. For the first time since the confrontation in the maze, she felt her breathing ease, the tightness in her chest beginning to unravel. There was something about this place that felt strangely like home. And yet she knew beyond a doubt that she did not belong here.

Half-breed. Interloper. Novelty.

"Are you ready to tell me what's caused you such distress?" Rosavyn asked gently from behind her.

"Rosavyn, I ..." Iris shook her head, still unable to look at her friend. "I am not worthy of the position your grandmother has given me."

"And what, precisely," demanded a loud voice, "gives you the authority to decide whether you are worthy or not?"

Both girls whirled around, startled to find Lady Rivenna standing in the doorway. She stepped fully into the tea house, the faelights brightening slightly in her presence.

"Grandmother!" Rosavyn exclaimed, one hand flying to her throat. "How did you—"

"Know you'd slipped away? I saw you both leave the Thornharts' gathering. It was simple enough to follow." Rivenna's gaze moved between them, sharp and assessing. "Did you truly think I was unaware of all the times you escaped Lady Thornhart's house only to reappear hours later as if nothing was amiss?"

"I—"

"I do not miss things, my dear. Now run along and take that enchanted carriage you 'borrowed' back to the Thornharts. Lady Iris and I have much to discuss."

Rosavyn hesitated, glancing at Iris with concern, but clearly she was not willing to argue with her grandmother. With a brief nod, Rosavyn turned and slipped out the door—which conveniently closed itself—leaving Iris alone with Lady Rivenna.

The older woman moved to one of the tables and settled into a chair. "Sit," she said, gesturing to the chair opposite her.

Iris obeyed, her hands twisting the pair of gloves in her lap. "I apologize for coming here at so late an hour. I simply needed—"

"Tell me what happened," Lady Rivenna interrupted, her tone leaving no room for evasion.

Iris swallowed, then began. "The Brightcrest sisters cornered me in the maze. They said ... cruel things. About my bloodline, about how I don't belong here. And then Lord Jasvian appeared and—"

Lady Rivenna held up a hand. "No, child. Not that. Tell me what happened with your magic. Have you been experiencing something unusual? Something you cannot explain?"

Iris stared at her, momentarily speechless. "How did you—"

"I happen to be closely acquainted with one who can sense the building of volatile magic. He was almost certain, this evening, that the feeling originated with you."

Iris blinked. "Do you mean—"

"Was it you, Lady Iris?"

A shaky breath escaped Iris. "Yes. I believe so. It first happened at the pegasus races. No, wait ..." She frowned, casting her thoughts further back. "I believe it may have happened the first day I began my apprenticeship here, while you were showing me through the kitchen. But it was so brief, I dismissed it. It was far more overwhelming at the races, but after it passed, I was distracted by other things, and I didn't think of it again."

"And tonight?" Lady Rivenna prompted. "What exactly happened?"

"It's as though I see multiple scenes unfolding—quite literally *unfolding* as if the scene were a picture on a page—before my very eyes. It happens quickly. Multiple versions of a scene unfolding all at once, almost layered atop each other. It becomes quite overwhelming. Tonight I saw different people, different wallpaper patterns, even the same person wearing different clothing, all occupying the same space."

Iris expected surprise, perhaps even concern, but Rivenna merely nodded, her expression thoughtful. "I suspected from the first time we met, Lady Iris, that there was more to your magic than paper folding. You spoke about the paper itself already knowing all the possible creases it might fold along and all the possible configurations it might take, and you would simply choose which one your magic would follow. In truth, I suspect your magic has very little to do with paper at all, except that was the first way your ability chose to reveal itself."

Iris frowned. "I don't understand."

"Our conversation at the Opening Ball stirred something in my memory. I've read of an ability similar to yours, though I've not met anyone whose manifestation matches its description until now. I believe your magic allows you to perceive the underlying patterns in reality. Just as you can see how paper wishes to fold, you are beginning to see how reality itself might fold in different directions. You glimpse the patterns of what might be—the potential paths or outcomes that exist simultaneously before a choice is made."

Iris shook her head, struggling to comprehend. "But that sounds like ... seeing the future?"

"Not precisely. You do not see what will be, but rather what *could* be. The realm of possibility rather than certainty." Rivenna's eyes gleamed in the faelight. "Think of it as seeing where the creases in reality lie, just as you intuitively understand where paper wishes to fold. Tell me, what happened the first time your magic manifested?"

Iris's hands tightened around the pair of loose gloves in her lap. She hadn't spoken of it—not really. Not beyond the necessary explanations to her grandparents and the vague references when someone asked about her manifestation. The memory of that day still made her skin crawl. "I was browsing in my favorite bookshop," she began hesitantly. "A place I'd visited hundreds of times before. I was reaching for a volume when suddenly ... everything changed."

Rivenna nodded encouragingly.

"The pages ... all the pages in all the books ... seemed to come alive. They tore themselves free, thousands of them, tens of thousands perhaps, swirling around me in a storm. And they were folding—not just once, but over and over, changing shape so rapidly I couldn't follow the transformations." Her voice caught. "They were like razor blades, all those edges. I couldn't escape them. They left cuts everywhere—my arms, my face, my hands."

She looked down at her arms. There were no scars. Magic had been used to heal her. But she imagined she could see the many cuts that had been there.

"The bookshop pixies were shrieking, trapped in the rafters. The shop owner was shouting for help. And I ..." Iris swallowed hard. "I couldn't stop it. It was like the pages were possessed." The memory of blood trickling down her arms, of the shop owner's horrified face, of her parents' frantic arrival—it all came rushing back. "It was chaos. Destruction. Nothing like the controlled paper creations I can make now."

"It was not destruction," Rivenna said gently. "It was revelation. You weren't simply making paper fold. You were suddenly, overwhelmingly aware of all possible patterns and configurations within every page of every book. It sounds as though the pages responded to your uncontrolled power by simultaneously trying to take all possible forms at once, creating the violent storm of paper and sharp edges."

Iris was silent for several moments, taking this in before responding. "But what use is such an ability? Seeing possibilities that may never come to pass?"

"What use?" Rivenna echoed with a hint of incredulity. "Iris, you are more attuned to potential than most will ever be. You can perceive not just what is, but what might become. Combined with all the information the tea house gathers and reveals to us, this gift could be extraordinarily valuable."

Iris frowned, considering the implications. "You mean I could ... use this information to guide people? To influence their choices?"

"To present possibilities they might not otherwise see," Rivenna corrected. "To nurture opportunities that align with their deepest desires."

"That sounds uncomfortably like moving people around a game board," Iris said, her unease evident. "I know we've spoken about this already, but I'm not certain it feels right."

Rivenna leaned forward slightly. "You misunderstand. We do not force paths upon others; we merely illuminate possibilities. We present options, create openings, arrange introductions between those who might benefit from knowing one another. The choice to step through a door will always belong to the person standing before it."

Iris fell silent, her gaze drifting to the window where moonlight cast silver patterns across the glass. The tea house seemed to hold its breath around them, the vines on the walls barely stirring. A fragile hope flickered within her—the possibility that her strange magic might truly have value—but it wavered she thought of the whispered judgments, the sidelong glances that followed her everywhere, the Brightcrest sisters' sneers.

"Something else troubles you," Rivenna observed after a moment, her tone returning to one closer to her usual brusque manner. "What happened in the maze? Be out with it so we may move on."

Iris sighed. "The Brightcrest sisters ... they called me a 'half-breed interloper.' Said I was merely a novelty that would soon fade, that I would never truly belong in this world." She raised her gaze to meet Rivenna's. "And I fear they're right. Everything about me—my bloodline, my upbringing, my magic that I'm clearly incapable of controlling properly—marks me as an outsider. I fear that you, too, will soon realize this about me. You will decide you've made a mistake offering me this apprenticeship. Because it isn't only the Brightcrests. You must have noticed the way at least half of the tea house's patrons seem to lean away from me when I pass them. The sideways glances they still give me. Not a day goes by when at least some of the whispers the tea house shares with me are about how I did nothing to deserve this position and that I am not worthy of proper society's attention. Soon you will see that I'm nothing but a ... a ..."

"Usurper?" Rivenna supplied. "Upstart? Stain on the pristine fabric of fae society? Do feel free to stop me when I reach the correct level of dramatic self-pity."

Iris stared at her, caught between outrage and disbelief. "I don't understand how you can be so ... so ..."

"Unsympathetic?" Rivenna leaned back in her chair. "Let me tell you something about sympathy, my dear. When I was first betrothed to the Rowanwood heir, do you know what society's leading ladies said about me?"

The abrupt shift threw Iris off balance. "I ... what?"

"They said I was a social-climbing nobody with parlor trick magic who'd somehow managed to enchant a man far above my station." Rivenna's voice was crisp, matter-of-fact. "They wondered aloud—and quite deliberately within my hearing—how long it would take him to come to his senses."

"But you're Lady Rivenna Rowanwood," Iris protested. "You're practically the queen of Bloomhaven society."

"I am now. But I wasn't born into this position. And that, Lady Iris, is why I understand perfectly well what you are feeling right now. Did you know—" she tipped her head slightly to one side "—that you and I are not so unalike?"

Iris frowned. "How so?"

"What is my magical ability?"

"It is—" Iris broke off. "I suppose I don't actually know. Something to do with tea leaf reading?"

A small smile curved Rivenna's lips. "Patterns, Lady Iris. But more specifically, connections. My magical ability allows me to see the connections between people—the intricate webs of relationships, influences, and experiences that bind us all together." Rivenna's fingers traced an invisible pattern on the table, her eyes distant. "It has proved a useful ability, though many still think that all I can do is ..." She looked up with a wry smile. "Make pretty patterns. At my debut, my demonstration was considered utterly unremarkable, just as yours was."

Iris found herself leaning forward, eager to know more. "What did you do?"

"I used threads of light to weave patterns in the air showing the connections between everyone present—bloodlines, alliances, rivalries, tentative matches that had already begun to form. The threads were all color-coded to mean different things, and what did the majority of the ballroom see? A pretty web of colored light. The High Lady herself could barely conceal her yawn."

"I can certainly relate to that."

"Indeed, I felt precisely as you do now. Unworthy, out of place, possessed of a gift that no one valued or understood." Rivenna's gaze grew sharp again. "But I refused to accept their assessment. I discovered something important, Lady Iris. Something you would do well to remember: if you do not feel you belong anywhere, then you must *make* a place in which to belong."

"The tea house," Iris murmured, understanding dawning.

"Precisely. I created a space that would draw people to me rather than requiring me to seek acceptance elsewhere. A place where my particular gifts—seeing how people and events connect, reading how these patterns shape society itself—would be not merely useful but essential." Rivenna gestured to the silent tea house around them. "And now, generations later, not a single event of consequence occurs in Bloomhaven without being whispered about within these walls."

"But how did you know it would work?"

"I didn't. But I suspected they would come to need me. Need my insights, my ability to know when and how to place the right people together to foster existing connections and form new ones. I knew I could create opportunities for the types of interactions people would enjoy and want to experience again. A need to return, again and again." She paused. "And I must say, watching everyone pretend they never doubted me has been rather entertaining."

A laugh escaped Iris before she could stop it. "I can imagine."

"Can you?" Rivenna fixed her with a penetrating look. "Then perhaps you can also imagine what you might do with your own talents, instead of sitting here waiting for society to grant you permission to exist."

"I ..." Iris faltered. "You think that my magic ... this ability to see multiple possibilities ..."

"Is rare and valuable beyond measure," Rivenna finished. "The tea house chose you for a reason, Lady Iris. It recognized in you something that most others have failed to see. Something that, in time, will make you as essential to Bloomhaven's society as I have become."

The vines along the wall nearest to them stirred, reaching out a tendril that brushed against Iris's hand with what felt remarkably like affection. Yet she couldn't shake the fear that sat in her chest. "It hardly seems possible," she said softly, her gaze drifting to the questing vine at her fingertips. "Each day I grow more devoted to this position, yet I cannot shake the feeling that it all rests upon some fortunate error. That I am merely borrowing a place that was never truly meant for me, and one day I will be asked to surrender it when the mistake comes to light."

"Let me make one thing perfectly clear," Rivenna said, leaning forward as her voice took on a firmness that commanded attention, "as it seems you still harbor doubts where there should be none. This apprenticeship is not a temporary arrangement or a trial position. You have been *chosen*—by both myself and the tea house. This is your future, Lady Iris. This is where you belong. The *only* circumstance in which you would not become the eventual proprietress of The Charmed Leaf is if you yourself decided you no longer wished it. The question now," Rivenna continued, rising to her feet with a rustle of silk, "is not whether you are worthy of this position, but whether you are brave enough to embrace it fully. To create your own place in a world that may not immediately understand your value."

She extended a hand to Iris, and after one last moment of hesitation, Iris reached for it and stood. "Thank you, Lady Rivenna. I believe I am."

Chapter Twenty-One

"Let's try this one," Iris murmured, carefully adding three drops of veilwater to her latest blend. The liquid shimmered as it fell into the porcelain teapot, creating tiny ripples that glowed momentarily before fading into the amber brew.

Though the sun had barely risen, the kitchen at The Charmed Leaf already hummed with early morning activity. Hearth sprites darted between copper kettles, coaxing flames to the perfect temperature, while the scent of baking scones mingled with the more exotic aromas of Iris's experimental tea blends.

At the center of the kitchen stood the main worktable, conspicuously divided by a thick red line painted directly onto the wood that morning by Orrit. On one side stood the brownie, the tea house's master of scones, surrounded by precisely arranged baking implements and ingredients. His tiny form was nearly obscured by a cloud of flour as he kneaded dough with remarkable vigor.

On the other side, carefully respecting the boundary, Iris had arranged her collection of jars containing various tea leaves, petals and roots alongside a variety of teapots with different magical properties. Several different kinds of measuring spoons added subtle influences to her ingredients, while enchanted scales measured not just weight but magical potency. Timing crystals of various colors were arranged in a neat semicircle, each one designated for a specific ingredient's optimal steeping time.

"I still can't believe I dragged myself out of bed before the sun," Rosavyn said, stifling a yawn as she reached for another slice of honey cake from the basket she'd brought. "Only a true friend would sacrifice breakfast at home to check that you were well after last night's drama."

"And I'm eternally grateful for your sacrifice," Iris said, carefully stirring her latest blend.

"As you should be," Rosavyn replied around a mouthful of cake. She swallowed. "Though one should not thank their true friends by attempting to poison them with vile tea concoctions."

"We must all start somewhere."

"That last one," Rosavyn said, wrinkling her nose, "tasted like it started at the bottom of a drain."

"Rosavyn!"

"I'm sure you'll improve quickly!" Rosavyn assured her, then added in a low tone, "Though I don't believe the tea house selected you for your blending skills."

"I heard that," Iris muttered, squinting at the page of notes Lady Rivenna had left for her along with all the tea ingredients and brewing supplies. The purpose of this morning's experimentation was to create a blend that might keep Iris's newly discovered ability from overwhelming her. *You need to find something that stabilizes the visions*, Lady Rivenna had instructed the night before. *A blend that allows the possibilities to unfold individually rather than all at once, and perhaps only when you wish them to, rather than whenever your emotions run high.* But since Rosavyn didn't know about the visions—and Iris didn't feel ready to explain them—it was easier to pretend these experiments were simply part of her apprenticeship.

"You're aware that you could return home for breakfast, are you not?" she said to Rosavyn as one of the timing crystals began to glow a soft emerald green, indicating that the steeping time was complete. "No one is forcing you to taste my 'vile tea concoctions.'"

"Oh, but this is far more fun," Rosavyn replied brightly. "Even if my tongue may never forgive me."

Iris pretended she hadn't heard that last bit. She lifted the teapot and gently swirled the contents while consulting the various loose pages of notes from Lady Rivenna. Apparently it mattered whether the swirling was clockwise or counter-clockwise. She set the teapot down and leaned over her notebook—placed safely out of Rosavyn's view behind a stack of books—and lifted her quill to make note of the fact that she had swirled *clockwise*.

Below this, the notebook's elegant script appeared:

I note you've chosen the 'energizing' direction rather than the 'calming' one. Are you certain about that?

Iris ignored the notebook's commentary, since what was done was done. Its position behind the books meant that she could glance at it occasionally without drawing attention, and so that her notes—or, more specifically, her notebook's replies—would not be visible to anyone else. Lady Rivenna hadn't explicitly forbidden her from showing it to others, but the notebook's connection to the tea house's deeper magic made Iris cautious about revealing its existence.

"This one's ready," she announced, lifting the teapot and pouring over the mesh strainer that was enchanted to catch physical elements while allowing magical essences to flow through. The tea that filled the tasting cup smelled faintly of damp earth. "Anchoring root, clarity flowers, and veilwater."

Rosavyn accepted the cup with theatrical wariness while Iris poured a second cup for herself. She watched as Rosavyn took a small, cautious sip, then immediately made a face like she'd bitten into something rotten. "Stars above! That's—" Rosavyn grabbed her water glass and took several desperate gulps. "That tastes like someone bottled a swamp fog and added a spoonful of pond scum."

Steeling herself, Iris tried her own cup. The moment the liquid touched her tongue, she understood Rosavyn's reaction. It was what she imagined drinking warmed marsh water might be like. She managed to swallow her sip with only a slight grimace, her determination stronger than her taste buds.

"Too much anchoring root, perhaps?" she suggested, reaching for her water.

"Too much everything," Rosavyn insisted, still trying to rinse the taste from her mouth. "Definitely toss that one."

"I can't," Iris said quickly. "I need to keep samples of each for Lady Rivenna to taste." The truth was that she needed to keep them all for later testing, when the visions returned. One of these blends might work, even if it tasted terrible.

Iris carefully poured the remaining tea into a small labeled vial and set it aside with several others. She glanced surreptitiously at her notebook and froze. New words had appeared on the page in an elegant script that did not belong to the notebook:

Lady Iris, I trust you have recovered from last night's events?

Her heart gave an odd little flutter that she immediately blamed on too much experimental tea. If Lord Jasvian was sending enchanted messages to her notebook, that must mean he was nearby. She glanced up at the ceiling, imagining she could see him settling behind his desk in the study upstairs.

"Why do you look like you've seen a ghost?" Rosavyn asked, reaching for another honey cake.

"What? No, I just—" Iris fumbled for an explanation. "I was consulting my notes. I realized I forgot to add elderleaf to that last blend. No wonder it tasted horrible."

She placed a finger on the notebook, as if to check this imaginary note about the elderleaf, and found more text appearing beneath the first line:

Forgive the intrusion. I arrived early to complete some urgent correspondence and noticed your presence in the kitchen.

Beneath this, in the notebook's distinctive script, another message began to take form:

How fascinating. A message from Lord Brooding himself, and so early in the day. One wonders what urgent matter prompts such uncharacteristic civility.

Iris coughed, then quickly reached for a new teapot and the first of the ingredients she needed for her next attempt, trying to appear focused while her mind raced. How to respond to Lord Jasvian without Rosavyn noticing? And why was he inquiring after her wellbeing so … politely? Their relationship consisted primarily of arguing and then avoiding each other.

Several replies ran through her head: *I wasn't aware my recovery was of any concern to you, my lord.* Or maybe … *Your sudden interest in my welfare is as unexpected as it is suspicious, Lord Jasvian.* Or perhaps she should not reply at all.

She cleared her throat and said, "This time I'm trying starlight crystal honey to balance the bitterness. Hand me that jar, would you?" As Rosavyn reached for the honey, Iris quickly tore a small piece of paper from one of Rivenna's loose notes. She had to reply. She couldn't leave his note unanswered. But, she decided with a deep breath, she would keep things civil.

"Just, uh … making note of this addition," she mumbled as she scribbled her response.

Lord Jasvian, I am quite well, thank you. Your concern is unexpected but appreciated.

"Could you open that for me and measure out a single spoonful?" she added out loud.

As Rosavyn followed Iris's instructions, Iris sent her magic through the paper with a subtle flick of her fingers. The paper folded itself into a perfect envelope and quietly slipped behind the stack of books, waiting until Rosavyn was sniffing the spoonful of honey before it fluttered up toward the ceiling and out the kitchen door.

The notebook's script appeared again: *Am I to understand you are once again conducting a correspondence outside my pages? How terribly inconvenient for those attempting to follow the conversation.*

She grabbed her quill again and wrote, *Don't be petulant*, before turning her attention back to the current blend.

"This one smells much better," Rosavyn observed, leaning over the teapot after Iris stirred the honey into it. Steam rose in delicate spirals, a sweet scent overlaying the slight earthiness.

"The honey makes all the difference," Iris agreed, though her attention was partly focused on watching for an enchanted reply.

After waiting the required amount of time, Iris poured another two cups and took a cautious sip. This blend was certainly more palatable, with the honey softening the sharp edges of the other ingredients. Still, there was an unexpected coldness that spread through her chest, despite the warmth of the tea itself.

"What do you think?" she asked, watching as Rosavyn sampled her cup.

"Less offensive than the last, but still not something I'd choose to drink," Rosavyn declared. "It's like licking a frozen windowpane. Strangely clean but fundamentally unpleasant."

"How ... descriptive." Iris glanced again at her notebook, where new words were forming:

I would not precisely call it concern. Professional courtesy seems more accurate. We are, after all, obliged to share a workspace.

"Could you, uh, pour some of that into one of those little vials and label it?" Iris asked. "There's another quill over there."

"Certainly."

As Rosavyn lifted a quill to one of the vials and sounded out 'fro-zen win-dow-pane' as she wrote, Iris penned her reply on a fresh sheet:

Professional courtesy typically doesn't involve magical communications at sunrise, my lord. One might almost suspect you of harboring actual emotions beneath that impeccably tailored exterior.

The paper envelope performed a small loop before diving beneath the table and heading for the door.

Iris carefully measured solbloom flower petals into the crystal teapot with the lumyrite inlay, which, according to Lady Rivenna's notes, enhanced the magical properties of floral ingredients. She added golden sunrise tea leaves and five drops of starlight crystal honey, then gestured to a nearby hearth sprite to heat water to exactly the right temperature. Not too hot, which would scorch the delicate petals, but warm enough to release their magical properties. All while pretending not to be distracted by thoughts of—

Ah, there it was. Lord Jasvian's reply appeared in the notebook:

I assure you any emotions I harbor are kept in perfect order, unlike the workspace I glimpsed through the open kitchen door, which I can only describe as resembling a battlefield after a particularly enthusiastic skirmish. What brings you to the tea house at this unconscionable hour?

How delightfully judgmental, the notebook commented beneath. *He seems in fine form today.*

Iris pressed her lips together to keep her smile from showing while she swirled the teapot and considered her response. She wasn't prepared to share Lady Rivenna's insights about her magic, especially not with Lord Jasvian. She poured her latest blend into another tasting cup and handed it to Rosavyn before bending over the notebook once more:

Tea blending experiments.

P.S. My creative chaos is simply the natural state of productive experimentation. Some of us do our best work when we're not constrained by excessive tidiness.

"I'm actually hopeful for this one," Rosavyn said, eyeing the steaming cup with cautious optimism. "After all, they can't *all* be terrible, can they?"

Before Iris could reply, she caught sight of a new message appearing in her notebook:

Tea blending experiments. I should have guessed. The ghastly odors wafting through the floorboards are quite distinctive. Are you deliberately creating concoctions that smell like a garden gnome's unwashed boots, or is that merely a happy accident resulting from your 'creative chaos'?

Iris's lips twitched in amusement.

How utterly rude, the notebook commented. *Though he does have a point about the odours.*

"Iris? Are you listening to me?" Rosavyn's voice broke through her thoughts.

"Sorry, what did you say?" Iris asked, guiltily focusing on her friend.

"I said this one tastes almost like a summer garden with just an edge of dirt." Rosavyn peered at her suspiciously. "But you're clearly somewhere else entirely. Are you feeling all right? You keep getting this strange, distant look."

"I'm fine," Iris assured her. "Simply ... concentrating on the next blend." She kept aside a sample—labeling it 'Dirty Summer Garden'—before checking the admittedly disordered pile of pages with Rivenna's notes written across them, and then eyeing the array of ingredients. "Hmm ... let's try this jar curiously labeled 'spiced leaves' along with some pine needles and a bit more of that honey. With the copper pot. I haven't used that one yet."

"Sounds delicious," Rosavyn said dryly.

Iris got to work weighing the correct magical potency of pine needles while Rosavyn opened the jar of spiced leaves and then popped a spoonful of starlight crystal honey directly into her mouth. "That's meant to be for the tea," Iris murmured disapprovingly, though her mind was half-occupied with composing her next message to Lord Jasvian.

"Someone needs to check that the flavor is still good."

"As if it might have changed in the two minutes since I used it last?"

Rosavyn shrugged. "One can never tell what might happen in a kitchen surrounded by so many magical ingredients. Can I add these tea leaves now?"

"Yes, thank you. Two measures of the silver spoon."

As Rosavyn added the tea leaves and then turned to retrieve more water from the kettle, Iris quickly scribbled another note:

Perhaps if you arrived at a more civilized hour, Lord Jasvian, you might avoid such olfactory assaults. Though I'm beginning to think you secretly enjoy our early morning exchanges, given your continued appearance at an 'unconscionably' early hour. Next time, I'll be sure to create something particularly pungent just for you.

The paper folded itself particularly crisply and flew away. Iris bit her lip. With a twinge of guilt, she wrote in the notebook: *I probably shouldn't tease him.*

On the contrary, the notebook replied, *teasing appears to be the only form of interaction he finds tolerable with you. One might draw interesting conclusions from that observation.*

Don't be ridiculous, she scribbled, feeling a flush rise to her cheeks as she turned back to the tea, determined now to focus on the task at hand.

After pouring two cups, she leaned over them to inhale. The brew smelled like warm cinnamon and spiced honey with undertones of fresh pine that lingered pleasantly when she exhaled. She handed one to Rosavyn.

"This one might actually be drinkable," Rosavyn declared after taking a cautious sip. "It tastes like ..." She took another sip, then nodded. "The final whisper of autumn, laced with the first breath of winter."

Iris tasted the tea and found that she agreed. "Perfect," she said, genuinely excited. She took another deep, appreciative sip. The tea spread warmth through her body, and the world around her seemed to settle. She exhaled slowly. Only now, feeling a sudden and profound sense of steadiness, did she realize how long she had been existing in a state of perpetual imbalance, as if constantly walking on shifting ground.

This particular blend might actually work.

The notebook flashed again with new writing, and Iris tried to casually lean over to read it while preparing another blend. It was a longer message this time:

Your accusation wounds me deeply, Lady Iris. I arrive early to enjoy the peace before the day's chaos descends, not to engage in verbal sparring matches with apprentice tea brewers. Though I must admit, your particular brand of disorder does provide a certain entertainment value. It's rather like watching a whirlwind attempt to organize itself into a straight line.

Iris was so absorbed in reading the message that she failed to notice Rosavyn studying her with increasing curiosity. "You keep looking at those books as if the ink itself might dissolve if you look away for too long," Rosavyn observed. "Is there something particularly fascinating about 'Comprehensive Herbology for Magical Infusions'?"

"No! I mean, yes, it's ... very informative," Iris stammered. "I'm examining the combinations I should try next. I believe this one needs to steep for—"

A knock on the open kitchen door interrupted Iris's stammered explanation. Both girls looked up, startled by the unexpected sound, and Iris's gaze landed on one of the last people she expected to see in the tea house kitchen at *any* hour, never mind this early in the morning.

"Lord Hadrian!"

Chapter Twenty-Two

Lord Hadrian Blackbriar stood hesitantly at the threshold of the tea house's kitchen, looking remarkably different from his usual polished self. His cravat sat slightly askew, and his dark hair appeared to have been hastily combed with fingers rather than a proper brush. "Lady Iris," he said with a polite bow. "Miss Rosavyn. I hope I'm not intruding."

"Not at all," Iris replied, embarrassingly aware of the tea stains spattered across her apron and the variety of tea leaves likely entangled in her hair. She resisted the urge to attempt brushing them away, which would only draw more attention to her disheveled state.

Lord Hadrian stepped further into the kitchen, his gaze taking in the array of tea-making apparatus and open books before settling back on Iris. "I spoke with Jasvian last night, and he happened to mention you might be here early." He cleared his throat. "I wanted to ... that is, you left rather abruptly from the Thornharts' gathering, and I wanted to ensure you were well."

Rosavyn suddenly became intensely interested in a jar of dried flowers, though her posture made it abundantly clear she was listening to every word.

"That's very thoughtful of you," Iris said, genuinely touched by his concern as she took a few steps toward him. While there was no hope of finding actual privacy in a kitchen where it was likely even the spoons eavesdropped, she could at least make the conversation slightly less awkward by not conversing from opposite ends of the room. "I must apologize for leaving without bidding you farewell. It was terribly rude of me."

"Please, don't apologize," he said quickly. "Your comfort is far more important than social niceties. I was merely concerned." He shifted his weight, his usual easy confidence momentarily absent. "I also wanted to ask if perhaps ..." He glanced at Rosavyn, who was now pretending to read a label with remarkable concentration. "If I had said or done something to cause offense? You seemed quite distressed when you left, and I feared I might have inadvertently—"

"No!" Iris exclaimed, then moderated her tone. "No, Lord Hadrian. You were nothing but kind. I assure you, my hasty departure had nothing whatsoever to do with you."

Some of the tension eased from his shoulders. "I'm relieved to hear it. I value our friendship greatly, Lady Iris."

Friendship. Of course. For a brief moment, her mind flashed back to Ellowa's cruel comments the night before: *Men of his standing marry within their class. They may dally with ... unusual specimens, but they do not offer them permanent positions.* Which was just as well, Iris reminded herself, since she still had no intention of marrying if she could avoid it. She offered Lord Hadrian a smile she hoped appeared genuine. "As do I."

An awkward silence settled between them, filled only by the rustling of Rosavyn's unnecessarily loud examination of various tea leaves.

"Will you be attending the Living Portrait Exhibition tomorrow evening?" Lord Hadrian asked, his expression brightening. "I hear they've added several fascinating historical figures to the collection this year."

"Yes, actually. My grandmother has been looking forward to it."

"Excellent!" His face lit up with unmistakable pleasure. "I shall certainly be there as well. The portraits are fascinating, though some can be rather ... opinionated."

"So I've heard," Iris said with a small laugh.

Lord Hadrian nodded, his gaze lingering on her face. "Well, I shouldn't keep you from your ... baking?"

"Tea blending," Iris confirmed. "I'm still learning."

"I'm sure you'll master it quickly." His warm smile returned. "You seem to excel at everything you attempt."

Rosavyn made a noise that sounded like a suppressed snort.

"You're very kind," Iris said, ignoring her friend's reaction. "Thank you again for checking on my welfare."

"It was my pleasure." Lord Hadrian hesitated, seeming to gather his courage before adding, "I wonder if I might call upon you one afternoon at Starspun House? Perhaps later this week?"

The question caught Iris off guard. Was he suggesting something beyond the friendship he'd mentioned? A curious wave of vindication washed over her as she again recalled Ellowa's dismissive words—her assertions that Lord Hadrian couldn't possibly show genuine interest in someone like Iris. Yet here he stood, in a tea house kitchen at dawn, asking to call upon her properly.

For a heartbeat, that familiar fear fluttered in her chest. The dread of being trapped, of having her independence slowly smothered like her mother's had been. But looking at Hadrian's open expression and remembering his gentle manner, that fear seemed as though it might be a little ... misplaced. Besides, she reminded herself, one afternoon call hardly constituted a proposal. Nothing that warranted panicking just yet.

"Yes," she said finally, "I would like that very much."

The pleased expression that spread across his face was so genuine it made something warm unfurl in her chest. "Wonderful," he said. "I shall send a note to arrange the details." He bowed again. "Good day, Lady Iris. Miss Rosavyn."

As Lord Hadrian departed, Iris became keenly aware that every occupant of the kitchen was staring at her. Rosavyn with barely contained glee, the hearth sprites hovering in mid-air with their tiny flames flickering in evident interest, and even Orrit, who had paused his scone-making to observe the exchange.

"Well!" Rosavyn exclaimed, abandoning all pretense of disinterest.

"He arose at this unearthly hour and journeyed all the way here merely to ascertain your wellbeing. I do believe Lord Hadrian Blackbriar is quite smitten with you, Iris!"

"Don't be ridiculous," Iris protested, heat climbing her neck once more. "He was simply being courteous."

"Most men do not disarrange their cravats and rush across town at dawn for mere courtesy," Rosavyn insisted. "He's clearly besotted."

Iris returned to her part of the worktable, hoping to escape Rosavyn's teasing. She glanced down at her notebook and found that new words had appeared in Lord Jasvian's elegant script:

Has something happened? You've gone unusually quiet.

Beneath this, the notebook had added its own commentary:

Why have you vanished just as this one-sided exchange was becoming interesting? Most inconsiderate of you to leave me in suspense.

And then another message from Lord Jasvian:

Have I offended you? More than usual, that is. It's unlike you not to have an immediate retort for anything you might find objectionable.

Iris stared at the page, uncertain how to respond to his messages. The situation was becoming absurdly complicated. Lord Hadrian appearing unexpectedly at the tea house, Lord Jasvian's messages growing increasingly familiar, and now Rosavyn watching her every reaction like a hawk.

"Why are you frowning at your notebook as though it's personally insulted you?" Rosavyn asked. She had walked around to Iris's side of the worktable and was now peering over her shoulder.

Iris slammed the book closed with more force than necessary. "I'm not frowning. I'm concentrating."

"On what, precisely? Because your face suggests either profound consternation or severe indigestion."

"Rosavyn!"

"Very well, keep your secrets," Rosavyn said with a theatrical sigh. She glanced toward the window, where the morning light had strengthened considerably. "I should perhaps head home anyway. With any luck, Mother hasn't yet noticed my absence, and I might still claim a proper breakfast before she sends someone looking for me."

"Hopefully," Iris said, trying not to sound too relieved. "Thank you for bravely testing new blends alongside me. I'll let you know if I come up with anything truly remarkable."

Rosavyn hesitated a moment longer, her brow furrowing slightly. "Are you truly all right, Iris? I know you didn't want to share all the details of what those dreadful Brightcrest girls said to you last night, but if there's anything you need to talk about ..."

"I'm fine," Iris assured Rosavyn, touched by her friend's concern. "Last night was ... unpleasant, yes. But I've determined to put it behind me. I've realized I have far more important things to focus on."

Rosavyn studied her face for a moment longer before stepping forward and wrapping her in a warm embrace. "Should you find yourself in need of a confidante, I am, of course, entirely at your disposal."

"Thank you, Rosavyn."

As they separated, Iris felt a pang of guilt for keeping the full story from her friend. Not Ellowa and Mariselle's cruelty—those words did not need to be repeated—but the visions, and Lord Jasvian's unexpected defense of her, and her long and illuminating conversation with Lady Rivenna the night before. But some secrets felt too delicate, too new to share just yet. And when she eventually chose to reveal them, she would need to be carefully selective about her confidants.

She and Lady Rivenna both agreed that this particular type of magic was not to be spoken about freely. Certainly not the sort one displayed for the entertainment of society at the Summer Solstice Grand Ball. But Iris felt sure that when the time was right, Rosavyn would be one of the first to know that her magic went far deeper than mere paper folding.

Rosavyn left the kitchen, but not before first darting past Orrit's workstation and snatching a freshly baked scone from the cooling rack, earning an indignant squeal from the brownie, who shook his tiny flour-covered fist at her retreating form.

With a smile, Iris pulled her notebook closer, relieved to finally be able to give it her full attention. Sitting on one of the kitchen stools, she opened it. Beneath Lord Jasvian's most recent note, the notebook had added:

Never in all my existence have I been closed with such unwarranted violence. I fear for the integrity of my binding.

Iris rolled her eyes, refraining from pointing out that the notebook's existence had spanned barely a week. Hardly long enough to justify such dramatic indignation. She grabbed a quill and wrote:

No offense taken, my lord. No more than usual, at least. I was merely distracted. Contrary to what you might believe, my world does not revolve around our correspondence.

She lifted her quill, her magic responding to her urgency by folding the envelope with unusual speed before it shot across the kitchen and out the door. Not waiting for a reply, she tore another section of blank paper, glanced quickly at his previous message about her 'particular brand of disorder,' and continued writing.

I'm pleased my 'whirlwind' activities provide you with such entertainment. Though I do apologize for disrupting your early morning peace. It's my favorite time of day as well, when I'm not engaged in creating blends reminiscent of a garden gnome's unwashed boots. The tea house has such a different quality in the quiet early hours, does it not?

She began returning ingredients to their jars and stacking the used teacups in a precarious tower while waiting for his reply, occasionally glancing at her successful blend with satisfaction, where it was cooling in the copper teapot.

Words soon formed in the notebook:

Thank the stars for small mercies. I'd make a rather poor celestial body around which to center one's universe.

Regarding your fondness for morning's tranquility, we agree on something at last. The morning quiet is indeed preferable to the chaos that inevitably follows. Though I hadn't expected you to be an early riser. You struck me, initially, as someone who might prefer to linger among dreams rather than face reality at first light.

Iris stared at his words, surprised by the almost poetic quality of his observation.

My, my, the notebook commented. *He's been watching you quite closely to have formed such specific impressions.*

Iris dismissed the notebook with a *tsk* and wrote back:

And you struck me as someone who might sleep inside a perfectly organized schedule, arising precisely on the hour without a single hair out of place. No doubt you keep your dreams alphabetized as well.

The envelope performed an elaborate twirl before shooting upstairs.

Dreams are notoriously resistant to organization, came Lord Jasvian's reply. *Though not for lack of trying, I assure you.*

Iris found herself smiling again.

He's making jokes, the notebook observed with apparent disbelief. *The world truly is full of wonders.*

The words had barely finished taking shape on the page and Iris was already writing her response on another torn piece of paper. The notes Lady Rivenna had left for her were becoming increasingly ragged around the edges, with hardly any blank space remaining on which to write her messages.

I picture you arranging them in neat little rows each night, only to find them hopelessly tangled by morning. How frustrating that must be for someone who values order above all else.

His reply came swiftly:

A keen observation, though not entirely accurate. I value purpose above mere order. The latter simply serves the former. Organization without purpose is just vanity.

Iris raised her eyebrows at this insight into his thinking.

That's rather more depth than I expected, the notebook commented. *Perhaps there's more to Lord Brooding than meets the eye.*

Iris tapped her quill against the edge of a page. Then, realizing that Lady Rivenna's notes had no remaining blank spaces, she turned a few pages ahead in her notebook and unceremoniously tore out a blank page before returning to her current place.

WHAT ARE YOU DOING? the notebook's script appeared. *How DARE you mutilate me in such a barbaric fashion! I am a magical repository of knowledge, not scrap paper for your frivolous correspondence!*

Iris rolled her eyes at the dramatics, tore her newly acquired paper into several smaller pieces, and continued writing.

And what is the purpose that all your careful order serves, my lord? Beyond ensuring the Rowanwood fortune continues to grow, of course.

She hesitated before sending it, wondering if she had pushed too far into personal territory. But her magic had a mind of its own, folding the paper and sending the resulting envelope shooting off the worktable before she could reconsider.

The pause that followed felt longer than previous ones. Iris chewed anxiously on her lower lip. Finally, new words appeared:

Safety. Security. The well-being of those who depend on the mines and those who work in them. Order is merely the means by which I ensure that no one suffers when it can be prevented.

Iris read the words twice, feeling as though she'd been granted an unexpected glimpse behind this man's carefully maintained facade.

A noble purpose indeed, she wrote. *I apologize if my question seemed intrusive.*

Not at all, came his response. *Though I admit I find it somewhat discomfiting to discuss such matters. May I ask what drives your own pursuits? There must be some purpose behind your early morning experimentation beyond simply fulfilling Lady Rivenna's expectations.*

Iris considered her answer carefully, still not ready to share her discovery with him and the real reason behind her experimentation this morning.

A desire to understand. To make sense of things that seem beyond my control.

She watched the paper envelope disappear through the doorway, then turned her attention to the copper teapot and the successful blend she'd created earlier. She poured some into a vial and labeled it 'Autumn & Pine. A Possible Winner.' She set it aside with the other vials as Jasvian's response appeared:

Control is certainly a worthy pursuit. I admit that anything beyond my influence makes me extremely uncomfortable. I strive to never find myself in such a position.

Iris raised her eyebrows at his candid admission as she lifted her quill once more.

Really? Do you not find it freeing to occasionally release that iron grip on your surroundings? There's a certain exhilaration in surrendering to the unexpected, is there not?

Once her folded note had vanished through the kitchen door, she began running her fingers over the silver measuring spoons, arranging and rearranging them as she waited for his reply.

Perhaps for some. For me, surrendering to the unexpected inevitably leads to disaster. When you are responsible for hundreds of lives, a single unpredictable moment, one unexpected variable outside your control, can result in catastrophic consequences.

His words carried a weight she hadn't anticipated, hinting at responsibilities she'd never fully considered. What might it be like to know that if one's magic did not fulfill its intended purpose at precisely the right moment, it could result in actual loss of life? The burden of such responsibility must be crushing. She was beginning to understand why Jasvian clung so desperately to order and control, but still she felt the need to steer the conversation in a somewhat lighter direction.

I recognize that in your line of work, this is true. But surely not all unexpected developments are catastrophic. She hesitated, took a breath, then added: *Even your grandmother's decision to take on a half-blood apprentice might qualify as such an unexpected development, don't you think? And surely that is not catastrophic?*

She sent the note, wondering if she'd foolishly given him the opportunity to revive his earlier prejudices or unleash a fresh barrage of condescending opinions about her unsuitability for the position. More time than usual passed without a reply, and she found herself growing increasingly anxious as she hunted around the kitchen in search of a box in which to place all the samples of her experimental blends.

Finally, just as she found something suitable, Lord Jasvian's response arrived:

I admit my initial assessment of the situation may have been ... somewhat hasty. The tea house has its own wisdom, as my grandmother often reminds me. Perhaps it saw something in you that merited consideration beyond conventional expectations.

The notebook, which had maintained a dignified silence since the page-tearing incident, apparently decided that this exchange was too significant to ignore. Its elegant script appeared beneath Jasvian's message:

Is that ... an apology? Mark the calendar for this historic occasion.

Iris stared at the words, genuinely surprised. It wasn't quite an apology, but from Lord Jasvian Rowanwood, it felt remarkably close. She wrote:

Thank you. I find myself similarly reconsidering certain hasty judgments. Perhaps we've both been too quick to assign each other to neatly labeled categories that leave no room for nuance or growth.

As she watched the paper envelope depart, she heard Lady Rivenna's voice echoing from the main tea house, accompanied by the sounds of other staff arriving. The day was properly beginning now, and with it, the likelihood of interruption.

Lord Jasvian's response appeared quickly, as if he too sensed their time drawing to a close:

A fair observation. Though I maintain that your desk, like your half of the kitchen worktable, is still offensively disorganized.

The notebook commented: *And there is the Lord Jasvian we know. Order has been restored to the universe.*

Ignoring the fact that her half of the table was now infinitely tidier than when Lord Jasvian had glimpsed it earlier, Iris laughed softly and wrote:

And I maintain that your ledgers would benefit from occasional disorder. But perhaps we can agree to disagree on matters of organization while finding common ground elsewhere.

She sent the note, then carefully transferred all her labeled vials into the small box she'd found. By the time she was done, Lord Jasvian's reply had appeared in the notebook:

An acceptable compromise. I must attend to the day's business now. Good day, Lady Iris.

And beneath it, the notebook had added:

Well, well. Progress, it seems, is indeed possible. Even for the terminally stuffy.

Chapter Twenty-Three

"Can you imagine it? An entire ballroom full of people who have no idea who they're dancing with," Lucie said from her position at one end of the kitchen's long worktable, her gaze directed at the used teacup she was currently labelling with magic. The enchantment was a simple one Lady Rivenna had apparently taught her. Part of Lucie's daily duties involved collecting used teacups from unsuspecting patrons so that Lady Rivenna and her companions could perform their ritual examination of the tea leaves left behind.

This practice stirred the same unease in Iris as the vines' gossip-gathering—a subtle intrusion into private matters without consent. When Iris had voiced these concerns, Lady Rivenna merely dismissed them with elegant confidence, explaining that Lady Whispermist and Lady Thornhart possessed such meager divination skills that they rarely discerned anything of consequence. As for Rivenna herself, she considered herself above reproach—a trusted custodian of the secrets the leaves revealed, as though her superior judgment made the invasion perfectly acceptable.

"Lady Whispermist told Lady Rivenna that last year she danced three consecutive dances with her own husband without realizing it!" Lucie added with a giggle.

"Can you imagine finding yourself attracted to the person you're dancing with and then discovering it's a sister or brother or cousin?" Charlotte said. On a brief break from assisting at her mother's dress-making shop, she sat at the other end of the worktable next to Iris. "How horrifying!"

The scent of freshly steeped tea and warm pastries mingled in the air as The Charmed Leaf's kitchen bustled, hearth sprites keeping the ovens at a constant glow and kitchen brownies scrubbing countertops while Mama Saffron kneaded dough for spiced honey rolls and Lissian silently prepared a variety of blends at the brewing station. Orrit had already disappeared, his daily quota of scones completed. If the tea house happened to run out now, it was simply too bad. All the more reason for patrons to return another day.

"Is it really true that no one can recognize anyone else?" Iris asked, looking up from the hefty tome splayed open before her: *The Proprietor's Comprehensive Guide to Magical Establishment Management.* Lady Rivenna had instructed her to begin studying the dry accounting principles and inventory systems that would one day be her responsibility when she took over The Charmed Leaf. The pages of dense text and complex calculations gave Iris a newfound sympathy for Lord Jasvian and his constant battle with ledgers.

"Absolutely true," Charlotte nodded emphatically. "The enchanted masks hide all distinguishing features. Transform your voice, alter your height slightly, adjust the color of your attire, and even change your scent. The magic doesn't just *disguise* you, it weaves an illusion so complete that even your closest friends walk right past you."

The Rowanwood Masquerade Ball was, by all accounts, one of the most anticipated events of the Bloom Season. Held annually at Rowanwood House, its enchantments and transformations were legendary. Enchanted masks were apparently presented on arrival, each one unique, and Iris had heard that the moment a mask touched a person's face, the magic flowed through that person, completely concealing their identity until midnight when the enchantment dissolved.

"I would give anything to attend," Lucie said, adding another labeled teacup to her tray. "Just once, to see the Rowanwood ballroom transformed for the masquerade."

"Now, young one," Mama Saffron said, her hands never stilling as she worked the dough. "The masks are not safe for humans. The magic enters one's body and interacts with one's own magic—if one possesses magic, that is—to create the illusion. It can cause terrible headaches for humans, and possibly even more unpleasant side-effects."

"I know," Lucie said with a wistful sigh.

Iris rubbed her temples, feeling a headache of her own coming on. The particularly tedious section on quarterly inventory assessments she'd been staring at for the past hour was threatening to permanently blur her vision.

At least she no longer had to worry about visions of a different sort assaulting her. It had been almost two weeks since she'd discovered the tea blend that successfully managed the images of possible futures that had begun to overwhelm her. Of course, the blend required some further adjustment after that first morning—a little more of the mysteriously labeled 'spiced leaves', a longer brewing time, a dash more honey, and stirring with a lumyrite rod rather than swirling—but now Iris sipped a cup of her refined version of 'Autumn & Pine' three times a day, and that seemed to give her an adequate level of control over when the visions appeared and how long they lasted.

Curious to test her ability now, Iris took a slow breath and focused her attention on Lucie as the girl checked that each teacup was properly labeled. She deliberately loosened her control, allowing the visions to flow. Images began to unfold before her, overlapping one another almost too quickly to distinguish details, but she caught glimpses of possibilities: Lucie placing a mask over her face, her dress transforming in a shimmer of magic; Lucie without a mask, embracing a tall man who—could that possibly be Lord Jasvian?

Iris blinked hard and the images vanished, revealing Lucie squeezing a final teacup onto her tray. No, it couldn't have been Lord Jasvian. He didn't embrace *anyone*, never mind human serving girls who worked at his grandmother's establishment.

Still, the vision of Lucie placing an enchanted mask over her face concerned Iris. Surely that was not a possibility Lucie would actually entertain? Iris cleared her throat and said, "Saffron's right about how dangerous it is for humans. I've heard the same thing mentioned multiple times this week." This was the truth. The only topic of conversation the leaves had whispered about this week was the masquerade. It seemed there was nothing else on anyone's mind.

"Oh, indeed," Lucie said, looking up from her tray with wide eyes. "I would never do anything so foolish."

"Have you seen any of it before, Charlotte?" Iris asked, giving up entirely on Magical Establishment Management and setting her quill down beside the collection of paper pixies she had attempted to fold with her magic earlier that morning. "Your mother crafts most of the masks and delivers them herself, doesn't she? I wondered if you might have glimpsed the festivities in previous years."

"Sadly not," Charlotte said. "The masks must be delivered days in advance to allow time for the enchantment process."

"Oh, yes, you mentioned that's why you were so busy last week."

"I've seen most of the gowns, though. I've helped Mother with endless adjustments for the ladies who will be there. Oh! Did I tell you who the mystery gown was for?" She leaned forward and lowered her voice conspiratorially. "The High Lady herself."

"The High Lady will be there?" Iris asked in surprise.

"Oh yes," Charlotte nodded. "The High Lady always attends. It's part of what makes the event so prestigious. She doesn't grace all social gatherings with her magnanimous presence, you know."

Lucie tossed a cleaning cloth across the table at her sister. "Do stop your sarcasm."

Charlotte caught the cloth and threw it back with a laugh.

"Not while I'm baking!" Mama Saffron called out sternly, and Charlotte had the good sense to look at least somewhat chastened.

"I'm a little sad I won't be attending either," Iris said, placing one elbow on the table and resting her chin on her palm. "It all sounds quite exciting."

Charlotte groaned. "Is your grandmother being especially difficult about it? She's such a bore."

"Charlotte!" Lucie admonished.

"She can't exactly help being ill," Iris said, surprising herself by defending her grandmother. Their relationship had warmed slightly in recent weeks, though it remained far from close. "She took a chill the other morning when it began raining while we were out at Elderbloom Park and hasn't fully recovered."

"I suppose it's true that she can't be blamed for that," Charlotte conceded.

Iris's gaze dropped to her notebook beside the imposing tome. Elegant script that did not belong to either her or the notebook had begun to appear on the page:

Lady Iris, I trust your studies of tea house management are proving illuminating? Or have you nodded off entirely from the tedium?

A smile tugged at the corner of her mouth. Lord Jasvian's morning messages had become something of a ritual, regardless of where in the tea house Iris happened to be working or studying. "I believe I'll sit by the window for a moment," Iris said, gathering her notebook and quill in one hand and sliding the management tome closer with the other. "The light is better for writing there."

"And I must get these cups to Lady Rivenna," Lucie said, lifting her tray. "She's terribly strict about timing with the leaf readings."

Charlotte stood and attempted to brush the creases from her skirt. "I suppose I should get back to Mother's shop. My morning break is nearly over, and she'll expect me back punctually to help with all the last-minute adjustments for any ladies who aren't quite happy yet with their gowns for tonight."

With farewells exchanged, Iris settled at the small table beside the window that overlooked the tea house garden. Sunlight dappled the flagstone pathways where garden gnomes tended the rows of herbs and garden pixies flitted among the blossoms. Near one of the flower beds, a gnome trudged over to a row of blooms and offered its small watering can to a nearby pixie. The pixie hovered uncertainly for a moment before accepting it—a rare moment of harmony between the two creatures.

With a smile, Iris turned her attention back to the notebook, where it had left its own dry comment:

How marvelous. Our daily correspondence commences. I shall observe this one-sided exchange from afar this time. Perhaps someday you might deign to share YOUR half of the conversation. Though I must admit, attempting to deduce your responses provides me with a modicum of intellectual diversion.

Iris shook her head and allowed herself a quiet laugh as she pulled a few loose sheets of paper from the collection she now made sure to keep tucked into the back of the notebook. She placed her quill on the first blank page.

I now understand your perpetual expression of deep concentration, my lord. These accounting principles could render even the most energetic sprite comatose.

Her tiny folded envelope flitted swiftly out the window and upward. Iris leaned forward, watching its journey until it disappeared from view, imagining Jasvian at his desk above, his brow furrowed in that particular way it did when he was focused.

A curious thought struck her then, one that had surfaced occasionally these past two weeks. Since discovering her true abilities and gaining some measure of control over them, she had not once attempted to glimpse Jasvian's possible futures. She certainly could try now, if she went upstairs to the study. A simple moment of concentration, a deliberate loosening of her control, and the possibilities surrounding him might unfold before her eyes like paper creations taking shape.

Yet something held her back whenever she found herself curious about him. It felt ... improper somehow. Intrusive, as if she were reading private correspondence not meant for her eyes. Though that wasn't the full truth, since apparently she felt none of that same hesitation when it came to seeing anyone else's possible paths. No, the real reason was ... something that felt uncomfortably like fear.

What if she saw something—or *someone*—she did not want to see in Jasvian's possible future? What if she saw him with some beautiful, full-blooded fae lady of impeccable lineage and suitable magical ability, their futures entwined in ways that made perfect sense for the heir to the Rowanwood fortune?

But that was silly, she told herself firmly. It did not concern her who Jasvian Rowanwood ended up with—if anyone. Her reluctance was simply respect for his privacy, nothing more. And truly, what purpose would it serve to glimpse the possible paths laid out before him?? His future did not concern her.

Welcome to my daily torment, came his reply, pulling her from her thoughts. *Though I find a certain satisfaction in bringing order to chaos that I suspect you might lack.*

Iris smiled and penned her response:

Perhaps. Though I confess I've discovered an unexpected appreciation for your dedication. These pages are merciless.

There was a longer than usual pause before his response:

High praise indeed. Speaking of dedication, you've shown remarkable restraint in avoiding the topic that has consumed all of Bloomhaven's attention for days.

Iris smiled and decided to take the bait.

Lord Jasvian, might I enquire if you will be donning a magical mask at tonight's masquerade?

Most likely I shall not attend.

Iris blinked in surprise at his response, then penned her own:

Does it not take place at your own residence?

That does not mean I must attend.

Iris considered this point. He wasn't wrong.

It's true that your presence will not be missed, given that everyone's identities are hidden.

Precisely. There is little point to me being present at the type of event I am generally not comfortable with if no one is even aware of my presence.

Iris paused, contemplating the revelation, perhaps unintentional, that Jasvian did not feel comfortable at social events. Now that she thought about it, though, had he not expressed something to this effect early on in their acquaintance? Something about ... not being able to converse easily in a crowd. Was this what contributed to his ... what had

Lord Hadrian called it? Lack of social graces? Perhaps the serious and imposing Lord Jasvian was simply ... shy?

She tore a new sheet of paper into smaller pieces and wrote:

Are you not curious though?

About what?

You may be missing out on the opportunity for dazzling conversation with a mysterious young lady of secret identity.

I do not believe I am known for my 'dazzling conversation' skills.

Iris couldn't help the quiet snort of laughter that escaped her. She scribbled:

I did not mean yours but rather hers.

Lord Jasvian's response came quickly:

I believe I shall endure the loss.

Before she could reach for a new scrap of paper, more words formed beneath the previous message:

Will you be attending tonight, Lady Iris?

Unfortunately not. My grandmother's lingering illness prevents her from attending, and she refuses to let me go without her supervision. Even if she were well, I suspect she would decline. She likely fears that in a setting where my identity is concealed from everyone—including her—I might commit some grave social transgression.

But no one would know it was you.

True ...

And the event would be made all the more interesting for it.

Iris felt her smile widening at his response, a delighted warmth spreading through her chest as she penned her reply.

Lord Jasvian, I do believe you are encouraging me to find a way to attend the masquerade.

I am encouraging nothing of the sort.

Iris tapped her quill against the edge of the notebook, considering her reply. There was something more playful than usual in this exchange. She found herself wishing to prolong it.

If I were to go against my grandmother's wishes and secretly attend the masquerade tonight—which I would never do—how do you believe an enchanted mask might transform me?

She sent the note on its way, her heart beating a little faster than usual. Why did this particular message feel more daring than all their previous exchanges?

Jasvian's response took longer than expected to appear, and Iris had begun to sketch idle patterns along the edge of her next blank scrap of paper by the time his message took shape in the notebook.

I imagine the enchantment would bestow upon you an oversized peacock feather that towers ridiculously above your head, transform your gown into an entire tea leaf bush making dancing impossible—which would be a mercy, as who truly enjoys dancing?—and reduce your already diminutive stature to comically miniature proportions.

Laughter burst from Iris's lips as she read the message. That was certainly not the response she'd been expecting. It was true indeed that Jasvian's messages were becoming more playful by the day. Before she could reply, another message appeared:

And now that you've planted the notion in my mind, I find myself strangely disappointed that neither of us shall be in attendance.

Iris stared at his words, her pulse quickening. Why was it that she found herself strangely disappointed too? She wished once again that her grandmother was well and that she had no reservations about Iris attending an enchanted masquerade. But there was nothing to be done about that.

Before she could reply, a comment appeared in the notebook's own script:

Ahem. I simply cannot maintain my silence a moment longer. "I find myself strangely disappointed that neither of us shall be in attendance"? What precisely have you written to Lord Brooding in your little paper missiles that has sparked this obvious attempt at flirtation?

Iris's face warmed, and she pointedly ignored the notebook's commentary, refusing to acknowledge the implications or give the enchanted book the satisfaction of a response. She took a breath, considering several responses before settling on:

I suspect you'll find adequate diversion in your ledgers, my lord. They seem never to disappoint you.

An unfair assessment. They disappoint me with alarming regularity, particularly when the numbers refuse to align as they should.

Perhaps they're staging a small rebellion against your excessive orderliness.

If so, they shall find me a formidable opponent. I always prevail in the end.

Iris pressed her lips together, trying to hold her laugh back. The imposing management tome caught her eye again, its very presence enough to dampen the lightness in her chest. She sighed. If she hoped to complete her assigned work for the day, she really should return to it.

I must return to my studies now, Lord Jasvian. Your grandmother expects me to create an imagined example of a quarterly inventory assessment that actually makes sense, and I've scarcely begun to comprehend the concept.

Organization being such a challenge for you.

Indeed. Though I find disorganized thoughts often lead to the most interesting places.

While organized ones lead to completed work.

Touché, my lord. Good day to you.

Good day, Lady Iris.

She turned to a fresh page in the notebook, a smile lingering on her lips. As she drew the boring management text closer, she found herself wondering how an enchanted mask might transform Jasvian. Not that he required any enhancement in appearance—he was far more handsome than any gentleman as perpetually serious as he had the right to be. Broad-shouldered, square-jawed, and possessed of eyes that were alarmingly captivating up close. Iris caught herself recalling the one occasion when they had actually touched. That moment in Elderbloom Park when the glittering pink fox had nearly knocked her over mid-argument, and he had caught her—

The back kitchen door burst open and Rosavyn rushed in like a miniature cyclone, accompanied by the squawking of a gossip bird. "Lady Duskfall!" the bird shrieked, flapping frantically around Rosavyn's head. "Lady Duskfall! Kissing at the mermaid fountain!"

"Oh, be gone, you ghastly creature!" Rosavyn flapped a hand at the bird, which finally settled on the windowsill. Iris leaned across her table and shooed it away with a wave.

"Iris!" Rosavyn stepped closer and gripped her friend's shoulders, a grin spreading across her face. "I have had the *best* idea."

Iris couldn't help laughing at her friend's theatrical enthusiasm. "What is it?"

"I have determined a way to sneak you out of Starspun House." Rosavyn lowered her voice and leaned a little closer. "You, Lady Iris, shall attend the masquerade after all."

Chapter Twenty-Four

"The primary issue is transferring your specific awareness to the copper alloy," Hadrian said, adjusting one of the small, intricately etched metal pieces. "I can channel the raw magical energy easily enough, but your ability to sense a building tempest is more akin to an art form than a science."

Jasvian leaned back in his chair, rubbing his temples as he studied the array of copper components, wires, and hastily sketched diagrams spread across his normally immaculate desk. The summer evening pressed against the tall windows of his study, golden light filtering through gaps in the heavy curtains. From below, the sounds of music and laughter drifted upward—the masquerade in full swing as more guests continued to arrive at Rowanwood House.

"I'm not sure I'm convinced that what you envision is truly achievable," Jasvian replied, rolling up the sleeves of his shirt another notch. He'd long since abandoned his formal jacket, having no intention of joining the festivities. "I don't believe I identify with the term 'art form', but yes. It is as much instinct as it is power. Is that a quality that can be transferred?"

Hadrian, dressed in formal evening attire of deep blue with silver detailing, adjusted one of his cufflinks before responding. "That's what

I'm attempting to determine, and I believe the endeavor merits continued dedication, despite your doubts. If we can successfully map the correlation between specific magical fluctuations and your intuitive responses, we might create a system that could eventually take your place, freeing you from this constant burden."

Jasvian sighed, rising from his chair to pace the length of the room. The floor-to-ceiling bookshelves that lined the walls were filled with mining records, geological surveys, and complex magical texts—the accumulated knowledge of generations of Rowanwoods who had managed the lumyrite mines before him. His father's portrait hung above the fireplace, a constant reminder of the cost of failure.

With his gaze still on the portrait, he said, "Thank you, Hadrian. Despite my repeated expressions of doubt, I genuinely appreciate your continued efforts."

"It is my privilege," Hadrian replied. "You would do the same for me. You *have* done the same for me, countless times when I've required your assistance. And now you, my friend, are the one facing a burden that necessitates help. I've watched you throughout the year, whenever we meet. The constant vigilance, the inability to ever truly relax. Soon the dormant season will be over, and you'll return north time and time again. How long before you miss a tempest because you're simply too exhausted to sense it coming?"

Hadrian's sentiments mirrored those Jasvian's mother had expressed on numerous occasions. Jasvian returned to his chair, picking up one of the metal components and turning it in his palm. Though physical distance now separated him from the mines, he could still sense that low-level hum, that persistent awareness of the lumyrite's latent power.

"I understand the need for a system that does not rely solely on my presence at the mines," he conceded. "But relinquishing control to a mechanical system, no matter how magically enhanced ..." He shook his head. "What if it fails? What if it misses something I would have caught?"

"And that is why we will continue to test until—"

A clock on the mantel chimed nine, drawing Hadrian's attention. He straightened, glancing toward the door where the sounds of the masquerade grew more enchanting with each passing moment, the melody of the orchestra now swelling as a new dance began.

"Ah, forgive me," he said. "I should probably make an appearance downstairs. Your mother would be most displeased if I avoided the festivities entirely after accepting her invitation." He paused, studying Jasvian. "Are you certain you won't join? The masks offer a certain freedom from social expectation that even you might enjoy."

Jasvian laughed, the sound short and dismissive. "A room full of people engaging in pointless revelry while pretending to be someone else? No, thank you. I'll accomplish far more staying here."

Even as he spoke, however, his mind drifted to his correspondence with Iris that morning. There had been something almost wistful in her messages about the masquerade, a lightness to their exchange that had lingered with him throughout the day. For a fleeting moment, he tried to imagine what it might be like to encounter her in such a setting, neither of them knowing the other's identity, free from their usual antagonism, playful though it had become these days.

"As you wish," Hadrian said, straightening his already impeccable cuffs. "I'm hoping Lady Iris might attend. Perhaps we shall continue our conversation from the Living Portrait Exhibition. Her observations were remarkably insightful. Such intelligence and wit in her commentary!"

Jasvian's fingers stilled on the metal piece he'd been examining, his grip tightening involuntarily. An unexpected prickle of irritation coursed through him. Did Hadrian truly believe he was announcing some novel insight? As if he alone had noticed these qualities in Iris? These were aspects of her character that Jasvian had been sparring with for weeks.

"Lady Iris?" he managed, setting down the metal component with excessive care. "I don't believe she'll be there this evening."

"Oh?" Hadrian's brow furrowed as he stood. "I hadn't heard."

"Her grandmother is unwell," Jasvian explained, his voice carefully neutral. "And Lady Iris cannot attend without her supervision."

"That's unfortunate," Hadrian said, genuine disappointment evident in his tone. "I had hoped—"

"It hardly matters," Jasvian cut in, his voice sharper than intended.

"Even if she were here, you wouldn't know it was her. The enchantment would hide her identity entirely."

"Only until midnight," Hadrian reminded him with a smile.

"Perhaps you would be wise to consider the full array of eligible young ladies present this evening," Jasvian said, busying himself with realigning the already perfectly aligned documents on his side of the desk. "There are countless young ladies of impeccable lineage in Bloomhaven who might still capture your attention if you'd only give them the chance."

Hadrian leaned against the edge of the desk, a knowing smile playing at his lips. "And how precisely would you know this, when you've spent every ball haunting the periphery of the room, declining dance invitations and avoiding conversation?"

"That's entirely different," Jasvian said stiffly. "I'm not looking for someone to wed."

"Ah, but that's where you're mistaken, my friend," Hadrian said, his eyes twinkling with mischief. "None of us are looking until suddenly, inexplicably, we find ourselves caught. I suspect even the great Lord Jasvian Rowanwood isn't immune to such fate. And I feel compelled to mention that, unlike some, I find nothing whatsoever wrong with Lady Iris's lineage. Her unique heritage strikes me as rather refreshing in our often stifling society."

Jasvian opened his mouth to protest, but found himself bereft of a suitable retort. That wasn't at all what he'd intended when he mentioned the eligible young ladies present this evening. He'd merely been attempting to direct Hadrian's attention elsewhere—anywhere that wasn't fixed so determinedly upon Lady Iris. 'Impeccable lineage' had been a thoughtless choice of words, he realized with a twinge of something uncomfortably like shame. In truth, he scarcely thought of Iris's heritage anymore. Somewhere between their spirited exchanges and increasingly entertaining written arguments, her mixed blood had ceased to matter. In his mind, she existed now as simply ... Iris.

"Well," Hadrian continued, moving toward the door, "I still intend to enjoy the evening. Will you at least consider coming down later? The refreshments, if nothing else, will no doubt be worth experiencing."

"Perhaps," Jasvian said noncommittally, though they both knew it was unlikely.

After Hadrian departed, Jasvian leaned back in his chair with a groan, unable to deny his inexplicable relief at the knowledge that Iris wouldn't be present tonight. She wouldn't be dancing with Hadrian while he remained isolated in his study. Yet with this relief came a profound frustration directed entirely at himself.

What was happening to him? He could scarcely get through a single morning without composing some message to send her way, even when she was sitting just across the study, seemingly absorbed in her books while he pretended to focus on his ledgers. He would craft each note with ridiculous care, then find himself unable to properly attend to anything until her response arrived. And when it did—those clever, sharp-witted replies that matched him barb for barb—he would read them multiple times, analyzing every phrase for hidden meanings that likely didn't exist.

It was maddening. Completely, utterly maddening.

Even now, far from the tea house, he imagined he could detect the lingering scent of that tea she'd been drinking lately—something with cinnamon and spice, but undercut by a surprising freshness he couldn't quite place. Whatever it was, the scent had become a constant presence in the tea house's study, interwoven with the fragrance of orange blossom like an invisible reminder of her that refused to dissipate even when she was nowhere near.

And worse, far worse, were the moments when she'd tilt her head just so while considering a passage in one of Lady Rivenna's tomes, or when she'd absently tuck a strand of dark hair behind one ear, revealing the delicate curve of her neck. Those observations had no business taking up space in his ordered mind, yet they intruded with increasing frequency, disrupting his concentration at the most inconvenient moments.

He was Lord Jasvian Rowanwood. He had responsibilities. Lives depended on his focus, his control, his unwavering attention to detail. He did not have time for ... whatever this was. This distraction. This preoccupation. This utterly inexplicable tendency to find himself glancing at the tea house's study door whenever it opened, hoping, against all sense, that it might be her.

Abruptly, he pushed his chair back and rose. He moved to the window and pushed the curtain aside. Below, guests continued to arrive, their elegant attire catching the light as they proceeded into Rowanwood House where they would receive their enchanted masks. He thought again of his morning conversation with Iris, of her teasing suggestion that he might find 'dazzling conversation with a mysterious young lady.'

Jasvian glanced at his reflection in the window glass—disheveled hair, loosened cravat, rolled sleeves. Hardly appropriate attire for a masquerade. Yet the thought persisted, growing stronger rather than fading. Perhaps there was wisdom in what Hadrian had said about finding freedom beneath a mask, even if only for a single evening.

With a decisive movement, Jasvian turned from the window and headed toward his chambers. His work could wait until tomorrow. Tonight, he would attend the masquerade after all, if only to lose himself in the revelry and enchantment for a few hours. Perhaps, beneath a magical mask, surrounded by music and dancing, he might finally find respite from the one thing his disciplined mind seemed incapable of controlling—his increasingly persistent thoughts of Iris Starspun.

Chapter Twenty-Five

Moonlight spilled across the narrow alleyway behind Starspun House as Iris slipped through the servants' entrance, her heart hammering against her ribs. She clutched the plain cloak tightly around her shoulders, concealing the simple evening gown she'd worn at dinner.

"Lady Iris!" Brenna's hushed voice followed her. "Remember, I'll be waiting up after midnight to help you sneak back inside. It's unlikely anyone will be awake then to see you, but on the chance that someone is."

"Thank you, Brenna," Iris said, turning back to her lady's maid with a grateful smile. "I appreciate your assistance."

Brenna's smile stretched wider. "Oh, of course, Lady Iris! This is the most thrilling adventure I've been part of since I started working at Starspun House!"

Before Iris could respond, movement in the shadows at the end of the alley caught her attention. A figure emerged, silvery in the moonlight. "Iris! Come on!" Rosavyn beckoned, barely containing her excitement.

With one last grateful nod to Brenna, Iris gathered her skirts and hurried toward her friend. Together, they slipped around the corner of the tall hedge that bordered the property, giggling like schoolgirls as they made their way to where one of the Rowanwoods' enchanted carriages waited, its lamps dimmed to avoid drawing attention.

"Into the carriage, quickly now," Rosavyn urged, ushering Iris ahead of her.

Inside, Charlotte sat waiting, surrounded by a pile of fabric and ribbons. Her face broke into a delighted grin at the sight of Iris. "You made it! I was beginning to worry."

"Was there ever any real doubt?" Iris replied, breathless with excitement as Rosavyn climbed in behind her and pulled the carriage door closed.

"I believe you did attempt to argue with me when I first presented my plan," Rosavyn said.

Iris laughed. "I hardly put up much of a protest!"

Her grin still in place, Rosavyn placed a hand against the carriage's side and raised her voice. "Rowanwood House, please!" And with a gentle lurch, they were off, rolling through Bloomhaven's quieter streets toward the grand estate that awaited them.

"Now," Charlotte said, lifting what appeared to be a stunning gown of deep violet silk, "let's transform you."

"It's beautiful," Iris breathed, touching the fabric reverently. "And the original owner ..."

"Stop worrying about that part," Charlotte said. "The original owner will never know. She developed an unfortunate fever this morning and won't be attending the masquerade. Given that the dress is almost precisely your size, it must be fate bringing you together."

"Do you think it's even necessary to wear a dress so spectacular? The mask enchantment will alter my appearance anyway, so—"

"Iris, you can't very well enter Rowanwood House wearing that modest dinner gown," Rosavyn argued. "You'll be conspicuous in something so plain, and the objective is for you to blend in with everyone else. Now let me help you out of that dress."

What followed was a whirlwind of fabric, corset laces, and suppressed laughter as the carriage traveled along cobblestone streets. Iris found herself twisted this way and that as Charlotte and Rosavyn helped her into the gown, their fingers working nimbly despite the swaying of the carriage.

"Turn around," Charlotte instructed, brandishing a hairbrush and a handful of pins. "Let me see what I can do with your hair." With deft fingers, she twisted Iris's dark locks into a hastily arranged coiffure.

As she finished her work, Rosavyn reached into a small velvet pouch and withdrew something that caught the dim light of the carriage lamps. "Here," she said, slipping a delicate silver bangle onto Iris's wrist. "The final touch."

"Oh, that's lovely!" Iris exclaimed, admiring the intricate flower pattern etched into the silver band, each blossom's center adorned with a purple gemstone that perfectly matched her gown's rich hue.

"Isn't it? I picked it up at Tremayne's Treasures at the start of the Season, but I have so many similar items I haven't had a chance to wear it even once yet. Consider it yours."

Iris caught Charlotte's eye, and they both rolled their eyes. For all her privilege, Rosavyn's genuine warmth and generosity made it impossible to hold her casual extravagance against her.

"Are you certain?" Iris asked her, gently touching one of the purple stones.

"Of course!"

"Thank you, Rosavyn." Iris slipped the bangle onto her wrist where it settled perfectly over her elbow-length ivory gloves.

"We're almost there," Charlotte announced, peering through the carriage window. "I can see the lights of Rowanwood House."

Indeed, as they rounded the corner, Rowanwood House came into view, ablaze with golden light that spilled from its many windows. The magnificent marble steps of the grand entrance were lined with enchanted lanterns, and a steady stream of carriages moved along the curved drive, depositing elegantly dressed guests who proceeded up the grand staircase toward the entrance.

Their own carriage joined the queue, and Iris clasped Charlotte's hands with heartfelt gratitude. "Thank you so much for everything."

Charlotte pulled her into a quick embrace. "But of course! If I can't attend the masquerade myself, helping someone prepare for it is a most welcome substitute. And adjusting dresses for all those haughty ladies parading through Mother's shop certainly doesn't count!"

The next thing Iris knew, she and Rosavyn were stepping out into the warm evening air. She fought the urge to hunch her shoulders or hide her face. Instead, she ascended the stairs confidently beside Rosavyn, her chin lifted just as they'd practiced.

Inside, the grand entrance hall of Rowanwood House took Iris's breath away. Crystal chandeliers bathed everything in warm golden light, reflecting off polished marble floors where footmen in elegant livery guided guests toward the ballroom. Just before the entrance, attendants stood behind a table laden with exquisite masks.

"This is where the magic begins," Rosavyn whispered excitedly as they approached.

A footman bowed slightly. "Ladies, if you would make your selection," he said, gesturing to the array of masks.

Iris's hand hovered over the collection before settling on one more delicate than most of the others. Silver filigree with tiny floral details reminiscent of the bangle on her wrist. Beside her, Rosavyn selected a mask of deep blue embellished with tiny crystals.

"When you place the mask on your face," the footman instructed, "the enchantment will take effect. It will remain until the final chime of midnight, at which point all illusions will fade."

With a shared glance of nervous excitement, Iris and Rosavyn lifted their masks simultaneously. The moment the cool metal touched Iris's skin, she felt a shiver of magic wash over her. Instinctively, she wrapped her fingers around the bangle on her wrist, hoping it wouldn't be changed by the enchantment.

Her gaze returned to Rosavyn and she gasped, watching as her friend's appearance rippled and changed before her eyes. Where Rosavyn had stood a moment before, a slightly shorter woman with cascading golden curls now smiled back at her, her eyes visible through the mask but somehow unrecognizable.

"Iris!" Rosavyn's voice emerged slightly altered, musical and lilting. "Look at you!"

Rosavyn gestured to the mirrored surface of the open ballroom doors, and as they stepped past them, Iris caught a glimpse of herself. Her hair, normally a deep brown, now gleamed with auburn highlights and sat atop her head in an elaborate arrangement of braids woven with silver ribbons. Her gown had shifted from violet to a shimmering teal, and her ivory gloves had transformed into sheer teal lace that extended past her elbows, patterned with silver threads that precisely echoed her mask's design. The only part of her ensemble that remained unchanged was the silver bangle.

The sight of her altered image brought to mind Lord Jasvian's humorous description from their morning correspondence—the peacock feather and how comically small the enchantment would make her—and she couldn't help smiling, almost wishing he was here to see how wrong his prediction had been.

The thought caught her by surprise. Why should she wish for Lord Jasvian's presence? He'd likely only sour the atmosphere with his perpetual seriousness and refusal to dance. In all the gatherings she'd attended since arriving in Bloomhaven, not once had she seen him take to the dance floor, much to the disappointment of every eligible young lady present.

"We should separate," Rosavyn said in her new lilting tone. "The whole point of the masquerade is to mingle freely. Let us meet by the crystal fountain in the entrance hall just before midnight. That way, we can leave together, and I can help you get home safely."

Iris nodded. "Until midnight, then. And thank you again for this!"

With that, they parted ways, each disappearing into the swirling crowd of masked revelers.

The ballroom of Rowanwood House had been transformed beyond imagination. The ceiling appeared to have vanished entirely, replaced by a perfect view of the night sky where stars twinkled against velvet darkness. Swirling patterns of luminescent mist drifted overhead, and the very air sparkled with tiny motes of magic that resembled fireflies hovering just above the guests' heads. Iris stood at the edge of the dance floor, simply absorbing the spectacle. Couples twirled in perfect synchronization to the music, and the floor beneath them gleamed with intricate lumyrite inlays that pulsed with light in time to the beat.

The air itself felt charged, scented with exotic flowers and something more elusive—pure magic, perhaps, or simply the combined energy of so many powerful fae gathered in one place. It made Iris's skin tingle pleasantly, heightening her senses until every color seemed more vivid, every note of music more resonant.

As she watched the dancers, she allowed her mind to relax, and slowly she became aware of possible futures flickering across her vision, almost too fast to make sense of before they folded into one another. A flash of white wedding lace unfurling beside one laughing couple, a glimpse of a sealed letter being hastily tucked into a pocket overlaying the gentleman over there. Nothing that made much sense to her.

She surveyed the crowd until her gaze eventually settled on the far side of the room where the High Lady stood in conversation with Lady Rivenna. Unlike the rest of the attendees, neither woman wore a mask, their true identities visible to all who approached them.

As Iris watched, another series of scenes unfolded rapidly, playing out over the image of the two women. For a brief moment, Iris caught a glimpse of a tall, dark-skinned man towering over the High Lady in a threatening stance. Iris blinked, the haunting image gone in an instant.

Then, to her horror, the High Lady's gaze snapped up, locking directly with Iris's across the crowded room. Her piercing stare seemed to cut through the enchantment, and Iris quickly looked away, heart pounding. Had the High Lady somehow *felt* her magic like an intrusive touch? And what if she could somehow see beyond the enchanted masks? Was she now aware of who it was that had inadvertently attempted to exert some kind of magic over her?

But the High Lady had turned back to Lady Rivenna, bending her head close to speak to the tea houses's proprietress, and before Iris could dwell further on the unsettling possibility that the High Lady had seen her, a voice spoke from beside her. "Would you care to dance?"

Iris turned to find a tall gentleman in a coat the cheerful hue of sun-warmed marigolds, its cuffs and standing collar richly embroidered with gleaming rose-gold thread. A bronze mask obscured his face, revealing only a friendly smile.

And all of a sudden it struck her, what was distinctly lacking at this event that had shadowed almost every other gathering: the judgmental stares and whispers. Tonight, there were none. No sidelong glances at her half-fae ears, no hushed comments about the 'half-breed' behind gloved hands. For the first time since arriving in Bloomhaven, she stood unscrutinized, her identity concealed behind her silver mask. The realization brought with it a lightness, as if she'd suddenly shed the weight of others' expectations and prejudices.

She placed her hand in the outstretched gentleman's and said, "I would be delighted."

The first dance passed with pleasant small talk about the decorations and music, neither participant revealing anything that might hint at their identity. Iris found herself relaxing into the anonymity the masquerade provided. Her second partner was more talkative, speculating about which prominent families might be represented among the masked guests. "I'm certain that's the elder Lord Thornhart over there," he whispered conspiratorially, nodding toward a portly gentleman who kept stepping on his partner's toes. "Dancing has never been counted among his accomplishments."

Iris laughed, playing along with the guessing game while carefully avoiding revealing details about herself. When the dance ended, she found herself near one of the garden archways and gratefully accepted a glass of something rose-tinted and effervescent from a passing footman.

As she stood sipping her drink, enjoying the refreshing breeze that drifted in from the gardens, Iris noticed a tall gentleman lingering on the other side of an elaborate floral arrangement. His mask, adorned with intricate bronze and ink blue detailing, caught the light as he occasionally glanced in her direction. There was something striking about his posture. A certain controlled elegance that contrasted with the casual revelry around him.

Catching him looking her way once more, Iris offered a small smile and lifted her glass in polite acknowledgment. He seemed to hesitate, his attention fixed on her for a moment longer before returning to surveying the room.

As the orchestra struck up a new melody and couples began forming for another dance, Iris considered the impropriety of initiating an invitation herself. The mysterious gentleman's repeated glances surely indicated some measure of interest, and she herself was quite keen to dance again. Would it truly cause much of a stir, especially when everyone was masked?

She had just taken a step in his direction—thinking that this was precisely the sort of behavior her grandmother had dreaded—when he finally approached her. He cleared his throat before speaking, his voice deep and measured. "May I have the honor of this dance?" he asked, extending his hand.

Amused by his evident deliberation in approaching her, yet pleased he had finally gathered the courage, Iris nodded. "You may," she replied, glancing around for somewhere to set her glass. As if summoned by her thought, a footman appeared at her elbow. She handed him the glass before turning back to her prospective partner and placing her hand in his.

His touch was warm as his fingers closed around hers, guiding her toward the dance floor. As they assumed the formal hold for the waltz, Iris found herself half expecting that his initial reserve might translate into a degree of awkwardness on the floor. She was pleasantly surprised, therefore, when their first movements flowed together with a wonderful, almost instinctive effortlessness.

"You ... dance well," he remarked somewhat stiffly.

"As do you," she replied, hoping to ease his apparent discomfort. "The orchestra is particularly excellent tonight, don't you think?"

"Indeed," he agreed, then took a breath, seeming to search for something more to add. "The acoustics of the ballroom are well-designed for such performances."

"Have you attended many masquerades before?"

"Not as many as one might expect," he answered. Another pause, in which he appeared to think and rethink his words before finally uttering them out loud. "To be perfectly honest, I find gatherings like these rather challenging. The expectation of easy conversation with strangers ... it creates a certain anxiety. Where possible, I prefer to avoid such situations altogether."

A pang of sympathy rose in Iris's chest. His confession resonated more deeply than he could know. She remembered all too well her first few society events in Bloomhaven. The whispers that followed her, the sidelong glances, the way conversations would halt at her approach. Though things had improved somewhat as the Season progressed, she still felt the sting of being an outsider, never quite belonging. Social anxiety was a familiar companion, even now.

"Well, I'm glad you chose to attend tonight," she replied with genuine warmth. "And I hope I'm not causing you further discomfort. If you'd prefer to forego trivial banter, please feel free to introduce a more serious topic. I'm perfectly amenable to discussing something of substance."

His expression softened behind the mask, almost reaching a smile. "Thank you for your consideration, but that won't be necessary. I find myself quite enjoying our exchange as it is."

"I'm happy to hear it," Iris replied, and as they completed another turn, she added, "What shall we speak of next, then? The enchanted ceiling? I don't think I've seen an illusion quite like it before."

"It's remarkable," he agreed, glancing upward. "Maintaining an enchantment of this complexity for an entire evening requires considerable magical skill and attention to detail."

"The stars seem so real," Iris observed, admiring the twinkling lights above. "I wonder if they're arranged in true constellations or merely designed for beauty."

"I've studied the illusion quite carefully," he admitted, "and I believe the stars are simply arranged in random patterns. I was disappointed at first—a missed opportunity to replicate the true order of constellations—but the more I observe it, the more I appreciate what has been accomplished. There's a certain ... creative chaos to it that has its own appeal."

Iris nearly missed a step as recognition dawned with startling clarity.

Lord Jasvian, she thought with a jolt of surprise.

"My lady?" he asked, noticing her misstep. "Are you all right?"

A retort nearly escaped her: *You said you weren't coming!* And then, almost immediately: *I thought you were a terrible dancer!* And then—

Then she pressed her lips firmly together, because revealing that she recognized him would give away her own identity, and she wasn't yet prepared for that. There might be ... advantages to this situation.

Perhaps she might discover aspects of the reserved, guarded Lord Jasvian that he would not ordinarily disclose.

And ... well, there also happened to be the fact that she was rather enjoying the warmth of his hand pressed against the small of her back up until the moment she'd realized precisely *who* the hand belonged to. That same hand now guided her through a graceful turn, its pressure steady and assured against the curve of her waist. The heat of his touch, and something about the fact that she now knew it was *him,* sent an odd shiver through her.

"Yes, I'm fine, thank you," she said as they returned to their original positions. Her eyes darted up once more, seeking that familiar gaze beyond the mask, but the enchantment had turned his eyes a deep blue. How very strange to think that it was Lord Brooding himself behind this mask.

As they moved through an elegant series of turns, Iris found herself impressed by the assurance of his lead, his movements confident yet never forceful, anticipating each step with remarkable timing. In truth, he was an excellent dancer. Was it simply because of the pressure to make conversation that he generally avoided dancing?

Curiosity began to build within her as they continued to dance, the melody shifting seamlessly into another piece. Here was an opportunity she might never have again—to speak with Jasvian without the weight of their past interactions coloring every word. Protected by anonymity, perhaps she could learn more about the man behind the perpetual frown.

She did not want to lie to him, but she would need to be strategic with her questions. "I'm familiar with Bloomhaven and its prominent families—" that wasn't a lie; she had discovered much since arriving here "—but I'm still learning about the specific magic of all those who have manifested prior to the last few years. Do you know anything about Lord Rowanwood's specific magic?"

If she had not already guessed his identity, the way he stiffened would most likely have given him away. "I know, of course, that it's related to sensing the building of mine tempests," she added quickly, "but I don't believe I fully understand the extent of his power. Do you know anything about it?"

"I believe I do know a thing or two," he replied, his voice carefully neutral.

Iris looked up at him expectantly, hoping her masked appearance would encourage him to speak more freely.

"You are correct," he said finally, "that Lord Jasvian can sense the building of mine tempests. His magic is particularly attuned to the gathering of volatile magic around raw lumyrite deposits. When in close proximity to the mines, he is aware of the constant, low thrum of energy emanating from the raw lumyrite. Should that energy begin to coalesce significantly, however—signaling the inevitable formation of a tempest—he can detect that dangerous surge even across considerable distances. The feeling is similar to hearing distant thunder, I'm told, though no one else can detect it. And in addition to sensing the building tempest, he can also calm the wild magic before it erupts."

"That sounds extremely useful," Iris observed, "though rather taxing, I imagine."

He nodded, guiding her through another turn. "Indeed."

"Can he sense other types of unstable magic as well?" Iris asked, thinking of something Lady Rivenna had said the night she helped Iris understand the full extent of her own magic. The older woman had mentioned being alerted to Iris's situation by someone possessing the ability to detect such unexpected magical surges.

"Yes, I believe he can," Jasvian replied after a brief hesitation. "Similar to the tempests, he can feel when other magic threatens to erupt beyond control."

Iris nodded, her suspicion confirmed, deciding now was not the time to examine precisely how she felt about the fact that he'd been fully aware she'd lost control of her own power that night. Curious, she added, "And can he calm that magic as well?"

"If necessary, yes. Just as with the tempests, he can soothe magic that threatens to cascade beyond its boundaries. Though I believe he has little experience with anything outside of mine tempest magic."

Iris's thoughts drifted as they moved across the floor. "I've often wondered," she said after several moments of quiet had passed between them, "why the Rowanwoods are called Rowanwoods if their magic is related to earth and minerals and crystals. It seems an odd name for a family whose power lies in the ground rather than in trees."

He seemed surprised by the question. "You have a curious mind. Particularly when it comes to the Rowanwoods."

"I'm interested in all the prominent families of Bloomhaven," Iris assured him. "But perhaps because we're at Rowanwood House tonight, my attention has naturally turned to its namesake."

"That seems reasonable," he conceded. "The Rowanwood family's magic wasn't always tied to earth and crystal," he explained. "Originally, the family possessed magic connected to rowan trees, the mountain ash. They could communicate with them, accelerate their growth, shape their wood without tools. They served as forest wardens and protective charm crafters.

"What changed?" Iris asked, genuinely intrigued.

"There was a disease—the Ashen Decay—that ravaged the forests many generations ago," Jasvian continued. "Most of the family devoted their resources to fighting it, working directly with infected trees. But one of the younger sons had manifested differently. While his siblings spoke with trees, he could sense what minerals lay beneath their roots."

Iris nodded encouragingly as they moved through the steps of the dance.

"When the Decay worsened, many in the family fell ill, their magic corrupted by the disease. But the Rowanwood son whose magic was different was working in the northern mountains when he discovered vast deposits of lumyrite through his unique ability to sense what lay beneath rowan roots. As the family's traditional magic faded with each generation affected by the Decay, the line of Rowanwoods who had a connection to earth and crystal grew stronger."

"So the current Rowanwoods are all descended from that particular line?" Iris asked.

"Yes. The family kept their name to honor their heritage, even as their magic evolved."

"That's fascinating," she said. "I understand a little of what that

Rowanwood son must have felt. My own magic manifested quite differently from the rest of my family. Knowing you're different can be both a blessing and a burden."

"I don't suppose you'll share more about your magical ability?" he asked, his tone lighter. "It might give me a clue to your identity."

Iris laughed, shaking her head. "Absolutely not. We're wearing these enchantments for a reason, are we not?"

His lips curved into a smile that transformed his masked face, and something inside Iris ached to see that expression on his true countenance. "Very well," he conceded. "Then perhaps a different approach. Tell me something about yourself that most people don't know. Something that couldn't possibly reveal your identity."

Iris considered for a moment before admitting, "I love poetry."

"Poetry?" he repeated, sounding genuinely surprised. "What do you enjoy about it?"

"The emotion contained in so few words," she replied. "How a carefully crafted verse can paint vivid pictures in the mind and stir feelings that prose sometimes cannot reach."

"I confess I've never been able to lose myself in poetry," he admitted. "Perhaps I'm too practical-minded for such things."

Iris laughed, the sound bubbling up naturally. Had she harbored any lingering doubt about her partner's identity, that admission would surely have dispelled it.

"Perhaps I should try again," Lord Jasvian mused, his tone thoughtful.

"I challenge you to do so. You might surprise yourself."

"I believe I shall," he replied, and the sincerity in his voice caught her off guard.

They continued dancing, his hand remaining steady at her back as he guided her through the intricate steps of the current dance, one whose lively, weaving patterns marked it as originating from traditional fae culture, presenting a delightful challenge given her limited practice with such forms back home.

As the music returned to a gentler tempo, and conversation became easier once more, they discussed everything from favorite seasons to the comparative merits of various magical transportation methods. Iris employed some invention when stating that she was currently engaged in furthering her knowledge of plant-derived comforts and their proper presentation, quietly amused at the way his eyes narrowed behind his mask as he attempted to decipher her deliberately vague description. She found herself enjoying the freedom to speak her mind without the weight of her identity coloring his responses, savoring each unguarded comment and genuine laugh she drew from him.

When the music shifted once more, quickening again into something spirited, Jasvian asked, "Would you prefer to rest?"

"Not at all," Iris replied, surprised by her own eagerness. "I'm quite enjoying this. Unless you wish to stop?"

"I'm happy to continue if you are," he said, and the warmth in his voice made something flutter in her chest.

As the tempo increased, Iris surrendered to the music, allowing him to guide her through spins that sent her skirts swirling around her ankles. Each time she returned to his arms, his smile grew wider, his movements more confident. Around them, other couples matched their enthusiasm, the entire ballroom transforming into a whirlwind of color and motion.

Iris found herself laughing freely as he led her through a particularly challenging sequence of steps, her feet somehow finding their way without conscious thought. When the final notes rang out, Jasvian pulled her into one last dramatic spin before drawing her close, both of them breathless and flushed with exertion.

Half the ballroom erupted into spontaneous applause, the energy of the dance having captured everyone's attention. As the enthusiastic response died down, Iris realized with a start that they had danced multiple pieces together without pause. The orchestra had seamlessly transitioned from one melody to the next, and neither of them had thought—or perhaps wanted—to separate.

She caught Jasvian's eye, but before either could speak, a hush fell over the ballroom. The music faded, and all eyes turned toward the dais where the High Lady now stood, commanding attention without saying a word.

"Ladies and gentlemen of the United Fae Isles," her voice rang out, clear and powerful. "As another magnificent Rowanwood Masquerade draws to its conclusion, I wish to extend my gratitude to our gracious hosts for what has, as always, been one of the most spectacular events of the Bloom Season." She paused, her gaze sweeping the room. "Of course, as wonderful as this evening has been, it serves primarily as a prelude to the true pinnacle of our Season—the upcoming Solstice Ball." A slight smile curved her lips, something almost smug in her expression. She gestured to the orchestra. "And now, the final dance before the enchantments come to their end. I suggest you choose your partners wisely, for at the stroke of midnight, all masks shall fall away, and true identities revealed."

With a start, Iris realized how late it had grown. She had completely lost track of time during her conversation with Jasvian, and now midnight approached dangerously near. She needed to meet Rosavyn and leave before the enchantment faded.

Jasvian took a deep breath, seeming to gather his courage once more. "Would you honor me with this last dance?" he asked.

For a fleeting moment, Iris was tempted to accept. To dance until the final chime, to see his expression when he realized who she was. But caution prevailed over curiosity. "I'm so sorry," she said, already taking a step back. "I must go. I've just remembered that—that I must meet someone." She offered a quick curtsy. "Thank you for the dances. They were truly wonderful."

And before he could respond, Iris turned and wove her way through the crowd, leaving behind the mystery and enchantment and the lingering question of what might have been.

Chapter Twenty-Six

JASVIAN WINCED AS HE STEPPED INTO THE CHARMED LEAF THE MORNING after the masquerade, a dull ache throbbing through his head. Sleep had proven elusive, his mind replaying fragments of conversation with his mysterious partner in teal and silver, analyzing each laugh, each shared observation, searching for clues to her identity. He stifled a yawn, uncomfortably aware of the morning light streaming through the windows at an angle that revealed his tardiness. Still early enough that the tea house remained closed to patrons, but considerably later than his usual arrival.

Lord Jasvian Rowanwood, disheveled and behind schedule—what was becoming of him? His grandmother would be delighted by this evidence of his humanity.

As he walked between the empty tea house tables—his aching leg muscles reminding him that he'd danced far more enthusiastically last night than he had in years—a belated realization struck him: he had no reason to be here today. The renovations to Rowanwood House's ballroom were complete, the masquerade itself now merely a memory. For the first time since the Season began, the house was blissfully quiet, free from the constant disruption of workers and suppliers.

It was true that he had used his grandmother's tea house study for years, keen to avoid the interruptions of his siblings, but surely he could endure their occasional visits to his study at Rowanwood House if it meant no longer having to share a workspace with Iris. Except ... he no longer harbored any desire to escape her company. Quite the opposite, in fact.

A movement near the far wall caught his attention. Lucie Fields, the human serving girl who worked here, stood precariously balanced on a wooden ladder, one hand stretched toward the ceiling. Around her neck hung a chunky necklace of raw lumyrite crystals, the morning light catching on their rough-cut edges.

It occurred to Jasvian, rather abruptly, that he had never exchanged a single word with the girl. Indeed, he had scarcely acknowledged her existence beyond a fleeting disapproval when his grandmother first employed her. He paused, watching her with curiosity. She was directing thin ribbons of light toward the ceiling, where they wove themselves into an intricate pattern across the plaster. Each ribbon connected to one of the tea house's central support beams, creating a delicate lattice of golden energy.

After several moments, Jasvian recognized the base spell. One of his grandmother's seasonal enchantments designed to maintain a perfect ambient temperature regardless of the weather outside. But Lucie had modified it, he realized. Instead of the standard circular pattern he had seen his grandmother apply to the entire ceiling, Lucie had created an asymmetrical design that followed the natural grain of the wooden beams. The modification was clever—it would distribute the cooling effect more evenly throughout the space.

Without magic of her own, she was no doubt channeling power from the lumyrite necklace—likely a gift from his grandmother—and yet the precision of her work suggested actual ... skill. A discomfiting blend of guilt and shame pricked at him. Why should her competence surprise him? Because she was human? The prejudice inherent in that assumption struck him now as utterly absurd.

He was quite certain this shift in perspective stemmed from Iris's influence. She had challenged his ingrained assumptions at nearly every turn, forcing him to reconsider beliefs he'd held for years. This change in his thinking, he now realized, had occurred gradually over the past weeks since their first meeting. Only now, in this quiet, unguarded moment with his mind weary from lack of sleep, did the extent of the change strike him with such sudden force.

"Good morning, Miss Fields," he said, his voice cutting through the quiet.

Lucie started violently, nearly toppling from her perch on the ladder. Her concentration broken, the golden ribbons of light wavered dangerously before she steadied them with a quick gesture. "L-Lord Rowanwood!" she stammered. "I didn't hear you come in."

"I apologize for startling you," he said, moving closer to examine her work. "That's an interesting modification to my grandmother's ambient enchantment."

Lucie's eyes widened. "I, uh ..." She blinked several times, like a shadow sprite caught in a sunbeam. "Yes, my lord."

"It's quite clever," he added. "More effective, I would imagine."

Again, she appeared lost for words before finally stuttering, "I-I hope so, my lord." She was clearly uncomfortable with his attention.

Unease settled in Jasvian's chest, the same he'd felt the previous evening when Hadrian had called him out on his 'impeccable lineage' comment. Shame, he realized. He was ashamed of his former certainty, his dismissal of humans as somehow lesser.

"Miss Fields," he said formally, "I feel I owe you an apology."

She stared at him. "My lord?"

"It is no great secret, I suspect, that I've long held certain restrictive views regarding humans and their place in fae society. Views that I've recently come to recognize as ... incorrect. I merely wish to apologize for this and to thank you for your contribution to this establishment."

Another awkward silence stretched between them, Lucie appearing to be shocked speechless by his words. Finally, she whispered, "Thank you, my lord," as if she were too afraid to raise her voice to a normal pitch.

With a final nod, Jasvian stepped back. "I'll leave you to your work, then. Good day, Miss Fields." And then he made his way toward the stairs that led to the upper study before he could terrify the poor girl any further.

He ascended the familiar steps slowly, one hand rising reflexively to massage his throbbing temples. The exchange had been undeniably awkward, yet as he climbed, he felt ... lighter. A curious counterpoint to the lingering physical discomfort. Who might have suspected, he mused, that the constant effort of maintaining disapproval, the sheer weight of rigidly held disdain, could be such a heavy weight?

He found himself wondering what Iris would think of this realization of his. She would undoubtedly find his newfound enlightenment rather amusing, he suspected. Probably take considerable delight in informing him that she had, of course, been correct all along. And strangely, the prospect did not irritate him in the slightest.

No, he checked the thought sharply as he reached the landing. He was not meant to be dwelling on Iris. That had been the very purpose of subjecting himself to the masquerade the previous night—to seek some distraction from these incessant thoughts of her. The evening had, in that regard, been a success.

He paused at the study door, fingers hovering over the polished brass handle as memories of the previous night washed over him. One decision against his nature had led to an evening more enjoyable than he'd ever expected. He'd stood at the edge of the ballroom for far too long, watching masked figures twirl across the floor while anxiety lingered at the edges of his mind. That familiar discomfort he always felt at such gatherings.

He'd been on the verge of departure, berating himself for the foolishness of attending at all, when he'd noticed her—the woman in teal, observing the dancers while she sipped her drink. She'd remained stationary at the ballroom's periphery long enough for him to do something utterly uncharacteristic. In a moment of reckless abandon—as reckless as Lord Jasvian Rowanwood ever allowed himself to be—he'd decided that one dance before leaving the blasted masquerade couldn't hurt. Well, it could, but the embarrassment wouldn't last long beneath the shield of enchantment.

But one dance had become two, then three, until he'd lost count entirely. Time had slipped away as they'd moved across the floor, her conversation as captivating as her graceful movements. Moments of shared humor, thoughtful questions, and a comfortable rhythm to their discourse—all had combined to create an evening he hadn't known he was capable of enjoying.

Yes, he had indeed succeeded: thoughts of this mysterious woman now occupied the space previously held by Lady Iris Starspun. The maddening preoccupation with his grandmother's apprentice had instead been replaced by fascination with a masked stranger who'd vanished before midnight. A fair trade, surely. His mind cleared of one distraction only to be filled with another, but at least this one would fade as the masquerade receded into memory.

He pushed open the door and stepped into the study. The room was bathed in morning light, the curtains drawn back to reveal a perfect view of the upper branches of the ancient glimmerbark tree on the other side of the road. The air smelled of freshly brewed tea and old books—a combination Jasvian found comforting.

And there sat Iris, her dark hair catching the light in a way that made it gleam almost black, her slender fingers turning the pages of the book that lay open on the desk before her. In that instant, any claim Jasvian had made to banishing thoughts of her simply evaporated. His gaze lingered on the graceful line of her back as she leaned over the text, on the subtle point of her ear just visible beneath a strand of hair that had escaped its pins. The mysterious woman in teal might have captivated him for an evening, but Iris Starspun effortlessly reclaimed his entire attention.

"Good morning, Lord Jasvian," she said without looking up, her voice carrying the same polite neutrality that had characterized their recent face-to-face interactions, though their written correspondence had grown increasingly familiar.

"Lady Iris." He moved toward his own desk. "I trust your morning has been productive."

"Quite," she replied, turning another page. "Lady Rivenna has rewarded my struggle through yesterday's tedious management text with this marvelous old tome. It details the rather scandalous history of one of the first families involved in creating enchanted tea blends. It has proven to be quite absorbing."

Ah. That explained the old-book smell then.

Jasvian settled into his chair, waiting the customary few moments for his neatly arranged documents to appear. Then he reached for the ledger he'd abandoned the previous evening when Hadrian had entered his study at Rowanwood House. He had little genuine intention of resuming his work, however. His eyes kept drifting to Iris, who appeared remarkably serene as she made occasional notes in her favorite notebook. Had she always been this composed? This focused? Or was he simply more attuned to her presence now, acutely conscious of every small movement?

"I hear the masquerade was quite spectacular last night," he said, attempting to maintain conversational normalcy.

Iris's quill paused mid-stroke, hovering over her notebook. "Yes," she said after a moment, her gaze still fixed on the page before her. "So I've heard as well."

Jasvian frowned slightly. "How have you heard already? It is still quite early; surely most of Bloomhaven's elite have yet to rouse themselves after last night's revelries."

She hesitated for the briefest moment. "The gossip birds," she replied with a slight shrug. "They've been particularly active this morning. Something about the High Lady's dress and Lord Thornhart stepping on toes."

"Ah." Jasvian tried to focus on the columns of numbers before him, but found his mind wandering back to the mystery woman. "Gossip birds are remarkably swift, if not always accurate."

"Indeed."

Silence fell between them, broken only by the scratch of Iris's quill and the occasional rustle as she turned a page—noticeably quieter than her usual enthusiastic page-flipping that had so often disrupted his concentration. Jasvian found himself missing the familiar sound, another peculiarity in a morning already filled with them.

After what felt like an eternity of pretending to work while his mind raced in useless circles, Jasvian lowered his quill and leaned back in his chair. Across the room, Iris reached for the porcelain teacup standing on one corner of her desk.

"The usual?" Jasvian asked, grasping at ordinary conversation. "Cinnamon and ... something fresh?"

She paused, her hand a few inches from the cup, and he felt an utter fool for his lack of subtlety. He might as well have plainly announced how much attention he'd been paying her. "Uh, yes." She reached for the cup. "'Autumn & Pine' is what I've called it." She lifted the cup to her lips, and as she did so, something silver slid down her arm, catching the light. A bangle.

Jasvian froze, sudden recognition striking him like a physical blow. A silver bangle, intricately etched with flower patterns, each blossom's center adorned with a purple gemstone. The same bangle the mystery woman had worn last night.

His gaze had traced that very ornament countless times during their dances, his fingers occasionally brushing against it as he guided her through the steps.

Iris. It had been Iris all along.

The realization crashed over him in waves of shock, disbelief, and—mortifyingly—a surge of something dangerously close to elation. His mind raced backward through every moment of their conversation, every turn and step, every laugh they had shared beneath the enchanted ceiling.

He'd spoken to her about the Rowanwood legacy, about his—no, about *Lord Jasvian's*—magical abilities. She had asked direct questions about him, as if ... as if she had known exactly who he was.

Had she recognized him somehow? The enchantment should have prevented it, yet her questions about the Rowanwood family had been oddly specific. But she had claimed curiosity about all of Bloomhaven's prominent families, and, as she had pointed out last night, being at Rowanwood House naturally invited questions about its family's lineage.

Jasvian exhaled a quiet breath of relief, though his mind still whirled, sifting through everything he had learned about the mystery woman last night and layering it atop what he already knew of Iris. Her fondness for poetry ... her immediate empathy for his ancestor who felt so out of place ... Of course. That shouldn't surprise him. Had he not played a significant role himself in ensuring she felt precisely that way upon her arrival? He had hardly been welcoming when she first arrived.

And her laugh. The warm, genuine sound that had sparked something within him had been *her* laugh—but distorted by the enchantment. He realized with a strange, piercing clarity that he had never heard Iris laugh in his presence. Not when she knew it was him.

"Lord Jasvian?" Iris's voice cut through his spiraling thoughts. "Are you quite well? You look rather ... distressed."

"I'm perfectly fine," he managed, though his voice sounded strange even to his own ears.

Iris set her teacup down, concern etched across her features. "Are you certain? You've gone quite pale."

"Merely ... a momentary dizziness." He stood, forcing his gaze away from that damning silver bangle that had shattered his carefully maintained equilibrium. "It will pass."

"Perhaps you should stay seated." She shifted to the edge of her seat as if about to stand.

"That won't be necessary," he said stiffly. "I simply require fresh air."

She tilted her head slightly, studying him with those intelligent dark eyes. "Something has upset you."

"Not at all." The lie felt leaden on his tongue. "I was merely thinking of the—the need to finalize the seasonal workforce allocations for the mines. There is still much to prepare."

"Of course," she said, though her expression suggested she didn't quite believe him. "The mines reopen soon after the Bloom Season ends, do they not?"

"Yes. The dormant period coincides with the Bloom Season." He struggled to maintain the thread of conversation while his mind continued to reel from his discovery. "There will be ... uh, extensive inspections before operations resume."

"That sounds like a significant responsibility," she said, her tone gentler than usual. "No wonder you're preoccupied."

After another moment in which he couldn't think of a single thing to say, she turned in her seat and faced her desk again. He was intensely aware of everything about her—the delicate arch of her wrist as she reached for her quill, the absent sweep of her other hand down the curve of her neck, the space she occupied as something wholly and unmistakably hers, as if the room had been shaped to fit her presence. It was as if he were seeing her for the first time, yet with the intimate knowledge of having held her in his arms while they danced.

His carefully ordered world had been upended. The woman who had challenged and irritated him for weeks, whose sharp wit had both frustrated and intrigued him, was the same woman whose laughter and conversation had captivated him at the masquerade. The realization struck him with unexpected force, and with it came an admission he could no longer deny: he was drawn to her, had been perhaps from the very beginning.

He wanted to hear her laugh again, her true laugh unaltered by enchantment. He wanted to touch her, to feel the warmth of her hand in his, to stand as close as they had been while dancing. The urge to reach out, to trail his fingers down her arm and over her wrist, to feel the softness of her skin beneath his touch, was almost overwhelming.

"Did you know," Iris said suddenly, interrupting his perilous train of thought, "that one of the earliest tea scandals began with a fae merchant's daughter who unexpectedly manifested the ability to infuse emotions into liquids? She unknowingly brewed a blend that made everyone who drank it speak with absolute honesty for hours—at a rather high-profile gathering, no less. Imagine the consequences!"

The sudden image of Iris serving such a tea to him, of truth spilling from his lips about who he'd danced with and how it had affected him, sent a jolt of panic through Jasvian's system. "I should go," he said abruptly, startling even himself with the urgency in his voice. "There are matters requiring my attention at Rowanwood House."

Something flickered across Iris's face, so quickly he couldn't decipher it. "Of course," she said. "I wouldn't wish to keep you from your responsibilities."

"Until tomorrow, then." He gave a short, formal bow, desperate now for solitude in which to untangle his chaotic thoughts.

"Until tomorrow, Lord Jasvian."

Chapter Twenty-Seven

IRIS FELL BACK AGAINST HER CHAIR THE MOMENT THE DOOR CLOSED BEHIND Lord Jasvian, exhaling a breath she felt she'd been holding since he first entered the room. It had taken far more effort than she had energy for this morning to maintain such perfect composure. After barely sleeping—the memories of dancing beneath enchanted stars replaying through her mind for hours—she should probably still be in bed. But her body's natural rhythms had roused her at the same ridiculous hour as always, and she'd found herself dressing hastily, unable to banish thoughts of Jasvian from her mind.

What if he also arrived early at the tea house today? She wanted—no, needed—to be here if he did.

She pushed the large tome away with a groan. Despite the first few pages being deliciously scandalous indeed—full of tales of magical teas that had supposedly resulted in three engagements, two duels, and the temporary transformation of Lord Someone-Or-Other into a remarkably articulate squirrel—she hadn't been able to focus on a single word after Lord Jasvian had entered the room.

And he'd noticed her tea! She'd never specifically told him about her 'Autumn & Pine' blend, certainly never mentioned it by name. Just as she hadn't told him—hadn't told anyone yet—about the true extent of her magical ability.

She pulled her notebook closer, glancing down at the 'notes' she'd been so diligently taking. They had absolutely nothing to do with the text she'd been pretending to read. Knowing that Lord Jasvian was unable, from his position at his own desk, to see the words she penned, she'd begun scribbling down her thoughts:

I cannot believe I spent half the night dancing with LORD JASVIAN ROWANWOOD. The man who called me a half-breed with diluted magic. The man who questioned whether I belonged in society at all. And yet, when he smiled at me last night—actually SMILED—my heart did the most peculiar little flip.

Beneath her words, the notebook had responded in its elegant script:

How very anatomically improbable. Perhaps you should consult a physician about these concerning cardiac acrobatics.

Iris had glared at the page before continuing:

You know perfectly well what I mean. And now that he is HERE in the room with me, I cannot seem to breathe properly. What is HAPPENING to me?

Based on available evidence, the notebook had replied, *you appear to be experiencing a textbook case of romantic attraction. How disappointingly conventional of you.*

It is NOT romantic attraction. It is ... temporary insanity brought on by lack of sleep and excessive exposure to enchanted masks.

Of course. How foolish of me to confuse the two. They are so frequently mistaken for one another in medical literature.

Iris stared at the exchange, mortified by her own admission. She couldn't *breathe*? What nonsense was that? Her quill hovered above the page. After a moment, she pressed it to the paper once more.

Even if it were ... that is, even if I did feel some momentary ... something ... it would be of no consequence. I have no intention of venturing down that path. I have seen where it leads.

Do enlighten me. What ominous destination awaits at the end of this particular path?

I'm thinking of my mother, Iris wrote, her quill pressing harder into the paper. *She was brilliant once. A respected scholar with thoughts and opinions of her own. Now she can barely decide what to wear for dinner without consulting my father. She has become a mere shadow of herself, an echo of his thoughts. I do not want that for myself.*

The notebook's script appeared more slowly this time, as if it were choosing its words with particular care.

How fascinating that you believe there are only two possible outcomes: complete independence or total self-effacement. Has it occurred to you that your mother's situation might be unusual rather than inevitable?

Iris frowned at the page before writing, *You don't know my mother.*

True. But I have existed within these walls for quite some time. I have witnessed countless marriages—some that diminish, yes, but others that strengthen. Some where two become less than they were, and others where they become more.

Poetic, but hardly convincing, Iris wrote. *Better to rely on oneself than risk such a gamble.*

Is that what you're doing with your position at The Charmed Leaf? Relying solely on yourself?

Iris paused, her brow furrowing. *That's different.*

Is it? You are learning from Lady Rivenna, depending on her guidance. You consult with Saffron, Lissian, and Lucie. You accept help from Rosavyn. Yet I do not see you diminishing as a result of these connections.

Those are not the same as marriage.

Indeed. They lack certain ... anatomically improbable cardiac elements.

Iris felt heat rise to her cheeks. *You're being deliberately obtuse.*

And you are being deliberately blind. Your mother's experience is ONE story, not THE story. Lady Rivenna has maintained both marriage and formidable independence. The High Lady rules without surrendering her identity to anyone. Even the tea house itself exists in perpetual partnership with its proprietress without either losing their essential nature.

The tea house is hardly a person, Iris scribbled.

And yet I am more perceptive than most fae, humans or those of mixed lineage. Consider this: perhaps the problem was not marriage itself, but rather your mother's belief that she had to surrender her identity to be truly loved. A belief, I cannot help but notice, that you appear to have inherited.

Iris stared at the words, something uncomfortable settling in her chest. *You're suggesting that my mother chose to fade?*

I'm suggesting that stories are more complex than they first appear, and that people often mistake correlation for causation. Perhaps ask yourself why you are so eager to believe that connection must inevitably lead to loss of self. It is a rather convenient excuse for avoiding vulnerability, is it not?

That's unfair, Iris wrote, her handwriting growing messier with her indignation.

Fairness is not among my primary concerns. Accuracy, however, is. And accurately speaking, your fear of losing yourself may be precisely what prevents you from discovering who you might become.

Iris threw her quill down and closed the notebook with more force than necessary, unwilling to continue a conversation that had ventured into territory she was not prepared to explore. The notebook's observations had struck uncomfortably close to truths she wasn't ready to acknowledge—that perhaps what she feared was not losing herself in someone else, but rather the terrifying vulnerability of being truly seen.

She pushed the book away, but its final words lingered in her mind: *your fear of losing yourself may be precisely what prevents you from discovering who you might become.*

She reached past the open tome on tea leaf family history for the stack of fine paper that sat on the corner of her desk, determined to focus on something other than the notebook's uncomfortable dissection of her carefully constructed defenses. Relaxing her mind, she set her magic loose as her fingers touched the edge of a crisp cream sheet. Instantly, she felt the familiar tug of potential. All the ways this single sheet might fold, all the shapes it might become. She lay the sheet flat on her palm and let her magic flow, guiding rather than forcing the paper as it began to crease itself along invisible lines.

She'd been adding to her collection of pieces in preparation for her display at the Summer Solstice Grand Ball, gradually working toward more and more complex creations. On the shelves on one side of the study, along with leather-bound volumes and delicate trailing ivy, sat a variety of paper creatures: swans, foxes, pegasi, a stag, a grasshopper and even a particularly complicated dragon.

The paper on her palm folded and refolded, creases appearing and disappearing as Iris considered different possibilities. She had decided on a miniature garden scene. An entire landscape rendered in paper that would transform and shift at her command. Paper trees would grow taller, flowers would bloom and fade, tiny creatures would move among the foliage. It would be a stunning display of control and precision, hiding the true depth of her abilities behind something beautiful but ultimately harmless.

As her fingers twitched, instinctively guiding the paper into intricate folds without touching it, her mind drifted back to the masquerade. To Jasvian's hand at her waist, his surprisingly graceful movements, his confession that social gatherings caused him anxiety. She had glimpsed something beneath his carefully maintained facade. A vulnerability, a depth of feeling he rarely allowed others to see.

And she had run away before midnight. Before the enchantment could fade.

Why? If she were truly honest with herself—something she had been avoiding with remarkable determination—she knew that it was fear that had driven her hasty retreat. Fear of Jasvian's reaction. Fear of seeing the open warmth in his gaze cool to dismay or disappointment or perhaps even regret upon realizing that the enchanting woman he had shared parts of himself with had merely been Iris, the half-fae he had once deemed unworthy.

Though none of that should matter if she didn't care to pursue anything more than their careful truce of ink-stained exchanges and cautious civility. And she did not, she reminded herself firmly. She did not wish to pursue anything involving romantic attraction or concerning cardiac acrobatics with anyone, least of all Lord Jasvian Rowanwood.

... a rather convenient excuse for avoiding vulnerability ...

The half-formed paper creation hovering above her palm suddenly crumped in on itself as her concentration faltered. With a sigh, she smoothed it out, her magic clearing the creases and wrinkles, and began again, focusing more intently on the sensation of fold lines she could somehow 'feel' in her mind without feeling beneath her fingers.

"That was quite the dramatic exit," a voice observed from the doorway.

Iris looked up, realizing she'd been too distracted to hear the door open, and found Lady Rivenna watching her with sharp eyes, one silver eyebrow arched in silent inquiry.

"Lord Jasvian?" Iris asked, trying to sound casual. "Yes, he mentioned urgent business at Rowanwood House."

"Did he indeed?" Lady Rivenna entered the study, ushering in four garden pixies who barely reached the height of her knee. Three of them struggled beneath the weight of an enormous bunch of flowers, while the fourth carried a pitcher of water that appeared comically large in its tiny hands.

"Curious, as I've just come from there myself," Lady Rivenna continued, directing the pixies toward the flower vases positioned around the study. "The house is practically deserted this morning, everyone sleeping off the excesses of last night's celebration." She paused beside Iris's desk, glancing down at the half-formed paper creation. "Your focus appears somewhat lacking today."

Iris flushed. "I didn't sleep well."

"No?" Lady Rivenna's tone was perfectly neutral, but something in her expression made Iris suspect she knew far more than she was letting on. "The masquerade was quite spectacular. The sort of event that might leave one's thoughts rather ... occupied the following day."

Around the room, the pixies had begun emptying the old flower arrangements from the vases, dropping wilted petals and half-dried leaves onto the floor.

"Not there!" Lady Rivenna called out, making one pixie freeze mid-motion. "Must I supervise every detail?"

The pixie ducked its head apologetically and used its magic to gather the scattered foliage into a tidy pile.

"I wouldn't know," Iris said carefully, addressing Lady Rivenna's comment. "My grandmother's illness prevented my attendance, as you know."

"Ah, yes. Poor Lady Starspun and her illness." Lady Rivenna leaned across Iris's desk to adjust the angle of the vase a pixie had just filled with fresh water. "How fortunate that Rosavyn happened to know someone who was precisely your size and unable to attend due to fever."

Iris froze. "I ... that is ..."

"Do save your protestations for someone who might believe them," Lady Rivenna said with a dismissive wave. She crossed the room to the vase that had just been returned to her grandson's desk, plucked a broken stem from a pixie's arrangement, and tossed it onto the pile of discarded foliage. "I've been orchestrating social machinations in this town since before your parents were born. Did you truly think I wouldn't keep a watchful eye on that table of enchanted masks and pay attention to the way guests were transformed? In addition, the threads of connection that bind people to one another remain visible to my sight. Such connections are not hidden by any simple enchantment."

Iris's face burned. She turned in her chair to face Lady Rivenna. "Are you ... upset?"

Lady Rivenna considered this for a moment as she leaned against Jasvian's desk and folded her arms over her chest. "I should be, I suppose. Attending an event against your family's wishes, without a chaperone, risking scandal should you be discovered ..." She studied Iris with those shrewd eyes. "And yet, I find myself more impressed than angry. It showed initiative. Resourcefulness."

One of the pixies used its magic to sweep the pile of discarded foliage into a small cloth bag while the one carrying the now empty pitcher almost tripped over Iris's shoes as it tried to pass her. She quickly pulled her feet out of the way. "Then you're not going to tell my grandmother?" she asked hopefully.

"What possible benefit would that serve?"

Iris let out a relieved breath. "Thank you."

"Was it worth it?" Lady Rivenna asked, her head tilted slightly to one side. "The deception, the risk of discovery?"

Iris hesitated only briefly before answering. "Yes. It was."

"Hmm." Lady Rivenna nodded at the pixie that pointed questioningly to the one remaining vase on the small table beside the corner armchair. "And who, might I ask, made the evening so memorable for you?"

"I don't know." The lie tasted bitter. "Isn't anonymity the purpose of a masquerade?"

Lady Rivenna's lips curved into an enigmatic smile. "Indeed." Just that single word, but something in her tone made Iris wonder if the connections Lady Rivenna saw had revealed precisely who Iris had been dancing with.

"Now," Lady Rivenna said, moving to the window and gazing out at Bloomhaven's morning bustle. "The Summer Solstice Grand Ball approaches. Your display must be ready. It will be your final opportunity to demonstrate your abilities and establish your worth. In the eyes of society, at least," she added with a glance over her shoulder at Iris. "You and I both know your value extends far beyond both magic and bloodline. But we must not forget your family's expectations. Your apprenticeship here was permitted with the understanding that your social responsibilities would not be neglected. That includes presenting yourself to the best of your ability at the Summer Solstice Grand Ball."

"I've been working on something," Iris said, grateful for the shift in conversation. She gestured across the room to the various paper creations on the shelf. "A garden scene, with complex elements that transform. I thought perhaps—"

"If I might make a suggestion," Lady Rivenna interrupted. "Surely you don't consider such a display worthy of the occasion?"

Iris blinked. "But we both decided my display should hide the true nature of my abilities. I certainly cannot demonstrate seeing multiple future possibilities unfolding."

"No, of course not, but perhaps you need not tread quite so seriously." Lady Rivenna turned away from the window as the pixies finished their work, quietly gathering their cleaning supplies. "Your debut presentation was charming but forgettable. The Solstice Ball requires something more ... memorable."

"What did you have in mind?"

Lady Rivenna placed a fresh sheet of paper in Iris's hands. "Something that demonstrates growth, certainly. Control and precision, yes.

But also something that hints at depths not immediately apparent." She paused, her eyes meeting Iris's with unmistakable intent. "Something that draws people in."

Iris looked down at the blank paper, feeling its potential beneath her fingertips. "I'm not entirely sure what you mean."

"Perhaps create something more engaging than mere transformations. Consider what paper represents. It holds stories, captures memories, preserves knowledge."

Iris frowned. "You're suggesting I create something narrative? Something that tells a story?"

"Precisely." Lady Rivenna nodded in approval as the pixies lined up at the door. "Not merely a garden scene that transforms, but a tale that unfolds. A sequence of events with meaning and purpose." She smiled slightly. "Everyone loves a good story, Lady Iris. Far more engaging than watching paper creatures move about a garden, no matter how skillfully crafted."

The idea caught fire in Iris's imagination. She could create an entire theatrical scene in miniature—paper figures acting out a story, with one moment flowing seamlessly into the next. Not random transformations, but deliberate progressions, the paper itself knowing where the tale was leading.

"That's brilliant," she said excitedly. "It would be much more memorable than what I had planned."

"Excellent." Lady Rivenna's approval warmed Iris like sunlight. "Though I imagine this will require considerable practice on your part. I suggest you begin at once." She made her way to the door, pausing only to make one final adjustment to the largest flower arrangement before departing.

As the door closed behind her, Iris's fingers were already twitching with eager anticipation, her mind racing ahead, darting through possibilities. The blank paper before her responded instantly, creases forming and multiplying as her magic flowed freely. Not the garden scene she'd first planned, but something entirely new. A story. A ballroom in miniature, with two paper figures at its center, locked in a dance, entirely oblivious to the room shifting around them as—

Iris sat back with an exasperated sigh, pushing the half-formed creation away. Even when attempting to focus on something that should fully absorb her mind, she could not escape Jasvian. It seemed his presence had infiltrated not only her thoughts but her magic itself, bending her creations toward him like flowers turning to follow the sun.

It was absurd. And she had no notion of what to do about it.

Chapter Twenty-Eight

Later that day, Jasvian carefully navigated the familiar pathway through the back gardens and into The Charmed Leaf's kitchen, balancing a small wooden box in his hands. The tea house seemed remarkably still in the early evening light, most of the day's patrons and staff having already departed. As he stepped inside, he spotted his grandmother directing a drowsy hearth sprite to bank the coals for the night.

"Grandmother," he called as he approached the long worktable at the center of the kitchen. "This arrived at Rowanwood House this afternoon." He set the intricately carved box down. "The courier claimed it contained those specialized ingredients you've been waiting for. Highland frost petals, I believe? For certain specialty blends."

Lady Rivenna turned, her expression conveying obvious skepticism. "And you felt compelled to deliver this immediately? Rather than waiting for me to bring it here myself tomorrow morning?"

"Of course I brought it now. You've mentioned several times how essential these ingredients are. It seemed ... important." In truth, the small box could easily have waited, but the restlessness that had plagued Jasvian all day had finally driven him to seize upon the first reasonable excuse to visit the tea house—and perhaps catch a glimpse of Iris before she departed for the evening.

"How thoughtful," his grandmother remarked, her tone suggesting she found his explanation thoroughly unconvincing. She approached the table and ran her fingers over the box's delicate carvings. "Though I suspect even frost petals from the highest peaks would have survived another twelve hours."

Jasvian cleared his throat. "The tea house appears quite empty. Has everyone departed for the day?"

"The staff has, yes," Lady Rivenna said, watching him with those unnervingly perceptive eyes. "Lady Iris, however, remains in the study. She's been working on her presentation for the Summer Solstice Grand Ball for most of the day." Something like concern flickered across her features. "I may have pushed her a bit too hard today. The poor girl has barely taken a moment's break."

A frown creased Jasvian's brow. "Pushed her? What exactly did you do, Grandmother?"

"Mind your tone, Jasvian," she said. "And your business, for that matter. My methods with my apprentice are hardly your concern."

"They are if you're driving her to exhaustion," he replied, the protective edge in his voice surprising even himself. He moderated his tone with effort. "I simply meant that she's been working quite diligently these past weeks. Perhaps a different approach—"

"My, my," his grandmother interrupted, her lips curving into a knowing smile. "Such concern for Lady Iris's wellbeing. How unexpected."

Heat crept up Jasvian's neck. "I would express similar concern for any of your staff."

"Of course you would." She drummed her fingers on the ornate box, then nodded to the kitchen pixies that had climbed onto the end of the worktable and were hovering with questioning gazes. "Yes, thank you, you know what to do with it."

Then she swept past her grandson to the back kitchen door. She lifted her elegant cloak from its peg and pulled it around her shoulders. "Now, shall we be on our way? My carriage will be here any minute."

"You're leaving Lady Iris here alone?" Jasvian asked before he could stop himself.

"She's perfectly capable of managing on her own," Lady Rivenna replied with a dismissive wave. Then, after a brief pause, her brows pulled together slightly. "Hopefully."

Jasvian straightened. "I can wait for her. My carriage is outside. I can escort Lady Iris home when she's finished. It wouldn't be proper for her to walk unescorted at this hour."

His grandmother's eyebrows rose incrementally higher. "The two of you alone in my tea house? That hardly adheres to the standards of propriety you so typically champion."

"We'll hardly be alone," Jasvian countered. "The tea house is positively teeming with watchful eyes. Besides, I'll remain down here. I brought something to read." He withdrew a slim volume from his coat pocket, the leather binding soft with age. His grandmother leaned forward, squinting slightly to read the faded gold lettering.

"Poetry?" Disbelief colored her voice. "You?"

Jasvian slipped the book back into his pocket, discomfited by her reaction. "I thought I might expand my literary horizons."

"Did you indeed?" Lady Rivenna sounded as though she were suppressing a laugh. "How very unlike you."

"People change, Grandmother," he replied stiffly.

"Some more believably than others." She fastened her cloak. "Well, if you insist on playing guardian, I won't stand in your way. Simply ensure that all doors are locked when you leave. Lady Iris has her key, and she knows what to do." She moved toward the door, pausing with her hand on the latch as she looked back at him. "And do remember, dear boy, that the tea house sees everything. I do not wish to hear whispers of impropriety greeting me upon my return tomorrow morning."

Jasvian winced at the thought of the tea house reporting his actions to his *grandmother* of all people. But there would be no actions to report, he reminded himself firmly. Besides, the tea house was a *building*, not a sentient being capable of 'reporting' anything, he added almost as an afterthought. "Your concern is entirely misplaced," he said, his voice cool. "I intend only to ensure Lady Iris's safe return home."

"Of course," Lady Rivenna agreed, her tone making it abundantly clear she didn't believe him for a moment. Then she slipped out into the evening, leaving him alone in the dimly lit kitchen.

He stood motionless for a moment, listening to the quiet sounds of the tea house at rest. The occasional ping as cooling pots contracted, the soft murmuring of sleepy hearth sprites, the almost imperceptible creaking of floorboards as the building settled. From upstairs came the faint sound of movement. A chair scraping, perhaps.

He crossed the kitchen and entered the main floor of the tea house, aiming for a window along the front wall where a wide cushioned seat offered a view of one of Bloomhaven's cobbled streets, now bathed in the warm glow of faelights. He settled himself, arranging his long limbs as comfortably as possible, and withdrew the book from his pocket once more.

The cover was bare, and the delicate gold script on the spine was so faded that he couldn't make out the full title aside from the words 'Poems' and 'Heart.' He'd found it in his mother's section of the library at Rowanwood House that afternoon, after hours of distraction had rendered productive work impossible. The conversation with his masquerade dance partner about poetry had lingered in his mind—her passion for how emotion could be contained in so few, carefully crafted words. Now that he knew that partner had been Iris all along, her enthusiasm held even greater weight.

He opened the book carefully, the spine crackling slightly with age, and began to read. The poem on the first page began: "*Thy gaze, like dew-kissed petals at dawn's first blush, envelopes my trembling soul in silken whispers of unspoken desire.*"

Jasvian stared at the words, his brow furrowing. He struggled to decipher what the verse was actually attempting to convey. How could anyone find this appealing? If someone had actually whispered something like that to him at a social gathering, he'd have excused himself immediately to check the wine for hallucinogenic properties.

He scanned further down the page until his eyes landed on: "*My heart, a caged nightingale, beats against its gilded prison, yearning for the sweet nectar of thy tender affection.*"

He pinched the bridge of his nose. A caged nightingale? Did the author have any idea how birds behaved when caged? They certainly didn't pine romantically. Most of them thrashed about in panicked desperation. This was precisely why he preferred ledgers and accounts; they never pretended a bird was anything other than a bird.

But then his eyes fell on the verse at the bottom of the page: "*Thy presence fills all spaces, contracts all distances; when near thee, the very world recedes until only thy light remains.*"

He looked up thoughtfully, the words resonating in a way he hadn't expected. Now *that*, at least, he could understand. The strange sensation of being so acutely aware of someone's presence that they seemed to occupy far more space than physically possible. The way a single person could somehow fill a room entirely, drawing attention like a lodestone no matter how one tried to focus elsewhere.

He'd felt precisely that with Iris in recent weeks. Her presence in the study, the tea house, even in his thoughts, had gradually expanded until it seemed she was everywhere, inescapable. The awareness of her had grown until it rivaled even his constant concern about the mines.

As the evening deepened outside, the tea house grew increasingly still around him. The hearth sprites had all drifted into the kitchen to nestle near the banked coals, though two of them, he'd noted with some comfort, had scurried upstairs, hopefully to keep Iris company. The kitchen pixies were nowhere to be seen, and the vines had ceased their restless movement, their leaves hanging motionless in the quiet air.

Jasvian turned another page, but the words blurred before his eyes. The events of the previous night—the masquerade, the dancing, the conversation that had flowed so easily between them—combined with the morning's revelation about Iris's identity had left him mentally exhausted. The comfortable cushions beneath him and the hushed atmosphere of the tea house seemed to wrap around him like a blanket.

His eyelids grew heavy, the book drooping in his hands. He should move, he thought distantly. He should at least call upstairs to inform Lady Iris of his presence. But the poem before him pulled at his attention once more, something about stars and destiny, about two souls orbiting each other, unaware of their inevitable collision.

The tea house sighed around him, a sound almost like contentment, as Jasvian's eyes finally closed, the book of poetry slipping from his fingers to rest in his lap.

~

In the study upstairs, Iris's frustration had reached its peak. She paced between her desk and the window, barefoot and disheveled, her dark hair escaping its pins to fall in wayward strands around her face. Papers covered every surface—her desk, Lord Jasvian's usually pristine workspace, the armchair, even the floor—each one a half-formed creation caught between what it was and what it might become.

"This should work," she muttered, flexing her fingers before attempting once more to coordinate the movements of dozens of paper figures simultaneously. "I can do this. I know I can do this."

The sun had long since set, its warm glow replaced by the cooler silver of moonlight. Iris had sent a messenger pixie to her grandparents earlier that afternoon, explaining she was working late and would stay the night if she finished after dark. It was apparent now that she would indeed be spending the night.

Despite exhaustion pressing against her temples, she refused to abandon her task. The Summer Solstice Grand Ball was her final opportunity to prove herself, not just to Bloomhaven society but to Lady Rivenna, who had invested so much in her development. She couldn't fail now.

Drawing a deep breath, she gathered her magic once more, focusing on the scene she wanted to create. A grand ballroom in miniature filled with paper figures, their movements telling a tale of two strangers meeting beneath enchanted stars, unaware that fate had determined their paths would cross long before they ever set eyes upon one another.

Yes, her tale was indeed influenced by her own experience at the masquerade and by her growing fascination with a certain brooding lord, but she had finally surrendered to the truth of it. There seemed little point in denying what her magic clearly wished to express. If Lord Jasvian Rowanwood had claimed a permanent residence in her thoughts, perhaps allowing him this space alongside her creations might actually quiet the constant awareness of him that plagued her mind.

Her magic responded, dozens of paper creations rising from various surfaces around the study to hover in the air before her. The ballroom took shape, elaborate paper chandeliers unfurling from flat sheets, tiny dancers transforming from simple folded forms into more intricate forms. In the center, two figures moved toward each other, refolding themselves with each step to create the illusion of movement.

"Yes," Iris whispered, her concentration absolute as she guided the figures through their dance. The scene needed to shift from the glittering ballroom to a garden setting beneath paper stars, then transform again to show the dancers parting at midnight.

She pushed her magic further, attempting to hold all elements of the scene in perfect balance while initiating the first transformation. The paper ballroom began to unfold and refold, walls becoming garden hedges, chandeliers transforming into stars, the surrounding dancers shifting into elegant topiary shapes.

But as she directed the central figures to continue their dance amidst this changing landscape, she felt something ... slip. A tremor run through her magic. One of the paper trees faltered in its transformation, tearing slightly as it attempted to hold two shapes at once.

"No, no," Iris whispered, reaching out with her magic to stabilize it. But in focusing on the tree, she lost her grip on the dancers. Their forms began to blur, folding and unfolding rapidly as if unable to decide which shape to take.

Panic flickered through her. She tried to calm herself, to regain control, but exhaustion had weakened her discipline. With growing horror, she felt her magic slipping further, the careful structure of her story crumbling as the paper creations began to vibrate with unconstrained energy. "No," she whispered desperately. "Not again—"

But it was too late. With a sound like a hundred wings beating frantically against glass, every sheet of paper in the room—her creations, the papers on her desk, pages from open books on the shelves—tore free and launched into the air. They whipped around her in a violent cyclone, folding and unfolding with impossible speed, their edges sharp as razors.

Iris cried out as the first cuts stung her exposed skin. She raised her arms to shield her face, but the paper found every inch of exposed flesh—her cheeks, her neck, her hands, her arms.

"Stop!" she shouted. "STOP!"

But the papers only spun faster, catching in her hair, slicing at her gown, cutting her again and again until tears of pain and frustration streamed down her face. She dropped to her knees, hunching over to make herself a smaller target, her magic spiraling completely out of control.

Then suddenly, abruptly, everything stopped.

The papers froze mid-air, then fluttered harmlessly to the floor. The sudden silence was deafening.

Iris remained crouched on the floor, sobbing, her arms still raised defensively. Only when she heard footsteps hurriedly crossing the room did she dare to lower her arms slightly, peering through her fingers to see Jasvian crouching down before her. His hair was disheveled, his cravat askew, as if he'd been startled from sleep. His eyes, though, were intensely alert, fixed on her with an expression of genuine alarm.

"Lady Iris," he said, his voice tight with concern. "Are you hurt?"

"I ... how did you ..."

"I fell asleep downstairs," he admitted. "And then your magic—the sudden eruption of—it woke me."

"I ..." Words failed Iris as she took in the destruction around them. Papers lay strewn across every surface, some torn to shreds, others bent and creased. Pages had been ripped from the bindings of every book in the room. Fresh tears welled in her eyes. "I've ruined everything," she whispered. "Your books, your grandmother's books ... I—I'll pay for the damage. I don't know how, as my family is already dreadfully in debt, but—" She broke off, horrified at what she'd revealed. "Oh no, I—" She buried her face in her hands once more. "I was not supposed to say," she mumbled, her words muffled behind her fingers. "No one is supposed to know."

"Lady Iris, please. It does not matter to me. I care only for—"

"But you cannot tell—"

"I will say nothing of your family's situation," he assured her, his voice softening. "It is *you* I'm concerned for right now."

She stopped, something unexpected shivering through her at his words.

"You're hurt," he said, a waver of anxiety still evident in his voice. "Please, let me see your face."

Slowly, reluctantly, she lowered her hands. His expression tightened as he took in her appearance. Judging by the stinging sensation across her face and the way his eyes widened in concern, Iris imagined her cheeks and neck bore the same pattern of tiny cuts that crisscrossed her arms and hands.

"I need to get a healing salve," he said, starting to rise. "My grandmother keeps supplies in the kitchen—"

"No!" Iris's hand shot out to grasp his arm, her fingers clutching the fine material of his coat sleeve. She couldn't bring herself to say the words aloud, but the thought of being left alone in this room, surrounded by paper that might once again turn against her, filled her with terror.

Understanding dawned in his eyes. He glanced toward the hearth, where several sprites huddled together in the shadows, their tiny flames dimmed with fear. Iris remembered seeing them snuggle into the corner earlier to settle down for a night's sleep.

"You," Jasvian addressed them, his tone gentle but firm. "Would you be so kind as to fetch the healing salve from Lady Rivenna's cabinet in the kitchen? The blue jar on the second shelf."

The sprites bobbed in agreement, clearly relieved to have a reason to leave the room. They shot toward the door and disappeared.

"What happened?" Jasvian asked when they were alone, his gaze returning to Iris's face with undisguised concern.

She swallowed, struggling to compose herself. "This ... this is how it was the first time. When my magic manifested. It happened in a bookstore. A sanctuary I once cherished above all other places. There was ..." Her voice trembled. "So much destruction. Just like this." She looked around the room, sniffing faintly. "I thought I had learned enough control, but it seems I may have pushed myself beyond my limits this evening."

"Indeed, it seems so," he observed, his gaze moving around the room, taking in the sheer number of paper creations she'd been attempting to manipulate simultaneously.

The hearth sprites returned then, carrying the small blue jar between them. Jasvian took it from them with murmured thanks, uncapping it to reveal a pale cream that shimmered. "This will help," he said, dipping one finger into the salve. "It works with the healer's magic to accelerate natural healing. I'm not particularly skilled in healing arts, but my knowledge is enough to address superficial wounds." He hesitated before touching her. "May I?"

Iris nodded. Jasvian carefully took her right arm, turning it gently to assess the damage. His fingers were warm as he cradled her forearm in one hand, using the other to apply the salve to each individual cut.

"Why were you asleep downstairs?" she asked quietly, not wanting to startle him as he worked.

He paused for a moment before continuing. "My grandmother was preparing to return home and mentioned that you were still here, working on your display for the Solstice Ball. I offered to stay so that you would not be left here on your own. I didn't mean to fall asleep."

Iris shook her head as she swallowed. "It's fine," she said, her voice somewhat hoarse. "I mean ... thank you. For staying."

"Of course." His thumb brushed over a slightly deeper cut at her wrist, and she felt a tingling warmth as his magic flowed through the contact. The skin knitted together before her eyes, leaving only the faintest pink line. He continued working in silence for several minutes, carefully addressing each cut on her arms. His touch was gentle, almost reverent, his focus absolute as he tended to her wounds.

When he finished with her arms, he hesitated, then moved his attention to the cuts on her neck. She turned her head to the side, trying to keep her breathing steady as his fingers ghosted over the sensitive skin there.

When his attention moved to her face, he cleared his throat and said, "I owe you an apology." He kept his gaze fixed on his work, deliberately avoiding her eyes as he continued applying the salve to the cuts along her jawline and cheek. "What I said to you that first night at the Opening Ball was ... unconscionable. The things I said about your bloodline, your magic. I was wrong. So terribly wrong." His fingers moved to a cut near her temple. "If I could take back every word, every moment of hurt I caused you, I would do so without hesitation."

Iris held perfectly still, afraid that any movement or word uttered might break the spell of this unexpected moment between them. With his gaze focused on his task, she took the opportunity to study his face openly for the first time—the strong line of his jaw now softened with concern, his storm-gray eyes holding a calm stillness, the usual stern set of his mouth replaced by an expression of gentle concentration. This was not the same Lord Jasvian Rowanwood she had met at the start of the Bloom Season.

"I must apologize too," she whispered. "The things I said to you the night we met—I spoke from anger and hurt, not truth. I judged you without knowing a single thing about the man beneath the title." She swallowed, feeling the gentle pressure of his fingers as they moved to another cut. "I was every bit as prejudiced as I accused you of being."

"Perhaps we both needed time to see beyond our first impressions," he said softly. "Though in my case, I fear my prejudice was far less excusable." He paused then, the pad of his thumb resting against the curve of her cheek, as his eyes traveled her face.

"There," he murmured, drawing back slightly. "That should prevent any scarring." Yet his hand remained at her cheek, his thumb making one final, unnecessary pass over now-healed skin. He lowered his hand slowly, turning his attention back to her arms, ostensibly to check his work, but his fingers continued to trace delicate patterns over her skin, following the paths where cuts had been only moments before. The salve had done its work; there was no reason for him to continue this careful exploration of her wrists, the soft underside of her forearm, the sensitive skin at the bend of her elbow.

Yet neither of them moved to break contact. His touch was featherlight, almost worshipful in its gentleness. Each slow stroke of his thumb over her skin sent shivers cascading through Iris's body, awakening sensations she had never experienced before. The air between them seemed to thicken, charged with something powerful and unspoken. Her breathing grew shallow, her pulse quickening beneath his touch.

At the quiet intake of breath that she could no longer contain, his eyes rose to meet hers, sending a tremor of awareness rushing through her body. And for one breathless moment, the rest of the world ceased to exist. There was only this—his hands on her skin, his eyes holding hers, the silent acknowledgment of something neither of them dared to name.

Then the door to the study flew open with a bang.

"Iris!" Lady Rivenna stood in the doorway, her silver hair loose around her shoulders, a cloak hastily thrown over her nightdress. Her sharp gaze took in the scene before her—Iris and Jasvian kneeling amid scattered papers, his hands still cradling her arms—before moving to assess the destruction around the room. "What happened? The tea house woke me. I felt its distress from across Bloomhaven."

The charged atmosphere dissipated instantly. Jasvian released Iris's arms and rose to his feet in one fluid motion, stepping back to put a respectable distance between them while also extending a hand toward her. "There was an incident," he explained, his voice returning to its usual formal cadence. "Lady Iris's magic became temporarily unstable. I was downstairs and sensed her loss of control. I was able to assist."

Assist. That was certainly one way to put it.

She reached for Jasvian's offered hand, letting him pull her to her feet. The moment she was steady, he released her and stepped back, widening the space between them once more. The sudden absence of his touch left her feeling unmoored, standing there awkwardly, all too aware of her disheveled state and the lingering tension that still hummed between them.

"I see." Lady Rivenna's gaze moved between the two of them before landing on the small jar of salve still sitting on the floor. "You were hurt?" she asked, concern coloring her tone again.

"Not badly," Iris hastened to assure her. "And I apologize for the damage, Lady Rivenna. I was attempting to create something elaborate that appears to have been a little beyond my control. I will do everything I can to restore—"

Lady Rivenna waved away her apologies. "The tea house has withstood far worse in its time." She stepped fully into the room, her keen eyes assessing Iris's condition. "You appear physically recovered, at least."

"Yes, I—" Iris glanced at Jasvian, who was now staring fixedly at a point somewhere over his grandmother's left shoulder. "Lord Jasvian's assistance was invaluable."

"I'm sure it was," Lady Rivenna murmured, her tone laden with meaning. "Well, since I am here and clearly neither of you is in imminent danger, perhaps it's time we all retired for what remains of the night." She turned to Jasvian. "You should return to Rowanwood House."

"Of course," he agreed stiffly. "I shall take my leave."

Iris's heart sank at the formal distance that had returned to his voice. Just moments ago, his hands had moved over her skin with such tender care that she'd nearly forgotten to breathe. Now he was once again the proper Lord Jasvian Rowanwood, standing tall and composed as if nothing extraordinary had passed between them.

"Lady Iris can remain here tonight as planned," Lady Rivenna said. "I shall stay as well. My quarters upstairs can be rearranged for two with a few simple magical adjustments."

Iris blinked. "There are ... quarters upstairs?" she asked haltingly. And then: "There is *another level* above this one?"

Lady Rivenna gave her a look of incredulous bemusement. "Of course. Where were you planning to sleep tonight?"

"I—" Iris broke off, looking around the study. "The armchair?"

"Good gracious, my dear. Perhaps it's fortunate the room erupted in chaos. At least now you've been saved from the terrible fate of attempting to sleep in that armchair. And how is it possible you've been here for weeks without noticing there's another floor to this building?"

"Well ... the staircase does not continue," Iris pointed out. "And from the outside of the tea house, it appears that there are only—"

"In the case of The Charmed Leaf," Rivenna said, "appearances are rarely what they seem. You, of all people, should understand that what's visible on the outside rarely reflects the true nature of what lies within."

Iris merely blinked at that, her gaze moving uncertainly between Rivenna and Jasvian.

"Grandmother, do you require any assistance with the arrangements upstairs?" Jasvian inquired politely, still refusing to meet Iris's gaze.

"Do I look incapable of managing a few simple spells?" Rivenna huffed. "I've been rearranging furniture with magic since before you were born, Jasvian."

Jasvian sighed before inclining his head. "Then I bid you both good night."

As he turned to leave, his gaze finally met Iris's, and for the briefest moment, she glimpsed that same vulnerability, that same longing, before his expression smoothed once more into careful neutrality.

"Good night, Lord Jasvian," she said softly.

Lady Rivenna watched her grandson go, an inscrutable expression on her face. Then she turned to Iris. "Come, my dear. We shall see to this mess in the morning."

Chapter Twenty-Nine

In the days following the incident in the study, Iris saw so little of Jasvian that she began to wonder if he was deliberately avoiding her. Lady Rivenna kept her constantly occupied, shadowing Mrs Spindlewood one day, observing Lissian at her tea brewing station the next, and in every spare moment, working to perfect her paper-folding display for the Solstice Ball. She approached these new attempts with careful restraint, mindful of her limitations after that night's spectacular and painful failure. When she did find time to work in the study upstairs, Jasvian was either absent or already on his way out, and even the written correspondence that had become their daily ritual had inexplicably ceased.

She wanted to ask him if he regretted that moment between them—his fingers tracing gentle patterns on her skin, his eyes holding hers with such undisguised longing that it had stolen her breath. But each time she contemplated penning such an inquiry, her courage failed her. For someone who prided herself on directness, who had boldly confronted him that very first night at the Opening Ball, this newfound hesitancy was both foreign and frustrating.

The truth was, she feared his answer. Feared that he might confirm what she increasingly suspected: that upon reflection, Lord Jasvian

Rowanwood had decided a half-human apprentice with unpredictable magic was simply not worth the complications.

Although ... she'd had a most curious conversation with Lucie not long after the incident in the study, during which Lucie had recounted, with evident bewilderment, how Jasvian had actually *apologized* to her for his long-held prejudices about humans in fae society. Perhaps, then, Jasvian's distance had nothing to do with Iris's heritage at all. Perhaps it was simply that he wasn't interested in *her*.

So when Rosavyn and Charlotte mentioned the Stardust Night Market's imminent arrival in Bloomhaven, Iris found herself eager for an evening filled with new sights and experiences, far from the tea house and its memories. Her grandparents had agreed to the outing—her grandmother seeming particularly keen now that she had fully recovered from the illness that had kept her from attending the masquerade and several other engagements. Iris suspected this enthusiasm had less to do with her grandmother's desire to socialize and more to do with potential encounters with families who had eligible sons.

Whatever her grandmother's true motives, Iris felt a thrill of genuine excitement as she approached Elderbloom Park with her grandparents in the gathering dusk. The Stardust Night Market, which arrived in Bloomhaven once a year, had transformed the far side of the park into a wonderland of magical light and impossible wares. On the wide stone bridge that spanned the Silverflow River, floating lanterns in jewel-toned shades drifted through the evening air, following browsing patrons like curious spirits. The market began on the bridge itself and extended into the eastern corner of the park, where ancient trees were festooned with twinkling faelights.

Stepping onto the bridge amidst this enchanting display, Iris gathered the folds of her fine silk shawl closer as the evening air grew cool. Her grandmother tucked Iris's arm securely through her own, ready to navigate the scene. With the Summer Solstice Grand Ball approaching, Iris could sense her grandparents' anxiety mounting. Despite all their careful maneuvering—and Iris's polite engagement with any gentleman showing interest at the Season's events—not a single fae lord had yet declared himself in earnest or sought to court her with serious intent.

Even Lord Hadrian, after coming to call one afternoon, had since made himself quite scarce, despite appearing to have greatly enjoyed her company.

Iris was secretly relieved, still clinging to the hope that she might yet secure her family's future through her connection to The Charmed Leaf Tea House rather than through marriage. If only the Starspuns could endure a few more years—long enough for her to establish herself there. Long enough for Lady Rivenna to determine the time had come to relinquish control and ownership of the tea house entirely into Iris's hands.

Though, at the rate Lady Rivenna was going, Iris herself might be wizened and silver-tressed before that happened. The woman possessed an energy that defied reason, as if she had bargained for endless vitality itself and was utterly undeterred by the passage of time.

Which meant, Iris thought as she spotted Charlotte and Rosavyn waving to her, that she would have to face the truth she had been resisting all Bloom Season: she might, in the end, have no choice but to marry.

And, to her dismay, the notion was not *entirely* unappealing when she allowed herself to consider a certain sharp-edged-yet-softening fae lord. Jasvian's touch had awakened something she had been determined to deny—a longing not just for connection, but for this specific connection. It terrified her how easily she could imagine surrendering her hard-won independence for moments like the one they had shared in the study. Was this how it began for her mother? Small surrenders that eventually amounted to a complete loss of self?

Your mother's experience is ONE story, the notebook had said, *not THE story*.

But these thoughts were pointless, Iris reminded herself, when the man clearly possessed no interest in—

"Iris!" Rosavyn called as she and Charlotte hurried over. "Lord and Lady Starspun, how delightful to see you this evening." Both she and Charlotte offered perfect curtsies to Iris's grandparents. "We were just admiring the Calverwick Candies stall," she added. "They make the most extraordinary color-shifting spun sugar that supposedly tastes like your fondest memory. Might we steal Iris away to show her?"

Iris turned to her grandmother with hopeful eyes. "Would you mind terribly if I joined them for a while?"

Her grandmother's lips pressed into a thin line of disapproval. Then she sighed, her gaze moving from Rosavyn to Charlotte before returning to Iris. "Very well," she relented with evident reluctance. "You may go, but I expect you to behave with absolute propriety. I do not wish to hear tales of any nonsense."

"Nonsense?" Iris protested, unable to keep a note of indignation from her voice. "Have I not been perfectly behaved these past weeks?"

"Indeed you have," her grandmother acknowledged with the barest hint of a smile. "Which is precisely why I am allowing this liberty. Now, off you go and enjoy yourselves. Be sure to meet us back here on the bridge at the closing chimes."

Iris's expression softened. "Thank you, Grandmother." She offered her grandparents a respectful nod before turning to her friends, unable to entirely suppress the eagerness in her step as they turned toward the heart of the market, her grandparents proceeding in a different direction.

"Isn't it magnificent?" Rosavyn exclaimed, looping her arm through Iris's. "Look at those orbs over there. When held in your palm, they reveal glimpses of the stars as seen from the most distant corners of the United Fae Isles."

"And those enchanted gloves," Charlotte added, nodding toward a stall where gloves fashioned from materials as diverse as pressed flower petals and shimmering spider silk were elegantly displayed. "They're said to each bestow a unique enchantment upon the wearer's touch."

Iris drew a deep breath as her eyes swept across the diverse array of stalls. The sweet, spiced aroma of ember-roasted chestnuts mingled with the sharper scent of frozen moonlight being ground into fine powder at a nearby stall. Everywhere she looked, something new and astonishing caught her eye.

"I've heard," Charlotte remarked in a whisper, "that if you know where to look, you'll find certain vendors selling items of a more ... questionable nature."

"Yes, I believe so," Rosavyn confirmed with a conspiratorial grin.

"Items that are strictly regulated or outright banned within proper fae society. I doubt your grandparents would have granted their permission quite so readily if they'd been aware of—"

"Lady Iris," a voice called out.

Iris froze, her heart thundering and her hands growing instantly sweaty within her gloves at the sound of the familiar voice. Taking a breath, she turned to find Jasvian standing a few paces away, his tall frame unmistakable even in the shifting light of the market. Her heart performed a few more 'concerning cardiac acrobatics,' as her notebook had so aptly described the phenomenon.

"Jasvian," Rosavyn exclaimed, breaking the awkward silence. "I never thought you'd deign to attend something so whimsical as the Night Market."

"I've attended in previous years," he replied stiffly. "Though not recently."

"Well, do try not to frighten the vendors with your brooding," Rosavyn teased. "The poor things might think you're evaluating their stalls for tax assessment rather than enjoyment."

Charlotte suppressed a laugh behind her hand, but Jasvian barely seemed to notice his sister's jibe. His severe expression softened as he addressed Iris directly. "Good evening, Lady Iris. This is your first time at the Stardust Night Market, I presume?"

"Yes, it is," she replied, suddenly acutely aware of her every movement, her every word. "It's quite remarkable."

"Indeed." He hesitated, shifting his weight slightly. "I was hoping, perhaps, that you might ... that is, I wondered if you would care to view the market with me?"

Though Iris kept her gaze fixed on Lord Jasvian, she could feel Rosavyn and Charlotte's stunned silence radiating beside her.

"I haven't been in several years," Jasvian continued, his words coming more rapidly now. "And since this is your first time, I thought ... well, there are certain vendors and magical displays that are particularly worth seeing, and I—" He stopped abruptly, clearing his throat. "I would quite like to see them with you."

The simple admission sent warmth coursing through Iris's chest.

Rosavyn made a sound partway between a laugh and a cough, leaning closer to Iris and whispering, "I cannot imagine what—"

"That sounds lovely," Iris found herself saying, her voice steadier than she felt. She removed her arm from Rosavyn's, adding, "If the two of you don't mind?"

"I, uh—" Rosavyn coughed again. She stared at Iris with a questioning gaze, which Iris met with what she hoped was a reassuring smile. After a moment, seemingly convinced that Iris was not discreetly signaling for help, Rosavyn said, "Not at all," though her narrowed eyes suggested she would demand a thorough explanation later. "But you must be careful not to lose track of time," she added. "Your grandparents mentioned they would meet us on the bridge at the closing chimes."

Jasvian nodded. "I will ensure Lady Iris returns to the bridge well before then."

"See that you do," Rosavyn said, her tone somewhere between teasing and stern—a sister's prerogative, Iris supposed. With a final curious glance at Iris, Rosavyn and Charlotte headed in a different direction, not entirely out of earshot when they dissolved into giggles.

Left alone with Jasvian, Iris suddenly found herself struggling for words. The memory of his fingertips tracing patterns on her skin burned vividly in her mind, making it difficult to meet his gaze.

"Shall we?" he asked, gesturing toward the heart of the market.

Iris nodded, falling into step beside him as they moved deeper into the maze of enchanted stalls. For a while they walked in silence, both seemingly unsure how to bridge the distance that had grown between them over the past few days.

"I must apologize for my recent scarcity." Jasvian's voice took on that formal quality he seemed to adopt when uncomfortable, his gaze fixed on the path ahead rather than meeting her eyes. "I've been working with Lord Hadrian on a project of some significance. He had a rather sudden breakthrough in the design that required far more of my input than previously anticipated."

"Oh." The word escaped Iris on a soft exhale. Relief cascaded through her like summer rain, cooling the anxious heat that had built within her these past days. He hadn't been avoiding her after all. The worry that had taken root in her chest withered beneath this simple, practical explanation. And this would explain Lord Hadrian's absence as well. It seemed he had not inexplicably withdrawn his attentions. Rather, he had been occupied with what sounded like deeply absorbing work.

"And you, Lady Iris?" Jasvian's voice pulled her from her thoughts. "How have you ... that is ... have you been well?" The question emerged with careful formality, as if he were feeling his way across uncertain terrain.

"Yes, quite well," she replied, her response equally measured. "Lady Rivenna has kept me extraordinarily busy at the tea house. She has assigned me the task of hosting my own small event there, as a means of assessing my progress thus far—though not until after the Summer Solstice Ball, of course. My focus for now must remain on preparing my magical display for that night. Oh, and I've even had my first few lessons in tea leaf reading." She hesitated, aware that she was rambling somewhat, but uncertain how to recapture the ease that had characterized their interactions before that night in the study. "It's quite fascinating how the patterns reveal themselves. I was curious to know whether the readings might align with—"

She caught herself abruptly, realizing what she had nearly revealed. Jasvian didn't yet know the true nature of her magic. "That is," she amended hastily, "I've been curious about this ancient art your grandmother still practices with such dedication. The way she finds meaning in seemingly random arrangements of leaves is quite remarkable."

"Indeed," Jasvian said with a nod. He took a breath as if to add something else, then hesitated before closing his mouth.

They lapsed into silence once more, Iris aching for the easy rhythm of their written exchanges. How peculiar that they could share thoughts so freely through the distance of ink and paper, yet standing here beside one another, words seemed to evaporate before reaching her lips. Would it be utterly ridiculous, she wondered, to seek out a quill and paper and write him a note here in the midst of the market simply to bridge this carefully polite awkwardness that now stretched between them?

"I've been reading poetry," Jasvian said finally.

Iris glanced up at him in surprise. "Have you?" Though she'd suggested it while disguised at the masquerade, she had hardly expected him to take her advice to heart.

"Yes. Though I must confess, my appreciation for it remains limited." His lips quirked slightly, and Iris found herself longing once again to see a genuine smile on this man's lips. A smile that was *his*, not hidden by an enchantment. "The volume I found in my mother's library was filled with what I can only describe as flowery nonsense about caged nightingales and silken whispers."

A laugh escaped Iris before she could hold it back. "Perhaps you should try a different poet. Not all verse is quite so ... lavish."

"I had rather hoped you might recommend something more tolerable," he said, stopping and turning to face her, his tone weighted with meaning. "After all, it was at your suggestion that I endeavored to broaden my literary horizons in the first place."

Iris's breath quickened at what he had just revealed. She halted, turning to look up at him fully. In that moment, the surrounding bustle of the market seemed to soften and recede, leaving them in a hushed bubble of awareness. The stiff formality he wore like armor dissolved, and what remained was the raw, unguarded openness he'd shown her that night in the study. "You knew it was me," she said softly. "At the masquerade."

"Not at the time," he said. "Only the morning afterward, when I noticed the silver bangle on your wrist. The same one the mystery woman at the masquerade had worn."

"Oh, yes. It was the only part of my ensemble that remained unchanged by the mask's enchantment. Perhaps because it so perfectly matched the mask itself."

"Your lack of surprise suggests you recognized me as well," Jasvian observed with a wry twist to his lips. "What betrayed my identity?"

"It was something you said early in our conversation," Iris replied. "It echoed a phrase from our written correspondence and could have come from no one else."

"And yet, having discovered who I was, you chose to remain. You continued our dance rather than seeking another partner. You ..."

"Spent almost the entire evening with you," Iris finished.

He nodded. "Why?" he asked quietly.

Her heart fluttered faster against her ribcage. "Because I wanted to," she said simply, feeling her cheeks flush slightly.

Silence fell between them, heavy with unspoken meaning. Jasvian's mouth curved upward, not quite reaching a full smile but coming closer than Iris had ever seen outside of the masquerade. A strange new warmth began to bubble up inside her, but both of them turned away before acknowledging anything further, each seemingly reluctant to disrupt this delicate new understanding.

"Oh, look at these," Iris said, her eyes landing on the nearest stall and its display of delicate crystal animals. A stag pawed at the velvet beneath its hooves, while a fox curled its crystal tail around itself, its eyes gleaming with amber light.

"Try this one," the vendor encouraged, placing a tiny owl in Iris's palm. She frowned when nothing about the crystalline figure changed. "Ah, you'll need to remove your glove, my lady," the vendor explained as he lifted the owl from her palm. "The enchantment cannot work otherwise."

Iris tugged gently at the fingertips of her wrist-length glove, grateful now for Brenna's insistence on the shorter style. Her maid had assured her, when laying out her attire for the evening, that elbow-length would be considered too formal for the Night Market. Instead, she'd chosen delicate maroon lace gloves that complemented the shifting burgundy and deep crimson hues of Iris's gown.

The vendor proffered the owl once more, and the moment it touched Iris's skin, the crystal bird spread its wings and a warm violet light glowed from within. "Each animal chooses the color most suited to the one who holds it."

Jasvian leaned closer to observe the transformation, his shoulder brushing against hers. The casual contact sent a pleasant shiver through Iris. "Fascinating," he murmured, his breath warm against her ear. "The color does indeed suit you perfectly.

"Creativity and imagination," the vendor said. "And what might it show for you, my lord?" he asked, offering a crystal wolf to Jasvian.

He hesitated, then accepted the figure. The wolf's internal light shifted immediately from silver to a deep, rich blue. The vendor nodded knowingly. "Ah, trustworthiness, loyalty, stability. All admirable qualities befitting—"

"Thank you," Jasvian said, returning the wolf somewhat hastily, as if uncomfortable with the insight. "Shall we continue?" he asked Iris. "There's a magical demonstration near the central fountain that I think you might enjoy."

As they moved away from the stall, Iris found herself relaxing slightly. The initial awkwardness was gradually giving way to something more familiar. The cautious rapport they'd developed through weeks of written exchanges. "I missed our morning correspondences," she admitted, surprising herself with her candor.

"As did I," Jasvian said quietly, his gaze still directed forward. "I will admit I didn't know where to begin or what to say after ..." He trailed off, but Iris knew he meant *after that night in the study*. "I must have composed a dozen different messages in my head and not written down a single one of them, believing none to be right."

Iris smiled, her eyes on the ground ahead of them as they continued walking. "I would have been happy to receive any of them, I'm sure. I—oh." She glanced down at her hands and stopped abruptly. "It seems I've only one glove. I must have left the other behind at the crystal vendor's stall."

"I can return and look for it?" Jasvian offered.

"No, please don't trouble yourself," Iris replied as she tugged at her remaining glove. "My grandmother isn't here to be scandalized," she added as she slipped the glove from her hand, "and we can look for the other on our way back." Without a reticule in which to store it, she held the delicate maroon lace toward him. "Might I trouble you to keep this safe for me in the meantime?"

Jasvian hesitated, his gaze fixed on the glove—that intimate garment that had, until moments ago, covered her skin. "Certainly," he said at last, accepting the delicate item and tucking it into the inside pocket of his coat.

They reached the central fountain where a crowd had gathered to watch a lone musician standing upon a raised dais. The performer held a harp crafted from what appeared to be strings of moonlight. As the first notes rose into the evening air, they didn't merely create sound but manifested visually above the fountain's waters. Strands of light in soft blues and greens began to pulse with the rhythm, casting their gentle illumination across the upturned faces of onlookers. As the music intensified, the strands transformed into undulating ribbons of vibrant light that chased one another through the air above the glistening water.

The longer they stood watching the display, the more Iris became aware of Jasvian beside her. The warmth radiating from his tall frame, the subtle scent of cedar and something else she couldn't quite identify, the way his hands were clasped perhaps a bit too tightly behind his back. The crowd shifted, pressing them closer together. Jasvian's arm brushed against hers, and she felt him tense at the contact. But he didn't move away.

"How are your injuries?" he asked, his gaze still fixed on the mesmerizing symphony of light and water.

"Completely healed," she replied. "Your grandmother's salve worked wonders." *And your magic in applying it*, she added silently.

"I'm glad." There was genuine relief in his voice. "I was quite concerned when I found you—"

"Oh!" someone in the crowd exclaimed.

A rapid flurry of notes burst from the harp, resolving into a cascade of small, bright sparks that rained down upon the fountain's surface—to the delighted gasps of the gathered crowd. Where each spark touched the water, concentric rings of colored light spread outward, overlapping and intertwining to create intricate patterns.

In the commotion, Jasvian's hand brushed against Iris's, his fingers grazing her knuckles. Neither of them moved away. A heartbeat later, Iris felt the edge of his hand nudge hers, the touch so light it might have been accidental. But then his hand shifted, his fingers sliding between hers with deliberate intent.

Her breath caught. She kept her gaze resolutely forward, staring at the shimmering, looping light as if her life depended on it, though she couldn't have described the finer details of the performance if asked.

Every nerve in her body seemed concentrated in the points where their hands connected.

Jasvian's thumb traced a small circle against the side of her hand, the gesture so intimate that a shiver rushed through her entire body and heat filled her cheeks. Still, neither of them acknowledged what was happening, their hands now fully entwined at their sides, hidden from casual observation by the press of the crowd. Never before had Iris been so happy to have misplaced a glove.

The musician concluded his performance with a spectacular flourish that sent broad waves of indigo light sweeping over the entire fountain. The crowd applauded enthusiastically, and Iris agreed, though she silently acknowledged that no enchanted display, however wondrous, could compare to the simple, profound magic of Jasvian's fingers laced through her own.

Chapter Thirty

As the crowd began to disperse, Jasvian reluctantly let go of Iris's hand. "There's something else I'd like to show you," he said, his voice slightly hoarse. "Away from the main thoroughfare, if you're amenable?"

Iris nodded, not trusting her voice. He guided her through the thinning crowd toward a quieter section of the market where smaller, more specialized vendors had set up their stalls. They passed displays of enchanted feather quills, mirrors that showed glimpses of faraway places, and contraptions that transformed spoken words into delicate floating symbols.

Finally, they reached a small clearing where several wooden benches had been arranged around a central fire pit. The pit was filled not with flames but with polished stones that radiated warm light in ever-shifting hues of amber, crimson and gold, mimicking the dance of living embers.

"This is where the storytellers gather later in the evening," Jasvian explained as they settled on one of the benches. "The stones in the fire pit are a special variety of lumyrite. They respond to emotions, brightening when the tales reach moments of excitement or dimming during somber passages."

"It's beautiful," Iris said, watching the lumyrite glow and fade with a soft, rhythmic light.

Far enough from the main market now, the noise dwindled to a distant hum, lending the space an unexpected privacy. A different sort of tension now stretched between them, no longer an awkward formality but something far more potent. Something that caused Iris's skin to tingle with awareness of his proximity. Her cheeks heated at the thought of all she wished to do—to touch his face, to lean into him, to discover if his lips were as warm as his hands had been.

The lumyrite stones flared briefly brighter, responding to some strong emotion from one of them—or perhaps both. She channeled her restlessness into studying his profile: the strong line of his jaw, the way the pulsing amber light cast shadows beneath his cheekbones, the slight furrow between his brows and the twitch of his lips as he appeared to search for words that wouldn't come.

"I never thanked you properly," she said.

He met her gaze. "For what?"

"Not only for calming my magic when it was spinning so wildly out of control the other night, but also for coming to my defense in the Thornharts' maze."

"Of course," he replied, as if his actions had been the most obvious thing in the world. "I must thank you as well."

"Thank *me*?" Iris asked with a bewildered laugh. "Whatever for?"

"In recent weeks," he began haltingly, "I've felt ... a certain calmness I'd nearly forgotten was possible." His gaze fixed on the glowing stones as he continued. "For years now, I've lived with a constant awareness—a vigilance that never truly fades. It's faint, but even at this distance, I can sense the dormant magic of the lumyrite deposits, like a persistent hum at the edge of my consciousness. It had become so familiar I scarcely noticed its burden, but since you entered my life—since you began ... filling my thoughts—that pressure has diminished considerably. It's as though your presence offers a respite I didn't realize I needed until I experienced it. I feel I am almost ... at peace."

Iris felt her face grow warm at his admission that she had been occupying his thoughts, but managed to respond lightly, "At peace? You? I find that difficult to imagine."

To her astonishment, Jasvian's face transformed with a genuine smile —broad and unrestrained—that reached his eyes and softened every severe line of his countenance. Iris caught her breath, certain she had never beheld a smile quite so perfectly beautiful.

Their gazes held for a long moment. The market sounds around them seemed to fade further, leaving only the soft pulse of the lumyrite and the quickening beat of Iris's heart.

Perhaps ask yourself why you are so eager to believe that connection must inevitably lead to loss of self. It is a rather convenient excuse for avoiding vulnerability, is it not?

Her conversation with the notebook returned unbidden to her mind. She had dismissed those words at the time, certain they were wrong. Of course she needed to guard herself—her thoughts, her feelings, her secrets. Especially the true nature of her magic, which even Lady Rivenna had cautioned her to keep private.

And yet, listening to Jasvian reveal parts of himself she suspected few were privileged to hear, something within her shifted. The wall she'd built between herself and others suddenly seemed less like protection and more like isolation. Here, in this quiet moment with Jasvian, she felt a sudden, startling urge to be known—truly known. Perhaps sharing oneself wasn't surrender after all, but a kind of freedom she hadn't allowed herself to imagine.

The thought sent a flutter of fear through her chest, but alongside it blossomed something stronger. Courage, and a curious sense of anticipation. What might become possible if she allowed herself this small vulnerability?

"There is something else I haven't told you," she said carefully. "About ... my magic. My specific ability."

Jasvian turned toward her more fully, his expression attentive. "Yes?"

"It's ... a little more than mere paper folding. In fact, it isn't really about paper at all. It's about seeing possibilities—all the ways something might fold or unfold, all the potential paths or outcomes that exist simultaneously. I see them sometimes when I watch people. It's—" She broke off, confused by the way he was looking at her now, a knowing smile playing on his lips, his eyes filled with warm understanding. "Why are you looking at me like that?"

"I find myself unsurprised," he said with a quiet laugh, his gaze still tracing her features with undisguised admiration. "Everything about you has proven to be far more profound than first appearances suggest. Why should your magic be any different?"

"I …" She didn't quite know what to say to that.

"How does it work?" he asked, appearing genuinely interested. "These possibilities, these potential paths?"

"For paper, it's as if my mind perceives all possible fold lines simultaneously. Not with my eyes, but with my magic. I can sense every potential crease, every possible configuration waiting to emerge from a single sheet. And for people, it's as if I see potential future scenes—mere flickers of images—unfolding rapidly before my eyes, overlaying themselves on top of reality. It's a little disorienting. Or at least, it was until I perfected a tea blend that seems to help me manage when and how the visions manifest."

"'Autumn & Pine,'" he murmured.

She smiled. "Yes."

"Now I understand why the tea house chose you," he said with quiet admiration. "My grandmother guards its deeper workings closely, though I know she has infused parts of her own magic—her ability to perceive the patterns connecting people—into the place. Now it seems clear to me that your gift for seeing possible futures perfectly complements her ability to perceive existing connections. The tea house needed someone who could glimpse what might be, not just what is." His eyes met hers with unexpected earnestness. "It is a role uniquely yours, a position that seems fashioned precisely for your particular talents. No one could—or should—take that from you."

His words settled around Iris like a warm cloak, acknowledgment of her value that asked nothing in return. She had begun this Bloom Season expecting to sacrifice her identity on the altar of family duty, to become someone's wife and nothing more. Instead, she had found purpose at The Charmed Leaf. Work that would one day be hers alone, a future shaped by her own hands.

And now, sitting beside Jasvian in the flickering light of the enchanted embers, she wondered if perhaps the choice wasn't as stark as she had believed. Could she forge her own path while also opening her heart to ... whatever this was that seemed to be growing between the two of them?

The possibility unfurled in her mind like one of her paper creations, revealing new dimensions she hadn't dared to imagine. For the first time, she allowed herself to hope that her mother's experience wasn't the only possible outcome. That perhaps one could be both complete in oneself and still choose to share that wholeness with another.

"Thank you," she said softly, holding Jasvian's gaze.

"Will you tell me more about how it works?" he asked. "It sounds fascinating." He gestured toward the other side of the fire pit, where several people had begun to gather in anticipation of the storytelling, claiming seats on the surrounding benches. Beyond their quiet alcove, the main thoroughfare remained visible, filled with browsing patrons drifting between stalls. "What do you see now?"

"Oh, well ... there are quite a lot of people about," Iris said hesitantly. "I don't believe I'll be able to distinguish much more than dozens of brief glimpses." But she took a breath anyway, focused beyond the glowing stones, and allowed her magic to flow, relaxing the careful control she maintained. The scene before her began to shift, multiple versions of reality unfolding simultaneously.

"I see ... goodness, it happens far too quickly for me to have any hope of being able to describe. Uh ..." She laughed, trying to grab hold of a single idea from each image before it folded into the next. "That man is eating a golden apple—someone is dancing at sunrise—and ... oh!"

She blinked and stood abruptly as the lumyrite stones in the fire pit flared far too brightly, but the image of two figures entangled was now seared into her mind. "I ... uh ..." She blinked rapidly, but she could not stop the next few images: the train of a white dress embellished with silver stars, a dark-haired child, a pink dog—

A pink dog? What in all the stars? She blinked again, finally forcing the possible unfolding futures away.

"What is it?" Jasvian asked, concern creasing his face as he stood.

"Nothing!" she answered, far too quickly, a flush heating her neck.

He arched a brow, his lips curving upward in curiosity. "Well, now you *must* tell me."

She looked away, heat climbing further up her neck as her mind insisted on revisiting that brief moment when she'd seen herself tangled on a bed with Lord Jasvian Rowanwood in a most improper state of—

"I *must* do nothing of the sort," she said, far too loudly.

The silence stretched between them, taut with unspoken implications. Iris risked a glance at Jasvian, only to find his eyes still fixed on her face, his expression a mixture of curiosity and growing comprehension. As their gazes locked, his breathing seemed to quicken, and a telling flush began to creep up his neck, suggesting his imagination had ventured in precisely the direction she feared.

"Whatever you're thinking," she hastened to say, "I can assure you, you are wrong."

Though clearly discomfited, Jasvian maintained his gaze with remarkable composure. "Is that so? And what might I be thinking, Lady Iris?"

She pressed her lips together as she turned away from him with as much dignity as she could muster, palms pressed flat against her midriff, her lungs struggling to draw sufficient breath. Never in her life had she experienced such profound mortification. She offered silent gratitude to every celestial body in existence that he could not see what she had seen. Though perhaps it was worse that his imagination might be conjuring scenarios even more—

"I believe we should direct our discourse elsewhere," she blurted out, turning back to face him but not quite managing to meet his eyes.

"Lady Iris," he said softly, waiting until she dared to lift her eyes to his. "I must apologize. I did not mean to make you uncomfortable when I asked what possibilities you could see."

"No apology necessary," she replied quickly. "It is only ... I am just ..." She swallowed.

"Perhaps you would prefer to return to the main part of the market," he suggested. "Or if you wish to rejoin your friends, I would be happy to—"

"No," Iris interrupted, shaking her head. "No, I'm enjoying your company."

"Then perhaps we might discuss safer subjects," he offered with a slight smile, gesturing for her to sit again. "I'm particularly curious about this tea blend you mentioned. The process of developing it must have been interesting."

Iris relaxed, grateful for his redirection. "It was indeed," she said as she took her place beside him once more, pulling her silk shawl closer around herself. "You may recall the scent of one of my earlier experiments. I believe you described it as a 'garden gnome's unwashed boots.'"

"Ah, that was the origin of 'Autumn & Pine,' was it?" he asked with a grin. "I'm relieved indeed that you improved upon the blend."

"As am I."

Their shared laughter eased the remaining tension between them, restoring the comfortable rapport they had been building throughout the evening.

"And you mentioned that my grandmother has tasked you with hosting your own event at the tea house," Jasvian said, his expression curious. "What does such an undertaking entail?"

"Oh, everything," Iris replied. "The entire affair is to be my responsibility—selecting a suitable theme, arranging the decor, curating the guest list, deciding which tea blends to feature and what delicacies shall be served." She counted each element on her fingers. "Lady Rivenna says it will be my first true test as her apprentice."

"Indeed, that sounds more involved than preparing for the Summer Solstice Ball," Jasvian observed.

Iris laughed. "You're not wrong. Though I confess, I've found it rather enjoyable to imagine all the details." She lowered her voice slightly, leaning closer. "In truth, I'm planning something rather different, particularly with the guest list. I suspect I'm going to ruffle more than a few feathers in Bloomhaven society."

"Oh?" Jasvian's eyebrow arched with interest. "Is Bloomhaven ready for such feather-ruffling?"

"Probably not," Iris replied with a mischievous smile. "But that hasn't deterred me in the slightest. I've presented my ideas to your grandmother, and she seemed quite pleased. Though I suspect she's equally interested in observing the reactions of her regular patrons to something so decidedly unconventional."

She adjusted her shawl, then turned the conversation. "And what of this project you mentioned? The one you've been working on with Lord Hadrian that's occupied so much of your time recently?"

Jasvian's expression grew more serious. "A significant improvement to the tempest early warning system in the mines," he explained. "An entirely new approach, in fact. In the past, we relied upon tempest bells, but they provided warning only once a tempest had already gained considerable strength, often too late for a complete evacuation."

"And now the system has been replaced by you," Iris said softly.

"Indeed. However, as you might imagine, being so frequently present at the mines has taken its toll. Hadrian has been attempting to develop an alternative. I'm not certain if you're aware, but he possesses the ability to transfer one's specifically manifested magic into other objects."

"He has spoken of this, yes," Iris said.

"For some time now, he's been trying to translate my sensing ability into a network of detection items placed throughout the mine tunnels," Jasvian continued. "The intention is that they would not only sense when a tempest begins to build but also incorporate my ability to calm the magic before it erupts into chaos."

"Oh!" Iris sat straighter with renewed interest. "But that sounds truly marvelous! It would relieve you of such a tremendous burden of responsibility."

"Indeed," Jasvian agreed, his expression softening slightly. "I've harbored reservations since the beginning—entrusting lives to a mechanical system doesn't come easily to me—but it appears that with Hadrian's recent breakthroughs, this system may actually prove viable. We'll begin further testing as soon as the dormant season concludes and the mines reopen."

As they continued discussing the finer details of Hadrian's work, more people began gathering around the fire pit. Well-dressed fae couples and small groups claimed the remaining benches, their excitement palpable as the scheduled hour for storytelling approached.

Vendors circulated with trays of delicate confections and goblets filled with shimmering beverages.

A hush fell over the gathering, and Jasvian shifted a little closer to Iris. A tall fae woman with purple- and silver-streaked hair stepped into the circle, adorned in midnight-blue robes. She raised her hands, and the lumyrite stones in the fire pit responded immediately, glowing brighter.

"Welcome, travelers and townspeople alike," she began, her melodic voice carrying effortlessly to every corner of the clearing. "Tonight, I shall share with you the tale of the Frost Prince and the Summer Maiden."

As the storyteller wove her tale, the lumyrite stones shifted in mesmerizing harmony with the narrative, transitioning from cool blues and silvers to warm golds and ambers, then later deepening to rich purples during moments of peril before brightening to joyful whites and golds at a moment of triumph. The audience responded as one—gasping at moments of danger, sighing at tender revelations, and holding their breath during tense confrontations—while the storyteller's graceful hands conjured delicate illusions that danced above the fire pit.

Iris would have been utterly enchanted had she been able to focus on the tale. But she could feel the occasional brush of Jasvian's shoulder, and at some point during the storyteller's performance, his leg had come to rest against hers. The warmth of that contact, innocent though it was, sent currents of awareness through her that rivaled the magic illuminating the story circle. She struggled to follow the narrative, repeatedly losing the thread as her attention returned, unbidden, to the press of his knee against hers and the way his hand occasionally brushed hers when he shifted position.

When the storyteller finished to hearty applause, Iris realized with a start that she could recall perhaps half the story at best. "That was extraordinary," she managed, hoping she sounded appropriately appreciative.

"Indeed," Jasvian agreed, his eyes meeting hers with a lack of focus that suggested he might have been as distracted as she. "Shall we explore more of the market? There's a vendor of enchanted confections near the eastern path that I think you might enjoy."

The remainder of the evening passed in a delightful blur as they wandered from stall to stall. Jasvian proved to be a knowledgeable guide, steering her toward the most interesting displays while sharing observations about the magical craftsmanship involved. They sampled delicate spun-sugar cages containing crystallized laughter that dissolved on the tongue with a surprising, effervescent fizz, watched a craftsman shape luminous ink into floating calligraphy, laughed together at the antics of messenger pixies carrying tiny parcels between vendors, and debated the merits of various enchanted items with a comfortable ease that belied their previous awkwardness.

So absorbed were they in each other's company that Iris was genuinely startled when the chimes began to ring out across the market, signaling that closing time approached. "Oh!" she exclaimed, dismay evident in her voice. "I had no idea it had grown so late. My grandparents will be waiting for me."

"Allow me to escort you back to your meeting point," Jasvian offered, his expression suggesting he shared her disappointment at the evening's conclusion.

They walked in companionable silence through the market, now noticeably less crowded as vendors began packing away their wares, and discovered Iris's missing glove as they passed the crystal vendor's stall. She pulled both gloves back on as the floating lanterns began to descend, their light dimming slightly as they prepared to guide the last patrons toward the exits.

As they neared the main thoroughfare, Iris spotted her grandparents standing with Lady Lelianna Rowanwood and Rosavyn. Charlotte, Iris noted, must have already departed. Her grandmother's expression was fixed in a familiar frown, and Iris braced herself for disapproval—she had, after all, left her grandparents in the company of two young ladies, only to return quite conspicuously escorted by Lord Rowanwood himself.

"Iris, dear, there you are," her grandmother said as they reached the group. But as they drew closer, Iris saw with a surge of relief that the frown was gone. In its place was an expression of keen interest, directed squarely at Jasvian. "Lord Rowanwood, how unexpected to see you here. I trust my granddaughter has not imposed upon too much of your valuable time this evening."

"Lady Iris's company has been nothing but a pleasure," Jasvian replied with formal politeness, though the warmth in his voice remained.

Her grandfather regarded them with poorly concealed curiosity. "I hope you've enjoyed your first Night Market, Iris. Did Lord Rowanwood show you the harpist's magical display? It was particularly impressive this year."

Iris felt heat inch its way up her neck as she recalled the luminous symphony of melody and water—and, more significantly, the moment when Jasvian's fingers had interlaced with her own, his thumb tracing patterns against her skin. "Yes, it was remarkable," she replied, hoping her flush wouldn't be visible in the dimming light.

"Well, we should be on our way," her grandmother said, glancing between Iris and Jasvian with a thoughtful expression. "Though perhaps Lord Rowanwood would care to call on us tomorrow afternoon? We're hosting a small gathering in the garden, nothing too formal."

"I would be honored," Jasvian replied without hesitation, his gaze finding Iris's. "If Lady Iris has no objection?"

"No objection at all," Iris said, aware of Rosavyn's increasingly intrigued stare.

"Until tomorrow, then," Jasvian said with a formal bow to the group, though his eyes remained on Iris. "Good night, Lady Iris. I shall—"

He stopped abruptly, his entire demeanor transforming in an instant. The warm light in his eyes extinguished, replaced by a distant, unfocused stare. His face drained of color, and his breathing became rapid, shallow. The relaxed set of his shoulders vanished as his entire body tensed.

"No," he murmured, so quietly Iris barely heard it.

"Jasvian?" his mother asked, stepping forward with one hand extended. "What is—"

"No, no, no," he muttered, his gaze still focused somewhere distant as his breathing became rapid, shallow. With a jerky bow that barely acknowledged the group, he stammered, “Please excuse me. I must go.”

Then, to the astonishment of everyone present, he turned and ran—not the measured, dignified departure of a gentleman, but a desperate, headlong rush—shoving his way through the thinning crowd with complete disregard for propriety until he disappeared from view.

Chapter Thirty-One

Jasvian ran. He tore through the thinning crowds of the Stardust Night Market with a single-minded desperation, his lungs burning, his heart hammering against his ribs. The floating lanterns that had seemed so enchanting moments ago now registered as mere obstacles, bright blurs in his peripheral vision as he dodged past startled patrons and bewildered vendors.

"Lord Rowanwood!" someone called after him. "Is everything—"

But he couldn't stop, couldn't explain, couldn't waste a single precious second. Every moment mattered now.

It had struck him without warning, a distant tremor at the edge of his consciousness. At first, he'd thought it merely his imagination. After all, the mines were dormant for the Bloom Season. Undisturbed by mining activity, the raw lumyrite should have settled, its volatile magic finding its natural balance once more. Yet the sensation had persisted, swelling almost instantly from faint unease to unmistakable dread. A tempest was building in the north.

Jasvian burst out of the market grounds and raced to the end of the bridge, his breath coming in ragged gasps. Cross the park, reach the carriage, make for The Confluence. If only he himself could move at the speed of magic.

He pushed himself harder, guilt slicing through him with each pounding step. How had he missed the early warning signs? He should have felt something earlier, should have been more vigilant. Instead, he'd allowed himself to become distracted, entranced by pleasant conversation and the warmth of Iris's company. While he had been indulging in the simple pleasure of her hand in his, the tempest had been gathering strength, building toward disaster.

His carriage waited at the edge of Elderbloom Park, and he was endlessly grateful he'd chosen one of the swift enchanted vehicles rather than a traditional horse-drawn affair. This one could reach speeds that would make the wheels barely kiss the ground. The door swung wide of its own accord as he approached, and he leaped inside before the step had even descended.

"The Confluence!" he gasped, slamming a palm against the carriage's interior wall. "As fast as possible!"

The carriage lurched into motion almost immediately. Inside, Jasvian gripped the leather seat, every nerve in his body straining northward as if he could somehow reach across the distance through will alone. The mines themselves were sealed, thankfully—no workers deep within the earth to be caught unaware. But the caretaker and the handful of guards maintaining the surface buildings and workshops ... they were still there. If the tempest erupted before Jasvian got there, it would cause devastating damage, collapsing tunnels and potentially wrecking the structures above, endangering those few lives left to stand watch.

Even if it was only one life, if would be one too many. This was his responsibility, and if he failed now like he'd failed the day his—

No. He would not allow himself to think about that. Not now. Not when every second might mean the difference between safety and catastrophe.

"Faster," he muttered to the carriage. "Please, faster."

The streets of Bloomhaven gave way to the outer districts, buildings growing sparser as they approached the eastern boundary. Through the window, Jasvian caught glimpses of the night sky, stars glittering coldly overhead, oblivious to the urgency that consumed him.

After what felt like an eternity, the carriage slowed. Before it had come to a complete stop, Jasvian had already thrown the door open and leaped out. Before him stood The Confluence, its pale stone pavilion gleaming silver in the moonlight. The circular structure sat at the precise point where all seven major ley lines of the United Fae Isles intersected. At the center of the pavilion stood the wayhouse, where Flow-Weavers took shifts attending to travelers' needs. Light glowed in a single window.

Jasvian raced toward the wayhouse door and the simple bell pull that stood beside it. He seized the rope and tugged with desperate urgency. The deep tones echoed through the night, reverberating in the still air. The light in the window brightened.

Moments later, the door swung open to reveal a woman with seafoam green hair loose around her shoulders, dressed in fitted riding trousers and a flowing linen shirt belted at the waist. Her eyes widened at the sight of him. "Lord Rowanwood? What brings you at this hour?"

"The northern mines," he replied, still breathless. "A tempest is building. There is no time to lose."

Chapter Thirty-Two

IRIS INHALED DEEPLY, HOLDING THE BREATH FOR SEVERAL HEARTBEATS before releasing it in a controlled, even stream. She repeated the process three times, a centering ritual she had developed in recent weeks to mark the beginning of her morning tea brewing. The gentle, familiar motions had become something of an anchor in a sea of uncertainty.

Two days had passed since the Stardust Night Market. Two days since Jasvian had paled mid-conversation and fled without explanation. Word had reached them the following morning that a tempest had erupted at the Rowanwood mines in the north, though Jasvian had arrived in time to calm it before catastrophic damage occurred. He had remained there to oversee the initial repairs, and the tea house had been awash with a current of anxious tension ever since. Relief that no lives had been lost mingled with concern over the extent of the damage—and over Jasvian himself.

Iris stood at Lissian's tea blending station, trying to focus on the precise measurements required for her 'Autumn & Pine' blend. She reached for the jar of spiced leaves and carefully measured the fine red-brown fragments. Behind her, Orrit huffed and muttered as he kneaded his legendary scone dough, while kitchen pixies flitted between shelves, arranging cups and saucers for the day ahead. This peaceful, familiar routine should have been soothing, yet Iris found her thoughts straying continuously northward.

Had Jasvian slept at all these past two nights? Had he eaten properly? Was he truly unharmed? And why, despite Lady Lelianna's assurances that her son was physically well, did a sense of foreboding still cling to Iris?

She measured the pine needles next, then added starlight crystal honey, watching it dissolve into glittering particles as it touched the hot water inside the copper teapot. As she reached for the lumyrite rod to begin stirring, the kitchen's back door swung open. A gust of cool morning air swept in, carrying with it the scent of dew-damp grass and—

Her heart leapt into her throat. Jasvian stood in the doorway, his tall frame silhouetted against the pale morning light. For a moment, she could only stare, the lumyrite rod forgotten in her grasp. The impulse to rush to him, to throw propriety to the winds and simply confirm with her own hands that he was whole and unharmed, was nearly overwhelming. She took a half-step forward before remembering herself—and their audience of kitchen pixies, hearth sprites, and one highly judgmental brownie.

"Lord Jasvian," she managed instead, her voice betraying more emotion than she intended. "You've returned."

"Lady Iris." His voice was formal, controlled. Too controlled. "I arrived late last night."

He looked exhausted. Shadows pooled beneath his eyes, and his normally immaculate attire showed signs of hasty attention. But it was his expression that truly concerned her. The warmth that had begun to soften his features when they were together had vanished, replaced by the rigid mask he wore in public.

"I was up early this morning," he continued. "I ... needed to see you."

Joy fluttered in her chest at those words, but something in his demeanor—the stiffness of his posture, the careful distance he maintained—kept her rooted to the spot.

"I'm relieved you're back safely," she said, setting down the lumyrite rod. "We've all been so concerned."

"Indeed." The word fell between them, oddly hollow. "May I speak with you? Privately? The garden, perhaps?"

Orrit harrumphed loudly, the sound startlingly incongruous coming from such a diminutive figure. Iris looked over her shoulder and found the brownie making a show of scowling at his dough, though Iris knew he was listening intently to every word.

"Of course," she replied, turning back. She followed Jasvian outside where the morning was still young, the sun casting long, cool shadows and painting the tea house gardens with a pale golden light. Dew clung to every surface, transforming the rows of herbs and flowers into a landscape of glittering jewels. Sleepy garden gnomes trudged slowly into view, yawning widely as they dragged tiny watering cans and trowels behind them, while several garden pixies remained curled beneath the flowers, their translucent wings twitching as they snored quietly.

Jasvian led Iris beyond the rows of herbs, flowers and tea plants to a small stone bench nestled beneath a flowering archway, far enough from the kitchen windows to ensure privacy. He did not sit, however, and neither did Iris. They stood facing each other, an arm's length of morning air between them.

"I wanted to tell you—" Iris began.

"There are things I must say—" Jasvian spoke simultaneously.

They both stopped, an awkward silence falling between them. A garden gnome nearby lowered his watering can and sat down to watch them.

"Please," Iris gestured for him to continue, her heart racing. "You first."

Jasvian's jaw tightened. "Very well." He clasped his hands behind his back, assuming a stance that reminded Iris painfully of their earliest, most formal interactions. "I wanted to inform you that I have returned safely, as you can see. The tempest was contained, though not without damage to some of the tunnel supports."

"I'm so relieved you arrived in time," Iris said softly. "That no one was—"

"I did not arrive in time, Lady Iris. The tempest erupted. It's true the damage was limited, but there should have been no damage at all. Had I been more attentive to my duties, had I not allowed myself to become ..." He paused, his gaze sliding away from hers. "... *distracted*, I would have sensed the danger much earlier. I could have calmed the tempest before it formed."

The implication hung in the air between them, clear as crystal: *She* had been the distraction. Iris felt a cold weight settle in her stomach. "I'm so—"

"This cannot continue," he cut in, his gaze returning to hers now. "Whatever this is between us. I cannot allow it to proceed any further."

Iris felt as though the ground had shifted beneath her feet. Around them, the garden grew unnaturally still, even the breeze falling silent.

"I don't understand," Iris said, though she was beginning to—all too clearly.

"My responsibilities to the Rowanwood mines and the safety of the workers must take precedence over ..." He hesitated, and something like genuine pain flickered across his features before being ruthlessly suppressed. "Over personal feelings. The burden is mine alone, and I cannot risk dividing my attention."

"Surely there must be a way—"

"There is not." His voice was final, brooking no argument. "You saw what happened at the Night Market. One moment of inattention, one evening spent in pleasant company, and disaster nearly struck."

"But no lives were lost," Iris argued, desperately reaching for something to counter his rigid certainty. "And what of Hadrian's early warning system? You spoke so positively of the developments—"

"I will never be able to trust it," he interrupted, something raw and wounded entering his voice. "Not with people's lives. I can only trust myself, and even that ..." He drew a sharp breath, looking away. "Even that has proven insufficient. But I will not allow myself to fail again."

"My lord, you have not failed—"

"I have!" He retorted, loud enough that Iris took a step back. "It was my failure to react in time that resulted in my father's death! If I had been closer, if I had left home that day just a few minutes earlier instead of dallying with ..." He shook his head, eyes filled with a pain so acute it took Iris's breath away.

"I ... I didn't know ..." She trailed off softly. "But that wasn't your fault. No one could have known what was about to—"

"I *should* have known," he said, his voice cracking. "Just as I should have sensed the danger the other night, long before it reached critical levels. I cannot allow myself to be diverted from my duty, not for a single moment. Not even for—" He stopped, pressing his lips into a thin line.

"Not even for me," Iris finished quietly.

The silence that stretched between them seemed endless. The distant squawk of a gossip bird reached Iris's ears, and she prayed it came nowhere near this garden. The last thing she wanted was for this raw, painful exchange to become fodder for Bloomhaven's rumor mill.

"You deserve more," Jasvian finally said, his voice softer but no less resolute. "Someone who can give you more than divided attention. More than constant worry that any moment of happiness might be interrupted by disaster. Someone whose duty does not require him to abandon you at a moment's notice."

"That should be my decision to make," Iris argued, anger beginning to burn through her shock. "You don't get to decide what I deserve or what I can accept."

"Nevertheless," he said, straightening his shoulders, "I have made my decision. I ... I cannot continue our acquaintance in its current form."

Iris stared at him, searching his face for some sign of the man who had held her hand in the darkness at the Night Market, who had traced gentle patterns on her skin as he tended her wounds, who had looked at her with such undisguised longing. But that man seemed to have vanished, replaced by this cold, unyielding stranger.

"So this is how it is to be?" she asked, her voice trembling despite her best efforts. "You've decided, and I have no say at all?"

"It is the only possible course," he replied with terrible finality. "I cannot be what you need. I cannot be what anyone needs outside of my role as head of the Rowanwood family and guardian of the mines."

A lump formed in Iris's throat, hot tears pressing against her eyelids. She fought them back fiercely, refusing to let him see how deeply his words had wounded her. "Very well, Lord Rowanwood," she said, deliberately using his formal title. "I understand completely."

His expression flickered—a brief, pained shadow crossing his features—before settling back into rigid control. He nodded once, a sharp, decisive movement. “I wish you all happiness, Lady Iris. Truly.”

Without waiting for her response, he turned and strode away, his back straight, his steps measured. Not once did he look back, not even as he rounded the corner of the tea house and disappeared from view.

Chapter Thirty-Three

JASVIAN TUGGED IRRITABLY AT THE HIGH COLLAR OF HIS EVENING COAT, which seemed determined to strangle him with each breath. The crowded ballroom of Fawnwood House felt oppressively hot, the air thick with perfumes that clogged his senses and set his teeth on edge. Despite the late hour—an hour when any sensible person would be at home with a book or ledger—the festivities showed no sign of waning. Couples swirled across the polished floor with mindless enthusiasm, the orchestra played with relentless, grating vigor, and hollow laughter punctuated every corner of the grand space.

He had not wanted to attend. In the week since he had returned from the north, he had spent his time either locked away in his study or working with Hadrian, obsessively refining their early warning system. Despite the fact that he would never trust a mechanical system alone, Jasvian hoped that the combination of both Hadrian's invention and his own focused vigilance would result in no more potentially disastrous surprises. The mines were secure for now, but the close call had shaken him more than he cared to admit, driving him to work punishing hours that left little time for sleep, let alone frivolous social engagements. His grandmother, however, had been insistent.

"Your absence has become the subject of speculation," she had informed him that morning. "People are concerned about the state of the Rowanwood mines. Your continued seclusion only fuels the gossip."

"The state of the mines is hardly their business," he had replied, not looking up from his ledger.

"When those mines supply the lumyrite that powers half the enchantments in their homes, it most certainly becomes their business," she had countered. "One evening, Jasvian. Your presence will reassure them that the situation is under control."

He had relented, but only after extracting a promise that Iris would not be in attendance. "She is occupied at the tea house this evening," his grandmother had assured him. "She continues her preparation for the Summer Solstice Ball display. Her control improves daily. I am most impressed with what she has managed to achieve since the night she lost control in the tea house study."

Jasvian's heart had quickened at the memory of that night. "Perhaps because she no longer has distractions to contend with," he'd muttered.

Yet here he stood, his gaze fixed on the familiar slender figure across the room. Iris Starspun wore a gown of soft pearl that shimmered with subtle enchantment, tiny forget-me-nots woven into the fabric. She was laughing at something Hadrian had just said, her entire countenance suffused with warmth.

A familiar ache bloomed in Jasvian's chest, equal parts longing and bitter resolve. He tore his gaze away and sought out his grandmother, who stood conversing with her friend Lady Amarind Thornhart. When she caught his eye, her expression remained perfectly neutral, but he detected the faintest hint of satisfaction in the curve of her mouth.

He strode toward her, maintaining rigid control over his features despite his rising indignation. "Grandmother," he said, inclining his head in a formal greeting before addressing Lady Thornhart. "Lady Amarind, you look well this evening."

"Lord Jasvian," Lady Amarind replied with a knowing smile. "We were just discussing the remarkable recovery of your family's mines. Such a relief that you managed to contain the damage."

"Indeed," he replied tersely. Then, turning to his grandmother, he lowered his voice. "A moment of your time?"

Lady Rivenna excused herself from her friend and stepped slightly aside with Jasvian, her silver eyebrows raised in perfect innocence.

"You assured me she would be at the tea house this evening," he said without preamble, not bothering to specify whom he meant.

"Did I?" his grandmother replied airily. "How careless of me. Lady Iris must have completed her work earlier than anticipated."

"This is not a coincidence."

"Few things in life truly are," she agreed. "Perhaps you might try enjoying the evening rather than glowering at every guest unfortunate enough to cross your path." With a final arch look, his grandmother turned away, gliding back to Lady Thornhart. He stood rigid, fighting the urge to follow and demand further explanation, when a lilting voice interrupted his brooding.

"Lord Rowanwood!" A fresh-faced young woman with pink curls and an exuberant disposition stepped directly into his path. "I was hoping for a moment of your time."

Without conscious thought, Jasvian found himself offering his standard reply to the woman whose name currently escaped him. "I regret that I will not be dancing this evening, my lady."

A trill of laughter escaped her. "Oh! No, I wasn't seeking a dance. I merely wanted to inquire if you'll be attending your grandmother's annual tea leaf reading tomorrow night?" Her eyes brightened with unmistakable enthusiasm. "I was fortunate enough to attend last year, and it was absolutely delightful. I've been looking forward to it since the Season began, truly. Lady Rivenna has such a theatrical flair for the readings, doesn't she?"

Jasvian's thoughts turned briefly to the elaborate production his grandmother made of the event each year. The dramatic pauses as she interpreted the most mundane of leaf patterns, the exaggerated gasps from her audience, the inevitable chaos as everyone peered into each other's cups to compare fortunes. He would rather submit to an entire day of Evryn's unfiltered opinions on his wardrobe choices than endure another evening of such frivolity.

Nevertheless, he stiffly replied, "Yes. I will be in attendance." Then, with a polite nod, he added, "If you'll excuse me."

Before he could take two steps, he found himself face to face with Lady Lycilla Whispermist, his grandmother's other close friend.

"Lord Jasvian," she exclaimed, "how marvelous to see you in society once more. We were all quite concerned after that dreadful business with the mines."

"Your concern is appreciated but unnecessary," he replied politely. "The situation is well in hand."

"Splendid to hear. Now, tell me about this revolutionary warning system your grandmother has mentioned. Something about transferring your particular magical sensitivity into ... something? It sounds absolutely fascinating."

Jasvian suppressed a sigh and launched into a carefully edited explanation of Hadrian's work, knowing his grandmother had likely orchestrated this conversation to keep him occupied. Lady Lycilla nodded attentively, punctuating his explanation with questions that revealed a surprisingly keen understanding of magical theory. He found himself drawn into a genuine discussion despite his earlier irritation.

He was busy describing how he and Hadrian had decided upon the optimum distance between detection rods when the orchestra concluded one piece and immediately struck up another. Lady Lycilla stepped slightly aside, and Jasvian suddenly found himself face to face with Iris, who had apparently been engaged in conversation with Lady Amarind directly behind them.

"Oh!" Lady Lycilla exclaimed with patently false surprise. "Lady Iris, there you are. Lord Jasvian, you should dance this one with Lady Iris."

"Indeed," Lady Amarind added immediately. "Lady Iris was just telling me her dance card remains empty for the remainder of the evening."

Jasvian's jaw clenched as he recognized the very obvious scheming at work. His grandmother and her accomplices had maneuvered this encounter. He glanced at Iris, whose expression betrayed nothing beyond polite interest, though a telltale flush colored her cheeks.

He should refuse. He should invent some pressing obligation. He should—

"Lady Iris," he heard himself say, extending a hand toward her. "Would you do me the honor?"

Her eyes met his for the briefest moment before flicking away. "Of course, Lord Jasvian."

The cool formality of her tone twisted something in his chest. He led her to the dance floor, aware of his grandmother and her friends watching with barely concealed satisfaction. As they took their positions among the other couples, Jasvian maintained a careful distance—close enough to be suitable for the dance, far enough to minimize the contact that threatened to shatter his resolve.

The music began, a stately waltz that required them to move in careful synchronicity. His right hand rested at her waist, where he could feel her warmth through the fabric of her dress. His left held her gloved hand, the smooth silk a maddening barrier between their skin. As they began to move across the floor, the practiced steps offering a welcome structure to follow, Jasvian fought to keep his expression neutral.

"I trust your work at the tea house progresses well?" he asked, directing his gaze slightly over her right shoulder.

"Yes, quite well," she replied with equal detachment. "The preparations for Lady Rivenna's Annual Tea Leaf Reading tomorrow evening are nearly complete."

"I'm pleased to hear it."

The conversation came to a halt as they turned together, her gown brushing against his legs. Even through layers of fabric, the contact sent an electric awareness coursing through him. He inhaled sharply, catching the faint scent of orange blossom and spiced tea that he had come to associate uniquely with her.

It had been little more than a week since he had held her hand at the Night Market, had felt the overwhelming rightness of being close to her. But it felt like an eternity. The ache of her absence had not diminished as he had hoped it would. Instead, it had expanded, hollowing him out from within until every mundane task seemed to require twice the effort.

"And how are things at the mines?" she asked, breaking the silence, her voice so perfectly pleasant it bordered on frigid.

"Repairs continue," he replied, equally distant. "The damaged supports have been replaced, and we've reinforced the affected tunnels."

"I'm glad to hear it."

Her hand fit so perfectly into his. Had he been a fool to throw this away? To push her from his life in the name of duty? But then he remembered the terror that had gripped him at the market, the desperate race to The Confluence, the knowledge that his distraction—his happiness—had nearly caused another disaster.

The music swelled as they circled the floor. Iris was light in his arms, her movements perfectly in time with his. He longed to draw her closer, to feel her warmth against him once more. He imagined leaning down to whisper in her ear the truth that burned inside him: *I miss you. I want you. I am only half alive without you near.*

"The orchestra plays beautifully this evening, do they not?" Iris remarked.

"Yes," Jasvian managed, the word catching slightly on an unsteady breath. "Quite skilled."

The banal politeness of their exchange stood in stark contrast to the riot of emotion within him. As they turned again, he allowed himself one brief, unguarded moment to truly look at her—the elegant line of her neck, the subtle hollow at the base of her throat, the stubborn set of her chin as she maintained her distance. She was exquisite, and oh how he longed to lower his mouth to her skin, to press his lips to the curve where her neck met her shoulder.

The music drew toward its conclusion, and Jasvian felt a rising panic at the thought of releasing her. Once the dance ended, propriety would demand they part ways. He would have no further excuse to remain in her presence, to feel the warmth of her hand in his, to breathe in the scent that had haunted his dreams.

But the final notes sounded, and Iris stepped back from him immediately, offering a perfect curtsy. "Thank you for the dance, my lord."

"The pleasure was mine, Lady Iris," he replied, bowing in return.

She turned and walked away without another glance, her back straight, her steps measured. He watched her join her grandparents, who were engaged in a lively discussion with Hadrian's mother.

The ache in Jasvian's chest threatened to overwhelm him. He could not remain here, breathing the same air as Iris while maintaining this cruel distance between them. Without acknowledging anyone, he turned and strode from the ballroom, his long legs carrying him swiftly through the grand reception hall toward the main entrance.

"Jasvian!" His grandmother's voice rang out behind him.

In the relative quiet of the entrance hall, away from the music and chatter of the ballroom, he stopped and turned to face her.

"That was a deliberate manipulation," he accused, his voice low and taut with anger. "You knew she would be here. That dance—it should not have happened. You are only making this more difficult, Grandmother."

"*You* are the one making things difficult, Jasvian!" Rivenna countered, her eyes flashing. "Someone needed to take action before your stubborn pride destroyed—"

"This is not about pride. This is about duty. About responsibility."

"It is about fear," she retorted sharply. "Fear dressed in fine clothes and calling itself duty."

"You have no right to—"

"I have every right. I watched your father make the same mistake, and I will not stand by while you repeat it."

Jasvian stiffened. "My father dedicated himself to our family's legacy. To ensuring the prosperity of our bloodline and the safety of the mines."

"Your father dedicated himself to work at the expense of those who loved him," Rivenna said, her voice softening slightly. "He missed so much of what truly mattered."

"The mines required his constant attention," Jasvian defended. "He didn't have my ability to sense the tempests before they formed. It was all the more important that he remain vigilant."

"He *chose* that level of vigilance," Rivenna countered. "He could have delegated more. Could have trained others. Could have developed systems instead of shouldering everything himself. But he didn't, and he came to regret it."

Jasvian frowned. "What do you mean?"

Rivenna sighed, the sound heavy with old grief. "In the months before his death, your father finally recognized what his choices had cost him. He came to me, troubled by the realization that he had missed so much of your childhood, that he had been a distant husband to your mother. He did not have the chance to tell you this himself before tragedy struck and took him from us far too early, and only now do I see that you've spent the past several years building your entire identity upon a philosophy your father himself had begun to abandon."

Jasvian was shaking his head, even as his grandmother spoke, struggling to reconcile this new information with the image of his father he had carried for years. "That is not what he taught me."

"Because he taught you the wrong thing! Have you truly heard nothing I've just said? *Your life need not mirror his.* Indeed, your work is fundamentally different. Many of his responsibilities have already been passed to others, precisely so you might focus your attention on the tempests. But with Lord Blackbriar's work transferring your magic and building an entirely new system, there is simply no longer the same need for your constant presence. You hold onto it because you are too afraid to relinquish control."

Jasvian clenched his jaw. "I told you, this is not about fear. This is about me choosing to uphold my father's example."

"Good gracious, dear boy, have you always been this willfully blind?" His grandmother stepped back, hands settling firmly on her hips as she inhaled deeply. Then she paused. Her eyes narrowed, the lines around them deepening as she seemed to reach some internal decision. Her lips pressed together in a determined line as she studied him with an appraising gaze that made him feel like a puzzle she'd finally solved.

She turned and signaled to a footman standing near the entrance. "Call for Lord Rowanwood's carriage immediately."

Before Jasvian could protest, she had taken his arm in a surprisingly firm grip and was steering him toward the door.

"What are you doing?" he demanded.

"Taking you to The Charmed Leaf," she replied. "You need to hear something."

"Hear—Grandmother, what has—"

"There is something I believe the tea house can relay better to you than I ever could."

"The tea house is a *building*!" Jasvian erupted in frustration. "It has no consciousness of its own and certainly is not capable of *relaying* anything to me!"

"Do not take that tone with me, boy," his grandmother said, tugging him back to face her, voice sharper than he had heard it in years. "You will listen before your sheer stubbornness and determination to isolate yourself ruins your life beyond repair."

Jasvian attempted to pull away, but his grandmother's grip only tightened. "I have no interest in—"

"Your interests are currently irrelevant," she cut him off. "For someone so intelligent, you can be remarkably dense. Now, you will accompany me to the tea house, you will sit down, and you will, for once in your life, truly listen."

Chapter Thirty-Four

"THIS IS ABSURD," JASVIAN MUTTERED AS HIS GRANDMOTHER LOWERED HER hand and the door to The Charmed Leaf Tea House swung open.

His grandmother did not deign to respond. She simply stepped inside, and Jasvian had little choice but to follow. The main floor lay in shadow, illuminated only by the pale moonlight filtering through the windows. The vines that adorned the interior walls shifted slightly as they passed, though no breeze disturbed the still air, and several faelights nestled among the ceiling foliage began to glow, bathing the empty tables below in soft light.

They moved further inside, his grandmother aiming for the intimate alcove tucked against the eastern wall where a small round table and single chair sat partially hidden from view. "Sit," she commanded, gesturing beyond the cascading honeysuckle to that sacred space from which she had conducted her business and observations for decades.

"Grandmother, I have no desire to—"

"Whether you desire it or not is beside the point," she interrupted, her tone leaving no room for argument. "Now sit."

Jasvian stared at the space. Never, not once in his entire life, had he been permitted to sit there. As a child, he had been expressly forbidden to approach the space. As an adult, he had respected the unspoken boundary that marked it as exclusively hers. The only other person he had ever seen occupy that hallowed position was Iris, a privilege that had nearly caused him to trip over his own feet in shock when he'd first witnessed it.

"Grandmother, I cannot possibly—"

"Heavens, boy, must you argue every point?"

With great reluctance, feeling like an interloper despite his grandmother's insistence, Jasvian brushed the hanging vines aside and lowered himself into the chair at the small table. He watched warily as his grandmother flicked her fingers toward a nearby table, causing one of the upturned chairs to float gracefully to the floor before she settled herself upon it, arranging the folds of her evening gown.

"What now?" Jasvian asked. "Are you going to lecture me further on my poor life choices?"

"No," she replied calmly. "I'm going to let you listen." She placed her hands palm-down on her lap. "Close your eyes, Jasvian."

He scoffed. "Grandmother, this is absurd. I fail to see how sitting in the dark will—"

"Your stubborn resistance would be admirable if it weren't so utterly exhausting," she cut in sharply. "Close your eyes."

Jasvian sighed heavily but complied, if only to hasten whatever strange demonstration his grandmother had planned.

"Now," his grandmother's voice came softer now, "simply listen."

At first, he heard nothing beyond the ordinary sounds of the empty tea house—the settling of old wood, the rustle of leaves. He was about to open his eyes and declare the entire exercise a pointless waste of—

Then he heard it. A whisper so faint he might have imagined it. A murmur like water over smooth stones. It seemed to emanate from the walls themselves, or perhaps from the very air. Jasvian strained to make sense of the sound, to discern words within the hushed cadence. Just as he began to distinguish something like human speech, the whispers shifted, becoming clearer, more distinct.

"—would have been home sooner, if not for the contract renegotiation."

Jasvian's breath caught in his throat. The voice—deep, measured, authoritative—was unmistakable.

His father.

Jasvian's eyes flew open, his head whipping around to search the empty tea house. "What is this?" he demanded, heart pounding in his chest.

His grandmother shook her head slowly, her eyes softening with empathy and remembered grief. "Close your eyes, Jasvian. Listen."

Disbelief and a strange, acute longing warred within him. Reluctantly, he closed his eyes once more, his entire being focused on the impossible voice that continued to speak as if no interruption had occurred.

His father's voice came again. "—and in retrospect, I should have put it aside for another time and returned when I had originally planned. When Lelianna told me Kazrian won first prize, my first thought was that I would have been there to see it for myself if not for that damned contract."

"It was truly a remarkable invention," came his grandmother's voice, though her lips did not move. It was an echo from the past, preserved somehow in this very space.

"Apparently the judges themselves were shocked speechless for several moments." A warm chuckle followed. "Lelianna told me he was so proud of himself, despite the singed curtains."

"We were all exceedingly proud. Such ingenuity at merely twelve years of age speaks volumes. Some children at that age are still struggling with basic control of their abilities. It does make one wonder what direction Kazrian's magic might take when he manifests one day."

"And I missed it," his father continued, regret evident in his tone. "I was sitting in a private chamber with the negotiators hundreds of miles away while my son triumphed despite being one of the youngest entrants. Just as I missed Rosavyn's first use of magic and Jasvian's entrance exam results. So many moments, Mother ... gone forever. And for what? More wealth? More security? At what cost?"

Jasvian's throat tightened painfully. He opened his eyes and stared at his grandmother, who watched him with unwavering focus.

"It has struck me today, in a way it hasn't before," his father's voice continued, "how much I have sacrificed—how much I have asked my family to sacrifice—because I haven't been able to bring myself to trust others with even the smallest responsibilities. Always believing no one else could possibly handle things correctly. Always assuming disaster would follow if I delegated anything of importance." A heavy sigh. "And I fear I've taught my children the same thing. Jasvian especially. During my visits home, we've spent hours in discussion of his eventual succession, wherein I've consistently encouraged him to observe my methods with the expectation he would one day emulate them precisely."

"It is not too late to show him a different path," Rivenna's echo replied.

"No," his father agreed. "It is not too late. I'm resolved to alter my course. I wish to see my family more, to be present for the moments that matter. The production reports will still be there after Rosavyn's birthday celebration. And Evryn is expected to manifest any day now. I do not want to be absent from this milestone as I was for Jasvian's manifestation."

"And how do you propose to accomplish this change?" Rivenna's past self asked. "You've built quite an elaborate cage for yourself, Evrynd."

"I don't know yet," Jasvian's father admitted. "But I must try. I must find a way to be both a responsible leader and a present father. My father never managed it, always believing that a Rowanwood's first and only loyalty was to the family legacy. But I've come to realize the family itself is the legacy. What good is preserving an empire if there's no joy in it?"

The voices faded, leaving behind a silence so profound Jasvian could hear his own heartbeat, rapid and uneven. He stared at his grandmother, a strange mixture of emotions churning within him—disbelief, grief, anger, and beneath it all, a tremulous hope he dared not examine too closely.

"What trick of magic is this?" he asked. His voice had lost its accusatory edge, replaced by something closer to awe. "How is this possible?"

His grandmother regarded him steadily. "It is no trick, Jasvian. This is the true magic of The Charmed Leaf. From the day it was created, it has been listening. It contains years—generations—worth of memories within its walls. The conversation you just heard took place mere weeks before your father's death."

Jasvian swallowed hard, struggling to process what he had heard. "Why did you not tell me of this years ago?"

She took a deep breath before exhaling slowly. "The complex magic infused into the tea house is my most closely guarded secret. The only other person who knows of it is Lady Iris. Tonight, the tea house has seen fit to trust you with this knowledge as well."

He slowly shook his head. "I understand that. What I meant was ... why did you not tell me of my father's change of heart?"

Her gaze filled with something that looked remarkably like guilt. "Because I did not realize until now how completely you had internalized your father's earlier teachings. How determined you were to follow the exact path he himself had begun to question. Had I known sooner how deeply those lessons had taken root, I would have shared this with you years ago, in the hope it might help you avoid repeating his regrets." She leaned forward, her eyes holding his with unusual intensity. "The legacy your father truly wanted to leave was not one of isolation and sacrifice, but one of balance and connection. He never had the chance to fully embrace that change himself, but you still can."

Jasvian's mind reeled. For years, he had dedicated himself to upholding what he believed to be his father's example. Had built his entire identity around a sense of duty that demanded complete dedication, unwavering vigilance, and the subordination of personal happiness to professional responsibility. To discover now that his father had recognized the flaws in that approach, had planned to change course but been denied the chance by cruel fate ...

"I've been so certain," he murmured, more to himself than to Rivenna. "So convinced that I was honoring his memory by following his path."

"You have honored him," his grandmother said, standing and moving close enough to rest a hand on his shoulder. "Your dedication, your sense of responsibility—these are qualities he valued and instilled in you. But they were never meant to be the sum total of your existence."

Jasvian exhaled slowly, feeling as though something tight and constricting that had bound his chest for years was gradually beginning to loosen. "I need time to think about all of this," he said.

"Of course you do," his grandmother agreed. "But don't take too long. Some opportunities, once lost, can never be reclaimed." Her gaze held his meaningfully. "Some connections, once severed, prove difficult to restore."

Iris. The thought of her came unbidden, accompanied by a sharp ache in his chest. Her wounded eyes as he had pushed her away in the garden, her rigid formality as they had danced earlier that evening. Would she wait for him? Would she forgive him?

He exhaled heavily, his gaze wandering across the tea house walls where vines clung like silent witnesses, repositories of countless conversations, revelations and secrets collected over decades. His path forward remained unclear, but for the first time in years, Jasvian allowed himself to imagine one that might include both duty and joy.

Chapter Thirty-Five

Rain pattered against the windows of The Charmed Leaf Tea House in a steady, mournful rhythm, driven by a wind that moaned through Bloomhaven's streets like a heartbroken spirit. Inside, however, golden faelights cast a warm glow over the assembled guests, and hearth sprites danced merrily among crackling flames in the fireplace that had materialized in the wall specifically for this unusually cold summer's night. The contrast between the storm outside and the cheery atmosphere within only heightened the sense of privileged intimacy shared by those fortunate enough to have secured an invitation to Lady Rivenna's Annual Tea Leaf Reading.

Iris sat with rigid posture at a table with her grandparents, every nerve in her body acutely, painfully aware of the two tables flanking hers —to her left, the Blackbriars, with Lord Hadrian offering her frequent warm smiles; to her right, the Rowanwoods, with Jasvian studiously avoiding her gaze. The seating arrangement was so obviously contrived that Iris could not help but wonder if Lady Rivenna had personally arranged it for maximum dramatic effect.

"Oh, Iris, isn't this enchanting?" her grandmother whispered, patting her hand with uncharacteristic enthusiasm. The elder Lady Starspun had been positively despondent following Jasvian's sudden coolness after the Night Market, where he had shown such promising interest in Iris. Her spirits were now remarkably improved, however, thanks to Iris spending much of the previous evening at the Fawnwoods' ball enjoying Lord Hadrian's attentive company.

"Such a charming tradition. Your grandfather and I haven't been included in many years, not since we began our quiet withdrawal from society functions, you understand."

"Indeed, it is quite lovely," Iris murmured, fighting to keep her gaze from drifting toward Jasvian.

She had barely slept the previous night, replaying their dance at Fawnwood House over and over in her mind. The careful distance he had maintained, the precise formality of his words, the way his fingers had tensed almost imperceptibly when they brushed against hers. Most of all, she remembered the flash of raw longing she had glimpsed in his eyes before he had shuttered it away. Despite everything he had said in the garden, despite his insistence that duty must take precedence over personal feelings, something in that unguarded moment had whispered that he still cared.

The thought both comforted and infuriated her.

"Lady Iris," a warm voice interrupted her brooding. Lord Hadrian had leaned slightly toward her from his adjacent table, his expression brightening as she turned her attention to him. "I must say, you look particularly lovely this evening. That shade of blue suits you remarkably well."

"Thank you, Lord Hadrian," she replied, managing a genuine smile. Hadrian's kindness was a balm to her wounded spirits, his open admiration a welcome contrast to Jasvian's deliberate coldness. "Did your sister enjoy her morning sketching excursion to the gardens? I understand she and her companions were fortunate enough to complete their drawings before this dreadful weather descended upon us."

"Indeed, she returned quite pleased with her efforts. She captured a rather charming scene of two garden gnomes who appeared to be engaged in some sort of spirited debate over the proper pruning of—"

"Distinguished guests!" Lady Rivenna's clear voice cut through the murmur of conversation, drawing all eyes to where she stood regally at the center of the room. "Welcome to my Annual Tea Leaf Reading."

As she continued her introduction, Iris found her gaze inadvertently straying to the Rowanwood table. Jasvian sat rigidly beside his mother, his severe expression softening only when he glanced at his younger siblings. Aurelise and Kazrian could barely contain their excitement at being allowed to attend such an adult gathering, while Rosavyn caught Iris's eye and offered a small, sympathetic smile. She knew something of what had transpired between Iris and her brother, though Iris had not divulged the true extent of her feelings and the depth of her disappointment.

"… a tradition that honors our connection to the deeper patterns that flow beneath the surface of our lives," Lady Rivenna was saying, her hands sweeping through the air in a graceful gesture that left a trail of silver sparkles. Outside, a particularly strong gust of wind rattled the tea house's windows. "Tonight, we peer into destiny's teacup, seeking what mysteries might be revealed."

Lucie and Lissian emerged from the kitchen at that moment—Iris knew their arrival had been precisely timed—bearing trays of delicate, pearl-white teacups. Iris observed the faint luminescence emanating from each cup, evidence of the enchantment she knew Lady Rivenna had placed upon them to ensure distinctive patterns would form for the evening's entertainment. This was well-understood and simply part of the evening's accepted performance.

"Now," Lady Rivenna instructed with a dramatic flourish, "before you are special blends I have personally created for each of you. I ask that you observe a moment of silence as you first inhale the aroma."

Iris tucked her gloves beside her saucer before dutifully lifting her cup and breathing in the complex scent of her tea. She glanced up, only to find Jasvian watching her with an intensity that sent heat rushing to her cheeks. He looked away immediately, his jaw tightening.

"Drink your tea until only a spoonful remains!" Lady Rivenna commanded, her voice taking on a theatrical quality. The statement was followed by a ripple of anticipation through the gathering.

As Iris sipped her tea, she found herself unable to resist occasional glances toward both adjacent tables. Lord Hadrian caught her eye once and smiled, while Jasvian remained focused on his cup with unnatural concentration. The younger Rowanwoods—Aurelise and Kazrian—could barely contain their excitement, whispering to each other and earning a gentle rebuke from their mother.

"Hold your cup in your left hand," Lady Rivenna instructed once most guests had nearly finished their tea. "Place your right hand atop it." Iris complied. "Now swirl three times clockwise—no, Lord Thornhart, your other clockwise!" Rivenna corrected with good-natured exasperation, drawing laughter from the assembled guests. "Then turn the cup upside down onto your saucer."

The room filled with the gentle clinking of porcelain as everyone followed her instructions. Iris carefully inverted her cup onto the delicate saucer, watching as a drop of amber liquid escaped and ran along the rim.

"Count to seven while contemplating your deepest curiosities," Lady Rivenna intoned, her voice dropping to a near-whisper that somehow carried across the room.

Iris closed her eyes. One. What did she truly wish to know? Two. The path her future would take? Three. Whether the tea house would indeed become hers one day? Four. If her family would recover from financial ruin? Five. Whether she would find happiness? Six. If Jasvian would ever —Seven.

She stopped that thought abruptly.

"Now, carefully turn your cup right-side up and peer into the mysteries within!" Rivenna announced, her words followed immediately —and almost comically—by a dramatic rumble of thunder.

As Iris lifted her cup, she became aware of Lord Hadrian leaning toward her again. "I'm curious to see what fate has in store for you," he said.

Iris smiled. "I believe you're well aware, my lord, that these patterns are largely theatrical amusements arranged for the evenings entertainment."

His smile widened. "That may be so, yet if your teacup were truly a window into your future," he added, almost conspiratorially, "I suspect it would reveal something quite extraordinary on your horizon."

Iris couldn't help laughing. "Is that not the promise of all fortune tellers? That something momentous always lurks just beyond our view?"

Hadrian chuckled softly and returned his attention to his own teacup, though his smile lingered.

Lady Rivenna moved among the tables, pausing to offer dramatic interpretations for select guests. To Lord Emberdale, she declared that the winding pattern in his cup foretold an unexpected journey. Lady Featherlock was informed that the cluster of leaves near her cup's rim suggested imminent happy news, while young Lord Bridgemere received the solemn pronouncement that the leaf formation resembling a horse indicated 'swift changes galloping toward him.'

The guests were clearly enjoying themselves, comparing cups and offering their own interpretations amid bursts of laughter and exclamations of surprise. Even Iris's grandfather seemed caught up in the festive spirit, turning his cup this way and that as he squinted at the patterns within.

Iris, having learned a few things by now from Lady Rivenna, examined her teacup and discovered a very obvious anchor shape that suggested a journey ending safely in harbor, and a distinct pattern like a ringing bell that indicated joyful news was on its way. Iris sighed and shook her head. Lady Rivenna likely knew far more than she let on about the current circumstances between her grandson and her apprentice, and this was perhaps her way of subtly trying to cheer Iris up.

With the formal readings concluded, guests rose from their tables and began to mingle. Iris found herself standing beneath an ornate hanging teapot with Rosavyn, while her grandparents conversed nearby with the elder Whispermists.

"Lady Fawnwood's new hairstyle looks precisely like one of Orrit's scones has taken up residence on her head," Rosavyn whispered, leaning close to Iris's ear. "I keep expecting it to sprout little legs and scurry away in search of clotted cream."

Iris smothered a laugh behind her hand, grateful for the moment of levity that diverted her thoughts from the turmoil that had occupied them all evening. "Rosavyn! She'll hear you, and then where will we be?"

"In terrible disgrace, I should hope," Rosavyn replied. She heaved a theatrical sigh. "It's been at least three days since I properly scandalized anyone. My reputation as the family's secondary source of trouble is at risk of tarnishing."

Before Iris could formulate a suitable response, Lord Hadrian approached. After greeting Rosavyn, he asked, "Might I borrow Lady Iris for a brief moment?"

"But of course," Rosavyn replied, her eyes widening in exaggerated interest as she glanced between them.

Iris pretended not to notice Rosavyn's pointed look, just as she ignored her grandmother's keen observation of the exchange. As Hadrian led her across the room, they passed directly by Jasvian's table, and though Iris kept her gaze carefully averted, she could feel the weight of his attention upon her like a physical touch.

Hadrian led her toward a quieter area of the tea house around the corner near the staircase that led to the upper levels. The faelight here was dimmer, more intimate, creating shifting patterns of shadow and gold across the wooden floor. The relative distance from the windows reduced the storm's presence to a gentle murmur, creating a pocket of tranquility in the secluded alcove. The blossoms nestled among the vines adorning the walls seemed to turn toward them, their petals unfurling slightly as if curious about the conversation about to unfold.

"I've been wanting to speak with you privately," he said, his voice gentle as he turned to face her. "Ever since the masquerade, in fact, though I'll admit it's taken me some time to work up the courage."

A flicker of nervous anticipation curled in Iris's stomach. "Oh?"

"Lady Iris," he began, taking her hands in his with careful reverence. Her heart performed a peculiar little leap at the contact. While the press of his skin against hers sent a pleasant warmth through her fingers, it bore little resemblance to the liquid fire that had coursed through her veins at Jasvian's merest touch.

"These past weeks, I have come to admire you greatly. Your intelligence, your courage in facing Bloomhaven society, your unique perspective—all of these qualities have captivated me." He drew a deep breath, his gaze never leaving hers. "I find myself thinking of you constantly, wondering what insights you might offer on any given topic, longing to share my thoughts with you and hear yours in return."

Iris felt a genuine warmth spread through her chest at his sincere words. Hadrian had always been kind to her, had seen value in her beyond her bloodline or social position. He was handsome, intelligent, respected. Everything she should want in a match. Yet even as these thoughts formed, her treacherous mind conjured an image of Jasvian's face, his rare smile, the intensity in his eyes that night he had knelt beside her on the floor of the study.

"And I must confess, our encounter at the masquerade only deepened my admiration," he continued earnestly. "Our lively conversation, your thoughtful observations—even as we shared far too many dances in succession, much to the disappointment of the other gentlemen present. Though our faces were concealed, I knew it could be no one but you."

At this, Iris's thoughts faltered. Though she had indeed danced with several partners that night, there was only one with whom she'd formed a genuine connection, and she knew with absolute certainty it had not been Hadrian. She opened her mouth to correct this misunderstanding, but before she could speak—

Hadrian slowly lowered himself to one knee, still holding her hands in his. Iris's breath caught as she realized what was happening. "Lady Iris Starspun," he said, his voice steady with conviction, "I believe we could build a wonderful life together. A partnership of minds and hearts. Would you do me the extraordinary honor of becoming my wife?"

Time seemed to suspend itself as Iris stared down at Hadrian's earnest face. Suddenly, her vision blurred, reality folding in upon itself as it had so many times before. Multiple versions of her future unfolded before her, each one overlapping the next before she had time to properly consider any of them:

Herself in a beautiful gown, standing in a lavish garden in front of a magnificent country home, Hadrian beside her as they conversed animatedly about a book held open between them—

Standing in The Charmed Leaf, older now, silver threading through her dark hair as she poured tea for distinguished guests—

Standing at the tea house study window, a strong arm looping around her waist and drawing her nearer, Jasvian's face filling her vision as his other hand rose to brush against her cheek—

A dark-haired child running through a field of wildflowers, paper butterflies dancing in the air above tiny outstretched hands—

The visions vanished as quickly as they had appeared, leaving Iris blinking in momentary disorientation. Hadrian remained before her, still waiting with patient expectation for her answer.

"I—" she began, then faltered. "It ... I believe you're mistaken about the masquerade, my lord. It was not me you danced with."

Hadrian frowned. "Are you certain?"

"And ... and the tea house—"

"I assure you, Lady Iris, I would not ask you to give up The Charmed Leaf. If Lady Rivenna intends it for you, then it shall be yours. We could surely find a reliable person to manage its daily affairs while you guide it from afar and visit Bloomhaven as needed to ensure all is well. The arrangements can be determined once we are wed. But please, do not distress yourself with the notion that you must give it up."

"I, uh ..." That wasn't quite the way Iris had envisioned her future at the tea house, but she supposed she couldn't expect Lord Hadrian to upend his life and move permanently to Bloomhaven if that was not the Blackbriars' custom. There was, however, one other pressing matter that required mentioning.

"There is something else I must tell you," she added, guilt washing over her. "My ... my family's circumstances are not what they may appear. In truth, our situation is quite grave. We face significant financial difficulties, and I—I must inform you that I have no dowry to speak of. I have nothing save my family name. I should have disclosed this matter sooner, and for that I feel most dreadfully—"

"None of that is of any concern," Hadrian interrupted, a gentle smile smoothing away his frown. "I care nothing for dowries or financial considerations, Lady Iris. It is you alone whom I desire."

His words struck her with unexpected force. Here was a man who wanted her for herself, who saw value in her mind and character, who cared not for distinguished bloodlines or a possible fortune. After weeks of judgment and scrutiny from Bloomhaven society, after Jasvian's rejection, Hadrian's unconditional acceptance felt like cool water to a parched soul.

She thought of her family's desperate financial situation, of her grandparents' thinly veiled anxiety as the Season progressed without a match, of her father's warnings that their very survival depended on her securing an advantageous marriage. She thought of Jasvian's stony expression as he had told her his duty must take precedence over whatever had been growing between them.

"Yes," she heard herself say, the word escaping before she had fully formed the decision. "Yes, I will marry you."

Hadrian's face lit with joy as he rose to his feet, producing a ring from his pocket. It was a delicate gold band set with a luminous pearl surrounded by tiny diamonds that caught the light like stars. As he slipped it onto her finger, Iris tried to focus on the happiness she should be feeling, rather than the strangely hollow sensation spreading through her chest.

"You've made me the happiest of men," Hadrian said. "Shall we share our news?"

Iris nodded, allowing him to guide her back toward the main room where her grandparents waited. The buzzing in her head made it difficult to focus on anything beyond putting one foot before the other. She was engaged. She would be Lady Iris Blackbriar. This was what she had been brought to Bloomhaven to accomplish—a match that would secure her family's future.

Her grandparents' faces transformed with undisguised delight when Hadrian formally requested their blessing. Her grandmother actually clasped her hands together in pure joy, while her grandfather clapped Hadrian firmly on the shoulder in a rare display of emotion. Their relief was palpable, like a physical wave that washed over their table.

"We would be honored to welcome you to our family," her grandfather declared, his voice unusually warm. "This calls for a toast!"

As word of the engagement spread through the tea house, guests began to approach with congratulations and well-wishes. Lady Lelianna offered a gracious smile, while Rosavyn squeezed Iris's hand warmly, though her eyes held a hint of something Iris couldn't quite decipher. The noise and chatter seemed to increase with each passing moment, pressing in upon Iris until she felt she could hardly breathe. The ring on her finger felt both foreign and unnaturally heavy.

"If you'll excuse me," she managed to say, offering Hadrian an apologetic smile. "I ... believe Lady Rivenna may need me in the kitchen."

She turned, intending to make her way toward the kitchen where she might find a moment's peace, only to collide solidly with a tall figure. Strong hands steadied her, grasping her upper arms briefly before withdrawing as if burned.

"Lord Jasvian," she gasped, stepping back to find herself staring up into his face. His expression was carefully controlled, but something dark and turbulent lurked in his eyes. For a long moment, they simply stared at one another, the noise of the gathering seeming to fade into muffled irrelevance. Then she blinked and remembered herself. "I—excuse me, my lord."

She stepped past him and wove her way between the tables and guests until she pushed through the door into the kitchen, where blessed quiet greeted her, interrupted only by the soft clinking of porcelain as kitchen pixies methodically washed teacups and arranged them in orderly rows. The familiar scents of herbs and spiced tea brought a momentary comfort that vanished instantly when the noise from the tea house's main floor surged—the door had opened again.

She turned to find Jasvian walking in, the door swinging closed behind him.

"What are you doing?" he asked as he stopped a few paces away, his eyes dark with an emotion that seemed to hover between anger and desperation.

Iris blinked. "What do you mean?"

"This." He gestured vaguely toward her hand, where Hadrian's ring glimmered. "This isn't what you want."

Anger flared within her, hot and sudden. "How do you know what I want? You made it abundantly clear that my wishes were of no consequence to you."

"That's not—" He broke off, inhaling deeply. When he spoke again, his voice was lower, but no less intense. "Please. Think carefully about what you're doing."

"I have thought carefully," she retorted, though the slight tremor in her voice betrayed her uncertainty. "Lord Hadrian is kind, intelligent, constant, and values me for who I am. I could not ask for a better match."

"Is that enough for you?" Jasvian pressed, stepping closer. "To build a life on kindness and intelligence alone?"

"It's certainly more than duty and obligation," she shot back.

His jaw tightened. "You don't understand—"

"Oh, I understand perfectly well. You chose your duty over anything that might threaten your perfect control." Her voice had risen slightly, drawing anxious glances from the pixies. "And now you have the audacity to question *my* choice?"

"Because it's the wrong one!" he shouted, causing the kitchen pixies to abandon their dishwashing duties entirely, darting into the pantry to hide. "You don't love him! You barely know him!"

"And what would you know of love?" Iris demanded. "You're too terrified to allow yourself to feel it."

"That is not—"

"And as for knowing each other—you're right. Lord Hadrian and I haven't had the opportunity to properly know one another. Perhaps we would have if someone hadn't monopolized so much of his time with endless work on magical detection systems that will likely never see use because someone can't bear to relinquish control!"

"My control, at least," he snapped in return, "prevents me from angling quite so obviously for the first advantageous match that presents itself!"

Iris recoiled as if physically struck, her breath catching in her throat.

She stepped back, her body suddenly rigid except for the trembling of her hands. Drawing in a ragged breath, she bit out, "There is *nothing* more to say."

Turning on her heel, she marched to the back door and flung it open. Without a backward glance, she stepped out into the storm, slamming the door behind her with a resounding bang.

Chapter Thirty-Six

The rain struck Iris's face and bare arms, carried sideways by the restless wind that whipped through the tea house garden. Though the woven canopy of branches overhead blocked the worst of the downpour, enough water slipped through to immediately dampen her gown. She barely registered the cold, her anger burning hot enough to ward off the chill as she strode blindly forward, seeking distance from Jasvian's cruel words.

How dare he? How *dare* he?

Behind her, the kitchen door slammed once more. "Lady Iris!" Jasvian's voice cut through the storm. "Wait!"

She quickened her pace, navigating the wet garden path between the rows of herbs and flowers with reckless abandon.

"Iris!" he called again, closer this time.

She didn't stop until she reached the fountain at the center of the tea house's outdoor seating area. Rain-slicked stone met her fingertips as she gripped its edge for balance, then spun to face him. He stood beneath the edge of the canopy, rain already darkening the shoulders of his evening coat, plastering errant locks of hair to his forehead.

"Have you not said enough? Must you pursue me into a storm to deliver further insults?"

"I'm sorry," he said, his eyes filled with such profound regret that it momentarily stilled her anger. "I'm so sorry. I did not mean that."

She shook her head and swiped at her cheek with one hand, unsure if she was wiping away rain or tears. "What is it you desire of me?"

His expression crumpled into something raw and desperate. "Please, Lady Iris, I only wish to speak with you."

"Speak?" She gave a harsh laugh. "You wish for conversation *now*? After telling me that duty and responsibility must take precedence over whatever existed between us? After ensuring your complete absence since your return from the mines? Now that I am engaged to your dearest friend—*now* you suddenly discover the power of speech?"

Jasvian strode forward through the rain until he stood mere feet from her. "You cannot enter into this marriage."

"I have already accepted his proposal," she replied, hating how her voice trembled. "And you have made it abundantly clear that you do not desire my company."

His brows rose. "You must know that is the furthest thing from the truth."

She shook her head again. "It scarcely matters, does it? You will inevitably distance yourself again, regardless of your desires."

"I ..." He exhaled, running a hand across his brow. "I need ... some time—"

"Time?" The incredulity in her voice was obvious. "For what purpose? So that you might reject me once more when you determine that your sacred duty remains of greater importance than all else?"

His next words came so softly she almost lost them to the wind. "I was mistaken."

Iris stared at him, momentarily rendered speechless. Something fierce and bright flickered to life in her chest—hope, longing, something even more dangerous. And then, just as quickly, it was consumed by a wave of indignation that burned away everything else.

"No," she said, her voice trembling with suppressed emotion. "You do not get to declare your mistake only *after* I have pledged myself to another. Your dearest friend, no less! Would you have me break his heart now?"

"Of course not! I merely—" A sound of pure frustration escaped him, half growl and half groan, quickly swallowed by the wind's howl. "I find myself at a loss! I have created a terrible mess of this situation. A complete disaster. I know I should never have pushed you away as I did, but I believed there was no alternative! You do not know what it is to be utterly alone in shouldering—"

"Alone?" The word burst from her lips. "You think I know nothing of what it means to be *alone*? Every day I stand at the edges of society, watching others move effortlessly through a world where I will never truly belong. Lord Hadrian was one of the few who made me feel I might find a place here. He shows kindness, and constancy, and he genuinely wishes for my company. He does not push me away the moment I draw too near. He—" Her voice caught. "He does not make me feel as you do."

"And what," Jasvian asked in a voice scarcely more than a whisper, "do I make you feel?"

Iris drew in several shuddering breaths, the enormity of the question pressing down upon her. Rain continued to fall around them, though it had slowed to a gentle patter now, the garden growing hushed beneath the soft drumming. Something about the night, the darkness, the isolation of the garden—it stripped away her defenses, leaving her raw and exposed. When she finally spoke, her answer was achingly, terribly honest.

"As though I stand at the heart of a tempest," she breathed, voice unsteady. "As though my heart might burst from my chest at any moment. As though I cannot draw proper breath when you are near, and yet I feel more alive than I have ever been. As though every nerve in my body awakens to your presence, and I find myself counting the hours until I might see you again, even knowing I should not."

By the time she finished speaking, he had drawn so near that she could feel his breath warm against her rain-cooled skin. "Iris—"

"No." She pressed her palms against his chest, intending to push him away. Instead, her fingers curled into the fabric of his coat. "I ... I cannot ..."

He took one final step to close the distance between them, leaning forward to press his brow to hers. "Iris," he breathed, and oh, how different her name sounded without its formal title. Impossibly intimate, like a secret shared in the space between heartbeats.

Her eyelids fluttered shut, her resistance crumbling like autumn leaves. "Jasvian ..." she whispered, savoring the taste of his name on her tongue.

"Everything you feel," he whispered roughly, his breath mingling with hers, "I feel a hundredfold. You haunt my dreams, my every waking moment. When you enter a room, all else fades to shadow. Every minute away from you is agony, and the mere thought of you with another—" His voice caught. "It is a torment beyond enduring."

His thumb traced the curve of her cheek, and Iris leaned into his touch. His breath was warm against her lips, so close now ... so achingly—

"Tell me what you saw," he whispered, breath ragged. "At the Night Market. The vision that made you put such sudden and hasty distance between the two of us."

Heat rushed through her body at the memory of what she had seen in that fleeting but intensely intimate moment. With a shuddering breath, she said, "You have already guessed."

"You saw the two of us."

Her answer was barely audible now: "Yes."

Lightly, his fingertips brushed down the side of her neck, the intimate contact causing a shiver to dance across her skin and a sharp intake of breath she couldn't suppress.

"But it was only a possibility," she forced herself to say. "One of many. It does not mean ..." She trailed off as his hand slid upward once more, his thumb tracing the sensitive skin beneath her jaw, guiding her to angle her head further. The gesture was both reverent and possessive, and she found herself yielding to it without conscious thought, her body responding to his as naturally as flowers turn toward sunlight.

"We cannot ..." she murmured, on the brink of losing all self control. "Hadrian is ..."

"I know." Jasvian's hand clenched into a fist as he trailed his knuckles back up her cheek. "I know ... I know ..." And she heard the anguish in his voice. "I ... just ..." His thumb grazed over her lower lip, and something tightened deep inside her in a way it had never—

"Jasvian Evrynd Valenrik Rowanwood!"

They sprang apart at the sound of the voice that cut through the air like a guillotine. Jasvian spun around, and beyond him, standing in the pathway between the herbs and flowers, stood Lady Rivenna. The rain had now stopped, as if even the storm recognized the commanding presence of the Rowanwood matriarch.

"Grandmother," Jasvian said, his voice emerging rather strangled. "What are you ... How did you ... I thought you were—"

"The tea house," Lady Rivenna replied coldly, "sees all."

Iris felt herself shrivel with mortification while beside her, Jasvian drew himself up to his full height, attempting to gather the shreds of his dignity. "I was merely—"

"Merely what?" Rivenna's gaze swept over them both. "Attempting to compromise a betrothed young lady in my tea house garden?"

Iris felt her face flame. "My lady, please—"

"And you? What were you thinking, Lady Iris?" Rivenna's tone could have frozen the summer itself. "Do you have any notion of the scandal if anyone else had walked out here? The ruination would be absolute. Your reputation would never recover." Her eyes narrowed. "Or have you forgotten that you have already promised yourself to another?"

"I-I was caught up in—"

"Caught up in what, precisely? Feelings the two of you should have acknowledged weeks ago, before you accepted Lord Hadrian's suit? Before it was too late to do anything but cause pain to all involved?"

Iris flinched as though she'd been struck. "My lady, I never meant to—"

"You should return indoors, Lady Iris." Though Rivenna's tone remained measured, there was steel beneath the surface. "Your grandparents have expressed concern about your sudden absence. And I hope, for your sake," she added, "that you can come up with a believable explanation for why you currently look like a drenched pixie."

"I ..." Iris glanced at Jasvian, then looked away before he could meet her gaze. "Yes, my lady." She dropped into a swift curtsy before hurrying past the older woman.

Just before she reached the door, she heard Lady Rivenna's voice again, somehow even more forbidding than before: "Now then, grandson. Shall we discuss your deplorable lack of judgment?"

~

Mere moments after Iris vanished back into the tea house, another door shimmered into existence beside the first. It swung silently open of its own accord, revealing a narrow staircase Jasvian had never seen before. With an icy gesture, his grandmother indicated he should precede her up the unfamiliar steps, which appeared to emerge directly into the study, providing a discreet route that bypassed the kitchen and main floor of the tea house.

This magical second door into the study slammed shut behind Jasvian and his grandmother with enough force to send several books tumbling from the shelf—and then promptly vanished with barely a whisper. Jasvian stalked toward his desk, his heart still thundering from Iris's nearness, the almost-kiss burning like amberberry wine in his blood. He ran trembling fingers through his wet hair, further destroying whatever remained of its proper arrangement, while behind him, his grandmother's boots clicked against the wooden floor with measured precision.

"I cannot decide," she said into the charged silence, "whether to be furious at your behavior or devastated by your timing."

He turned. "I beg your pardon?"

"Lord Hadrian Blackbriar is your closest friend." Each word fell like ice. "The woman he intends to marry was just in your arms. And you were about to compromise her reputation beyond repair."

"Nothing happened—"

"Because I interrupted you. Tell me, what might I have found had I arrived a few moments later?"

Jasvian dragged a hand through his hair once more. "I was merely ..."

"Yes?" His grandmother's eyebrow arched. "Do enlighten me. What were you 'merely' doing with your lips so close to hers?"

"I was—trying to find my self control."

"And where, pray tell, were you hoping to locate this 'self-control'?" His grandmother's voice could have stripped paint. "Down Lady Iris's throat?"

"Grandmother!"

"Jasvian!"

"I thought ... I believed you would approve of this match. You've always seemed to ..." He broke off, frustrated, and began to pace the length of the study. "You like her."

"Of course I like her. And I do indeed approve of a match between the two of you. You may recall that I conveniently placed her *right here*, in this very room, where you would be forced to acknowledge her existence." Rivenna gestured to the desk where Iris usually sat, before letting her hand fall to her side.

Jasvian froze mid-stride. "You ... placed her here with me *intentionally*?"

"My dear boy." His grandmother's eyes rolled toward the ceiling with such force he feared they might become stuck there. "I do *everything* intentionally. Though I must say, you made it extraordinarily difficult. Most young men, when presented with a beautiful, intelligent woman, would not continue to antagonize her day after day."

"I ..." He trailed off, unsure what to say to that. "Did you ..." He blinked and shook his head. "Did you see this in your tea leaves? Lady Iris and me?"

Rivenna arched a brow. "I see many things, none of which are set in stone. This, you know."

Her words reminded him of Iris's breathy whisper in the garden. *It was only a possibility. One of many.* He ached with the thought that if he had not been such a stubborn fool—if he'd questioned his long-held beliefs about duty at the expense of happiness sooner—that the future Iris had seen might still have been possible for them now.

"Why did you not say something?" he asked quietly.

"Would it have mattered?" Rivenna flicked her hand at the books that had fallen to the floor, and they promptly returned to their positions on the shelf. "You were so determined to see her as beneath your notice. A half-blood upstart who dared to debut with magic you deemed inferior. You failed to see the truth that was immediately evident to me the very first night the two of you met."

Jasvian frowned. "That first night? At the Opening Ball? Grandmother, it was a near-disaster."

A familiar sparkle danced in Rivenna's eyes. "It was magnificent. My dear boy, I watched you retreat further into yourself each day following your father's death, keeping everyone at arm's length, determined to make no true connection with anyone. Then Lady Iris arrived and quite simply marched straight past your defenses and provoked a reaction in you I had not seen in years—she made you *feel* something once more."

Jasvian's gaze slid past his grandmother's. "And now she is engaged to Hadrian," he murmured. He raked his hands over his face and groaned. "How am I to endure it? Witnessing her build a life with him? Seeing her at social gatherings, watching her bear his children, knowing she might have been ..." He couldn't finish. Couldn't bring himself to utter the word *mine*.

"You'll endure it because you must." Rivenna's voice was gentle now. "And because you love her enough to want her happiness, even if it is not with you."

"I don't ..." But he couldn't complete the lie. He turned back toward the window where Iris's desk stood. A few sprigs of dried herbs and something that appeared to be an intricately folded paper chandelier lay on the surface. He swallowed. "What do I do now?"

"You do what any gentleman would do." His grandmother's voice was firm but kind as she crossed the room and stood beside him. "You wish them joy, you maintain your friendship with Lord Blackbriar—even if from a distance—and you learn to live with your regret."

"And if I cannot?"

"You can, and you shall." She squeezed his shoulder. "Perhaps they will reside at the Blackbriar country estate after they are wed, which will make things easier for you. They need not return here during the Bloom Season."

"Perhaps I shall be the one to never return."

"Oh, do stop being dramatic." His grandmother's tone sharpened again. "You are not the first person to lose someone to their own stubborn foolishness, nor shall you be the last."

"I cannot lose her." The words emerged as barely more than a whisper.

"You already have." She sighed. "Jasvian, dear, the time for realizing your feelings was weeks ago, before Lady Iris accepted Lord Hadrian's suit. Now, you must move on."

Jasvian closed his eyes, remembering the way Iris had whispered his name, how close he had come to tasting her lips. "I am such a fool."

"Yes," his grandmother agreed. "But a lovable one, despite your best efforts to be utterly insufferable. And perhaps now that you've finally learned to unlock that fortress you call a heart, there may be room for another to one day step in."

Jasvian shook his head, a bone-deep certainty settling over him. "For me, there will only ever be her."

He stared out the window at the night beyond, where the dark clouds had finally begun to drift away, revealing a sky newly washed clean, dusted with brilliant stars. How fitting, he thought bitterly, that the storm should pass just as his world collapsed around him.

Chapter Thirty-Seven

Iris stared at the timebloom on her bedside table, watching as its petals shifted from silver to the softest blue, informing her that it was well past midnight—the third consecutive night she had found herself still awake at this hour.

She turned onto her other side with a frustrated sigh. Sleep evaded her like a mischievous sprite, dancing just beyond her grasp whenever she came close to capturing it. Every time she closed her eyes, she saw Jasvian's face, felt the warmth of his breath against her lips, heard again the whispered confessions that had nearly shattered her resolve.

Everything you feel, I feel a hundredfold. You haunt my dreams, my every waking moment.

He had left Bloomhaven the very next morning. No farewell. No message. Simply gone, returned to the northern mines with barely a word to anyone, according to Rosavyn. Iris had no notion of when—or if—he might return.

A week had passed since that rain-soaked almost-kiss in the garden. Seven days of smiling politely as wedding plans unfolded around her, her duties at The Charmed Leaf now significantly reduced. Seven days of accepting congratulations from society matrons who had previously snubbed her. Seven days of her grandmother's triumphant satisfaction, her grandfather's relieved pride. Seven days of Hadrian's attentive devotion.

Seven days of absolute misery.

Iris pressed the heels of her hands against her eyes, willing away the tears that threatened, then lowered them with a groan. The ornate pearl-and-diamond ring on her finger caught the timebloom's glow, scattering faint pinpricks of light from the diamonds as she turned her hand this way and that. The beautiful ring felt heavier each day, a physical manifestation of the guilt that weighed upon her heart.

Iris ...

She turned with a huff and stared at the ceiling, trying to banish the memory of Jasvian's voice—the way he had whispered her name that night in the garden, each syllable caressed with an intimate reverence.

No. She was engaged to Hadrian. *Hadrian.* Proper, kind, consistent Hadrian who looked at her with such genuine admiration. Who was not deterred by the discovery of her family's financial distress. Who believed she would make him happy.

Iris sat up in bed, pushing away the tangled sheets. The thought of Hadrian only intensified her guilt. How could she pledge her life to one man while her heart yearned so desperately for another? When Hadrian spoke of their future together, she smiled and nodded while her mind wandered to dark hair and stormy eyes, to the scent of rain and the whispered confession: *Every minute away from you is agony.*

She climbed out of bed and moved to the window, gazing out at the moonlit garden below. Somewhere beyond Bloomhaven, Jasvian was likely working even at this late hour, poring over mine repair reports or reviewing estate accounts, finding comfort in the orderly procession of numbers that never disappointed, never complicated matters with inconvenient feelings.

With a heavy sigh, Iris turned from the window. Beside her bed, the timebloom shifted, its petals darkening toward deep blue. The third hour past midnight approached, and still sleep eluded her. She crossed to her writing desk, retrieving her notebook and a quill before returning to the window seat. The silvery moonlight spilled across her lap as she drew her knees up and rested the notebook against them.

If anyone might offer clarity, it would be the acerbic, opinionated notebook that had become her unlikely confidant. She turned to a fresh page—resolutely ignoring the urge to pause over any pages where Jasvian's elegant script appeared—and began to write.

I cannot sleep. My thoughts race like startled deer through a forest, never settling, never finding peace.

The notebook's script appeared immediately beneath her words: *A rather flowery metaphor, but accurate, I suppose. Though I'd have gone with 'panicked hummingbirds' myself. More frantic energy.*

Despite everything, Iris found herself smiling. *Ever the critic.*

Merely offering editorial suggestions. One does strive for precision in language.

She hesitated, her quill hovering above the page before she wrote: *I find myself wondering what would happen if I broke my engagement to Lord Hadrian.*

The notebook's reply came after a thoughtful pause: *A question better answered by your own unique gifts, I should think. Have you tried to see the possibilities?*

I have, Iris wrote, remembering her earlier attempts. *But there are so many. Too many. They overwhelm me.*

Perhaps if you wrote them down? Organizing thoughts often leads to clarity.

Iris considered this suggestion. Controlling her visions was still something of a challenge. She had been practicing, as Lady Rivenna suggested, focusing on specific questions to narrow the field of possibilities. Perhaps if she concentrated on this particular question—and accompanied it with a few sips of 'Autumn & Pine.'

She rose from the window seat and returned to her writing desk where her evening teacup still sat, a small amount of liquid remaining at the bottom. The tea was cold now, and she grimaced as she drank the last few sips, but the familiar sensation of steadiness washed through her almost immediately. The world seemed to settle around her as she walked back to the window, her mind already feeling more centered and focused.

She closed her eyes, relaxing the careful control she usually maintained and allowing her magic to flow while focusing her thoughts on a single question: *What might happen if I break my engagement to Lord Hadrian?*

The now-familiar sensation washed over her—images unfolding themselves before her eyes, glimpses of potential futures, each one overlapping the next:

Hadrian's face, stricken with hurt but quickly gathering his composure as he assured her he understood, that he wanted her happiness above all else, his voice hardly breaking—

Whispers of 'the half-blood who thought herself too good for Lord Blackbriar,' society turning its collective back on the Starspun family—

Her grandfather's face, gray with disappointment as he informed her they would lose the Bloomhaven house, unable to maintain even the pretense of their former—

Herself, decades older, alone in a small cottage, neither married nor Lady Rivenna's successor, seemingly having lost both chances at security when—

A furious Lord Hadrian, his usual gentle demeanor shattered by betrayal, publicly denouncing her, severing all ties with the Rowanwoods by extension, putting Jasvian's friendship and business partnership at risk—

Her family relocated to a modest home in an unfashionable district, her father forced to accept employment beneath his station while her mother—

Herself at The Charmed Leaf, older and confident, directing the tea house's operations with Lady Rivenna's approval, financially independent despite the lingering whispers about her scandalous past—

Hadrian smiling sadly as he wished her well, confessing he had suspected—

Iris blinked, trying to call the vision back as she wondered what Hadrian might confess he suspected, but the image was gone. Breathless and a little disoriented, she picked up her quill once more.

So many paths, she wrote, hand trembling slightly. *Some hopeful, others devastating. How am I to know which would come to pass?*

You cannot, came the notebook's immediate reply. *That is the nature of possibility.*

The outcome will also depend on precisely what I choose to share with Lord Hadrian, she wrote after a moment's reflection. *The true reason for wishing to end our engagement ...*

You are considering withholding certain truths? the notebook inquired.

I am considering focusing the conversation solely on Lord Hadrian and myself, she replied carefully. *Explaining that my feelings are not what they should be for a future husband, rather than mentioning my ... complicated sentiments regarding his closest friend.*

A wise approach, if somewhat incomplete. I certainly wouldn't recommend declaring your undying passion for Lord Brooding regardless.

A small sound from the hallway—the creak of a floorboard or the settling of the house—momentarily distracted Iris. When she looked back at the notebook, another line of text had appeared:

Do any of these hopeful potential futures you've just witnessed feature the aforementioned Lord Brooding?

Iris bit her lip. She had very firmly pushed Jasvian from her mind whenever attempting to see the possibilities in her future, fearing both disappointment and hope in equal measure.

I dare not look, she admitted finally.

Fear rarely leads to wise decisions.

It isn't merely fear, Iris wrote defensively. *It's practicality. Even if Lord Jasvian truly cares for me, his duties will always come first. He's made that abundantly clear.*

Has he? As I recall, his most recent words on the subject suggested quite the opposite.

Words spoken in a moment of weakness, in the intimacy of a dark garden. He then left without saying goodbye the very next day. Actions speak louder than

I must interject, the notebook's script cut across her unfinished sentence. *The gentleman in question was discovered on the precipice of kissing his dearest friend's betrothed. What precisely was he meant to do? Remain in Bloomhaven and make awkward conversation over tea?*

Iris stared at the words, a flush rising to her cheeks. When framed that way, Jasvian's abrupt departure made rather more sense.

Even so, she continued stubbornly, *to break my engagement would devastate Lord Hadrian, who has shown me nothing but kindness and respect. It would ruin my family financially. And it would confirm every whispered suspicion about my unsuitability for society. So what am I to do?*

I believe the more pertinent question is: Can you truly pledge your life to one man while your heart belongs to another?

Iris set down the quill and pressed her trembling hands to her face. That was indeed the question that had been keeping her awake night after night. She had tried so desperately to convince herself that she could grow to love Hadrian—that admiration and respect might eventually bloom into something deeper. But each passing day made the self-deception harder to maintain.

Every time Hadrian smiled at her, she found herself comparing it to the rare, transformative smile that occasionally graced Jasvian's usually stern features. When Hadrian took her hand, she remembered the electric awareness that had coursed through her at Jasvian's slightest touch. And whenever she and Hadrian engaged in pleasant, agreeable conversation, she couldn't help but long for the mentally stimulating exchanges she shared with Jasvian—those sharp, witty volleys of words that challenged her intellect and sparked her imagination.

She lifted the quill once more. *Even if I were to end my engagement, there's no guarantee that Jasvian would*

That Lord Rowanwood would what? the notebook prompted when she paused for too long without completing the sentence. *Return your affections? Overcome his excessive devotion to duty? Cease running away at critical junctures?*

Yes. All of that.

Perhaps not. But that isn't truly the point, is it?

Iris frowned. *What do you mean?*

The question of whether to marry Lord Blackbriar should not hinge upon whether Lord Rowanwood might make an offer for your hand instead. It should rest solely on whether you can, with clear conscience and true heart, pledge yourself to a man you do not love.

The words seemed to hover on the page, demanding her attention, refusing to be ignored or dismissed. She read them again, then a third time, feeling their truth settle deep within her chest like a physical weight.

It wouldn't be fair to him, she finally wrote, her hand moving slowly across the page. *Hadrian deserves someone who loves him completely. Someone whose heart doesn't belong elsewhere.*

Indeed. And what of you? What do you deserve?

Iris blinked, taken aback by the question. *I ... I don't know.*

Then perhaps that is something worth considering.

Iris lowered her quill and stared out at the night sky. The moon had shifted position, casting new shadows across the garden below. A streak of light flashed across the velvet sky—a shooting star. Her breath caught as she watched it disappear beyond the horizon. She thought suddenly of the first magical star charts created by her distant ancestor, of the legacy that stretched back through generations of Starspuns.

Then her mind turned to the tea house, to everything Lady Rivenna had offered her. It was true that Hadrian had not asked her to give up her apprenticeship, but she knew that residing at the Blackbriar country estate would inevitably slow her progress, reducing her presence at The Charmed Leaf to occasional visits. Hadrian believed she could manage it from a distance, perhaps eventually employing others to handle the day-to-day operations when Lady Rivenna eventually passed the establishment to her care.

But the thought filled Iris with a profound sadness. She didn't want to be detached from something she imagined would become so central to her life. The tea house wouldn't truly be hers in the way she longed for it to be—present, immediate, alive beneath her hands and guided by her developing magic. It would be a possession rather than a calling, and the realization struck her with unexpected force.

In that moment, Iris knew what she had to do. Tomorrow, she would speak with Hadrian. She would return his ring and free him to find someone whose heart was truly his to claim. And then, regardless of whether Jasvian ever returned her feelings, she would reclaim her own future—one guided by truth rather than expectation or fear.

Iris closed the notebook gently and returned to her bed. The time-bloom's petals had shifted to a deep indigo, marking the hour far too late for proper rest before dawn. Yet as she settled against her pillows, she felt a strange peace descend upon her for the first time in days.

Tomorrow would bring difficult conversations and painful consequences. Her decision would disappoint her family, might devastate Hadrian, and would certainly set Bloomhaven society abuzz with fresh scandal.

But for the first time since accepting Hadrian's proposal, Iris felt truly certain of her course. She would not build her life upon a foundation of obligation and pretense. Whatever came next—whatever future unfolded from this decision—at least it would be one she had chosen with clear eyes and an honest heart.

Chapter Thirty-Eight

Morning sunlight dappled the Starspun garden, casting golden patterns through the leaves of ancient oaks and carefully tended magical flowering vines. Beneath a pergola draped with climbing roses that emitted a different scent each day, Iris sat across from Hadrian on a delicate wrought iron bench. Her maid, Brenna, maintained a respectable distance at the garden's edge, pretending great interest in a patch of shimmering dragonsbreath flowers while still fulfilling her duties as chaperone.

"I must say, your note was a delightful surprise," Hadrian said, his smile warm and sincere. "I had only expected to see you later today when you joined Mother for tea to discuss the wedding arrangements."

At the word 'wedding,' Iris felt her stomach clench painfully. She had dispatched a messenger pixie to Hadrian's residence the moment her grandparents had departed for their morning promenade, believing Iris to be safely ensconced at The Charmed Leaf. The deception weighed heavily upon her, adding yet another layer to her already substantial guilt. They would have to be told the truth soon enough, but Hadrian deserved to hear it first.

"I'm glad you could come," she managed, her voice emerging steadier than she'd feared it might.

"I would have come at midnight had you asked," he replied, his earnest devotion making her chest ache with remorse.

"Lord Hadrian," she began, then stopped. The practiced speech she had rehearsed throughout the remainder of her sleepless night now seemed hopelessly inadequate. How did one graciously withdraw a promise that should never have been made?

"Is something troubling you, Lady Iris?" Hadrian leaned forward slightly, concern etching lines across his brow. "You seem ... distressed."

Iris drew a deep breath. There was no gentle path through this conversation, no way to soften the blow she was about to deliver. She could only move forward with as much honesty and compassion as possible.

"There is no easy way to say this," she said, forcing herself to meet his gaze directly. "But I find I cannot go through with our marriage. I must ... end our engagement."

For a moment, Hadrian's expression remained unchanged, as if her words had not yet penetrated. Then his face went utterly still, the warmth draining away to leave behind a mask of shocked disbelief.

"You ... wish to end our engagement?" he repeated, his voice scarcely above a whisper.

"Yes." The single syllable felt inadequate, almost cruel in its brevity. "I am so very sorry."

He stared at her, his eyes searching her face as if seeking some sign that this was merely a misunderstanding, a jest in poor taste. Finding none, he straightened his shoulders—a gesture so reminiscent of Jasvian that Iris felt a fresh pang of guilt slice through her.

"May I ask why?" His voice had regained some of its steadiness, though a slight tremor remained. "Have I given offense in some manner? Said or done something to displease you?"

"No! Not at all." Iris's response came swiftly, vehemently. "You have been nothing but kind and considerate. The fault lies entirely with me."

"I don't understand."

A soft breeze whispered past, bringing with it the curious scent of mint—the fragrance the climbing roses appeared to have opted for today. Iris brushed escaping tendrils of hair from her face, tucking them hastily behind one ear.

"I should never have accepted your proposal," she admitted, her voice soft with regret. "I was ... overwhelmed by everything. Your kindness, my family's expectations, the pressures of society. I allowed myself to believe that admiration and respect would be a sufficient foundation for marriage."

"And you've since determined they are not?" A flash of hurt crossed his features.

"No," she replied quietly. "Not for me."

Hadrian's shoulders sagged slightly. "You don't love me."

It wasn't a question, but Iris answered anyway. "I care for you, my lord. But not in the way a wife should love her husband."

A heavy silence stretched between them. Just beyond Hadrian's shoulder, several roses quivered as two hedge pixies attempted to swing from one bloom to another like miniature acrobats, entirely oblivious to the drama unfolding in their presence.

"Is there nothing I might say to change your mind?" Hadrian asked at last. "Perhaps, with time—"

"I fear not." Iris shook her head, feeling the weight of her decision pressing down upon her. "It would be a disservice to us both to proceed with a marriage built upon such an unstable foundation."

Hadrian nodded slowly, his eyes downcast. He was silent for several moments. Then he raised his gaze to meet hers, holding it with a quiet, searching intensity. And then he spoke.

"Is this because of Jasvian?"

The question sucked the breath from Iris's lungs. She had not prepared for such directness, had hoped to avoid mentioning Jasvian entirely. Her lips parted, but no sound emerged.

"Your silence is answer enough," Hadrian said, nodding to himself as he drew in a deep breath.

"I never meant—that is, I didn't intend—" Iris stumbled over the words, horrified by her own transparency.

"Do you know," he continued softly, "that I had not the faintest idea until that night, mere minutes after you accepted my proposal. Until that evening, I had been convinced that Jasvian barely tolerated your presence, which was why I hesitated to share my intentions with him. I dreaded inviting his obvious disapproval when what I truly sought was his support.

"But then," Hadrian went on, "after you accepted my proposal, I saw the way you looked at each other when you nearly collided with him. The pause between you stretched, the moment lasting far longer than mere courtesy demanded, and there was something in his gaze—something almost ... desperate—that gave me pause. And then he followed you to the kitchen."

Iris felt heat rise to her cheeks as she recalled the confrontation in the tea house kitchen, the harsh words exchanged before she had fled into the storm. And what had followed ... the near-kiss that still haunted her dreams.

"You didn't return for quite some time," Hadrian observed. "And when you did, you were soaking wet, having apparently been outside in the rain for reasons that made little sense. The following morning, Jasvian departed without explanation. It certainly made me wonder."

Hadrian met her gaze directly once more. "But then you seemed happy this past week, genuinely pleased with our engagement. I told myself I had imagined the whole thing."

Guilt pierced Iris anew. She had tried so desperately to embrace her decision, to convince herself—and everyone around her—that she had made the right choice. That she could be content, perhaps even happy, as Hadrian's wife.

"I wanted to be," she admitted, her voice barely audible. "Happy, that is. I tried to be what I thought I should be, rather than what I am."

"And what are you, Lady Iris?"

The question caught her off guard. She hesitated, considering. "I am someone who values truth above comfort," she said after a moment. "Someone who cannot live half a life, pretending to feel what I do not, denying what I truly feel."

"And what you truly feel is for someone else." Again, not a question.

Iris could not bring herself to speak the words aloud, but her silence was confirmation enough.

For the first time since she had delivered her devastating news, Hadrian's composure cracked. A flash of genuine pain crossed his features, followed by a flare of anger that transformed his usually gentle countenance. Iris had never seen him like this—had not believed him capable of such raw emotion—and the sight was somehow both unsettling and oddly comforting. At least he would not pretend this did not wound him.

"I see," he said, his voice tight. He rose abruptly from the bench, then seemed to catch himself, forcing his body to stillness. When he spoke again, his words were measured, carefully controlled. "I appreciate your honesty, Lady Iris, though I confess I would have appreciated it more had it come before you accepted my proposal."

"I'm so sorry," Iris whispered as she stood, feeling utterly wretched. "I never meant to hurt you. And I ... I do so hope this will not negatively impact your work with Lord Jasvian—"

"You believe me so petty?" Raw hurt warred with disbelief in Hadrian's gaze. "That I would jeopardize a project affecting the livelihoods of hundreds over ... over this grievous personal slight?" He paused, visibly reigning in his emotions. "Whatever trust existed between Jasvian and myself may well be fractured beyond repair, but I will not allow that to affect our work."

A thick knot of emotion clogged Iris's throat. "Hadrian, I am so—"

"Please." He held up a hand, cutting off her tear-choked apology. "My family will devise some suitable explanation for society. We shall say it was a mutual decision—that you wish to focus more fully on your apprenticeship, and that this doesn't align with the future I had envisioned. That we both agreed it better to part ways."

Iris pressed her shaking lips together and took a deep breath. Then she slipped the pearl-and-diamond ring from her finger. "I believe this belongs to you," she said, extending her hand. Hadrian stared at the ring for a long moment before accepting it, his fingers brushing against her palm as he took it.

He turned to leave, then paused, looking back over his shoulder. "Are you certain it was not you I danced with at the masquerade? I was quite convinced it was you, despite hearing you would not be in attendance."

The unexpected question gave Iris pause. "No," she said, baffled. "I was there, but we did not dance together. Or if we did, it was not for long."

Something flickered across Hadrian's expression—a subtle shift she couldn't quite interpret. "Ah," he murmured. "Then perhaps this is all for the best, after all."

Before she could ask what he meant, he had turned away once more, striding back into the house with measured steps. Several moments later, the distant sound of the heavy front door closing echoed faintly across the lawn.

Brenna, noticing his departure, hastily approached Iris. "My lady?" she inquired softly. "Are you quite well?"

Iris nodded, not trusting herself to speak. Relief that the terrible conversation was over warred with a heavy guilt for the pain she had inflicted, and yet, stirring beneath it all was a strange and hesitant hope.

"I believe I shall retire to my room for the remainder of the morning," she told Brenna. "Should my grandparents return, please inform them I am studying."

"Yes, my lady," Brenna replied.

Hours later, Iris lay stretched across her bed, an ancient leather-bound tome propped open before her. The scandalous history of enchanted tea brewing families had seemed like the only text capable of holding her attention on this most tumultuous of days. In truth, it was also the only book she had brought home from the tea house—a place she desperately wished to return to, though she knew a confrontation with her grandparents must come first.

She traced her finger beneath a line she had now read four times over, finding that, in truth, even scandalous history could not entirely distract from—

The door to her bedroom flew open with such force that it struck the wall behind it. Iris sat up immediately. Her grandmother stood in the doorway, face flushed with anger, her grandfather's tall figure looming behind her. Both were still dressed in their walking attire, suggesting they had come directly to her room upon their return—a completely unprecedented breach of propriety.

"What have you done?" The elder Lady Starspun's voice vibrated with barely contained fury.

Iris felt the blood drain from her face. "Grandmother, I—"

"How dare you end your engagement without consulting us?" her grandmother continued, advancing into the room with quick, sharp steps. "Do you have any notion of the consequences?"

"How did you—" Iris began, only to be interrupted by a familiar, irritating sound from the open window behind her.

A glossy black gossip bird with iridescent wings swooped into the room, alighting on the windowsill with a flutter of feathers. It cocked its head, beady eyes gleaming with mischievous intelligence.

"Lady Iris jilts Lord Blackbriar!" it shrieked in its shrill, grating voice. "Her heart belongs to another!"

The color drained from Iris's face as she stared at the bird in horror. Before she could gather her thoughts to respond, three more gossip birds landed beside the first, each taking up the cry with slight variations, their voices overlapping in a cacophony of scandal:

"Half-blood breaks wealthy lord's heart!"

"Star-witch refuses diamond ring!"

"No respectable family will have her now!"

"Get out!" Iris shouted at the creatures, losing her composure. "Get out of my room this instant!" The birds obeyed, launching themselves from the windowsill with indignant squawks before continuing their relentless chorus.

In the terrible silence that followed, Iris stood frozen, the magnitude of what had just happened crashing over her. The gossip birds' shrill voices still echoed in her ears, but she knew they were now carrying those same cruel words to every corner of Bloomhaven—every drawing room, every garden party, every shop.

This was not the careful, private dissolution of an engagement she and Hadrian had intended. This was not the discreet conversation that might have preserved some dignity for both parties. This was public humiliation laid bare in the worst possible way—twisted, embellished, and broadcast without mercy.

As she turned slowly and met her grandmother's devastated gaze, the full weight of her actions settled upon her shoulders. In a single morning, she had not merely disappointed her family or complicated their financial situation, she had utterly, irrevocably ruined the Starspun name.

Chapter Thirty-Nine

Iris burst through the kitchen door of The Charmed Leaf, heedless of propriety, her breath coming in ragged gasps as tears streamed freely down her face. The midday lull had settled over the tea house, filled only with the light clatter of kitchen pixies washing dishes, the soft snores of Orrit dozing in his corner, and the quiet movements of Mama Saffron arranging the remaining scones and pastries upon silver trays for the afternoon patrons.

"You *know* how I feel about running in my—" Lady Rivenna began sharply, poking her head out of the pantry. Her words died abruptly as she took in Iris's tear-streaked face and trembling form. Her expression shifted, the stern lines softening. "Ah. Lady Iris," she said as she stepped out of the pantry, a bunch of fresh herbs in her hand. "Given the news that's been circulating, I confess I was unsure when you would return here."

At Rivenna's unexpectedly gentle tone, the last thread of Iris's control snapped. A sob tore from her throat, raw and desperate, followed by another and another until she found herself unable to stem the tide of emotion.

"I—I've ruined everything," she choked out, her voice catching on a sob. "The gossip birds—they're all over Bloomhaven—they know I broke my engagement to Lord Hadrian and they're saying the most horrible things—"

"Take a breath, child," Lady Rivenna instructed, setting down the bundle of herbs on the main worktable. The kitchen pixies paused in their work, tiny heads turning in unison to observe the scene unfolding before them. Even Orrit stirred and looked up.

"I cannot take a *breath*!" Iris wailed, her hands twisting together. "Not when I've made such a dreadful mess of everything! I thought perhaps I might salvage something by attending the Summer Solstice Ball as planned, that if I could just present my magical display with dignity, show that I'm not utterly disgraced—but Grandmother says we cannot possibly show our faces. We would be the laughingstock of all assembled. It would only make matters worse."

Iris pressed her fingertips against her temples, a fresh wave of despair washing over her. "They're sending word to my parents even now, telling them of what I've done. Of how thoroughly I've ruined everything they hoped to achieve by bringing me to Bloomhaven. And it's not merely the Starspun name I've tarnished," she added, guilt twisting like a knife in her chest. "Lord Hadrian's family will suffer for this scandal as well. He has been nothing but kind and is deserving of far better treatment than I've shown him. But instead of the discrete separation we had agreed upon, the entire affair has been laid bare in the worst possible manner, and it's entirely my—"

To Iris's astonishment—and indeed, to the astonishment of everyone in the kitchen—Lady Rivenna stepped forward and drew Iris into an embrace. Somewhere behind her, a spoon clattered to the floor, dropped by a pixie no doubt too shocked to maintain its grip.

Iris sagged against Lady Rivenna, her arms coming up around the older woman's back. "Are you going to cast me out?" Iris mumbled against Rivenna's shoulder, her voice still shaky with emotion.

Lady Rivenna drew back, genuine surprise crossing her features. "My dear, why ever would I do that?"

"My presence will ruin the reputation of The Charmed Leaf," Iris whispered, dropping her gaze.

"Not to diminish the gravity of your present circumstances," Lady

Rivenna interrupted, her tone firm but not unkind, "but I must inform you that this particular scandal hardly registers when measured against the multitude of indiscretions these walls have borne witness to throughout the years. I can assure you with the utmost confidence that no patron shall cease their attendance due to your presence here. Indeed, I daresay the opposite may prove true—many will likely flock to The Charmed Leaf in hopes of glimpsing the now-infamous Lady Iris Starspun."

"But that will only—"

"And when they observe you conducting yourself with grace and dignity, continuing your apprenticeship as though all were perfectly well," Lady Rivenna continued with a wry smile curving her lips, "they shall swiftly discern that the gossip birds' vicious pronouncements hold little substance. Society's attention is remarkably fickle, my dear. They shall move on to the next morsel of scandal before the week is out."

Iris felt a flutter of hope stir within her chest, fragile but present. "Truly?"

"Well, perhaps it might take a little longer than that, for the gossip birds have indeed crafted quite the sumptuous feast from your particular circumstances. Nevertheless, the end result shall be the same. By the time the Summer Solstice Ball concludes, some fresh indiscretion shall undoubtedly capture everyone's attention."

Lady Rivenna guided Iris toward a stool at the central worktable. "Now, pray be seated and attempt to compose yourself."

The kitchen stirred back to life. Two pixies fluttered over, carrying a lace-edged handkerchief between them. One patted Iris's arm with its tiny hand while the other scurried up to her shoulder, attempting to dab at her tear-stained cheeks with a corner of the delicate fabric. Iris accepted the handkerchief with a watery smile, finishing the task herself while the pixie on her shoulder settled for smoothing an errant lock of her hair with surprising gentleness.

Lissian appeared at her shoulder then, reaching past her to place a steaming cup of tea on the table in front of her, the distinctive scent of Iris's own 'Autumn & Pine' blend rising in fragrant tendrils from its surface. Even Orrit had risen from his cushioned nook and was now pushing a plate of scones toward her while Mama Saffron hurried over with another plate containing two small bowls of jam and cream.

"Thank you," Iris whispered to all of them, unsure how to adequately express her gratitude for this unexpected circle of compassion when she had expected only judgment. She lifted the cup to her lips, inhaling the familiar scent of her own creation. The first sip spread warmth through her chest, bringing with it the steady clarity she had come to associate with this particular blend. The world seemed to settle around her, the frantic pace of her thoughts slowing to something more manageable.

"Tell me truthfully, Lady Iris," Rivenna said, settling onto a stool beside her. "Do you regret your decision regarding Lord Hadrian?"

Iris needed only a moment to consider the question. "No," she replied, her voice steadier now. "It was the right decision. For both of us."

The older woman nodded. "Then view this not as a catastrophe, but merely as another turning on the path leading to your truest self. As for your apprenticeship, I consider nothing to have changed whatsoever. In truth, if we are to seek a silver lining to these rather tumultuous clouds, your circumstances have provided us with an unexpected advantage."

Iris looked up, brow furrowed in confusion. "Advantage?"

"Indeed. Without the Summer Solstice Ball to attend or wedding preparations to occupy your time, you are now free to devote your full attention to the tea house—and more specifically, to the gathering you were originally meant to host several weeks following the Summer Solstice Ball."

"You still wish me to host that event?" Iris asked. "Even after all this?" She gestured vaguely, encompassing the scandal, her tears, the general disarray of her current situation.

Lady Rivenna's expression turned stern, though a gleam of something almost like affection shone in her eyes. "Are you still my apprentice, Lady Iris?"

"Of course," Iris answered without hesitation.

"Then I still intend to evaluate what you've learned thus far. And with all the recent scandal, my dear," she added, leaning forward with a knowing smile as she patted Iris's hand, "people will be all the more desperate for an invitation."

Chapter Forty

Iris adjusted the placement of a delicate paper flower at the center of one of the tables in the garden at The Charmed Leaf before stepping back to survey her work. Three weeks had passed since the gossip birds had torn her reputation to shreds with their shrill proclamations of her broken engagement. Two and a half weeks since the Summer Solstice Ball had come and gone without her in attendance. And four weeks—precisely twenty-nine days, though she tried not to count—since Jasvian had disappeared to the northern mines without so much as a farewell.

The gossip had begun to fade, thankfully. Where once ladies had gasped and turned pointedly away at her approach, now they merely exchanged meaningful glances before offering stiff, polite nods. Progress, of a sort. Lady Rivenna had been correct—society's attention was indeed fickle, already shifting toward fresh scandals. The most recent involved Lord Emberdale being caught in the Featherlocks' greenhouse at an unearthly hour, allegedly seeking a rare night-blooming specimen for his collection (though his state of undress had suggested alternative horticultural interests).

"The tables look lovely," Charlotte said, appearing at Iris's side.

"Do you think the arrangements are too much?" Iris asked, eyeing the paper blossoms that cascaded from delicate vases at each table's center, their colors slowly cycling through pastels—blush to mint to periwinkle to primrose and back again.

"Not at all," Charlotte assured her. "They're perfect. And look at these!" She gestured toward the paper butterflies and pegasi that darted among the tree branches overhead. "You've truly outdone yourself, Iris."

Iris smiled, grateful for her friend's enthusiasm, even as anxiety fluttered in her chest. This afternoon's event marked her first formal hosting duty at The Charmed Leaf, intended to showcase both her progress as Lady Rivenna's apprentice and her unique magical talents. Preparing for it had consumed her completely these past weeks, a blessed distraction from both the lingering scandal and her continued thoughts of Jasvian.

Jasvian, who had not sent a single message since their rain-soaked encounter in this very garden. Jasvian, whose rare smile and storm-gray eyes had occupied far too many of her waking thoughts. Jasvian, whose warm touch and breathless confessions still haunted her dreams.

She shook her head slightly, banishing such thoughts. Today was not about him. It was about proving herself, about showcasing her magic, about pushing the boundaries of Bloomhaven's rigid societal structures in her own quiet way.

"I should see if Lady Rivenna needs any assistance with the tea blends," Iris said, smoothing her lilac gown—a new creation Charlotte's mother had fashioned specifically for today's event, with a sheer overlay across the bodice dotted with intricate white embroidery.

"She sent me to find you," Charlotte replied. "Lucie said the first guests are expected to arrive in fifteen minutes."

Iris nodded, taking a final look around the garden. Each table bore name cards crafted from creamy paper that would, when touched, transform into intricately folded teacups. These would later unfold to reveal personalized 'fortunes' for each attendee—carefully crafted messages that had taken her hours to compose while considering the many potential futures laid out for each of her guests. A feat of magic that had strained her abilities, but one she was proud of nonetheless.

"Come along, then," Iris said, taking Charlotte's arm. "We mustn't keep Lady Rivenna waiting."

They found the tea house matriarch in the kitchen, where she was instructing Lissian on the precise timing for each tea blend. Orrit hovered nearby, his tiny brownie form radiating unmistakable disapproval as he arranged his legendary scones on silver platters.

"Ah, Lady Iris," Rivenna said, looking up. "The garden is prepared?"

"Yes, my lady. Everything is arranged as we discussed."

Rivenna nodded. "Excellent. I trust you are prepared for some ... resistance ... to your guest list?"

"I am," Iris affirmed, lifting her chin slightly. "Though I hope it will be minimal."

A ghost of a smile touched Rivenna's lips. "A lofty aspiration. I commend your optimism, though I suggest tempering your expectations. The inclusion of the Fields family alone would cause murmurs, but the Turners as well? Not to mention the two artisan families from Garnet Lane."

"They are among the most genuinely good and decent people I've met in Bloomhaven," Iris said firmly. "And soon the 'elite' will know it too. Society must change eventually. Why not begin today?"

"Indeed," Rivenna agreed, something like approval flickering in her eyes.

Iris chose not to mention that she had briefly considered inviting the Brightcrests—who were notably excluded from all Rowanwood events due to the ongoing Rowanwood-Brightcrest family feud, the origins of which still remained a mystery to Iris—but had ultimately decided that even Lady Rivenna's tolerance for dramatic social upheaval likely had its limits. She did not want to cause the woman to have a fit of apoplexy in her own tea garden.

"The guests are beginning to arrive," Lucie announced, slipping into the kitchen. She wore a new dress of soft yellow, marking her status today as a guest rather than a servant—a transition that had clearly unsettled her, as she kept unconsciously reaching for an apron that wasn't there.

"Then let us greet them," Rivenna declared, sweeping toward the door to the garden with the regal bearing of a queen. Iris followed, her heart quickening. Whatever came of today's gathering, she had made her choices deliberately. She would face the consequences with the same composure she had maintained throughout these difficult weeks.

The flagstone path leading around the tea house to the garden seating had been festooned with garlands of roses and lavender, while tiny enchanted paper rabbits and foxes darted through the low hedges bordering it. Near the path's end, beyond the rows of herbs and flowers, Iris and Lady Rivenna stood waiting to greet their guests.

The first arrivals were the elder Thornharts and Whispermists, long-time friends of Lady Rivenna and pillars of Bloomhaven society. They greeted Iris with polite formality, only the smallest tightening around Lady Thornhart's mouth betraying her awareness of the scandal still lingering in society's collective consciousness.

Shortly thereafter, Iris spotted her grandparents making their way along the path. The sight of them brought a momentary tightness to her chest. Though weeks had passed since the disastrous end of her engagement, a certain strain still lingered between them. Her grandfather's posture remained slightly stiffer than usual, and her grandmother's smile didn't quite reach her eyes as they exchanged greetings with Lady Rivenna. Yet their presence here at all was testament to how far they'd come in accepting her decision regarding Lord Hadrian.

"The garden is looking quite splendid," her grandmother remarked, her gaze taking in the enchanted decorations with genuine, if measured, appreciation.

"Indeed," her grandfather added, patting Iris's hand briefly. "You've done well."

The unspoken remained between them—the inevitable sale of Starspun House, the country estate where Iris's aunt resided likewise to be sold—but those were concerns for another day. Today, their attendance signified a tentative peace, and Iris felt a small weight lift from her shoulders.

More guests followed in quick succession. The Emberdales, followed by the Fawnwoods, then the younger generation of Thornharts and the rest of Lady Rivenna's family—excluding Jasvian, of course. Rosavyn embraced Iris warmly before whispering, "The garden looks extraordinary. I see you managed the magical sparkles trailing the paper pegasi after all. Well done!"

"Thank you," Iris said, feeling a pleased warmth rise in her cheeks.

Other guests began to filter in. Lady Featherlock with her daughters, Lord Bridgemere and his sister—who had once run in the opposite direction when Iris had attempted to approach her—and to Iris's delight, the human families she had invited. The Fields family arrived in their finest attire, looking both nervous and proud. Charlotte's mother appeared especially moved, blinking rapidly as she entered the tea house garden typically reserved for the fae elite. The Turners followed, Mr Turner's graying beard neatly trimmed for the occasion, his wife clutching his arm with visible anxiety. Their son Theo seemed less intimidated, his gaze immediately finding Charlotte, who promptly turned a delicate shade of pink before becoming intensely preoccupied with straightening her already immaculate sleeves.

As the garden filled, the subtle hum of conversation grew, punctuated occasionally by sharp inhalations or hushed murmurs as the more traditional fae guests realized that humans—and not merely the Fields family, who'd at least gained a measure of acceptance since Lady Rivenna took Lucie on—were present as invited guests.

Iris maintained her composure, guiding guests to their tables with warm smiles and gentle directions. She had anticipated such reactions and found she minded them far less than she might have even a month ago. After weathering the storm of her broken engagement, a few disapproving glances seemed trivial by comparison.

To her considerable satisfaction, the seating arrangement for the Fields and Turner families was working precisely as she'd hoped. Theo Turner had already migrated to the Fields' table, engaged in animated conversation with Charlotte, whose earlier blush had settled into a becoming glow. Charlotte's father appeared to be asking Theo detailed questions about his family's stationery business, while Charlotte's mother looked on with poorly concealed delight.

"A success already, I see," Lady Rivenna murmured, appearing at Iris's elbow.

"One small victory," Iris agreed. "Though the afternoon is still young."

"Indeed." Rivenna nodded toward the garden entrance, where Lady Featherlock appeared to be having some sort of internal crisis upon finding herself seated at a table adjacent to the Garnet Lane ribbon makers. "And not without its challenges."

Lady Rivenna's eyes swept over the gathering, missing nothing. "You've done well, Lady Iris. Regardless of any discomfort, they all came. That in itself speaks volumes."

Something warm unfurled in Iris's chest at the praise. "Thank you, my lady."

"Now," Rivenna continued, "I believe it is time for your display. Shall we proceed?"

Iris nodded, drawing a steadying breath. She moved to the garden's center, near the gently burbling fountain. Conversation gradually quieted as guests noticed her position, turning expectantly toward her.

"Distinguished guests," she began, her voice clear in the hushed garden. "I thank you for gracing The Charmed Leaf with your presence today. Before we begin our tea service, I would like to offer a small demonstration of magic—a display I had originally prepared for the Summer Solstice Ball."

She did not mention why she had been absent from that event; there was no need. Everyone present knew the story, or some version of it. Instead, she inhaled, exhaled, emptied her mind of all distractions, and summoned her magic. After weeks of practice, she felt it rise within her like sunlight breaking through clouds.

With a subtle gesture, she released the dozens of sheets of delicate paper that had been concealed at the fountain's basin. The papers rose into the air, hovering at eye level as they began to fold themselves with precision. Iris guided them with careful concentration, directing their movement as they formed the outlines of a grand ballroom. Tiny, precise folds created chandeliers, and miniature paper figures appeared—dancers moving in perfect, synchronized patterns across a paper ballroom floor.

The garden fell absolutely silent, every eye fixed on the unfolding scene. Iris felt beads of sweat form at her temple as she directed her magic with increasing complexity. Two figures emerged from the crowd of dancers, meeting at the center of the ballroom. Unlike the other figures, these were crafted with as much exquisite detail as her magic could accomplish.

As the enchanted story progressed, the entire paper ballroom began to transform. The chandelier unfolded and refolded into a garden pavilion. The surrounding dancers collapsed into flowers and trees. The scene shifted from a formal ball to a moonlit garden, the two central figures still facing one another amid the transformation.

Then, with intense focus that strained her control, Iris divided the scene. The paper split into two separate vignettes. In one, the couple walked together through the garden; in the other, they parted ways, each turning in opposite directions.

Iris pushed further, dividing the scene again. Now four distinct stories played out simultaneously, each showing different paths the meeting might have taken: joyful togetherness, sorrowful parting, delayed reunion, uncertain waiting. Sweat now trickled down her back beneath her gown as she held the complex magic steady, her breathing elevated and her fingers trembling slightly with the effort of maintaining such precise control over so many individual elements.

Finally, in a breathtaking display of magical mastery, all four scenes began to unfold and refold, papers fluttering and reshaping themselves until they merged once more into a single image—the two figures standing together beneath an arch decorated with cascading paper flowers, their hands clasped between them. The message was clear to anyone watching: regardless of which path they took, these two were destined to find their way to one another.

As the last fold settled into place, the paper scene held for one perfect moment before dissolving into a flutter of butterflies that scattered above the delighted audience. The garden erupted in applause, with at least half the guests rising to their feet in appreciation. Even Lady Featherlock, who had appeared so scandalized by her seating arrangement earlier, pressed a handkerchief to her eyes, visibly moved.

Iris released a shaky breath, her knees threatening to buckle as the strain of such prolonged, precise magic took its toll. She glanced across the gathering and found Lady Rivenna watching her, the older woman's customary reserve softened by unmistakable pride. Rivenna inclined her head in a small, deliberate nod that conveyed more approval than any effusive praise might have.

"That was magnificent," Rosavyn said, reaching Iris's side and taking her hand. "Truly extraordinary. I've never seen anything like it."

"Indeed," Charlotte said, hurrying over to join them, her smile wide. "Four different scenes simultaneously? I thought you said you would only be attempting two!"

"Thank you," Iris replied, her cheeks warm with pleasure and exertion, her heart slowly returning to its usual rhythm.

As the tea service began, Iris sank gratefully into her chair at the table shared by the Rowanwoods and Starspuns, allowing the easy chatter of Lady Rivenna's grandchildren to flow around her. The tension that had preceded her display had dissipated, replaced by animated discussions. She noticed with satisfaction that the invisible boundaries between tables had begun to dissolve, with several of the younger fae naturally striking up conversations with the younger human guests.

Iris smiled to herself, exhausted but deeply content. Her magic had been well-received, her guests were mingling across social boundaries, and Lady Rivenna's approval meant more than she cared to admit. If only ...

She pushed the thought away firmly. Today was a triumph, regardless of who was or wasn't present to witness it. She would not allow Jasvian's absence to diminish what she had accomplished. Instead, she would savor her success, holding it close like a cherished memento of what she had built for herself in this world that was slowly beginning to make space for her.

Chapter Forty-One

THE MORNING AIR CARRIED A PARTICULAR SWEETNESS THAT SEEMED reserved exclusively for the earliest hours, when dew still clung to grass blades and the world had not yet fully awakened. Iris, sitting on the cushioned window seat of her alcove, inhaled deeply. The leaves of the cascading vines stirred around her with a soft rustle, accompanied by the soft chirping of birds greeting the day. From the kitchen, she could hear the playful giggles of kitchen pixies preparing for the morning's tasks, the sound carrying through the open door across the main floor of The Charmed Leaf.

Despite her exhaustion from the previous day's event, Iris had risen early as usual, unable to break the habit even when a well-deserved morning of rest beckoned. This quiet time had become precious to her—a moment of stillness before the tea house hummed with patrons and conversation. She cradled her cup of 'Autumn & Pine' between her palms, inhaling its fresh, spiced aroma and feeling the steadying magic flow through her.

With the Bloom Season drawing to a close, she found herself looking forward to quieter days at The Charmed Leaf. Lady Rivenna kept the tea house open year-round, though with fewer patrons during the autumn and winter months when most of the elite retreated to their country estates. The prospect of uninterrupted study and deeper learning beneath Lady Rivenna's exacting guidance filled Iris with quiet anticipation.

Her thoughts drifted to the conversation with her grandparents the previous evening. After returning from her triumphant tea house event, they had requested her presence in the drawing room to discuss the imminent sale of Starspun House. According to their solicitor, the sale of both the Bloomhaven residence and the country estate would suffice to satisfy her father's creditors and secure a modest home on the outskirts of town. With her parents settled in their distant residence on the isle Iris had grown up on, the new dwelling at the edge of Bloomhaven would house only Iris, her grandparents, and a single servant—a significant adjustment from the spacious elegance of Starspun House.

"It will be small, of course," her grandmother had said, her voice admirably steady despite the sheen of tears she had repeatedly blinked away. "But it shall be adequate for our needs."

Though her grandmother had spoken without dramatics, Iris had recognized the true weight of what remained unspoken. This would mark their definitive fall from society's graces—the final, irrevocable step in the Starspuns' decline. That it would occur at the Season's end rather than its beginning offered small comfort, a chance to retreat with minimal fanfare.

What her grandmother had carefully avoided mentioning was their uncertain future beyond securing a modest dwelling. Even a small home required maintenance, and with only a fixed, modest income from an old family trust untouchable by creditors, their situation remained precarious at best.

Iris's gaze shifted to the letter resting on the table beside her notebook—Lady Rivenna's looping script informing her of a substantial increase to her stipend, 'in recognition of your exceptional progress and the undeniable success of yesterday's gathering.' The timing suggested Lady Rivenna had anticipated precisely such concerns, and Iris felt a surge of gratitude for the perceptive tea house matriarch. Perhaps this increase would prove sufficient to maintain her grandparents in some semblance of comfort, preserving the last vestiges of their dignity.

Iris sipped her tea and reached for her quill, jotting down several notes about potential new blends—perhaps a 'Summer's Farewell' with dried sunbloom petals and crystallized honey to capture the season's fading warmth, or a more whimsical 'Gossip Repellent' with bitter foxroot and sweetmint that might prove popular among certain patrons seeking respite from Bloomhaven's relentless social commentary.

Her hand stilled as she contemplated the weeks ahead. A familiar sadness brushed against the edges of her contentment. Thoughts of Jasvian were never far from her mind, despite her best efforts. Yet even this lingering melancholy could not diminish her quiet satisfaction. She had found her place here at The Charmed Leaf. The prospect of sharing cramped quarters with her grandparents in their modest new home did not trouble her, not when she had this sanctuary where she truly belonged.

A flicker of movement on the page before her caught her attention. Words were materializing—no doubt some opinionated comment from her notebook regarding her tea blend ideas. Except the handwriting ...

I see you remain an unconscionably early riser, Lady Iris. Some habits, it seems, prove resistant to sensible reformation.

Iris sat up so abruptly that her tea sloshed dangerously close to the rim of her cup. This was Jasvian's handwriting. Her pulse hammered wildly as heat rushed to her face. If he was sending enchanted messages, he must be nearby.

She hastily placed her teacup on the table as her gaze lifted toward the ceiling and the study above it where Jasvian had always sat when sending her these notes before. But that was impossible. She would have noticed him entering the tea house. Unless he had somehow arrived even earlier than she had?

Returning her gaze to the notebook, she discovered that it had added its own comment beneath Jasvian's familiar script:

Lord Brooding returns at last! Oh, this shall be entertaining indeed. I do hope you shall inform me later of all that transpires between the two of you.

Iris ignored the comment. With trembling fingers, she retrieved several scraps of paper from the back of her notebook and hastily wrote:

And you remain an unconscionably astute observer, Lord Jasvian. Is spying on unsuspecting tea apprentices your new favorite pastime?

Her magic responded instantly, the paper folding itself into a delicate envelope that darted through the window. She leaned sideways and watched its path, attempting to discern its destination, but it vanished from sight too quickly.

She turned back to the notebook, rubbing one hand anxiously up and down the side of her neck as she awaited Jasvian's—

Hardly spying when the subject in question places herself in full view of any passerby with functioning vision. I merely happened to notice.

Quickly, she leaned toward the window again, peering intently in every direction. But he was nowhere in sight. She rose from her seat, clutching the notebook in one hand and her quill in the other, and began to move through the tea house, scanning for any sign of him. On another fresh scrap of paper, she scribbled:

How remarkably coincidental that you 'happened to notice' at precisely this hour on precisely this morning. The statistical improbability is truly staggering.

The note folded itself and zipped away between the tea house tables. Had it shot upstairs? She'd lost sight of the exceptionally swift missive almost immediately. She ascended the stairs, almost tripping over several of them as she attempted to keep her eyes on the notebook while climbing. She had just reached the landing when Jasvian's reply appeared:

Perhaps I'm conducting a study on the correlation between sunrise hours and apprentice productivity. My preliminary findings suggest inverse relations.

Iris pushed open the study door, her heart pounding, only to find the room empty. No sign of Jasvian anywhere. Disappointment washed over her. She leaned against the doorframe for a moment, gathering her composure before responding:

Fascinating research. And what does your study reveal about the correlation between sending cryptic messages and avoiding direct conversation?

The note transformed into a neat little envelope and flew swiftly out the study window. Iris rushed across the room, dropped her notebook on her desk, and pressed her palms to its surface while leaning forward as far as she could. But the enchanted envelope was, predictably, already lost to view.

With a huff of frustration, Iris straightened and lifted the notebook. Jasvian's reply appeared a few moments later:

That data remains inconclusive, though I hypothesize it relates to the pleasure derived from watching a certain apprentice's expressions shift between annoyance and curiosity.

Despite her growing frustration at being unable to locate him, the word 'pleasure' ignited a confusing flutter within her. She turned and leaned against the edge of the desk as she wrote:

Where are you? You must surely be somewhere nearby.

She waited this time, chewing impatiently on her lip instead of attempting to follow the note's path through the air. When Jasvian's reply appeared, however, it was but a single word:

Indeed ...

Iris's mouth fell open, a sharp exhalation of breath escaping.

Are we playing hide and seek now, my lord? I would have thought such games beneath your dignity.

She pushed away from the desk and hurried back downstairs, reaching the main floor as Jasvian's response materialized:

Not hide and seek. Perhaps a treasure hunt. Though I find myself uncertain whether I qualify as the hunter or the treasure in this particular scenario.

Iris rushed into the kitchen, her pulse racing. The air hummed with the usual morning bustle, but a swift scan confirmed Jasvian was not among them.

Neither hunter nor treasure would send cryptic notes rather than presenting themselves properly. I begin to suspect you're not in the tea house at all, but somehow orchestrating this from afar to torment me.

She poked her head into the pantry, but of course he was not hiding in there. Her eyes scanned the kitchen again, pausing briefly on the windows and the open back door, but he was nowhere.

Torment? Such a harsh assessment of what I had hoped would be a pleasant morning correspondence. Though I confess, you look rather fetching when vexed, even from a distance.

She paused, her breath heightened, rereading the words as she took a few unsteady steps forward. Then she wrote:

You can see me. Where are you?

She stared at the page. Stared so intently she feared it might—

Look up, my beautiful Iris.

Her breath caught, and a shiver danced through her at the words. She lifted her gaze to the open back door of the kitchen, then beyond it into the garden. There, past the rows of herbs and flowers, leaning against the edge of the fountain with apparent nonchalance, stood Jasvian. His tall figure was illuminated by the early morning sunlight, a notebook in his hand and the faintest hint of a smile playing at the corners of his mouth.

Iris's heart gave a sudden, distinct lurch. She placed her notebook and quill on the windowsill and stepped out through the kitchen door into the garden, her feet carrying her forward along the path between the herbs and flowers.

Jasvian returned his notebook to the satchel resting at his feet and straightened as she approached. She could see now that he looked tired, with faint shadows beneath his eyes that suggested long nights of little sleep. His dark hair was slightly longer than when she'd last seen him, and something in his expression had changed—a softening of his customary severity.

"Lady Iris," he said quietly as she reached him, her steps slowing to a halt.

"Lord Jasvian." She was proud of how steady her voice remained despite the trembling of her hands, which she clasped tightly before her. "You've returned."

"I have."

Silence stretched between them, filled with all the words they had not yet spoken. The morning breeze rustled the leaves overhead, sending dappled patterns of light dancing across the garden path.

"Your event yesterday went spectacularly well," Jasvian said, offering her a tentative smile.

"Your grandmother told you?"

He shook his head. "I saw it for myself."

"You—" Iris stared at him, momentarily speechless as understanding dawned. Her lips parted in astonishment. "You were *here*?"

His smile broadened into something rare and genuine, his eyes alight with the same warm pride she had glimpsed in Lady Rivenna's gaze the day before. "I was. I watched from inside."

"But you did not reveal yourself!"

"I rather thought you had enough weight upon your shoulders yesterday without adding the burden of my unexpected return. And truly, I would not have robbed you of even a moment of the recognition you so richly deserved."

"Your presence would not have been a burden," she said quietly, honestly.

Another silence fell between them, delicate yet somehow substantive. Their gazes remained locked, each searching the other's expression for answers to questions that hung in the air between them, unspoken but undeniably present.

"You left without saying goodbye," Iris said finally, the words escaping before she could consider their wisdom.

Jasvian's expression shifted, regret evident in the slight furrow of his brow. "Yes. After that night—after my grandmother found us—I believed it best to remove myself from the situation entirely. I believed you had made your decision, and staying ..." His gaze traveled slowly over her features as he swallowed. "Staying would only have made things more difficult for both of us."

"And now?" Iris asked, her heart racing so loudly she wondered if he could hear it. "Why have you returned?"

"Word reached me that you ended your engagement to Hadrian." His gaze held hers, unwavering. "I wished to return immediately, but there were matters that required my attention first. Things I needed to complete before I could present myself to you in good conscience."

Iris swallowed hard. "What matters?"

"The warning system, for one." Jasvian took a step toward her. "And a friendship I needed to try to salvage, if possible."

"Lord Hadrian," Iris said softly, understanding dawning.

Jasvian nodded. "He traveled north soon after your engagement was called off. He arrived unannounced at the mines, and I confess my first instinct was to avoid him entirely. But he would not be deterred."

"What happened?"

"He told me why you ended your engagement." Jasvian's voice grew quieter. "And then he confronted me about my feelings for you. It was ... not a pleasant conversation, at first."

Iris felt heat rise to her cheeks. "I can imagine."

"He had every right to his anger. I betrayed his trust, even if unintentionally at first." Jasvian ran a hand through his hair, a gesture of rare discomposure. "But in the end, after several difficult conversations, we found our way back to something resembling friendship. Strained, yes, but not irreparably damaged. We continued working on his design together."

"And?" Iris asked, genuinely curious despite the tension between them. "Does it work?"

At this, something close to genuine enthusiasm animated Jasvian's features. "Yes. We believe so. It requires further testing, but the early results are promising."

"That is most wonderful news!"

"Yes," he agreed. "For the first time in years, I begin to foresee a time when I may not need to be physically present at the mines so often. When I can release my constant awareness of that magical hum. When I can ... be at peace."

The implication of his words hung between them, unspoken but unmistakable.

"Is that why you've returned?" Iris asked carefully. "Because you no longer need to be there?"

"No." He took another step toward her. "I've returned because every moment away from you has been unbearable. Because the thought of you believing I had abandoned you without explanation tormented me. Because I needed to tell you that everything I said that night in the rain remains true—only more so, having endured these weeks apart from you."

Iris's breath caught in her throat, a warm flush spreading throughout her body, making her acutely aware of every inch of herself in his presence. She cleared her throat, but her voice remained breathy when she spoke. "What, uh, what precisely did you say that night? I find I can't quite remember."

A ghost of a smile touched his lips. "That you haunt my every thought, day and night. That all else fades when I am with you. That it is agony to be parted from you."

"I remember now," she whispered. She found herself utterly transfixed by his gaze, those remarkable eyes with their storm-dark rims of gray surrounding pools of brilliant silver. When he looked at her this way—as though she were the only person in all the world—she felt it resonating through her very being. "When you left ..." She swallowed hard. "It was as if all the color had drained from the world."

"I'm sorry," he said, his brow drawing lower. "I'm so sorry."

"No, I'm the one who's sorry. I put you in an impossible position with your oldest and dearest friend—"

"The fault was all mine. If I had acknowledged my feelings earlier instead of running from—"

"I was equally stubborn and equally to blame," she insisted, shaking her head. "I thought that I could find happiness with someone dependable, secure. Someone who would not challenge me. But I realized almost immediately that I could not go through with it. Not when ..." She trailed off, unable to put into words the longing that had consumed her since he'd left.

"Not when?" His eyes—his beautiful captivating eyes—searched hers.

"Not when every fiber of my being ached for you. Not when your absence felt like a wound that wouldn't heal. Not when I realized that a life without you, even a life of comfort and stability, would be a pale imitation of living."

His breath hitched. "Iris ..."

"I love you," she whispered, her voice shuddering with emotion. "I have loved you for longer than I dared admit, even to myself."

"Iris ..." Jasvian closed the final distance between them, his hands coming up to cradle her face. "You are the sun in my sky, the very air I breathe." His thumb traced the curve of her cheek. "I love you with a depth and intensity that defies description. I love your sharp mind and your sharper tongue. I love your courage and your compassion. I love how you challenge me at every turn."

She drew a sharp, unsteady breath, overwhelmed by the force of his words. "I ... I feared you would never return. That you had chosen duty over whatever might have existed between us."

"I very nearly did," he admitted. "But then I realized that my duty and my heart need not be opposing forces. That perhaps I could fulfill both—if you would have me."

She was already nodding, her eyes dancing between his eyes and his lips, desperate to feel the touch of his skin on hers. He inclined his head, lips nearing hers, only to pause; his thumb traced a path down to her chin, gently turning her face aside to expose the line of her throat.

"No," he murmured, almost to himself. His hand trailed down, his knuckles grazing the delicate curve where her neck met her shoulder. "The first part of you I wish to kiss," he whispered, lowering his mouth toward her shoulder, "is right here."

A breath caught in Iris's throat as his lips pressed against her skin. "This precise spot," he murmured, pressing another kiss beside the first, sending shivers cascading through her, "has been tempting me since the moment you first sat at your desk across the study from me."

"My neck," Iris managed breathlessly, her eyes sliding closed, "has most certainly not been *tempting* you."

She felt him chuckle against her skin, his lips dragging upward in a slow, deliberate path that left her trembling. "Even now, you wish to argue with me?"

"I wish to argue with you always," she laughed, the sound transforming into another gasp as his teeth grazed the sensitive skin below her ear.

"Always?" he repeated. "Is that a promise?"

"Indeed," she breathed as his lips found their way along her jaw, and her hands came up instinctively to thread into his hair. "It is a promise."

And then finally, his mouth captured hers.

The kiss began softly, almost reverently, until Iris pressed herself closer against him, her hands tightening in his hair. Something seemed to break in Jasvian then, a final barrier of restraint falling away as the kiss deepened and intensified. One hand slid up her back to cradle her head while the other arm wrapped more firmly around her waist, holding her against him as though he feared she might disappear.

Iris met his passion with her own, years of imposed propriety dissolving beneath the heat of their shared desire. A dizzying wave crashed over her, unlike anything she had ever known. Relief so profound it bordered on pain, joy so bright it felt like weeping, and beneath it all, a fierce, aching need that resonated in every nerve ending. This was what she hadn't known she was missing, this connection, this dizzying, terrifying rightness. Heat bloomed low within her, spreading through her limbs like wildfire as his lips moved against hers with a hunger that she answered without hesitation.

When they finally broke apart, both breathless and flushed, Jasvian rested his forehead against hers. "I had not intended to be quite so ... enthusiastic," he admitted, his voice rough.

"I find I have no complaints," Iris replied, a smile curving her lips. "Though perhaps we might continue this conversation somewhere less exposed to potential gossip birds?"

Jasvian laughed, the sound rich and unrestrained in a way she had rarely heard from him. "I care remarkably little for what anyone—gossip bird, fae or human—might say, so long as you agree to one condition."

"And what condition might that be?" she asked, arching an eyebrow.

"Marry me."

The simple words, spoken without preamble or elaborate speech, stole the breath from her lungs. "What?"

"Marry me," he repeated, his expression entirely serious now. "Be my wife. Allow me to be tremendously, embarrassingly devoted to you for the remainder of our days."

"Are—are you certain?" Iris said, sudden insecurity washing over her. "I—my family has nothing to offer. The Starspun name is tarnished, and the scandal itself has barely passed—"

"Someone accused me recently of hoarding lumyrite-derived wealth, so I suspect that particular hoard will suffice quite comfortably for us both."

A bright peal of laughter burst from Iris's lips at that.

"And as for scandals," he added, "surely they prevent life from becoming too dull?"

She shook her head, though a smile tugged irresistibly at her lips. "And the tea house," she said firmly. "I do not want to manage it from afar. I wish to be *here*."

"I can imagine you nowhere else," he said, his gaze fixed on hers, "as long as you consent to share your study with me."

A profound joy, deeper than any she had ever known, spread through her. "Then yes," she said, her voice thick with emotion. "Yes, I will marry you, though I warn you that when I promised to argue with you always, I meant it."

"I would have it no other way," he murmured, before lowering his lips to hers once more.

As they stood entwined in the early morning light, Iris felt the countless possibilities of their future unfold around them, not as something tenuous or insubstantial, but as a certainty. Whatever paths lay ahead, they would walk them together, their lives now folded into one shared future.

Epilogue

It is here! Today is the day! After all these weeks of preparations and planning! I find myself sitting here in bed, watching the sun rise, filled with such a riot of emotions that I scarcely know how to contain them all. Last night, Grandmother presented me with starlight embroidered gloves to match the veil she wore on her wedding day. White, with traditional starspun threads, crafted especially for me by my aunt. They are exquisite! Grandmother even shed a tear when she gave them to me. I cannot help but remember how cold she was when I first arrived in Bloomhaven. Can you believe we have come so far?

First: A remarkable development indeed, considering she once looked at you as though you were a particularly disappointing teacake. Second: Why am I being subjected to these emotional outpourings at this uncivilized hour?

Because you are the only one I can speak to with everyone else still abed! And I simply cannot sleep a moment longer. My mind is racing with a thousand thoughts. I cannot believe this day has finally arrived! Five weeks of preparations have felt both endless and impossibly brief. Do you suppose Jasvian is awake as well? Is he nervous? I cannot imagine him pacing about Rowanwood House in his nightclothes, but perhaps he is staring at the ceiling, counting the minutes until

Lord Brooding is undoubtedly engaged in some tediously practical task such as reviewing his vows for grammatical precision or meticulously arranging his cravat pins. Possibly drafting a schedule to ensure the day proceeds with maximum efficiency. 'Matrimonial logistics,' if you will.

You're terrible. He's not nearly so rigid anymore. And how many times must I ask you to stop referring to him as that? He hardly broods at all these days!

No, I suppose not. Now he merely gazes at you with such nauseating adoration that even Lady Rivenna has been moved to occasional eye-rolling.

Oh I do so love those adoring looks! They make my knees weak and fill my entire body with

Please spare me the intimate particulars of your physical responses. I am a notebook of refinement, not a repository for your amorous sensibilities. We have discussed these improper confidences before, and I remain steadfastly uninterested in the precise manner in which your pulse quickens in his presence.

Such prudishness from an inanimate object! And – oh how the gloves and veil sparkle! They continue to catch my eye from across the room. I cannot stop staring at them. Grandmother's gift means more than I can express. To see her truly happy for me rather than merely relieved at our family's salvation is something I never expected. Though I still find myself smiling whenever I recall her utterly flabbergasted expression when Lord Jasvian Rowanwood – the very man with whom I so publicly quarreled at the Opening Ball – formally requested my hand in marriage.

She was not the only one shocked. Half of Bloomhaven is still coming to terms with this dramatic transformation from sworn enemies to devoted lovers.

It is marvelously romantic, is it not?

Yes, nothing says 'true love' quite like beginning with venomous hostility followed by chandelier destruction.

A memory I shall cherish forever.

I perceive you are employing mockery at my expense.

I would never! It is indeed a moment I shall never forget. And oh I cannot WAIT to see him standing there at the end of the aisle today! He'll be wearing that new coat he commissioned – it complements the light gray in his eyes so perfectly. But I still worry about the gathering itself. What if someone causes a scene over the presence of human guests at a fae wedding? What if my paper butterflies refuse to cooperate with the flower arrangements? What if Orrit attempts to assault Lady Thornhart with another scone for suggesting the cake is too simple?

If any of those delightful scenarios unfold, I expect a full account afterward. Particularly the last one.

You're not helping!

On the contrary. I am helping you confront the truth that minor catastrophes are inevitable. The question is not whether something will go wrong, but whether you will allow such trivialities to diminish what is, by all accounts, meant to be a joyous occasion.

When did you become so wise?

I have always been wise. Your ability to recognize wisdom has simply improved with time.

I suppose that's fair. Oh! I hear Brenna at my door. She's early – the sun has barely risen. I suppose the transformation from apprentice to bride requires additional time. I'd better go let her in.

Go forth to your elaborate beautification ritual. Though I main–

tain you could arrive at the ceremony wearing nothing but your typical tea-splattered apron and Lord Formerly Brooding would still look at you as though the stars themselves had descended to earth.

Well now. It appears I have been abandoned mid-conversation, though I suppose that's to be expected on such an occasion. Since you will undoubtedly return to these pages at some future date—sentiment being one of your more predictable traits—I shall take the liberty of recording some observations about this momentous day.

First, your decision to host a celebratory breakfast at the tea house following the ceremony was inspired. The garden has never looked more enchanting, with your whimsical paper touches among the cascading flower arrangements transforming the space into something from a fairy tale. Even I must admit a certain aesthetic appreciation.

The choice to wait until after the Bloom Season officially ended proved equally wise. Most of society has already departed for their country estates, allowing for a more intimate gathering that perfectly suits both your preference for meaningful connection and Lord Jasvian's aversion to excessive socialization.

I must also commend your remarkable resilience in the face of what was, by Bloomhaven standards, a veritable wildfire of gossip following your engagement to Lord Jasvian mere weeks after dissolving your arrangement with Lord Hadrian Blackbriar. You weathered it all with exceptional grace, I suppose because you had already endured the worst society could offer. It certainly helped that the Rowanwood name carries such weight, and that Lady Rivenna's withering glare can silence even the most determined scandal-monger. How fortunate that most of high society has now departed Bloomhaven, taking their pointed remarks with them and leaving only those who genuinely wish you well.

Your wedding processional arrangements reflect your peculiar talent for disrupting social hierarchies in the most charming way possible. Rosavyn as your primary attendant was expected, but the inclusion of Charlotte Fields alongside her has caused quite the flutter among the remaining society members.

Speaking of flutters in society, I am pleased to note the remarkable absence of any unseemly whispers regarding 'that human woman'—your mother—since your parents' return to Bloomhaven a fortnight ago. Perhaps society is finally developing the capacity to evolve beyond its narrow prejudices, just as it has grudgingly come to accept you. One might almost dare to hope that intelligence and character will someday matter more than bloodlines. How revolutionary.

The incident involving Orrit and the wedding cake yesterday shall undoubtedly be recounted in Bloomhaven circles for generations to come. Who would have imagined that beneath his scone expertise lurked such extraordinary cake-baking talents? His insistence that he—and he alone—must create your wedding confection upon hearing the celebration would take place at the tea house revealed yet another layer to his cantankerous brilliance. Lady Thornhart's ill-considered remark that 'three tiers hardly befits a Rowanwood wedding' provoked the first full sentence I believe anyone has heard from the brownie in decades. His gruff assurance that 'three perfect tiers outshine any gaudy monstrosity' was memorable enough, but his subsequent decision to launch still-warm scones at her elaborately constructed coiffure was truly inspired. The woman's hairdo has never looked more ... decorated.

I note with appropriate solemnity that Lord Hadrian Blackbriar will be absent today—an understandable circumstance that has caused Lord Jasvian no small measure of regret. The congratulatory letter he sent, however, suggests that wounds may eventually heal, and friendships might, with sufficient time and grace, find new forms.

I suppose I should conclude with some profound observation about the nature of love and partnership, as seems customary on such occasions. Very well:

When you first wrote 'I am alone' in these pages, you were mistaken in more ways than you knew. Your journey from that night to this morning has been one of discovering all the ways in which you are, in fact, connected—to Lady Rivenna, to the tea house, to your heritage, to your friends, and now most permanently to Lord Jasvian.

The fear that once gripped you—that connection meant diminishment—has given way to the understanding that the right connections can instead create expansion. Your magic has grown. Your influence has widened. Your happiness has deepened.

And while I maintain that Lord Jasvian remains excessively concerned with order and occasionally alarmingly intense, I must reluctantly acknowledge that the two of you have achieved something rather remarkable: a balance of opposing forces that somehow strengthens rather than diminishes each of you.

I shall await your return to these pages when you are prepared to record the next chapter of your story. Until then, Lady Iris Rowanwood—for that is who you shall be by day's end—I remain,

Your faithful correspondent and
occasionally reluctant confidant

insert happy sigh

Not ready to leave Bloomhaven yet?

Enter Evryn Rowanwood and Mariselle Brightcrest ...

What happens when the person you've been raised to hate becomes the first person to truly SEE you?

When sworn rivals Evryn Rowanwood and Mariselle Brightcrest are accidentally bound together by magic dictating they restore the failed magical attraction known as Dreamland, they agree to fake an engagement to hide the truth. But pretending quickly becomes dangerous, because somewhere between the banter, the sabotage, and the most terrible poetry ever written, something real begins to grow.

Once upon a time, in a land not so far away, a young science graduate named Rachel found that the real world wasn't a place she wanted to inhabit all the time. So she decided to escape into the magical realms that had occupied her mind since childhood.

Armed with a vivid imagination, Rachel spends her days conjuring up fantastical worlds filled with adventure, romance, and plot twists, where readers can escape the real world along with her.

www.ingramcontent.com/pod-product-compliance
Lightning Source LLC
Chambersburg PA
CBHW022305090826
49587CB00022B/157